Something Borrowed

Emily Giffin

arrow books

Published by Arrow Books in 2004

14 16 18 20 19 17 15

First published in Great Britain in 2004 by
Arrow Books
Random House, 20 Vauxhall Bridge Road,
London SW1V 2SA

Addresses for companies within The Random House Group Limited can be found at: www.randomhouse.co.uk/offices.htm

The Random House Group Limited Reg. No. 954009

A CIP catalogue record for this book
is available from the British Library

ISBN 9780099461463

The Random House Group Limited supports The Forest Stewardship Council (FSC®), the leading international forest certification organisation. Our books carrying the FSC label are printed on FSC® certified paper. FSC is the only forest certification scheme endorsed by the leading environmental organisations, including Greenpeace. Our paper procurement policy can be found at www.randomhouse.co.uk/environment

Typeset by SX Composing DTP, Rayleigh, Essex

Printed and bound in Great Britain by Clays Ltd, St Ives plc

SOMETHING BORROWED

'I absolutely loved it and read it in two sittings because I could not put it down . . . this is a book which takes a clear-eyed look at the rivalry which exists in even the best of friendships . . . a compelling, engrossing and uplifting book'
Marian Keyes

'Here's a heroine you'll root for and a book you won't want to put down. I loved it!'
Lauren Weisberger, author of *The Devil Wears Prada*

'Emily Giffin brings a fresh new voice to women's fiction. *Something Borrowed* is a deftly written and convincing tale of a friendship gone comically – and at times poignantly – awry'
Meg Cabot, author of *The Princess Diaries*

'It's a winner. It has a rare depth, plus the writing is enviously controlled'
Valerie Frankel, author of *Smart Vs Pretty*

Emily Giffin graduated from Wake Forest University and the University of Virginia School of Law. She practiced law in New York City for several years before moving to London, where she began writing full time. She now lives in Atlanta with her husband and two sons. *Something Borrowed* is her first novel and is now a major motion picture starring Kate Hudson and Ginnifer Goodwin.

For my mother, with love

ACKNOWLEDGEMENTS

I would like to thank my parents, family and friends for their love and support.

I am grateful to my agents, Stephany Evans and Lorella Belli, and my editor, Kate Elton, for believing in me.

I owe a huge debt to my earliest readers, Sarah Giffin, Mary Ann Elgin and Nancy LeCroy Mohler, for their tireless input on every draft of the manuscript.

And most of all, I thank Buddy Blaha, for everything.

SOMETHING BORROWED

ONE

I was in the fifth grade the first time I thought about turning thirty. My best friend Darcy and I came across a perpetual calendar in the back of the phone book, where you could look up any date in the future, and by using this little grid, determine what the day of the week would be. So we located our birthdays in the following year, mine in May and hers in September. I got Wednesday, a school night. She got a Friday. A small victory, but typical. Darcy was always the lucky one. Her skin tanned more quickly, her hair feathered more easily, and she didn't need braces. Her moonwalk was superior, as were her cartwheels and her front handsprings (I couldn't do a handspring at all). She had a better sticker collection. More Michael Jackson pins. Forenza sweaters in turquoise, red, *and* peach (my mother allowed me none – said they were too trendy and expensive). And a pair of fifty-dollar Guess jeans with zippers at the ankles (ditto). Darcy had double-pierced ears and a sibling – even if it was just a brother, it was better than being an only child as I was.

But at least I was a few months older, and she would never quite catch up. That's when I decided to check out my thirtieth birthday – in a year so far away that it sounded like science fiction. It fell on a Sunday, which meant that my

3

dashing husband and I would secure a responsible baby-sitter for our two (possibly three) children on that Saturday evening, dine at a fancy French restaurant with cloth napkins, and stay out past midnight, so technically we would be celebrating on my actual birthday. I would have just won a big case – somehow proven that an innocent man didn't do it. And my husband would toast me. 'To Rachel, my beautiful wife, the mother of my children and the finest lawyer in Indy.' I shared my fantasy with Darcy as we discovered that her thirtieth birthday fell on a Monday. Bummer for her. I watched her purse her lips as she processed this information.

'You know, Rachel, who cares what day of the week we turn thirty?' she said, shrugging a smooth, olive shoulder. 'We'll be old by then. Birthdays don't matter when you get that old.'

I thought of my parents, who were in their thirties, and their lackluster approach to their own birthdays. My dad had just given my mom a toaster for her birthday because ours broke the week before. The new one toasted four slices at a time instead of two. It wasn't much of a gift. But my mom had seemed pleased enough with her new appliance; nowhere did I detect the disappointment that I felt when my Christmas stash didn't quite meet expectations. So Darcy was probably right. Fun stuff like birthdays wouldn't matter as much by the time we reached thirty.

The next time I really thought about being thirty was our senior year in high school, when Darcy and I started watching the show *Thirtysomething* together. It wasn't one of our favorites – we preferred cheerful sitcoms like *Who's the Boss?* and *Growing Pains* – but we watched it anyway. My big problem with *Thirtysomething* was the whiny characters and their depressing issues that they seemed to bring upon themselves. I remember thinking that they should grow up, suck it up. Stop pondering the meaning of life and start making grocery lists. That was back when I thought my teenage years were dragging and my twenties would surely last forever.

Then I reached my twenties. And the early twenties did seem to last forever. When I heard acquaintances a few years older lament the end of their youth, I felt smug, not yet in the danger zone myself. I had plenty of time. Until about age twenty-seven when the days of being carded were long gone and I began to marvel at the sudden acceleration of years (reminding myself of my mother's annual monologue as she pulled out our Christmas decorations) and the accompanying lines and stray gray hairs. At twenty-nine the real dread set in, and I realized that in a lot of ways I might as well be thirty. But not quite. Because I could still say that I was in my twenties. I still had something in common with college seniors.

I realize thirty is just a number, that you're only as old as you feel and all of that. I also realize that in the grand scheme of things, thirty is still young. But it's not *that* young. It is past the most ripe, prime child-bearing years, for example. It is too old to, say, start training for an Olympic medal. Even in the best, die-of-old-age scenario, you are still about one-third of the way to the finish line. So I can't help feeling uneasy as

I perch on an overstuffed maroon couch in a dark lounge on the Upper West Side at my surprise birthday party, organized by Darcy, who is still my best friend.

Tomorrow is the Sunday that I first contemplated as a fifth-grader playing with our phone book. After tonight my twenties will be over, a chapter closed forever. The feeling I have reminds me of New Year's Eve, when the countdown is coming and I'm not quite sure whether to grab my camera or just live in the moment. Usually I grab the camera and later regret it when the picture doesn't turn out. Then I feel enormously let down and think to myself that the night would have been more fun if it didn't mean quite so much, if I weren't forced to analyze where I've been and where I'm going.

Like New Year's Eve, tonight is an ending and a beginning. I don't like endings and beginnings. I always prefer to churn about in the middle. The worst thing about this particular end (of my youth) and beginning (of middle age) is that for the first time in my life, I realize that I don't know where I'm going. My wants are simple: a job that I like and a guy whom I love. And on the eve of my thirtieth, I must face that I am 0 for 2.

First, I am an attorney at a large New York firm. By definition this means that I am miserable. Being a lawyer just isn't what it's cracked up to be – it's nothing like *LA Law*, the show that caused applications to law schools to skyrocket in the early nineties. I work excruciating hours for a mean-spirited, anal-retentive partner, doing mostly tedious tasks, and that sort of hatred for what you do for a living begins to chip away at you. So I have memorized the mantra of the law firm associate: *I hate my job and will quit soon.* Just as soon as I pay off my loans. Just as soon as I make next year's bonus. Just as soon as I think of something else to do that will pay the rent. Or find someone who will pay it for me.

Which brings me to my second point: I am alone in a city of millions. I have plenty of friends, as proven by the solid turnout tonight. Friends to Rollerblade with. Friends to summer with in the Hamptons. Friends to meet on a Thursday night after work for a drink or two or three. And I have Darcy, my best friend from home, who is all of the above. But everybody knows that friends are not enough, although I often claim they are just to save face around my married and engaged girlfriends. I did not plan on being alone in my thirties, even my early thirties. I wanted a husband by now; I wanted to be a bride in my twenties. But I have learned that you can't just create your own timetable and will it to come true. So here I am on the brink of a new decade, realizing that being alone makes my thirties daunting, and being thirty makes me feel all the more alone.

The situation seems all the more dismal because my oldest and best friend has a glamorous PR job and is freshly engaged. Darcy is still the lucky one. I watch her now, telling a story to a group of us, including her fiancé. Dex and Darcy are an exquisite couple, lean and tall with matching dark hair and green eyes. They are among New York's beautiful people. The well-groomed couple registering for fine china and crystal on the sixth floor at Bloomingdale's. You hate their smugness, but can't resist staring at them when you're on the same floor searching for a not-too-expensive gift for the umpteenth wedding you've been invited to without a date. You strain to glimpse her ring, and are instantly sorry you did. She catches you staring and gives you a disdainful once-over. You wish you hadn't worn your tennis shoes to Bloomingdale's. She is probably thinking that the footwear may be part of your problem. You buy your Waterford vase and get the hell out of there.

'So the lesson here is: if you ask for a Brazilian bikini wax, make sure you specify. Tell them to leave a landing strip or else you can wind up hairless, like a ten-year-old!' Darcy finishes her bawdy tale, and everybody laughs. Except Dex who shakes his head, as if to say, what a piece of work my fiancée is.

'Okay. I'll be right back,' Darcy suddenly says. 'Tequila shots for one and all!'

As she moves away from the group toward the bar, I think back to all of the birthdays we have celebrated together, all of the benchmarks we reached together, benchmarks that I always reached first. I got my driver's license before she did, could drink legally before she could. Being older, if only by a few months, used to be a good thing. But now our fortunes have reversed. Darcy has an extra summer in her twenties – a perk of being born in the fall. Not that it matters as much for her: when you're engaged or married, turning thirty just isn't the same thing.

Darcy is now leaning over the bar, flirting with the twenty-something, aspiring actor/bartender whom she has

8

already told me she would 'totally do' if she were single. As if Darcy would ever be single. She said once in high school, 'I don't break up, I trade up.' She kept her word on that, and she always did the dumping. Throughout our teenage years, college, and every day of our twenties, she has been attached to someone. Often she has more than one guy hanging around, hoping.

It occurs to me that I could hook up with the bartender. I am totally unencumbered – haven't even been on a date in nearly two months. But it doesn't seem like something one should do at age thirty. One-night stands are for girls in their twenties. Not that I would know. I have followed an orderly, Goody Two-shoes path with no deviations. I got straight As in high school, went to college, graduated magna cum laude, took the LSAT, went straight to law school and to a big law firm after that. No backpacking in Europe, no crazy stories, no unhealthy, lustful relationships. No secrets. No intrigue. And now it seems too late for any of that. Because that stuff would just further delay my goal of finding a husband, settling down, having children and a happy home with grass and a garage and a toaster that toasts four slices at once.

So I feel unsettled about my future and somewhat regretful about my past. I tell myself there will be time to ponder tomorrow. Right now I will have fun. It is the sort of thing that a disciplined person can simply decide. And I am exceedingly disciplined – the kind of child who did her homework on Friday afternoons right after school, the kind of woman (as of tomorrow, I am no longer any part girl) who flosses every night and makes her bed every morning.

Darcy returns with the shots but Dex refuses his, so Darcy insists that I do two. Before I know it, the night starts to take on that blurry quality, when you cross over from being buzzed to drunk, losing track of time and the precise order of things. Apparently Darcy has reached that point even sooner because she is now dancing on the bar. Spinning and gyrating in a little red halter dress and three-inch heels.

'Stealing the show at your party,' Hillary, my closest friend from work, says to me under her breath. 'She's shameless.'

I laugh. 'Yeah. Par for the course.'

Darcy has always upstaged me, but I've never really minded. I have no desire to be the focal point of a room and, frankly, I enjoy watching her as much as the next person. She entertains; I make a good audience. This is my role in our friendship, and it is one that I have long acknowledged and often embraced. But tonight, for some reason, perhaps because it is my thirtieth birthday, I feel a flicker of irritation.

Darcy lets out a yelp, claps her hands over her head, and beckons me with a come-hither expression that would appeal to any man who has ever fancied girl-on-girl action. 'Rachel! Rachel! C'mere!'

Of course, she knows that I will not join her. I have never danced on a bar. I wouldn't know what to do up there besides fall. She screams my name again. I shake my head and smile, a polite refusal. We all wait for her next move which is to swivel her hips in perfect time to the music, bend over slowly, and then whip her body upright again, her long hair spilling every which way. The limber move reminds me of her perfect imitation of Tawny Kitaen in the Whitesnake video 'Here I Go Again', how she used to roll around doing splits on the hood of her father's BMW, to the delight of the pubescent neighborhood boys. I glance at Dex, who in these moments can never quite decide whether to be amused or annoyed. To say that the man has patience is an understatement. Dex and I have this in common.

'Happy birthday, Rachel!' Darcy yells. 'Let's all raise a glass to Rachel!'

Which everyone does. Without taking their eyes off her.

A minute later, Dex whisks her down from the bar, slings her over his shoulder, and deposits her on the floor next to me in one fluid motion. Clearly he has done this before. 'All right,' he announces. 'I'm taking our little party-planner home.'

Darcy plucks her drink off the bar and stamps her foot. 'You're not the boss of me, Dex! Is he, Rachel?' As she asserts her independence, she stumbles and sloshes her martini all over Dex's shoe.

Dex grimaces. 'You're wasted, Darce. This isn't fun for anyone but you.'

'Okay. Okay. I'll go . . . I'm feeling kind of sick anyway,' she says, looking queasy.

'Are you going to be okay?'

'I'll be fine. Don't you worry,' she says, now playing the role of brave little sick girl.

11

I thank her for my party, tell her that it was a total surprise – which is a lie because I knew Darcy would capitalize on my thirtieth to buy a new outfit, throw a big bash, and invite as many of her friends as my own. Still, it was nice of her to have the party, and I am glad that she did. She is the kind of friend who always makes things feel special. She hugs me hard and says she'd do anything for me, and what would she do without me, her maid of honor, the sister she never had. She is gushing, as she always does when she drinks too much.

Dex cuts her off. 'Happy birthday, Rachel. We'll talk to you tomorrow.' He gives me a kiss on the cheek.

'Thanks, Dex,' I say. 'Good night.'

I watch him usher her outside, holding her elbow after she nearly trips on the curb. *Oh, to have such a caretaker*. To be able to drink with reckless abandon and know that there will be someone to get you home safely.

Some time later Dex reappears in the bar. 'Darcy lost her purse. She thinks she left it here. It's small, silver,' he says. 'Have you seen it?'

'She lost her new Chanel bag?' I shake my head and laugh because it is just like Darcy to lose things. Usually I keep track of them for her, but I went off duty on my birthday. Still, I help Dex search for the purse, finally spotting it under a bar stool.

As he turns to leave, Dex's friend Marcus, one of his groomsmen, convinces him to stay. 'C'mon, man. Hang out for a minute.'

'Yeah, you should stay for a while,' I say. 'She'll be fine.'

So Dex calls Darcy at home and she slurs her consent, tells him to have fun without her. Although she is probably thinking that such a thing is not possible.

Gradually my friends peel away, saying their final happy birthdays. Dex and I outlast everyone, even Marcus. We sit at the bar making conversation with the bartender/ actor who has an 'Amy' tattoo and zero interest in an aging lawyer. It is after two when we decide that it's time to go. The night feels more like midsummer than spring, and the warm air infuses me with sudden hope: *this will be the summer I meet my guy*.

Dex hails me a cab, but as it pulls over he says, 'How about one more bar? One more drink?'

'Fine,' I say. 'Why not?'

We both get in and he tells the cabbie to just drive, that he has to think about where next. We end up in Alphabet City at a bar on Seventh and Avenue B, aptly named 7B.

It is not an upbeat scene – 7B is dingy and smoke-filled. I like it anyway – it's not sleek and it's not a dive striving to be cool because it's not sleek.

Dex points to a booth. 'Have a seat. I'll be right with you.' Then he turns around. 'What can I get you?'

I tell him whatever he's having, and sit and wait for him in the booth. I watch him say something to a girl at the bar wearing army-green cargo pants and a tank top that says 'Fallen Angel'. She smiles and shakes her head. 'Omaha' is playing in the background. It is one of those songs that seems melancholy and cheerful at the same time.

A moment later Dex slides in across from me, pushing a

beer my way. 'Newcastle,' he says. Then he smiles, crinkly lines appearing around his eyes. 'You like?'

I nod and smile.

From the corner of my eye, I see Fallen Angel turn on her bar stool and survey Dex, absorbing his chiseled features, wavy hair, full lips. Darcy complained once that Dex garners more stares and double takes than she does. Yet, unlike his female counterpart, Dex seems not to notice the attention. Fallen Angel now casts her eyes my way, likely wondering what Dex is doing with someone so average. I hope that she thinks we're a couple. Tonight nobody has to know that I am only a member of the wedding party.

Dex and I talk about our jobs and our Hamptons share that begins in another week and a lot of things. But Darcy does not come up and neither does their September wedding. Our conversation is easy and natural as it always is, although it has been a long time since we were alone, uninterrupted.

After we finish our beers we move over to the jukebox, fill it with dollar bills, searching for good songs. I push the code for 'Thunder Road' twice because it is my favorite song. I tell him this.

'Yeah. Springsteen's at the top of my list, too. Ever seen him in concert?'

'Yeah,' I say. 'Twice. *Born in the USA* and *Tunnel of Love*.'

I almost tell him that I went with Darcy in high school, dragged her along even though she much preferred groups like Poison and Bon Jovi. But I don't bring this up. Because then he will remember to go home to her and I don't want to be alone in my dwindling moments of twenty-somethingness. Obviously I'd rather be with a boyfriend, but Dex is better than nothing.

'When's the last time we hung out alone?' I ask, remembering when Dex and I became friends during our first year in law school. I think of how we used to meet for coffee or lunch in the student lounge, or go for strolls around Washington Square Park between classes. That was before I introduced Dex to Darcy. After they began to date, my friendship with Dex changed somewhat, although we continued to do things alone, in the context of law school. But after graduation, even the chats over coffee ended, and our friendship only involved Darcy. She filled it up, like she does everything else. I accepted the new order, barely notice it anymore. Yet I am aware of how peaceful it is now, without her.

Dex looks at me intently. 'It's been a while, hasn't it?'

I feel a quickening of my pulse as I nod, hold his gaze.

'Too long,' Dex says, his green eyes shining in the glow of the jukebox.

'Too long,' I echo, identifying a nervous feeling in my stomach. It is the way I felt when I first met Dex, when I was so conscious of his good looks and vigilant not to fall for him. But after a while, he was just Dex, my friend. Safe ground. And then he became the boyfriend of my best friend. Even safer ground.

'We had some fun times while being tortured in hell,' Dex says fondly. It is how we always refer to those years in law school. They were excruciating, yet also rosy and

15

exhilarating. With every day I was one step closer to becoming a real attorney – my dream that hadn't yet soured. Dex and I would always share a bond from those memories. Memories that have nothing to do with Darcy.

It is last call at 7B. We get two more beers and return to our booth. We talk and laugh and reminisce. My nervous feeling is gone. I am only happy, and wish that the night could last forever.

'Happy birthday, Rachel,' Dex says, after a stretch of comfortable silence. He smiles, his whole face warm and luminous.

'Thanks, Dex.' I smile back at him.

'Was it a good night?' He leans across the table, closer to me, waiting for my answer.

I feel my smile stretch wider. 'Yes,' I say. Nothing more. We both know what has made it good. Big parties aren't my thing. I prefer one-on-one interaction – real conversation rather than drunken whooping it up. I prefer this moment, right here.

We finish our beers and soon afterward we are in a cab again, going north on First Avenue. 'Two stops,' Dex tells our cabbie, because we live on opposite sides of Central Park. Dex is holding Darcy's Chanel purse, which looks small and out of place in his large hands. I glance at the silver dial of his Rolex, a gift from Darcy. It is just shy of four o'clock.

We sit silently for a stretch of ten or fifteen blocks, both of us looking out of our respective side windows, until the cab hits a pothole and I find myself lurched into the middle of the back seat, my leg grazing his. Then suddenly, out of nowhere, Dex is kissing me. Or maybe I kiss him. Somehow we are kissing. It is surreal, made more surreal in the hazy aftermath of too many drinks. I am watching myself, hearing my inward *Stop!* and then a more urgent *Don't stop!* And so I don't. My mind goes blank as I listen to the soft sound of our lips meeting again and again.

At some point, Dex taps on the Plexiglas partition and tells the driver, between kisses, that it will just be one stop after all. We arrive on the corner of Seventy-third and Third, near my apartment. Dex hands the driver a twenty and does not wait for change. We spill out of the taxi, kissing more on the sidewalk and then in front of José, my doorman. We kiss the whole way up in the elevator. I am pressed against the elevator wall, my hands on the back of his head. I am surprised by how soft his hair is.

I fumble with my key, turning it the wrong way in the lock as Dex keeps his arms around my waist, his lips on my neck and the side of my face. Finally the door is open, and we are kissing in the middle of my austere studio, standing upright, leaning on nothing but each other. We stumble over to my made bed, complete with tight hospital corners.

'Are you drunk?' His voice is a whisper in the dark.

'No,' I say. Because you always say no when you're drunk. And even though I am, I have a lucid instant where I consider clearly what was missing in my twenties and what I wish to find in my thirties. It strikes me that, in a sense, I can have both on this momentous birthday night. Dex can be my secret, my last chance for a dark twenty-something chapter, and he can also be a prelude of sorts – a promise of someone

17

like him to come. Darcy is in my mind, but she is being pushed to the back, overwhelmed by a force stronger than our friendship and my own conscience. Dex moves over me. My eyes are closed, then open, then closed again.

And then, somehow, I am having sex with my best friend's fiancé.

TWO

I wake up to my ringing phone, and for a second I am disoriented in my own apartment. Then I hear Darcy's high pitched voice on my machine, urging me to pick up, pick up, *please pick up*. My crime snaps into focus. I sit up too quickly, and my apartment spins. Dexter's back is to me, sculpted and sparsely freckled. I jab hard at it with one finger.

He rolls over and looks at me. 'Oh, Christ! What time is it?'

My clock radio tells us it is seven-fifteen. I have been thirty for two hours. Correction – one hour; I was born in the central time zone.

Dex gets out of bed quickly, gathering his clothes, which are strewn along either side of my bed. The answering machine beeps twice, cutting Darcy off. She calls back, rambling about how Dex never came home. Again, my machine silences her in mid-sentence. She calls back a third time, wailing, 'Wake up and call me! I *need* you!'

I start to get out of bed, then realize that I am naked. I sit back down and cover myself with a pillow.

'Omigod. What do we do?' My voice is hoarse and shaking. 'Should I answer? Tell her you crashed here?'

'Hell, no! Don't pick up – lemme think for a sec.' He sits

19

down, wearing only boxers, and rubs his jaw, now covered by a shadow of whiskers.

Sick, sobering dread washes over me. I start to cry. Which never helps anything.

'Look, Rachel, don't cry,' Dex says. 'Everything's going to be okay here.' He puts on his jeans and then his shirt, efficiently zipping and tucking and buttoning as if it is an ordinary morning. Then he checks the messages on his cell phone. 'Shhhit. Twelve missed calls,' he says matter-of-factly. Only his eyes show distress.

When he is dressed, he sits back on the edge of the bed and rests his forehead in his hands. I can hear him breathing hard through his nose. Air in and out. In and out. Then he looks over at me, composed. 'Okay. Here's what's going to happen. Rachel, look at me.'

I obey his instructions, still clutching my pillow.

'This will be fine. Just listen,' he says, as though talking to a client in a conference room.

'I'm listening,' I say.

'I'm going to tell her I stayed out until five or so and then got breakfast with Marcus. We got it covered.'

'What do I tell her?' I ask. Lying has never been my strong suit.

'Just tell her you left the party and went home . . . Say you can't remember for sure whether I was still there when you left, but you think I was still there with Marcus. And be sure to say 'you think' – don't be too definite. And that's all you know, okay?' He points at my phone. 'Call her back now. . . I'll call Marcus as soon as I leave here. Got it?'

20

I nod, my eyes filling with tears again as he stands.

'And calm down,' he says, not meanly, but firmly. Then he is at the door, one hand on the knob, the other running through his dark hair that is just long enough to be really sexy.

'What if she already talked to Marcus?' I ask, as Dex is halfway out the door. Then, more to myself, 'We are so screwed.'

He turns around, looks at me through the doorway. For a second, I think he is angry, that he is going to yell at me to pull myself together. That this isn't life-or-death. But his tone is gentle. 'Rach, we are not screwed. I got it covered. Just say what I told you to say . . . And Rachel?'

'Yeah?'

'I'm really sorry.'

'Yeah,' I say. 'Me too.'

Are we talking to each other, or to Darcy?

As soon as Dex leaves, I reach for the phone, still feeling dizzy. It takes a few minutes, but I finally work up the nerve to call Darcy.

She is still hysterical. 'The bastard didn't come home last night! He better be laid up in a hospital bed! . . . Do you think he cheated on me?'

I start to say no, that he was probably just out with Marcus, but think better of it. Wouldn't that look too obvious? Would I say that if I knew nothing? I can't think. My head and heart are pounding, and the room is still spinning intermittently. 'I'm sure he wasn't cheating on you.'

She blows her nose. '*Why* are you sure?'

'Because he wouldn't do that to you, Darce.' I can't believe my words, how easily they come.

'Well, then, where the fuck is he? The bars close by four or five. It's seven freaking thirty!'

'I don't know . . . But I'm sure there is a logical explanation.'

Which, in fact, there is.

She asks me what time I left and whether he was still there and who he was with – the exact questions that Dex prepped me on. I answer carefully, as instructed. I suggest that she call Marcus.

'I already called him,' she says. 'And that dumbass didn't answer his goddamn cell.'

Yes. We have a chance.

I hear the click of call-waiting and Darcy is gone, then back telling me that it is Dex and she'll call me when she can.

I stand and walk unsteadily to my bathroom. I look in the mirror. My skin is blotchy and red. My eyes are ringed with mascara and charcoal liner, and they burn from sleeping in my contact lenses. I remove them quickly just before dry-heaving over my toilet. I haven't thrown up from drinking since college, and that only happened once. Because I learn from my mistakes. Most college kids say 'I will never do this again', and then do it the following weekend. But I stuck to it. That is how I am. I will learn from this one too. *Just let me get away with it.*

I shower, wash the smoke from my hair and skin with my phone resting on the sink, waiting to hear from Darcy that everything is okay. But hours pass and she does not call.

Around noon, the birthday well-wishers start dialing in. My parents do their annual serenade and the 'guess where I was thirty years ago today?' routine. I manage to put on a good front and play along, but it isn't easy.

By three o'clock, I have not heard from Darcy, and I am still queasy. I chug a big glass of water, take two Advil, and contemplate ordering fried eggs and bacon, which Darcy swears by when she's hungover. But I know that nothing will kill the pain of waiting, wondering what is going on, if Dex is busted, if we both are.

Did anybody see us together at 7B? In the cab? On the street? Anyone besides José, whose job it is to know nothing? What was happening on the Upper West Side in their apartment? Had he gone mad and confessed? Was she packing her bags? Were they making love all day in an attempt to repair his conscience? Were they still fighting, going around and around in circles of accusation and denial?

Fear must supersede all other emotions – stifling shame or regret – because crazily enough, I do not seem to feel guilty about betraying my best friend. Not even when I find our used condom on the floor. The only real guilt I can muster is guilt over not feeling guilty. But I will repent later, just as soon as I know that I am safe. *Oh, please, God. I have never done anything like this before. Please let me have this one pass. I will sacrifice all future happiness. Any chance of meeting a husband.*

I think of all those deals I tried to strike with Him when I was in school, growing up. *Please don't let me get any lower than a B on this math test. Please, I will do anything – work in a soup*

23

kitchen every Saturday instead of just once a month. Those were the days. To think that a C once symbolized all things gone wrong in my tidy world. How could I have ever, even fleetingly, wished for a dark side? How could I have made such a huge, potentially life-altering, utterly unforgivable mistake?

Finally I can't take it any longer. I call Darcy's cell phone, but it goes straight to voice mail. I call their home number, hoping she will pick up. Instead Dex answers. I cringe.

'Hi, Dex. This is Rachel,' I say, trying to sound normal.

You know, the maid of honor in your upcoming wedding – the woman you had sex with last night?

'Hi, Rachel,' he says casually. 'So did you have fun last night?'

For a second, I think that he is talking about us and am horrified by his nonchalance. But then I hear Darcy clamoring for the phone in the background, and realize that he is only talking about the party.

'Oh yeah, it was a great time – a great party.' I bite my lip.

Darcy has already snatched the phone from him. Her tone is chipper, fully repaired. 'Hey. I'm sorry I forgot to call you back. You know, it was high drama over here for a while.'

'But you're okay now? Everything's all right with you – and Dex?' I have trouble saying his name. As if it will somehow give me away.

'Um, yeah, hold on one sec.'

I hear her close a door; she always moves into their bedroom when she talks on the phone. I picture their four-poster bed, which I helped Darcy select from Charles P. Rogers. Soon to be their marital bed.

'Oh yeah, I'm fine now. He was just with Marcus. They stayed out late and then ended up going to the diner for breakfast. But of course, you know, I'm still working the pissed off angle. I told him he's totally pathetic, that he's a thirty-four-year-old engaged man and he stays out all night. Pathetic, don't you think?'

'Yeah, I guess so. But harmless enough.' I swallow hard and think, yes, that *would* be harmless enough. 'Well, I'm glad you guys made up.'

'Yeah. I'm over it, I guess. But still . . . he should have called. That shit does not fly with me, you know?'

'I hear you,' I say, and then bravely add, 'I told you he wasn't cheating on you.'

'I know . . . but I still pictured him with some stripper bimbo from Scores or something. My overactive imagination.'

Is that what last night was? I know I'm not a bimbo, but was it some conscious choice of his to get laid before the wedding? Surely not. Surely he wouldn't choose Darcy's maid of honor.

'So anyway, what did you think of the party? I'm such a bad friend – I get wasted and leave early. And, oh shit! Today's your actual birthday. Happy birthday! God, I'm the worst, Rach!'

Yeah, you're the bad friend.

'Oh, it was great. The party was so much fun. Thank you for planning it – it was a total surprise . . . really awesome . . .'

I hear their bedroom door open and Dex say something about being late.

25

'Yeah, I actually gotta run, Rachel. We're going to the movies. You wanna come?'

'Um, no thanks.'

'Okay. But we're still on for dinner tonight, right? Rain at eight?'

I totally forgot that I had plans to meet Dex, Darcy, and Hillary for a small birthday dinner. There is no way I can face Dex or Darcy tonight – and certainly not together. I tell her that I'm not sure I'm up to it, that I am really hungover. Even though I stopped drinking at two, I add, before I remember that liars offer too much extraneous detail.

Darcy doesn't notice. 'Maybe you'll feel better later . . . I'll call you after the movie.'

I hang up the phone, thinking that it was way too easy. But instead of feeling relieved, I am left with a vague dissatisfaction, wistfulness, wishing that I were going to the movies. Not with Dex, of course. Just someone. How quickly I turn my back on the deal with God. I want a husband again. Or at least a boyfriend.

I sit on the couch with my hands folded in my lap, contemplating what I did to Darcy, waiting for the guilt to come. It doesn't. Was it because I had alcohol as an excuse? I was drunk, not in my right mind. I think of my first year criminal law class. *Intoxication, like insanity, infancy, duress, and entrapment, is a legal excuse, a defense where the defendant is not blameworthy for having engaged in conduct that would otherwise be a crime*. Shit. That was only *involuntary* intoxication. Well, Darcy made me do those shots. But peer pressure does not constitute involuntary intoxication. Still, it is a mitigating circumstance that the jury might consider.

Sure, blame the victim. What is wrong with me?

Maybe I am just a bad person. Maybe the only reason I have been good up to this point has less to do with my true moral fiber and more to do with the fear of getting caught. I play by the rules because I am risk-averse. I didn't go along with the junior-high shoplifting gags at the White Hen Pantry partly because I knew it was wrong, but mostly because I was just sure that I would be the one to get caught. I never cheated on an exam for the same reason. Even now I don't take office supplies from work because I figure that somehow the firm's surveillance cameras will catch me in the act. If that is what motivates me to be good, do I really deserve credit? Am I really a good person? Or just a cowardly pessimist?

Okay. So maybe I am a bad person. There is no other plausible explanation for my lack of guilt. Do I have it in for Darcy? Was I driven by jealousy last night? Do I resent her perfect life – how easily things come to her? Or maybe, subconsciously, in my drunken state, I was getting even for past wrongs. Darcy hasn't always been a perfect friend. Far from it. I start to make my case to the jury, remembering Ethan back in elementary school. I am on to something . . . *Ladies and gentlemen of the jury, consider the story of Ethan Ainsley . . .*

Darcy Rhone and I were best friends growing up, bonded by geography, a force greater than all else when you are in elementary school. We moved to the same cul-de-sac in Naperville, Indiana, in the summer of 1976, just in time to

27

attend the town's bicentennial parade together. We marched side by side, beating matching red, white, and blue drums that Darcy's father bought for us at KMart. I remember Darcy leaning in to me and saying, 'Let's pretend we're sisters.' The suggestion gave me goose bumps – *a sister*! And in no time at all, that is what she became to me. We slept over at each other's house every Friday and Saturday during the school year and most nights of the week during the summer. We absorbed the nuances of each other's family life, the sort of details you only learn when you live next door to a friend. I knew, for example, that Darcy's mother folded towels in neat thirds as she watched *The Young and the Restless*, that Darcy's father subscribed to *Playboy*, that junk food was allowed for breakfast, and the words 'shit' and 'damn' were no big deal. I'm sure she observed much about my home too, although it is hard to say what makes your own life unique. We shared everything – clothes, toys, yards, even our love of Andy Gibb and unicorns.

In the fifth grade we discovered boys. Which brings me to Ethan, my first real crush. Darcy, along with every other girl in our class, loved Doug Jackson. I understood Doug's appeal. I appreciated his blond hair that reminded us of Bo Duke. And the way his Wranglers fit his butt, his black comb tucked neatly inside the back left pocket. And his dominance in tetherball – how he casually and effortlessly socked the ball out of everyone's reach at a sharp upward angle.

But I loved Ethan. I loved his unruly hair and the way his cheeks turned pink during recess and made him look like he belonged in a Renoir painting. I loved the way he rotated his number two pencil between his full lips, making symmetrical little bite marks near the eraser whenever he was concentrating really hard. I loved how hyper and happy he was whenever he played four square with the girls (he was the only boy who would ever join us – the other boys stuck to tetherball and football). And I loved that he was always kind to the most unpopular boy in our class, Johnnie Redmond, who had a terrible stutter and an unfortunate bowl cut.

Darcy was puzzled, if not irritated, by my dissent, as was our good friend Annalise Giles, who moved to our cul-de-sac two years after we did (this delay and the fact that she already had a sister meant she could never quite catch up and reach full best-friend status). Darcy and Annalise liked Ethan, but not like *that*, and they would insist that Doug was so much cuter and cooler – the two attributes that will get you in trouble when you choose a boy or a man, a sense that I had even at age ten.

We all assumed that Darcy would land the grand Doug prize. Not only because Darcy was bolder than the other girls, strutting right up to Doug in the cafeteria or on the playground, but also because she was the prettiest girl in our class. With high cheekbones, huge, well-spaced eyes, and a dainty nose, she has a face that is revered at any age, although fifth-graders can't pinpoint exactly what makes it nice. I don't think I even understood what cheekbones and bone structure were at age ten, but I knew that Darcy was pretty and I envied her looks. So did Annalise, who openly told Darcy so every chance she got, which seemed wholly unnecessary to me. Darcy already knew she was pretty, and in my opinion she didn't need daily reinforcement.

29

So that year, on Halloween, Annalise, Darcy and I assembled in Annalise's room to prepare our makeshift gypsy costumes – Darcy had insisted that it would be an excellent excuse to wear lots of make-up. As she examined a pair of rhinestone earrings freshly purchased from Claire's, she looked in the mirror and said, 'You know, Rachel, I think you're right.'

'Right about what?' I said, feeling a surge of satisfaction, wondering what past debate she was referring to.

She fastened one earring in place and looked at me. I will never forget that tiny smirk on her face – just the faintest hint of a smug smile. 'You're right about Ethan. I think I'm going to like him, too.'

'What do you mean, "going to like him"?'

'I'm tired of Doug Jackson. I like Ethan now. I like his dimples.'

'He only has one,' I snapped.

'Well, then I like his dim-*ple*.'

I looked at Annalise for support, for words to the effect that you couldn't just *decide* to like someone new. But of course she said nothing, just kept applying her ruby lipstick, puckering before a hand-held mirror.

'I can't believe you, Darcy!'

'What's your problem?' she demanded. 'Annalise wasn't mad when I liked Doug. We've shared him with the whole grade for months. Right, Annalise?'

'Longer than that. I started liking him in the summer. Remember? At the pool?' Annalise chimed in, always missing the big picture.

I glared at her, and she lowered her eyes remorsefully.

That was different. That was Doug. He belonged in the public domain. But Ethan was exclusively mine.

I said nothing else that night, but trick-or-treating was ruined. The next day in school, Darcy passed Ethan a note, asking him if he liked me, her, or neither – with little boxes next to each selection and instructions to check one. He must have checked Darcy's name because they were a couple by recess. Which is to say that they announced that they were 'going out' but never spent any real time together, unless you count a few phone calls at night often scripted ahead of time with Annalise giggling at her side. I refused to participate in or discuss her fledgling romance.

In my mind, it didn't matter that Darcy and Ethan never kissed, or that it was only the fifth grade, or that they 'broke up' two weeks later when Darcy lost interest and decided that she liked Doug Jackson again. Or that, as my mother told me for comfort, imitation is the sincerest form of flattery. It only mattered that Darcy stole Ethan from me. Perhaps she did it because she really did change her mind about him; that's what I told myself so I would stop hating her. But more likely Darcy took Ethan just to show me that she could.

So, ladies and gentlemen of the jury, in a sense, Darcy Rhone had this coming to her. What goes around comes around. Perhaps this is her comeuppance.

I picture the faces of the jury. They are not swayed. The male jurors look bewildered – as if they miss the point altogether. Doesn't the prettiest girl always get the boy? That

31

is precisely the way the world *should* work. An older woman in a sensible dress purses her lips. She is disgusted by the mere comparison – a fiancé to a fifth-grade crush! Good heavens! A perfectly groomed, almost beautiful woman, wearing a canary-yellow Chanel suit, has already identified and allied herself with Darcy. There is nothing I can say to change her mind or mitigate my offense.

The only juror who seems moved by the Ethan tale is a slightly overweight girl with a severe bob the color of day-old coffee. She slouches in the corner of the jury box, occasionally shoving her glasses up on her beak of a nose. I have tapped into this girl's empathy, her sense of justice. She is secretly satisfied by what I did. Maybe because she, too, has a friend like Darcy, a friend who always gets everything she wants.

I think back to high school, when Darcy continued to get any boy she wanted. I can see her kissing Blaine Conner by our locker and recall the envy that would well up inside me when I, boyfriendless, was forced to witness their shameless PDA. Blaine transferred to our school from Columbus, Ohio in the fall of our junior year, and became an instant hit everywhere but the classroom. Although he wasn't bright, he was the star receiver on our football team, the starting point guard for our basketball team, and, of course, our starting pitcher in the spring. And with his Ken-doll good looks, the girls loved him. Doug Jackson, part two. But alas, he had a girlfriend named Cassandra back in Columbus to whom he claimed to be '110 percent committed' (a jock expression that has always bugged me for its obvious mathematical impossibility). Or so he was before Darcy got in the mix, after we watched Blaine pitch a no-hitter against Central, and she decided that she had to have him. The next day she asked him to go see *Les Misérables*. You'd think a three-sport jock like Blaine wouldn't be into musicals, but he enthusiastically agreed to escort her. After the show, in Darcy's living room, Blaine planted a large hickey on her neck. And the following morning, one Cassandra of Columbus, Ohio, was dumped on her ear.

I remember talking to Annalise about Darcy's charmed life. We often discussed Darcy, which made me wonder how much they gossiped about me. Annalise contended that it wasn't only Darcy's good looks or perfect body; it was also her confidence, her charm. I don't know about the charm, but looking back I agree with Annalise about the confidence. It was as if Darcy had the perspective of a thirty-year-old while in high school. The understanding that none of it really mattered, that you only go around once, that you might as well go for it. She was never intimidated, never insecure. She embodied what everyone says when they look back on high school: 'If I only knew back then.'

But one thing I have to say about Darcy and dating is this: she never blew us off for a guy. She always put her friends first, an amazing thing for a high school girl to do. Sometimes she blew her boyfriend off altogether, but more often she just included us. Four of us in a row at the theater. The flavor of the month, then Darcy, then Annalise and me. And Darcy always directed her whispered comments our way. At the time, I thought she just didn't love them enough. She was brash and independent, unlike most high school girls who allow their feelings for a boy to swallow them up. But maybe Darcy just wanted to keep control, and by being the one who loved the least, that is what she had. Whether she did care less or just pretended to, she kept every one of them on the hook even after she cut them loose. Take Blaine, for example. He is living in Iowa with a wife, three kids, and a couple of chocolate Labradors, and he still emails Darcy on her birthday every year. Now that is some kind of power.

To this day Darcy talks wistfully of how great high school was. I cringe whenever she says it. Sure, I have some fond memories of those days, and enjoyed moderate popularity – a nice fringe benefit of being Darcy's best friend. I loved going to football games with Annalise, painting our faces orange and blue, wrapping up in blankets in the bleachers, and waving to Darcy as she cheered down on the field. I loved our Saturday-night trips to Colonial Ice Cream where we always ordered the same thing – one turtle sundae, one Snickers pie, one double-chocolate brownie – and then split them among us. And I loved my first boyfriend, Brandon Beamer, who asked me out during our senior year. Brandon was a rule-follower too, a Catholic version of me. He didn't drink or do drugs, and he felt guilty even discussing sex. Darcy, who lost her virginity our sophomore year to an exchange student from Spain named Carlos, was always instructing me to corrupt Brandon. 'Grab his penis like this, and I guarantee, it's a done deal.' But I was perfectly happy with our long make-out sessions in Brandon's family station wagon, and I never had to worry about safe sex or drunk driving. So if my memories weren't glamorous, at least I had a few good times.

But I also had plenty of bad times: the awful hair days, the pimples, the class pictures from hell, never having the right clothes, being dateless for dances, baby fat that I could never shed, getting cut from teams, losing the election for class treasurer. And the overwhelming feeling of sadness and angst that would come and go willy-nilly (or, more accurately, once a month), seemingly out of my control. Typical teenager stuff really. Clichés, because they happen to everyone. Everyone but Darcy, that is, who floated through those tumultuous four years unscathed by rejection, untouched by the adolescent ugly stick. Of course she loved high school – high school loved her.

Many girls with this view of their teenage years seem to really take it on the chin later in life. They show up at their ten-year reunion fifteen to twenty pounds heavier, divorced, reminiscing about the long-gone glory days. But the tide of glory days hasn't ebbed for Darcy. No crashing and no burning. In fact, life just keeps getting sweeter for her. I once overheard my mother tell my father that Darcy has the world by the balls. It was unlike my mother to talk like that so it always stuck in my mind. It was the perfect description. Whether it was her looks or her confidence or her sheer determination, Darcy always got what she wanted. And now she has Dex, the dream fiancé.

I leave Darcy a message on her cell, which will be turned off during the movie. I say that I am too tired to make it to dinner. Just getting out of going makes me less queasy. In fact, I am suddenly very hungry. I find my menus and call to order a hamburger with cheddar and fries. Guess I won't be losing five pounds before Memorial Day. As I wait for my delivery, I picture Darcy and me, playing with the phone book all those years ago, wondering about the future and what age thirty would bring.

And here I am, without the dashing husband, the responsible baby-sitter, the two kids. Instead my benchmark birthday is forever tainted by scandal . . . Oh, well. No point beating myself up over it. I hit redial on my phone and add a large chocolate milk shake to my order. I see my girl in the corner of the jury box wink at me. She thinks the milk shake is an excellent idea. After all, doesn't everyone deserve a few weak moments on her birthday?

THREE

When I wake up the next morning, the cavalier girl sucking down a milk shake is gone, caved to guilt and thirty years of rule-following. I can no longer rationalize what I did. I committed an unspeakable act against a friend, violated a central tenet of sisterhood. There is no justification.

So on to Plan B: I will pretend that nothing happened. My transgression was so great that I have no choice but simply to will the whole thing to go away. And by proceeding with business as usual, embracing my Monday-morning routine, this is what I seek to accomplish.

I shower, dry my hair, put on my most comfortable black suit and low heels, take the subway to Grand Central, get my coffee at Starbucks, pick up the *New York Times* at my newsstand, and ride two escalators and one elevator up to my office in the MetLife Building. Each part of my routine represents one step farther from Dex and the Incident.

I arrive at my office at eight-twenty, way early by law-firm standards. The halls are quiet. Not even the secretaries are in yet. I am turning to the Metro section of the paper, sipping my coffee when I notice the blinking red message light on my phone – usually a warning that more work awaits me. Some jackass partner must have called me on the one

37

weekend in recent memory when I failed to check my messages. My money is on Les, the dominant man in my life and the biggest jackass partner amid six floors of them. I enter my password, wait . . .

'You have one new message from an outside caller. Received today at seven forty-two a.m. . . .' the recording tells me. I hate that automated woman. She consistently bears bad news and does so in a chipper voice. They should adjust that recording at law firms, make the voice more somber. *'Uh-oh'* – (*with ominous* Jaws *music in background*) – *'you have four new messages . . .'*

What is it this time? I think, as I play the message.

'Hi, Rachel . . . It's me . . . Dex . . . I wanted to call you yesterday to talk about Saturday night but – I just couldn't. I think we should talk about it, don't you? Call me when you can. I should be around all day.'

My heart sinks. It never occurred to me that Dex might want to discuss what happened. Why can't he just learn some good old-fashioned avoidance techniques and ignore it, never speak of it again? That was my game plan. No wonder I hate my job; I am a litigator who hates confrontation. I pick up a pen and tap it against the edge of my desk. I hear my mother telling me not to fidget. I put the pen down and stare at the blinking light. The woman demands that a decision be made with respect to this message – I must replay it, save it, or delete it.

What does he want to talk about? What is there to say? I replay, expecting the answers to come to me in the sound of his voice, his cadence. But he gives nothing away. I replay

38

again and again until his voice starts to sound distorted, just as a word changes in your mouth when you repeat it enough times. *Egg, egg, egg, egg.* That used to be my favorite. I'd say it over and over until it seemed that I had the altogether wrong word for the yellow substance I was about to eat for breakfast.

I listen to Dex one final time before I delete him. His voice definitely sounds different. This makes sense because, in some ways, he is different. We both are. Because even if I try to block out what happened, even if Dex drops the Incident after a brief, awkward telephone call, we will forever be on one another's List – that list every person has, whether recorded in a secret spiral notebook or memorized in the back of the mind. Whether short or long. Whether ranked in order of performance or importance or chronology. Whether complete with first, middle, and last names or mere physical descriptions, like Darcy's List: '*Delta Sig with killer delts*' . . .

Dex is on my List for good. Without wanting to, I suddenly think of us in bed together. For those brief moments, he was just Dex – separate from Darcy.

I knew him first. It is no more ironclad than the Ethan defense, but I can't help clinging to it. I picture my sympathetic juror, leaning forward as she absorbs this revelation. She even raises the point during deliberations. *Rachel knew him first! Doesn't that give her some kind of pass?* The other jurors stare at her incredulously, and Chanel Suit tells her not to be ridiculous. That it has nothing to do with anything. But somehow my girl can't help thinking that this is pertinent. *After all, if it weren't for Rachel, Dex and*

Darcy would never have met. Rachel deserved one time with him.

I think back to when I first met Dex. Unlike most law students, who come straight from college when they can think of nothing better to do with their stellar undergrad transcripts, Dexter Thaler was older, with real life experience. He had worked as an analyst at Goldman Sachs, which blew away my nine-to-five summer internships and office jobs filing and answering phones. He was confident, relaxed, and so gorgeous that it was hard not to stare at him. I was positive that he would become the Doug Jackson and Blaine Conner of law school. Sure enough, we were barely into our first week of class when the buzz over Dexter began, women speculating about his status, noting either that his left ring finger was unadorned or alternatively worrying that he was too well dressed and handsome to be straight.

But I dismissed Dex straightaway, convincing myself that his outward perfection was boring. Which was a fortunate stance because I also knew that he was out of my league. (I hate that expression and the presumption that people choose mates based so heavily upon looks, but it is hard to deny the principle when you look around – partners generally share the same level of attractiveness, and when they do not it is noteworthy.) Besides, I wasn't borrowing thirty thousand dollars a year so that I could find a boyfriend.

As a matter of fact, I probably would have gone three years without talking to Dex, but we randomly ended up next to each other in torts, a seating-chart class taught by the sardonic Professor Zigman. Although many professors at

40

NYU used the Socratic method, only Zigman used it as a tool to humiliate and torture students. Dex and I bonded in our hatred of our mean-spirited professor. I feared Zigman to an irrational extreme, whereas Dexter's reaction had more to do with disgust. 'What an asshole,' he would growl after class, often after Zigman had reduced a fellow classmate to tears. 'I just want to wipe that smirk off his pompous face.'

Gradually, our grumbling turned into longer talks over coffee in the student lounge. We began to study together in the hour before class, preparing for the inevitable – the day Zigman would call on us. I dreaded my turn, knowing that it would be a bloody massacre, but secretly couldn't wait for Dexter to be called on. Zigman preyed on the weak and flustered, and Dex was neither. I was sure that he wouldn't go down without a fight.

I remember it well. Zigman stood behind his podium, examining his seating-chart, a schematic with our faces cut from the first-year look book, practically salivating as he picked his prey. He peered over his small, round glasses (the kind that should be called spectacles) in our general direction, and said, 'Mr. Thaler.'

He pronounced Dex's name wrong, making it rhyme with 'taller'.

'It's Thaa-ler,' Dex said, unflinching.

I inhaled sharply; nobody corrected Zigman. Dex was really going to get it now.

'Well, pardon me, Mr. Thaaa-ler,' Zigman said with an insincere little bow. 'Palsgraf v. Long Island Railroad Company.'

Dex sat calmly with his book closed while the rest of the

class nervously flipped to the case we had been assigned to read the night before.

The case involved a railroad accident. While rushing to board a train, a railroad employee knocked a package of dynamite out of a passenger's hand, causing injury to another passenger, Mrs. Palsgraf. Justice Cardozo, writing for the majority, held that Mrs. Palsgraf was not a 'foreseeable plaintiff' and, as such, could not recover from the railroad company. Perhaps the railroad employees should have foreseen harm to the package holder, the Court explained, but not to Mrs. Palsgraf.

'Should the plaintiff have been allowed recovery?' Zigman asked Dex.

Dex said nothing. For a brief second I panicked that he had frozen, like others before him. *Say no*, I thought, sending him fierce brain waves, *Go with the majority holding*. But when I looked at his expression, and the way his arms were folded across his chest, I could tell that he was only taking his time, in marked contrast to the way most first-year students blurted out quick, nervous, untenable answers as if reaction time could compensate for understanding.

'In my opinion?' Dex asked.

'I am addressing you, Mr. Thaler. So, yes, I am asking for your opinion.'

'I would have to say yes, the plaintiff should have been allowed recovery. I agree with Justice Andrews's dissent.'

'Ohhhh, really?' Zigman's voice was high and nasal.

'Yes. Really.'

I was surprised by his answer, as he had told me just

42

before class that he didn't realize crack cocaine had been around in 1928, but Justice Andrews surely must have been smoking it when he wrote his dissent. I was even more surprised by Dexter's brazen 'really' tagged onto the end of his answer, as though to taunt Zigman.

Zigman's scrawny chest swelled visibly. 'So you think that the guard should have foreseen that the innocuous package measuring fifteen inches in length, covered with a newspaper, contained explosives and would cause injury to the plaintiff?'

'It was certainly a possibility.'

'Should he have foreseen that the package could cause injury to *anybody in the world*?' Zigman asked with mounting sarcasm.

'I didn't say "anybody in the world". I said "the plaintiff". Mrs. Palsgraf, in my opinion, was in the danger zone.'

Zigman approached our row with ramrod posture, and tossed his *Wall Street Journal* on to Dex's closed textbook.

'Care to return my newspaper?'

'I'd prefer not to,' Dex said.

The shock in the room was palpable. The rest of us would have simply played along and returned the paper, mere props in Zigman's questioning.

'You'd prefer not to?' Zigman cocked his head.

'That's correct. There could be dynamite wrapped inside it.'

Half of the class gasped, the other half snickered. Clearly, Zigman had some tactic up his sleeve, some way of turning the facts around on Dex. But Dex wasn't falling for it. Zigman was visibly frustrated.

'Well, let's suppose you *did* choose to return it to me and it *did* contain a stick of dynamite and it *did* cause injury to your person? Then what, Mr. Thaler?'

'Then I would sue you, and likely I would win.'

'And would that recovery be consistent with Judge Cardozo's rationale in the majority holding?'

'No. It would not.'

'Oh, really? And why not?'

'Because I'd sue you for an intentional tort and Cardozo was talking about negligence, was he not?' Dex raised his voice to match Zigman's.

I think I stopped breathing as Zigman pressed his palms together and brought them neatly against his chest as though he were praying. 'I ask the questions in this classroom. If that's all right with you, Mr. Thaler?'

Dex shrugged as if to say, have it your way, makes no difference to me.

'Well, let's suppose that I accidentally dropped my paper onto your desk, and you returned it and were injured. Would Mr. Cardozo allow you full recovery?'

'Sure.'

'And why is that?'

Dex sighed to show that the exercise was boring him and then said swiftly and clearly, 'Because it was entirely foreseeable that the dynamite could cause injury to me. Your dropping the paper containing dynamite into my personal space violated my legally protected interest. Your negligent act caused a hazard apparent to the eye of ordinary vigilance.'

I studied the highlighted portions of my book. Dex was

quoting sections of Cardozo's opinion verbatim, without so much as glancing at his book or notes. The whole class was spellbound – nobody did this well, and certainly not with Zigman looming over him.

'And if Ms. Myers sued,' Zigman said, pointing to a trembling Julie Myers on the other side of the classroom, his victim from the day before. 'Should she be allowed recovery?'

'Under Cardozo's holding or Justice Andrews's dissent?'

'The latter. As it is the opinion you share.'

'Yes. Everyone owes to the world at large the duty of refraining from acts which unreasonably threaten the safety of others,' Dex said, another straight quote from the dissent.

It went on like that for the rest of the hour, Dex distinguishing nuances in changed fact patterns, never wavering, always answering decisively.

And at the end of the hour, Zigman actually said, 'Very good, Mr. Thaler.'

It was a first.

I left class feeling jubilant. Dex had prevailed for all of us. The story spread throughout the first-year class, earning him more points with the girls, who had long since determined that he was totally available.

I told Darcy the story as well. She had moved to New York at about the same time I did, only under vastly different circumstances. I was there to become a lawyer; she came without a job, or a plan, or much money. I let her sleep on a futon in my dorm room until she found some roommates – three American Airlines flight attendants looking to squeeze a fourth body into their heavily partitioned studio. She borrowed money from her parents to make the rent while she looked for a job, finally settling on a bartending position at the Monkey Bar. For the first time in our friendship, I was happy with my life in comparison to hers. I was just as poor, but at least I had a plan. Darcy's prospects didn't seem great with only a 2.9 GPA from Indiana University.

'You're so lucky,' Darcy would whine as I tried to study.

No, luck is what you *have*, I'd think. Luck is buying a lottery ticket along with your Yoo-hoo and striking it rich. Nothing about my life is lucky – it's all about hard work, it is all an uphill struggle. But of course, I never said that. Just told her that things would soon turn around for her.

And sure enough they did. About two weeks later a man waltzed into the Monkey Bar, ordered a whiskey sour and began to chat Darcy up. By the time he finished his drink, he had promised her a job at one of Manhattan's top PR firms. He told her to come in for an interview, but that he would (wink, wink) make sure that she got the job. Darcy took his business card, had me revise her résumé, went in for the interview, and got an offer on the spot. Her starting salary was seventy thousand dollars. Plus an expense account. Practically what I would make *if* I did well enough in school to get a job with a New York firm.

So while I sweated it out and racked up debt, Darcy began her glamorous PR career. She planned parties, promoted the season's latest fashion trends, got plenty of free everything, and dated a string of beautiful men. Within seven months, she left the flight attendants in the dust and moved in with her co-worker Claire, a snobbish, well-connected girl from Greenwich.

Darcy tried to include me in her fast-track life, although I seldom had time to go to her events or her parties or her blind date setups with guys she swore were 'total hotties' but that I knew were simply her castoffs.

Which brings me back to Dex. I raved about him to Darcy and Claire, told them how unbelievable he was – smart, handsome, funny. In retrospect I'm not sure why I did it. In part because it was true. But perhaps I was a little jealous of their glamorous life and wanted to juice mine up a bit. Dex was the best thing in my arsenal.

'So why don't *you* like him?' Darcy would ask.

'He's not my type,' I'd say. 'We're just friends.'

It wasn't until the following semester that Darcy and Dex met. A group of us from school, including Dex, planned an impromptu Thursday evening out. Darcy had been asking to meet Dex for weeks, so I phoned her and told her to be at the Red Lion at eight. She showed up, but Dex did not. I could tell Darcy viewed the whole outing as wasted effort, complaining that the Red Lion wasn't her scene, that she was over these grungy undergrad bars (which she had been into just a few short months ago), that the band sucked, and could we please leave and go somewhere nicer where people valued good grooming.

At that moment Dex sauntered into the bar wearing a black leather coat and a beautiful, oatmeal-colored cashmere sweater. He walked straight over to me and gave me a kiss on the cheek, which I still wasn't used to – Midwesterners don't kiss and greet like that. I introduced him to Darcy, and she turned on the charm, giggling and playing with her hair and

47

nodding emphatically whenever he said anything. Dex was pleasant back to her but didn't seem overly interested and, at one point, as she was dropping Goldman names – *Do you know this guy or that guy?* – Dex actually appeared to be suppressing a yawn. He left before the rest of us, waving goodbye to the group and telling Darcy it was nice to meet her.

On the walk back to my room, I asked her what she thought of him.

'He's cute,' Darcy said, giving the minimum endorsement. Her lackluster response irritated me. She couldn't praise him because he hadn't been dazzled enough by her. Darcy expected to be the one pursued. And that's what I had come to expect too.

The next day, as Dex and I had coffee, I waited for him to mention Darcy. I was sure he would, but he didn't. A small – okay, a *big* – part of me enjoyed telling Darcy that her name hadn't come up. For once, somebody wasn't falling all over themselves to be with her.

I should've known better.

About a week later, out of the blue, Dex asked me what the story was with my friend.

'Which friend?' I asked, playing dumb.

'You know, the dark-haired woman from the Red Lion?'

'Oh. Darcy,' I said. And then cut right to the chase. 'You want her phone number?'

'If she's single.'

I delivered the news to her that evening. She smiled coyly. 'He *is* pretty cute. I'll go out with him.'

It took Dex another two weeks to call her. If he waited on purpose, the strategy worked wonders. She was in a frenzy by the time he took her to Union Square Cafe. The date obviously went well, because they went to brunch the next morning in the Village. Soon after that, Darcy and Dex were both off the market.

In the beginning, their romance was turbulent. I always knew Darcy loved to fight with her boyfriends – it wasn't fun unless high drama was involved – but I viewed Dex as this rational, cool creature, above the fray. Maybe he had been that way with other girls, but Darcy sucked him into her world of chaos and high emotion. She'd find a phone number in one of his law-school notebooks (she was a self-proclaimed snoop), do the research, trace it back to an ex-girlfriend and refuse to speak to him. One day he came to class looking sheepish, with a cut on his forehead, right above his left eye. Darcy had hurled a wire hanger at him in a jealous rage.

And it worked the other way, too. We'd all go out and Darcy would cozy up to the bar with another guy. I'd watch Dex steal casual glances their way until he could stand it no longer. He'd go to collect her, looking angry but composed, and I'd overhear her justifying her flirtations with some tenuous connection to the guy: 'I mean, we were just talking about our brothers and how they were in the same freaking fraternity. Jesus, Dex! You don't have to overreact!'

But eventually their relationship stabilized, the fights grew less intense and more infrequent, and she moved into his apartment. Then, this past winter, Dex proposed. They picked a weekend in September, and she picked me as her maid of honor.

I see Chanel Suit shaking her head. *Her maid of honor! The ultimate betrayal!*

I work late that night, delaying my call back to Dex. I even consider waiting until tomorrow morning, mid-week, not calling at all. But I decide that the longer I wait, the more awkward it will be when I inevitably see Dex. So I force myself to sit down and dial his number. I hope for voice mail. It is ten-thirty. With any luck, Dex will be gone, home with Darcy.

'Dex Thaler,' he answers, his tone all business. He is back at Goldman Sachs, having wisely chosen the banker route over the lawyer route. The work is more interesting, and the money much better.

'Hi, Dex. It's Rachel.'

'Rachel!' He sounds genuinely happy to hear from me, although somewhat nervous, his voice a bit too loud. 'Thanks for calling. I was starting to think I wasn't going to hear from you.'

'I've been meaning to call. It's just that . . . I've been really busy . . . Crazy day,' I stammer. My mouth is bone dry.

'Yeah, it's been nuts here too. Typical Monday,' he says, sounding a bit more relaxed.

'Yeah . . .'

An awkward pause follows – well, it feels awkward to me. *Does he expect me to bring up the Incident?*

'So. How do you feel?' His voice becomes lower.

'How do I feel?' My face is burning, I'm sweating, and I

can't rule out the possibility of regurgitating my sushi dinner.

'I mean, what do you think about Saturday?' His voice is lower still, almost a whisper. Maybe he is just being discreet, making sure nobody in the office hears him, but the volume translates as intimate.

'I don't know what you're asking me . . .'

'Do you feel guilty?'

'Of course I feel guilty. Don't you?' I look out my window at the lights of Manhattan, in the direction of his downtown office.

'Well, yeah,' he says sincerely. 'Obviously. It shouldn't have happened. No question about that. It was wrong . . . and I don't want you to think that, you know, that it's typical practice for me. I've never cheated on Darcy before. Never . . .You believe that, don't you?'

I tell him that of course I believe him. I want to believe him.

Another silence.

'So, yeah, that was a first for me,' he says.

More silence. I picture him with his feet up on his desk, his collar loosened, tie thrown over his shoulder. He looks good in a suit. Well, he looks good in anything. And nothing.

'Uh-huh,' I say. I am gripping the phone so tightly that my fingers hurt. I switch hands and wipe my sweaty palm on my skirt.

'I feel so bad that you've been friends with Darcy forever, and this thing that happened between us . . . it puts you in a really atrocious position.' He clears his throat and continues. 'But at the same time, I don't know . . .'

51

'What don't you know?' I ask, against my better judgment to end the conversation, hang up the phone, choose the flight instinct that has always served me well.

'I don't know. I just . . . well, in some ways . . . well, objectively speaking, I know what I did was so wrong. But I just don't feel guilty. Isn't that awful? . . . Do you think less of me?'

I have no idea how to answer this one. 'Yes' seems mean and judgmental; 'no' might open the floodgates. I find safe middle ground. 'I have no room to judge anyone, do I? I was there . . . I did it too.'

'I know, Rachel. But it was my fault.'

I think about the elevator, the feel of his hair between my fingers.

'We were both at fault . . . We were both drunk. It must have been the shots – they just sneaked up on me and I hadn't really eaten much that day,' I ramble, hoping that we are nearly finished.

Dex interrupts. 'I wasn't that drunk,' he states plainly, almost defiantly.

You weren't that drunk?

As though he has read my mind, he continues. 'I mean, yes, I had a few drinks – my inhibitions certainly were lowered – but I knew what I was doing, and on some level, I think I wanted it to happen. I suppose that's a rather obvious statement . . . But what I mean is that I think I *consciously* wanted it to happen. Not that it was premeditated. But it had crossed my mind at various points before . . .'

At various points? When? In law school? Before or after he met Darcy?

I suddenly recall one pre-Darcy occasion when Dex and I were studying for our torts exam in the library. It was late and we were both punchy, almost delirious from lack of sleep and too much caffeine. Dex started imitating Zigman, quoting certain pet phrases of his, as I laughed so hard that I started to cry. When I finally got a hold of myself, he leaned across the narrow table and wiped a tear off my face with his thumb. Just like a scene in a movie, only usually those are sad tears. Our eyes locked.

I looked away first, returning my eyes to my book, the words jumping all over the page. I couldn't for the life of me focus on negligence or proximate cause. Only the feel of his thumb on my face. Later, Dex offered to walk me back to my dorm. I politely declined, telling him that I'd be fine on my own. As I was falling asleep that night, I decided that I had imagined his intent, that Dex would never care for me as more than a friend. He was only being nice.

Still, I sometimes wondered what would have happened if I hadn't been so guarded. If I had said yes to his offer that night. I am wondering now in a big way.

Dex keeps talking. 'Of course, I'm well aware it can never happen again,' he says with conviction. 'Right?' The last word is earnest, almost vulnerable.

'Right. Never *ever* again,' I say, immediately regretting my juvenile choice of words. 'It was a mistake.'

'But I don't regret it. I should, but I just don't,' he says.

This is so weird, I think, but say nothing. Just sit dumbly, waiting for him to speak again.

'So anyway, Rachel, I'm sorry for putting you in this

position. But I just thought you should know how I feel,' he finishes, then laughs nervously.

I say okay, well now I know, and I guess we should move on and put this behind us, and all of those other things that I thought Dex was calling to tell me. We say goodbye, then I hang up and stare out my window in a daze. The call that was supposed to bring closure only ushered in more uneasiness. And a tiny little stirring inside me, a stirring that I resolve to squelch.

I stand up, turn off my office light, and walk down to the subway, trying to put Dex out of my head. But as I wait on the subway platform, my mind returns to the kiss in the elevator. The feel of his hair. And the way he looked sleeping in my bed, half-covered by my sheets. Those are the images that I remember most. They are like the photographs of ex-boyfriends that you desperately want to throw away, but you can't bring yourself to get rid of them. So instead you store them in an old shoebox, in the back of your closet, figuring that it doesn't hurt to save them. Just in case you want to open that box and remember some of the good times.

FOUR

We are days away from the official start of summer and all Darcy can talk about is the Hamptons. She calls and emails me constantly, forwarding information about Memorial Day parties, restaurant reservations, and sample sales where we are guaranteed to find the cutest summer clothes. Of course, I am absolutely dreading all of it. Like the four previous summers, I am in a house with Darcy and Dex. This year we are also sharing with Marcus, Claire and Hillary.

'You think we should've gotten a full share?' Darcy asks for at least the twentieth time. I have never known such a second-, third-, fourth-guesser. She has buyer's remorse when she leaves Baskin Robbins.

'No, a half share is enough. You never end up using the full share,' I say, the phone tucked under my ear as I continue to revise my memo summarizing the difference between Florida and New York excess insurance law.

'Are you typing?' Darcy demands, expecting my full attention.

'No,' I lie, typing more quietly.

'You better not be . . .'

'I'm not.'

'Well, I guess you're right, a half share is better . . . And we have a lot of wedding stuff to do in the city anyway.'

The wedding is the only topic I wish to avoid more than the Hamptons. 'Uh-huh.'

'So do you want to drive out or take the train?'

'Train. I don't know if I can get out of here at a decent hour,' I say, thinking that I do not want to be stuck in a car with her and Dex. I have not seen Dex since he left my apartment. Have not seen Darcy since the betrayal.

'Really? 'Cause I was thinking that we should definitely, *definitely* drive . . . Wouldn't you rather have a car the first weekend out? You know, especially because it's going to be a long weekend. We don't want to be stuck with cabs and stuff . . . C'mon, ride with us!'

'We'll see,' I say, just as a mother tells a child so that the child will drop the topic.

'Not "we'll see". You're comin' with us.'

I sigh and tell her that I really should get back to work.

'Okay. Sheesh. I'll let you go work at your oh-so-important job . . . So we still on for tonight?'

'What's tonight?'

'Hello? *Ms. Forgetful!* Don't even tell me you have to work late – you promised. Bikinis? Ring a bell?'

'Oh, right,' I say. I had completely forgotten my promise to go bathing suit shopping with her. One of the least pleasant tasks in the world. Right up there with scrubbing toilets and getting a root canal. 'Yeah. Sure. I can still do it.'

'Great. I'll meet you at the yogurt counter in the

basement of Bloomie's. You know, next to the fat women's clothes. At seven sharp.'

I arrive at the Fifty-ninth Street station fifteen minutes after our designated meeting time and run into the basement of Bloomingdale's, nervous that Darcy will be pouting. I do not feel up to cajoling her out of one of her moods. But she looks content, sitting at the counter with a cup of strawberry frozen yogurt. She smiles and waves. I take a deep breath, reminding myself that there is no scarlet letter on my chest.

'Hi, Darce.'

'Hey, there! Omigod. I'm going to be so bloated trying on suits!' She points at her stomach with her plastic spoon. 'But whatever. I'm used to being a fatty.'

I roll my eyes. 'You're not fat.'

We go through it every year during bathing suit weather. Hell, we go through it virtually every day. Darcy's weight is a constant source of energy and discussion. She tells me what she is weighing in at – always hovering around the mid to high twenties – always too fat by her rigorous standards. Her goal is one-twenty, which I maintain is way too thin for five nine. She emails me as she eats a bag of chips: 'Make me stop! Help! Call me ASAP!' If I call her back, she'll ask, 'Is fifteen fat grams a lot?' Or, 'How many fat grams equal a pound?' The thing that irritates me, though, is that she is three inches taller than I am but five pounds lighter. When I point this out, she says, 'Yes, but your boobs are bigger.' 'Not five pounds bigger,' I say. 'Still,' she'll say, 'you look perfect the way you are.' *Back to me.*

I'm far from fat, but her using me as a sounding board on this topic is like me complaining to a blind woman that I have to wear contacts.

'I am so fat. I totally am! And I chowed at lunch. But whatever. As long as I'm not a fat cow in my wedding dress . . .' she says, finishing her last spoonful of yogurt and tossing the cup into the trash. 'Just tell me I have plenty of time to lose weight before the wedding.'

'You have plenty of time,' I say.

And I have plenty of time before the wedding to stop thinking about the fact that I had sex with your husband-to-be.

'I better rein it in, you know, or else I'm gonna have to shop here.' Darcy points at the plus size section without checking to see if any larger women are within earshot.

I tell her not to be ridiculous.

'So anyway,' she says, as we ride the escalator up to the second floor, 'Claire was saying that we're getting too old for bikinis. That one-pieces are classier. What do you think of *that*?' Her expression and tone make it clear what she thinks of Claire's view on swimwear.

'I don't think there are precise age limits on bikinis,' I say. Claire is full of exhausting rules; she once told me that black ink should only be used for sympathy notes.

'Ex-*act*-ly! That's what I told her . . . Besides, she's probably just saying that because she looks kind of bad in a bikini, don't you think?'

I nod. Claire works out religiously and hasn't touched fried food in years, but she is just destined to be lumpy. She is redeemed, however, by impeccable grooming and expensive clothing. She'll show up at the beach in a three-hundred-dollar one-piece with a matching sarong, a fancy hat, and designer glasses and it will go a long way toward disguising an extra roll around her waist.

We make our way around the floor, searching the racks for acceptable suits. At one point, I notice that we have both selected a basic black Anne Klein bikini. If we both end up wanting it, Darcy will either insist that she found it first or she'll say that we can get the same one. Then she will proceed to look better in it all summer. No thanks.

I am reminded of the time that she, Annalise, and I went shopping for backpacks the week before we started the fourth grade. We all spotted the same bag right away. It was purple with silver stars on the outside pocket – way cooler than the other bags. Annalise suggested that we get the same one and Darcy said no, that it was way too babyish to match. Matching was for third-graders.

So we rock-paper-scissored for it. I went with the rock (which I have found to be a winner more than its share of the time). I pounded my jubilant fist over their extended scissor fingers and swept my purple book bag into our shared cart. Annalise balked, whining that we knew purple was her favorite color. 'I thought you liked red better, Rachel!'

Annalise was no match for me. I simply told her, yes, I did prefer red, but as she could plainly see, there were no red bags. So Annalise settled for a yellow one with a smiley face on the pocket. Darcy agonized over the remaining choices and finally told us that she was going to sleep on the decision and come back with her mom the next day. I forgot about Darcy's bag choice until the first day of school. When I got to the bus stop, there stood Darcy with a purple bag just like mine.

I pointed at it, incredulous. 'You got my bag.'

'I know,' Darcy said. 'I decided I wanted it. Who cares if we match?'

Hadn't she been the one to say that matching was babyish?

'I care,' I said, feeling the rage grow inside me.

Darcy rolled her eyes and smacked her gum. 'Oh, Rachel, like it matters. It's just a bag, after all.'

Annalise was upset too, for her own reasons. 'How come you two get to be twins and I'm left out? My bag is gay.'

Darcy and I ignored her.

'But you said we shouldn't match,' I accused Darcy, as the bus pulled around the corner and screeched to a stop in front of us.

'Did I?' she said, fingering her stiff, feathered hair, freshly sprayed with several layers of Breck. 'Well, who cares?'

Darcy used 'who cares' (later replaced by 'whatever') as the ultimate passive-aggressive response. I didn't recognize her tactic as such at the time; I only knew that she always managed to get her way and make me feel stupid if I fought back.

We boarded the bus, Darcy first. She sat down and I sat behind her, still furious. I watched Annalise hesitate and then sit with me, recognizing that I had right on my side. The whole purple backpack issue could have escalated into a full-fledged fight, but I refused to let Darcy's betrayal ruin the first day of school. It wasn't worth going to battle with her. The end result was seldom satisfying.

I covertly replace the Anne Klein suit on the rack as we make our way to the long lines for the dressing rooms. When one becomes available, Darcy decides that we should share a room to save time. She strips down to her black thong and matching lace bra, contemplating which suit she should try on first. I steal a look at her in the mirror. Her body is even better than it was last summer. Her long limbs are perfectly toned from her wedding work-out regimen, her skin already bronzed by routine applications of tanning cream and an occasional trip to the tanning beds.

I think of Dex. Surely he compared our bodies after (or even during, since he 'wasn't that drunk') our night together. Mine isn't nearly as good. I am shorter, softer, whiter. And even though my boobs are bigger, hers are better. They are perkier, with the ideal nipple-to-areola-to-breast ratio.

'Stop looking at my fat!' Darcy squeals, catching my glance in the mirror.

Now I am forced to compliment her. 'You're not fat, Darce. You look great. I can tell you've been working out.'

'You can? What body part has improved?' Darcy likes her praise to be specific.

'Just everywhere. Your legs look thin – good.' That is all she is getting from me. I have long since grown out of my adolescent jealousies and accepted that she is prettier than I am, but her endless fishing for compliments makes me weary.

She studies her legs, frowning at the reflection.

I undress, noting my own cotton underwear and non-matching, slightly dingier cotton bra. I quickly try on my first suit, a navy and white tankini, revealing two inches of midriff. It is a compromise between Claire's one-piece edict and Darcy's preference for bikinis.

'Omigod! That looks so awesome on you! You gotta get it!' Darcy says. 'Are you getting it?'

'I guess so,' I say. It doesn't look awesome, but it's not bad. I have studied enough magazine articles about suits and body flaws over the years to know which suits will look decent on me. This one passes.

Darcy puts on a tiny black bikini with a triangular top and bare coverage in the bottom. She looks straight-up hot. 'You like?'

'It's good,' I say, thinking that Dex will love it.

'Should I get it?'

I tell her to try the others on before making a decision. She obeys, taking the next one off the hanger. Of course, every suit looks amazing on her. She falls into none of those categories of body flaws in the magazines. After much discussion, I settle on the tankini and Darcy decides on three tiny bikinis – one red, one black, and one nude-colored number that is going to make her look naked from any kind of distance.

As we go to pay for our suits, Darcy grabs my arm. 'Oh! Shit! I almost forgot to tell you!'

'What?' I ask, unnerved by her sudden outburst, even though I know she isn't going to say, 'I forgot to tell you that I know you slept with Dex!'

'Marcus likes you!' We might as well be in the tenth grade, from her tone and use of the word 'likes'.

I am intentionally obtuse. 'I like him too,' I say. 'He's a nice guy.' *And a hell of an alibi.*

'No, silly. I mean, he *likes* you. You must've done a good job at the party because he called Dex and got your number. I think he's going to ask you out for this weekend. Of course, I wanted it to be a double date, but Marcus said no, he doesn't want witnesses.' She drops her bikinis onto the counter and fumbles in her purse for her wallet.

'He got my number from Dex?' I ask, thinking that this is quite a development.

'Yeah. Dex was cute when he told me about it. He was . . .' She looks up, searching for the right word. 'Sort of protective of you.'

'What do you mean by "protective"?' I ask, way more interested in Dex's role in this exchange than in Marcus's intentions.

'Well, he gave Marcus the number, but when he got off the phone he asked me all these questions, like were you seeing anyone and did I think you would like Marcus. And you know, was he smart enough for you. Stuff like that. It was really cute.'

I digest this information as the store clerk rings up Darcy's bikinis.

'So what did you tell him?'

'I just said that you were *totally* single, and that of course you'd be into Marcus. He's such a sweetie. Don't you think?'

I shrug. Marcus moved to New York from San Francisco only a few months ago. I know very little about him, except that he and Dex became friends at Georgetown, where Marcus's claim to fame was graduating dead last. Apparently

63

Marcus never went to class and got high all the time. The most infamous story is that he overslept on the day of his statistics final exam, showed up twenty minutes late only to discover that he had thrown his remote control into his backpack instead of his calculator. I haven't yet determined whether he is a free spirit or simply a buffoon.

'So are you psyched? If you get a date in with him before our share starts, you will have dibs on him over Claire and Hillary.'

I laugh and shake my head.

'Seriously.' Darcy signs her receipt and flashes a smile at the clerk. 'Claire would love to sink her nails in him.'

'Who said I'm going on a date?'

'Oh, puh-lease. Don't even start with that shit. You're going. (A) he is such a cutie. And (B) Rachel, no offense, but you can't exactly afford to be all picky, Ms. Haven't Been Laid in, what? Over a year?'

The store clerk looks up at me sympathetically. I glare at Darcy as I slide my tankini across the counter. *Yeah – a year.*

We leave Bloomingdale's and look for a cab on Third Avenue.

'So, you'll go out with Marcus?'

'I guess so.'

'Promise?' she asks, getting her cell phone out of her purse.

'You want me to take a blood oath? Yes, I'll go,' I say. 'Who are you calling?'

'Dex. He bet me twenty bucks that you wouldn't go.'

That is all I need to know to say yes to Marcus when he calls the next afternoon to ask me to dinner at Gotham Bar and

Grill. Darcy's right – I have nothing else going on. But, more important, Dex said I wouldn't go. And just in case he thought he had cast some sort of spell over me and I was going to turn Marcus down because I'm preoccupied with the Incident, I will go on the date with Marcus.

But then I start obsessing about what Marcus *really* knows. Did Dex tell him anything? I decide that I must call Dexter and find out. I hang up three times before I can dial the full number. My stomach is churning when he answers on the first ring. 'Dex Thaler.'

'What does Marcus know about what happened last Saturday?' I blurt out, my heart racing.

'Well, hello to you too,' he says.

I soften slightly. 'Hi, Dex.'

'Last Saturday? What was last Saturday? Refresh my memory.'

'I'm being serious! What did you tell him?' I am horrified to find myself talking in the girly, whiny way that Darcy has perfected.

'What do you think I told him?' he asks.

'Dexter, tell me!'

'Oh, relax,' he says, his tone still one of amusement. 'I didn't tell him anything . . . What do you think this is? A high school locker room? Why would I tell anyone our business?'

Our business. *Our. We. Us.*

'I was just wondering what he knew. I mean, you told Darcy you were with him that night . . .'

'Yeah. I said, "Marcus, I was with you last night and we

65

had breakfast together this morning, all right?" And that was that. I know that's not how it works with you girls – women.'

'What is that supposed to mean?'

'I mean you and Darcy share every exhaustive detail with one another. Like what you ate that day and what brand of shampoo you plan on purchasing.'

'And like when you sleep with one another's fiancé? That sort of detail?'

Dex laughs. 'Yeah, that would be another example.'

'Or like your bet that I'd say no to Marcus?'

He laughs again, knowing that he is busted. 'She told you that, did she?'

'Yeah. She told me that.'

'And did it offend you?'

I realize that I am starting to relax, almost enjoying the conversation. 'No . . . but it made me say yes to Marcus.'

'Oh!' he laughs. 'I see how it works. So had she not shared that piece of information with you, you would have turned my boy down?'

'Wouldn't you like to know?' I ask coyly, hardly recognizing myself.

'I would actually. Please enlighten me.'

'I'm not sure. . . . Why did you think that I'd say no?'

'Wouldn't you like to know,' he retorts.

I smile. This is full-fledged flirtatious banter.

'Okay. I thought you'd say no because Marcus doesn't seem to be your type,' he finally says.

'And who is?' I ask, and then feel instantly remorseful. Flirting like this is not the path to redemption. It is no way to

66

right the wrong I committed against Darcy. This is what my brain tells me, but my heart is galloping as I await his answer.

'I don't know. I've been trying to figure that out for about seven years.'

I wonder what he means by this statement. I twist the cord around my fingers and can think of nothing to say in response. We should hang up now. This is going in a bad direction.

'Rach?' His voice is low and intimate.

I feel breathless, hearing him say my name like this. The one syllable is familiar, warm. 'Yeah?'

'You still there?' he whispers.

I manage to say, 'Yes, I'm still here.'

'What are you thinking?'

'Nothing,' I lie.

I have to lie. Because what I am thinking is, *Maybe you are my type just a little bit more than I once thought.*

FIVE

Maybe I don't have a type at all. When I consider my past relationships there is no composite picture. Not that the sample would be considered statistically significant – other than Brandon in high school, I have had only three boyfriends.

My real dating history began my first semester of college at Duke. I lived in a co-ed dorm, and every night we all gathered in the lounge to study (or pretend to), hang out, and watch shows like *Beverly Hills, 90210* and *Melrose Place*. It was in that lounge that I developed a serious crush on Hunter Bretz from Mississippi. Hunter was scrawny and nerdy, but I was crazy about him. I loved his intelligence, his slow, smooth drawl, and the way his brown eyes fixed on you when you talked, as though he really cared about what you had to say. My roommate Pam, a Jersey girl with big hair, declared my feelings a 'total fucking mystery' but still encouraged me to ask Hunter out. I didn't, but I did work hard at developing a friendship, cracking through his shy exterior to talk to him about poetry and literature. I really believed I was making progress with Hunter when Joey Merola came in for the kill.

Joey was the opposite of Hunter – a boisterous sports guy with a loud laugh. He played every intramural sport in the book and was always strolling into the lounge all sweaty with a story about how his team came from behind in the last second to win the game. He was the kind of guy who was proud of how much he could eat and the fact that he could get by in literature classes without ever reading a book.

One Thursday night, Joey, Hunter, and I were the last three in the lounge, talking about religion, the death penalty, and the meaning of life, the stuff I had imagined discussing in college, away from Darcy and her more shallow pursuits. Joey was an atheist and pro-death penalty. Like me, Hunter was Methodist and against the death penalty. All three of us were unclear on the meaning of life. We talked and talked, and I was determined to outlast Joey and end up with Hunter. But some time after two, Hunter threw in the towel. 'Awright y'all, I have an early class.'

'C'mon, man. Skip it. I never make my eight o'clock,' Joey said proudly.

Hunter laughed. 'I figure I'm payin' for it, I should go.'

This was another thing I liked about Hunter. He was paying for his own education, unlike the rich kids at Duke. So he said good night, and I wistfully watched him amble out of the lounge. Joey didn't miss a beat, just kept yapping, rehashing the fact that we were both from Indiana – just two towns apart – and that both of our fathers had attended Indiana (his dad had been a walk-on for the basketball team). We played the name game and got two hits. Joey knew Blaine, Darcy's ex-boyfriend, from reading the local sports page. And we both knew of Tracy Purlington, a promiscuous girl from the town between ours.

69

Finally, when I said I really must get to bed, Joey followed me upstairs and kissed me in the stairwell. I thought of Hunter, but I still kissed Joey back, excited to be getting some real collegiate experience. Annalise had already met her now-husband Greg (and lost her virginity to him), and Darcy had hooked up with four guys by my latest count.

The next morning I regretted kissing Joey. Even more so when I spotted Hunter hunkered down in the library stacks, his head bent over a textbook. But not enough to keep me from kissing Joey again that weekend, this time in the laundry room as we waited for our clothes to dry. And so it continued until everybody in our dorm, including Hunter, knew that Joey and I were an item. Pam was psyched for me – said that Joey blew Hunter away and had the cutest butt in the dorm. I wrote to Darcy and Annalise, telling them about my new boyfriend and how I was over Hunter (only partly true) and how happy I was (happy enough). They both had one question: was I going to go *all the way* with Joey?

I was ambivalent on the subject of sex. Part of me wanted to wait until I was deeply in love, maybe even married. But I was also intensely curious to find out what all the fuss was about, and desperately wanted to be sophisticated and worldly. So after Joey and I had been together a respectable six weeks, I marched over to the school health clinic and returned to my dorm with a prescription for Lo-Ovral, the birth control pill that Darcy guaranteed would not cause weight gain. A month later, with the added protection of a condom, Joey and I did the great deed. It was his first time too. The earth didn't move during those two and a half minutes, as Darcy claimed it did during her first time with Carlos. But it also didn't hurt as much as Annalise had warned me it would. I was relieved to have it out of the way and happy to join my hometown friends in all their womanly glory. Joey and I embraced in my bottom bunk and said that we loved each other. Ours was a better first time than most.

But that spring, there were two red flags indicating that Joey wasn't the man of my dreams. First, he joined a fraternity and took the whole thing way too seriously. One night when I teased him about his secret handshake, he told me that if I disrespected his brotherhood, I was disrespecting him. *Please*. Second, Joey became obsessed with Duke basketball, sleeping out in tents for tickets to big games and painting his face blue, jumping up and down courtside with the other 'Cameron Crazies'. The whole scene was a bit much, but I guess I would have been fine with his enthusiasm if he had been from New Hampshire or another state with no huge basketball ties. But he was from Indiana. Big Ten country. His father played for the Hoosiers, for God's sake. And there he was, this sudden die-hard 'I've liked Duke since the dawn of time and I'm all tight with Bobby Hurley because he once drank at my frat house' kind of a fan. But I looked beyond these imperfections, and we forged ahead to sophomore and then junior year.

Then one night, after Wake Forest beat Duke in hoops, Joey showed up at my place in a foul mood. We began to argue about nothing and everything. First it was petty matters: he said that I snored and hogged the bed (how can you *not* hog a twin bed?); I complained that he consistently

71

mixed up our toothbrushes (who makes that mistake?). The arguing escalated to more significant issues. And there was no turning back when he called me a boring intellectual and I called him a shameless bandwagoner who actually believed that his painted blue face contributed to Duke's championships. He told me to lighten up and get some school pride before storming off.

He returned the next day with a solemn face and his scripted 'we need to have a talk' introduction followed by the 'we'll always be close' conclusion. I was more stunned than sad, but I agreed that maybe we should be having a more diverse college experience, which really meant dating other people. We said we would always be friends, even though I knew we didn't have enough in common for that to happen.

I didn't shed a tear until I saw him at a party holding hands with Betsy Wingate, who had also lived in our freshmen dorm. I didn't want to be holding his hand, so I knew my reaction was only a mix of nostalgia and hurt pride. And regret that maybe I should have stuck with Hunter, who had long since been snatched up by another discerning undergraduate.

I phoned Darcy in a rare case of role reversal, seeking comfort from the relationship pro. She told me not to look back, that I had some good, rah-rah college memories with Joey, something I wouldn't have had with Hunter, who would have dragged me down socially. 'Besides,' she said earnestly, 'Joey taught you the basics of predictable, missionary-style sex. And that's worth something, right?' It was her idea of a pep talk. I guess it helped a little.

I kept hoping that Hunter and his girlfriend would break

72

up, but it never happened. I didn't date again at Duke, nor did I through most of law school. The long drought finally ended with Nate Menke.

I met Nate our first year of law school at a party, but for the next three years we barely talked, only said hello in passing. Then we both found ourselves in the same small class: The Empowered Self: Law and Society in the Age of Individualism. Nate spoke in class often, but not just to hear himself speak, as half the people in law school did. He actually had interesting things to say. After I made a decent point one day, he asked if I wanted to grab a coffee to discuss it further. He ordered his black, and I remember copying him because it seemed more sophisticated than dumping milk and sugar into my cup. After coffee, we took a long walk through the Village, stopping in CD stores and used-book shops. We went to dinner after that, and by the end of the evening it was clear that we were going to become a couple.

I was thrilled to have a boyfriend again and became quickly enthralled with most things about Nate. I liked his face, for one. He had the coolest eyes that turned up slightly in a way that would have made him look Asian but for his light coloring. I also liked his personality. He was soft-spoken, but strong-willed and politically active in a defiant, angry sort of way. It was hard to keep track of all his causes, but I tried, even convinced myself that I felt the same way. Compared to Joey, who could only muster passion for a basketball team, Nate seemed so real. He was intense in bed too. Although he had had few partners before me, he seemed very experienced, always urging me to try something new.

73

'How's this?' 'How's that?' he would ask, and then would memorize his position and get it just right the next time.

Nate and I graduated from law school and spent the summer in the city, studying for the bar exam. Every day we went to the library together, breaking only for meals and sleep. Hour after hour, day after day, week after week, we crammed thousands of rules and facts and laws and theories into our crowded brains. We were both driven less by the desire to succeed than by an all-pervasive fear of failure, which Nate chalked up to our being only children. The relentless ordeal brought us closer. We were both miserable, but happy in our misery together.

But that fall, only one of us stayed miserable. Nate began working as an assistant district attorney in Queens, and I started my law firm job in Midtown. He loved his job, and I hated mine. As Nate interviewed witnesses and prepared for trial, I was relegated to document productions – the lowliest task in the legal profession. Every night I'd sit in conference rooms studying piles of papers in endless cardboard boxes. I'd look at the dates on those documents and think, *I was just getting my driver's license when this letter was typed, and here it is, still caught in an endless cycle of litigation*. It all seemed so pointless.

So my life was bleak – except for my relationship with Nate. I began to rely on him more and more as my sole source of happiness. I often told him that I loved him, and felt more relief than joy when he said it back. I started to think about marriage, even talked about our theoretical children and where we all might live.

Then one night Nate and I went to a bar in the Village to

hear a folk singer from Brooklyn named Carly Weinstein. After her performance, Nate and I and a few other people chatted with her as she put her guitar away with the gentleness of a new mother.

'Your lyrics are beautiful . . . what inspires you?' Nate asked her, big-eyed.

I was instantly worried; I remembered that look from our first coffee date. I became even more distressed when he bought a copy of her CD. She wasn't *that* good. I think Nate and Carly went on a date a week later, because there was one night when he was unaccounted for and didn't answer his cell phone until after midnight. I was too afraid to ask where he had been. Besides, I already knew. He had changed. He looked at me differently, a shadow over his face, his mind somewhere else.

Sure enough, we had the big talk soon after that. He was very forthright. 'I have feelings for someone else,' he said. 'I always promised that I would tell you.'

I remembered those conversations well, remembered liking the strong, confident way I sounded as I told him that if he ever met someone else, he should just tell me outright, that I could handle it. Of course, I didn't think at the time that it would ever leave the hypothetical realm. I wanted to suck back all of my cavalier instructions, tell him instead that I would greatly prefer a gentle lie about needing some space or some time apart.

'Is it Carly?' I asked, a catch in my throat.

He looked shocked. 'How did you know?'

'I could just tell,' I said, unable to fight back sobs.

'I'm so sorry,' he said, hugging me. 'It kills me to hurt you like this. But I had to be honest. I owe you that.'

So he got a new girl, *and* he got to be noble. I tried to be angry, but how can you be mad at someone for not wanting to be with you? Instead I just sulked around, gained a few pounds, and swore off men.

Nate kept calling for a few months after our break-up. I knew he was just being nice, but the calls gave me false hope. I could never resist asking about his girlfriend. 'Carly is fine,' he would say sheepishly. Then once, he answered, 'We're moving in together . . . and I think we're going to get engaged . . .' His voice trailed off.

'Congratulations. That's great. I'm really happy for you,' I said.

'Thank you, Rachel. It means a lot to hear you say that.'

'Yeah . . . Best of luck and all, but I don't think I want you to call me anymore, okay?'

'I understand,' he said, probably relieved to be off the hook.

I haven't heard from Nate since that conversation. I'm not sure if or when they married, but I still look for Carly Weinstein sometimes when I'm shopping for CDs. So far she hasn't made it big.

Looking back, I question whether I really loved Nate, or just the security of our relationship. I wonder if my feelings for him didn't have a lot to do with hating my job. From the bar exam through that first hellish year as an associate, Nate was my escape. And sometimes that can feel an awful lot like love.

A reasonable time passed after Nate. I lost my break-up

weight, got my hair highlighted, and agreed to a string of blind dates. At worst they were awful. At best, simply uncomfortable and forgettable. Then I met Alec Kaplan at Spy Bar, down in SoHo. I was with Darcy and some of her friends from work and he and his oh-so-hip friends approached us. Alec, of course, wooed Darcy at first, but she pushed him my way – literally, with her hand in the small of his back – with firm directions to 'talk to my friend'. To her, it was the ultimate in generosity. Even though she had Dex, she was never one to turn down male attention. 'He's really cute,' Darcy kept whispering. 'Go for it.'

She was right, Alec was cute. But he was also all about image. He was the kind of guy who turns in his college cool-boy uniform of filthy, intentionally broken-in baseball caps, fraternity party T-shirts, and woven leather belts, and swaps it for his twenty-something urban cool-boy uniform of gripping, cotton-spandex T-shirts, tight black pants with a slight sheen and loads of hair gel. He told too many 'a guy walks into a bar' jokes (none funny) and 'I'm a badass trader' war stories (none impressive). When he bought me a drink on that first night, he threw down a one-hundred-dollar bill and told the bartender in a loud voice that he was sorry but he didn't have anything smaller. In a nutshell, he epitomized what Darcy and I call 'TTH', for Trying Too Hard.

But Alec was smart enough, fun enough, and nice enough. So when he asked for my number, I gave it to him. And when he called and asked me out to dinner, I went. And when he propositioned me, four dates later, ribbed condom in hand, I shrugged inside but said yes. He had a great body, but the sex was just average. My mind often wandered to work, and once, when I heard *SportsCenter* in the background, I even pretended he was Pete Sampras. Many times I came close to breaking up with him, but Darcy kept telling me to give him another chance, that he was rich and cute. Way richer and cuter than Nate, she'd point out. As if that was what it was all about.

Then one night, Claire spotted Alec kissing a petite, somewhat trashy-looking blonde at Merchants. When the girl went to the bathroom, Claire confronted Alec, warning him that if he didn't confess his infidelity, she would tell me herself. So the next day Alec called and sputtered an apology, saying he was getting back together with his ex, who I assume was the girl at Merchants. I almost told him that I had wanted to break up too – it was the truth. But I cared so little that I didn't bother setting the record straight. I simply said okay, best of luck. And that was that.

Every now and then I run into Alec at the New York Sports Club near work. We are very cordial to each other – once I even used the StairMaster beside his, not caring that my face was broken out or that I was wearing my sloppiest gray sweats (Darcy says they should never be worn in public). On that occasion, we made small talk. I even inquired about his girlfriend, letting him ramble on about their upcoming trip to Jamaica. It took no effort at all to be nice, another clear indication that I'd had nothing real invested in our relationship. In some ways, in fact, I shouldn't even put Alec in the serious boyfriend category. But because I slept with him (and see myself as the sort of woman who would only sleep with someone in a legitimate relationship), I put him in that unfortunately exclusive club.

I review my three boyfriends, the three men I slept with in my twenties, searching for a common thread. Nothing. No consistent features, coloring, stature, personality. But one theme does emerge: they all picked me. And then dumped me. I played the passive role. Waiting for Hunter and then settling for Joey. Waiting to feel more for Nate. Then waiting to feel less. Waiting for Alec to go away and leave me in peace.

And now Dex. My number four. And I am still waiting.

For all of this to blow over.

For his September wedding.

For someone who gives me that tingly feeling as I watch him sleeping in my bed early on a Sunday morning. Someone who isn't engaged to my best friend.

SIX

On Saturday night, I cab down to Gotham Bar and Grill with an open mind and positive attitude – half the battle before any date – thinking that maybe Marcus will be the someone I am looking for.

I walk into the restaurant and spot him right away, sitting at the bar wearing baggy jeans and a slightly wrinkled, plaid green shirt with the sleeves rolled up haphazardly – the opposite of TTH.

'Sorry I'm late,' I say, as Marcus stands to greet me. 'Had some trouble getting a cab.'

'No worries,' he says, offering me a stool next to his.

I sit down. He smiles, exposing two rows of very white, straight teeth. Possibly his best feature. Either that or the cleft in his square chin.

'So what can I get you?' he asks me.

'What are you having?'

'Gin and tonic.'

'I'll have the same.'

He glances toward the bartender with a twenty extended and then looks back at me. 'You look great, Rachel.'

I thank him. It's been a long time since I've received a

proper compliment from a guy. It occurs to me that Dex and I didn't get around to compliments.

Marcus finally gets the bartender's attention and orders me a Bombay Sapphire and tonic. Then he says, 'So, last time I saw you we were all pretty wasted . . . That was a fun night.'

'Yeah. I was pretty out of it,' I say, hoping that Dex told me the truth about keeping Marcus in the dark. 'But at least I made it home before sunup. Darcy told me that you and Dex were out pretty late that night.'

'Yeah. We hung out for a while,' Marcus says, without looking at me. This is a good sign. He is covering for his friend but has trouble lying. He takes his change from the bartender, leaves two bills and some coins on the bar, and hands me my drink. 'Here you go.'

'Thanks.' I smile, stir, and sip from the skinny straw.

An emaciated Asian girl wearing leather pants and too much lip liner taps Marcus on the arm and tells him that our table is ready. We carry our drinks, following her to the quieter restaurant area behind the bar. As we sit, she hands us two oversized menus and a separate wine list.

'Your server will be with you shortly,' she says before flipping her long, black hair and waltzing off.

Marcus glances at the wine list and asks if I want to order a bottle.

'Sure,' I say.

'Red or white?'

'Either.'

'Do you think you're going to have fish?' He looks at the menu.

81

'Maybe. But I don't mind red with fish.'

'I'm not very good at picking wines,' he says, cracking his knuckles below the table. 'You wanna have a look?'

'That's okay. You can pick. Whatever is fine.'

'All right then. I'll wing it,' he says, flashing me his 'I never skipped a night wearing my retainer' smile.

We study our menus, discussing what looks good. Marcus slides his chair closer to the table, and I feel his knee against mine.

'I almost didn't ask you out, since we're in the same summer house and all,' Marcus says, his eyes still scanning the menu. 'Dex told me that's one of the cardinal rules here. Don't get involved with someone in your house. At least not until August.'

He laughs as I store away this fact for later analysis: *Dex discouraged our date.*

'But then I thought, you know, what the hell – I dig her, I'm going to call her. I mean, I've been thinking about asking you out since Dex first introduced us. Right when I moved here. But I was seeing this girl from San Francisco for a minute in there and thought I should wrap things up before I called you. You know, just to make it all neat and kosher. So I finally ended that deal . . . And here we are.' He wipes his forehead with the back of his hand as if he is relieved to make this confession.

I smile, feeling myself warm to him. He doesn't evoke the feelings Dex gives me, but he is pleasant and easy to be with. 'I think you made the right decision.'

'To wait?'

'No. To call.' I give him my most alluring smile, fleetingly reminding myself of Darcy. She doesn't have the market cornered on female attractiveness, I think. I don't always have to be the serious, dowdy one.

Our waitress interrupts the moment. 'Hello. How are you this evening?'

'Fine,' Marcus says cheerfully, and then lowers his voice. 'For a first date.'

I laugh, but our waitress musters only a stiff, tight-lipped smile. 'Can I tell you about the specials?'

'Go for it,' Marcus says.

She stares into the space just above our heads, rattling off the list of specials, calling everything 'nice' – 'a nice sea bass', 'a nice risotto' and so on. I nod and only half listen while I think about Dex telling Marcus not to ask me out, wondering what that means.

'So would you like to start with something to drink?'

'Yeah . . . think we're going with a bottle of red. What do you recommend?' He squints at the menu.

'The Marjorie Pinot Noir is *superb*.' She points down at the wine list.

'Fine. That one then. Perfect.'

She flashes another prim smile my way. 'And are you ready to order?'

'Yes, I think we are,' I say, and then ask for the garden salad and tuna.

'And how would you like that done?'

'Medium,' I say.

Marcus orders the pea soup and the lamb.

'Excellent choices,' our waitress says with an affected tilt of the head. She gathers our menus and turns on her heels.

'Man,' says Marcus.

'What?'

'That chick has zero personality.'

I laugh.

He smiles. 'Where were we? . . . Oh yeah, the Hamptons.'

'Right.'

'So Dex says it's never a good idea to go out with someone in your own house. And I'm like, "Dude, I'm not playin' by your dumb East Coast rules." If we end up hating each other, we hate each other.'

'I don't think we're going to hate each other,' I say.

Our waitress returns with the wine, uncorks the bottle, and pours some into his glass. Marcus takes a healthy sip and reports that it's great, skipping the usual pretentious ceremony. You can tell a lot about a guy by watching him take that first sip of wine. I hate when he does the whole swirling thing, burying his nose into the glass, taking a slow, thoughtful sip, pausing with a furrowed brow followed by a slight nod so as not to appear too enthusiastic, as if to say, this passes, but I have had plenty better. If he is truly a wine connoisseur, that's one thing. But it is usually just a bunch of show, painful to observe.

As our waitress pours my wine, I ask Marcus if he knows about the bet.

He shakes his head. 'What bet?'

I wait until we are alone again – it's bad enough that our waitress knows this is a first date. 'Dex and Darcy had a bet about whether I'd say yes when you asked me out.'

'Get outta here.' He drops his jaw for effect. 'Who thought you'd go and who thought you'd diss me?'

'Oh. I forget.' I pretend to be confused. 'That's not the point. The point is—'

'That they are so up and in our business!' He shakes his head. 'Bastards.'

'I know.'

He lifts his glass. 'To eluding Dex and Darcy. No sharing details of tonight with those nosy bastards.'

I laugh. 'No matter how great – or how bad – our date is!'

Our glasses touch and we sip in unison.

'This date is *not* going to be bad. Trust me on that.'

I smile. 'I trust you.'

I do trust him, I think. There is something disarming about his sense of humor and easy, Midwestern style. And he's not engaged to Darcy. A nice bonus.

Then, as if on cue, Marcus asks me how long I've known Darcy.

'Twenty-some years. First time I saw her she was all dressed up in this fancy little sundress, and I was wearing these dumb Winnie-the-Pooh shorts from Sears. I thought, now *there's* a girl with style.'

Marcus laughs. 'I bet you looked cute in your Pooh shorts.'

'Not quite . . .'

'And then you were the one who introduced Darcy and Dex, right? He said you were good friends in law school?'

Right. My good friend Dex. The last person I slept with.

'Uh-huh. I met him first semester of law school. I knew

85

right away that he and Darcy would make a good match,' I say. A bit of an exaggeration, but I want to set the record straight that I never considered Dex for myself. Which I didn't. And still don't.

'They even look alike . . . No mystery as to how their kids will turn out.'

'Yes. They will be beautiful.' I feel an inexplicable knot in my chest, picturing Dex and Darcy cradling their newborn. For some reason, I had never thought beyond the wedding in September.

'What?' Marcus asks, obviously catching my expression. Which doesn't mean he is perceptive, necessarily; my face is less than inscrutable. It is a curse.

'Nothing,' I say. Then I smile and sit up a bit straighter. It is time for a transition. 'Enough about Dex and Darcy.'

'Yeah,' he says. 'I hear you.'

We start the typical first-date conversation, discussing our jobs, our families and general backgrounds. We cover his Internet start-up that went under and his move to New York. Our food arrives. We eat and talk and order another bottle of wine. There is more laughter than silence. I am even comfortable enough to take a bite of his lamb when he offers it to me.

After dinner, Marcus pays the bill. It is always an awkward moment for me, although offering to pay (whether sincerely or with the fake reach for the wallet) is so much more awkward. I thank him and we make our way to the door, where we decide to get another drink.

'You pick a place,' Marcus says.

I choose a new bar that just opened near my apartment. We get in a cab, talking the whole way to the Upper East Side. Then we sit at the bar, talking more.

I ask him to tell me about his hometown in Montana. He pauses for a beat and then says he has a good story for me.

'Only about ten percent of my senior class went to college,' he starts. 'Most students don't even bother with SATs at my high school. But I took the thing, did fine on it, applied to Georgetown and got in. Of course, I didn't mention it to anyone – just went about my business at school, hanging out with my boys and whatnot. Then the faculty catches wind of the Georgetown thing and one day my math teacher, Mr. Gilhooly, takes it upon himself to announce my news to the class.'

He shakes his head as if the memory is painful. 'So everyone was like, "So what? Big fucking deal."' Marcus imitates his bored classmates by folding his arms across his chest and then patting his mouth with an open hand. 'And I guess their reaction pissed Mr. Gilhooly off. He wanted them to truly grasp the depth of their inadequacies and future doom. So he proceeded to draw this big graph on the board showing my earning potential with a college degree versus their earning potential bussing tables at Shoney's.'

'No way!'

'Yeah. So they're all sitting there like, "Fuck Marcus," right? Like I think I'm hot shit 'cause I'm going to make six figures some day. I wanted to kill that dude.' Marcus throws up his hands. 'Thanks for nothing, Mr. Gilhooly. Way to win me some friends.'

87

I laugh.

'So what the fuck am I supposed to do now? I gotta fight the image of dork gunner boy, right? So I go out of my way to show everybody I don't give a shit about academics. Started smokin' weed every day and never stopped the practice in college. Hence, well, you know, my finishing next to last at Georgetown. I'm sure you've heard about the remote?' he asks, peeling the label off his Heineken.

I smile and tap his hand. 'Yeah. I know the story. Except the version I heard was that you were dead last.'

'Aww, man!' Marcus shakes his head. 'Dex never gets that shit right. My one point six seven beat someone out! Next to last, dude! Next to last!'

After two drinks, I glance at my watch and say it's getting late.

'Okay. I'll walk you home?'

'Sure.'

We stroll over to Third Avenue and stop in front of my apartment.

'Well, good night, Marcus. Thank you so much for dinner. I had a really nice time,' I say, meaning it.

'Yeah. So did I. It was good.' He licks his lips quickly. I know what is coming. 'And I'm glad we're in the same house this summer.'

'I am too.'

Then he asks if he can kiss me. It is a question I don't usually like. *Just do it*, I always think. But for some reason it doesn't bother me coming from Marcus.

I nod as he leans over and gives me a medium-long kiss.

We separate. My heart isn't palpitating, but I am content.

'You think Darcy and Dex bet on that?' he asks.

I laugh. I had been wondering the same thing.

'How did it go?' Darcy yells into the phone the next morning.

I am just out of the shower, dripping wet. 'Where are you?'

'In the car with Dex. We're on our way back to the city,' she says. 'We went antiquing. Remember?'

'Yes,' I say. 'I remember.'

'How did it go?' she asks again, smacking her gum. She can't even wait until she gets home to get the scoop on my date.

I don't answer.

'Well?'

'We have a bad connection. Your cell is breaking up,' I say. 'I can't hear you.'

'Nice try. Give me the goods.'

'What goods?'

'Rachel! Don't play dumb with me. Tell me about your date! We're dying to know.'

I hear Dex echo her in the background. 'Just *dying*!'

'It was a lovely evening,' I say, trying to wrap a towel around my head without dropping the phone.

She squeals. 'Yes! I knew it. So details! Details!'

I tell her that we went to Gotham Bar and Grill, I ordered the tuna, he had lamb.

'Rachel! Get to the good stuff! Did you hook up?'

'I can't tell you that.'

89

'Why not?'

'I have my reasons.'

'That means you did,' she says. 'Otherwise you'd just say no.'

'Think what you want.'

'C'mon, Rachel!'

I tell her no way, I am not going to be her car ride entertainment. She reports my words to Dex and I hear him say, 'Bruce is our car ride entertainment. Tell her that.'

Tunnel of Love is playing in the background.

'Tell Dexter that's Bruce's worst album.'

'They're all bad albums. Springsteen sucks,' Darcy says.

'Did she just say this album is bad?' I hear Dex ask Darcy.

Darcy says yeah and a few seconds later 'Thunder Road' is blaring. Darcy shouts at him to turn it down. I smile.

'So?' Darcy asks. 'Are you going to tell us or not?'

'Not.'

'If I promise not to tell Dex?'

'Still not.'

Darcy makes an exasperated sound. Then she tells me she will find out one way or another and hangs up.

The next I hear from Dex is on Thursday night, the day before we are scheduled to leave for the Hamptons.

'Do you want a ride? We have room for one more,' he says. 'Claire's coming with us. And your boyfriend's in.'

'Well, in that case, I'd love a ride,' I say, trying to sound breezy and casual. I need to show him that I've moved on. I *have* moved on.

*

At five o'clock the next day, we are assembled in Dexter's car, hoping to get ahead of the traffic. But the roads are already clogged. It takes us an hour to get through the Midtown Tunnel and nearly four hours to make the 110-mile drive to East Hampton. I sit in the backseat between Claire and Marcus. Darcy is in a giddy, hyper mood. She spends most of the car ride facing the three of us in the backseat, raising various topics, asking questions, and generally carrying the conversation. She makes things feel celebratory; her good moods are as infectious as her bad ones. Marcus is the second most talkative in our group. For a thirty-mile stretch, he and Darcy are a running comedy routine, making fun of each other. She calls him lazy, he calls her high maintenance. Claire and I chime in occasionally. Dex says virtually nothing. He is so quiet that at one point Darcy yells at him to stop being such a bore.

'I'm driving,' he says. 'I need to concentrate.'

Then he looks at me in the rearview mirror. I wonder what he's thinking. His eyes give nothing away.

It is getting dark when we stop for snacks and beers at a gas station on Route 27. Claire sidles up to me in front of the chips, loops her arm through mine, and says, 'I can tell he really likes you.' For a second I am startled, thinking that she means Dex. Then I realize she is talking about Marcus.

'Marcus and I are just friends,' I say, selecting a can of Pringles Light.

'Oh, c'mon now. Darcy told me about your date,' she says.

91

Claire is always in the know about everything – the latest trends, the hot new bar opening, the next big party. She has her manicured fingers on the pulse of the city. And knowing the details of Manhattan's singles is part of her bag too.

'It was just one date,' I say, happy that Darcy has not determined what happened with Marcus, despite a barrage of questioning. She even probed him with an email; he forwarded me the message with his subject line reading, 'nosy bastards'.

'Well, the summer is long,' Claire says wisely. 'You're smart not to commit until you see what else is out there.'

We arrive at our summer house, a small cottage with limited charm. Claire found it when she came out alone in mid-February, disgusted with all of us for not sacrificing a free weekend to house-hunt. She organized everything, including setting up the other half of the share. As we tour the house, she apologizes again for the lack of a pool, and laments that the common areas aren't really large enough for good parties. We reassure her that the big backyard with a grill makes up for that. Plus, we are close enough to the beach to walk, which, in my opinion, is the most important thing about a summer house.

We unpack the car and find our bedrooms. Darcy and Dex have the room with the king-sized bed. Marcus has his own room, which could come in handy. And Claire has her own room – a reward for her efforts. I am rooming with Hillary, who blew off work today and took the train in last night. Hillary is always blowing off work. I don't know anyone more laid back about work, particularly at a big firm. She comes to work late every day, closer and closer to eleven with each passing year, and she refuses to play the games that other associates play, like leaving a jacket on the back of their chair or a cup full of coffee on their desk before leaving at night so that partners will think they've only left for a short break. She billed fewer than two thousand hours last year and therefore received no bonus. 'Do the math and you'll realize that making a bonus comes out to less per hour than flipping burgers at McDonald's,' she said this year, on the day checks were handed out.

I call her on my cell now. 'Where are you?'

'Cyril's,' she shouts over the crowd. 'Want me to stay here or meet you guys somewhere?'

I pass along the question to Darcy and Claire.

'Tell her we're going straight to the Talkhouse,' Darcy says. 'It's already late.'

Then, as I expected, Claire and Darcy insist on changing their clothes. Marcus says he thinks he'll change too. So Dex and I sit in the den, opposite each other, waiting. He holds the remote control but does not turn the TV on. It is the first time we have been alone since the Incident. I have been worrying about this moment for what feels like a very long time. I swallow nervously, conscious of sweat accumulating under my arms. Why am I nervous? What happened is behind us. It was a one-off. It is over. Over. I must relax, act normal. As I try to remember what normal felt like before the Incident, he asks me, 'Aren't you going to doll up for your boyfriend?' He says it quietly, still without looking at me.

'Very funny.' Even the mere exchange of words now feels illicit.

'Well, aren't you?'

'I'm fine in this,' I say, glancing down at my favorite jeans and black knit top. What he doesn't know is that I already put much thought into this outfit when I changed after work.

'I'm being serious – you and Marcus make a swell couple.' He glances furtively at the staircase.

'Thanks. So do you and Darcy.'

We exchange a lingering look, too loaded with potential meaning to begin to interpret. And then, before he can respond, Darcy bounds down the stairs in a curve-hugging chartreuse sheath. She hands Dex a pair of scissors and crouches at his feet, lifting her hair. 'Can you cut the tag, please?'

He snips. She stands and spins.

'Well? How do I look?'

'Nice,' he says, and then glances at me sheepishly as if the one-word compliment to his fiancée might somehow upset me.

'You look awesome,' I say, to show him that it doesn't. Not in the least.

We pay the cover and make our way through the massive crowd at Stephen's Talkhouse, our favorite bar in Amagansett, saying hello to all the people we know from various circles back in the city. We find Hillary at the bar with a Budweiser, wearing cutoff jeans, a white scooped neck T-shirt, and the kind of plain blue flip-flops that Darcy and Claire would only wear to their pedicurist. There is not a pretentious bone in Hillary's body, and as always, I am so happy to see her.

'Hey, guys!' she yells. 'What took you so long?'

'Traffic was a bitch,' Dex says. 'And then certain people had to get ready.'

'Well, of *course* we had to get ready!' Darcy says, looking down to admire her outfit.

Hillary insists that we need a kick-start to our evening and orders a round of shots. She hands them out as we stand in a tight circle, ready to drink together.

'To the best summer ever!' Darcy says, tossing her long, coconut-scented hair behind her shoulders. She says it at the start of every summer, expressing wildly high expectations that I never share. But maybe this summer she will be right. Maybe I will fall in love. With Marcus, of course.

We all throw back our shots, which taste like straight vodka. Then Dex buys another round, and when he hands me my beer, his fingers graze mine. I wonder if he does it on purpose.

'Thank you,' I say.

'Anytime,' he murmurs, holding my gaze as he did in the car.

I count to three silently and then look away.

As the night wears on, I find myself watching Dex and Darcy interact. I am surprised by the territorial pangs I feel as I observe them together. It is not exactly jealousy, but something related to it. I notice little things that didn't used to register. Like once, she slipped her four fingers into the back of his jeans right at the top. And another time, when he was standing behind her, he gathered all of her hair in one hand and sort of held it up in a makeshift ponytail before dropping it back at her shoulders.

Right now, he leans in to say something to her. She nods and smiles. I imagine that his words were 'I want you tonight' or something along those lines. I wonder if they have had sex since he and I were together. Surely, yes. And that bothers me in some weird way. Maybe that happens whenever you watch someone on your List with someone else. I tell myself that I have no right to be jealous. That I had no business adding him to my List in the first place.

I try to focus on Marcus. I stand near him, talk to him, laugh at his jokes. When he asks me to dance, I say yes without hesitation. I follow him onto the crowded dance floor. We work up a good sweat, dancing and laughing. When I feel his body against mine, I realize that although there is no great chemistry I am having fun. And who knows? Maybe this will lead to something. But is it enough? Would I be settling? Am I only using Marcus to bother Dex? I tell myself not to overanalyze. Stop thinking. Just have fun.

'They're dying to know what happened on our date,' Marcus says into my ear.

'Why do you say that?' I ask.

'Darcy inquired again.'

'She did?'

'Yup.'

'When?'

'Tonight. Right after we got here.'

I hesitate and then ask, 'Did Dex say anything?'

'No, but he was standing right next to her looking pretty darn interested.'

'Some nerve,' I say playfully.

'I know, the nosy bastards . . . And don't look now, but they're staring at us.' His face touches mine, his whiskers scratching my cheek.

I drape my arms over his shoulders and move my body flush against his. 'Well then. Let's give them something to look at.'

SEVEN

'So what's the deal with you and Marcus?' Hillary asks me the next morning as she picks through the pile of clothes that have already accumulated beside her bed. I resist the urge to fold them for her.

'No deal, really.' I get out of bed and promptly start to make it.

'Potential?' She pulls on a pair of sweats and ties the drawstring, cinching them at hip level.

'Maybe.'

Last year Hillary broke up with Corey, her boyfriend of four years, a nice, smart, all around great guy. But Hillary was convinced that, as good as the relationship was, it wasn't good enough. 'He's not *the One*,' she kept saying. I remember Darcy informing her that she might revise that opinion in her mid-thirties, a statement Hillary and I both rehashed at length later. A classic, tactless Darcyism. Yet, as time passes, I can't help wondering if Hillary made a mistake. Here she is, one year later, embroiled in the fruitless blind-dating scene while, rumor has it, her ex has moved into a Tribeca loft with a twenty-three-year-old med student who is a dead ringer for Cameron Diaz. Hillary claims that it doesn't bother her. I find that very hard to believe, even for someone with her moxie.

In any case, she doesn't seem to be in a hurry to find a Corey replacement.

'Summer potential or long-term potential?' she asks me, running her hands through her short, sandy hair.

'I don't know. Maybe long-term potential.'

'Well, you looked like a total couple last night,' she says. 'Out there dancing.'

'We did?' I ask, thinking that if we looked like a couple, Dex must know that I'm not dwelling on him.

She nods, finds her 'Corporate Challenge' T-shirt and sniffs the armpits before tossing it over to me. 'Is this clean? Smell it.'

'I'm not gonna smell your shirt,' I say, throwing it back. 'You're gross.'

She laughs and puts on her obviously clean enough shirt. 'Yeah . . . You two were out there whispering and laughing. I thought for sure you were going to hook up last night, and that I would get the room to myself.'

I laugh. 'Sorry to disappoint.'

'You disappointed him more.'

'Nah. He just said good night when we got home. Not even a kiss.'

Hillary knows about the first kiss. 'Why not?'

'I don't know. I think we're both proceeding with caution. We'll have a lot of contact between now and September . . . You know, he's in the wedding party too. If things blow up, it could be bad.'

She looks as if she is considering my point. For one second I am tempted to tell Hillary everything about Dex. I

99

trust her. But I don't share, reasoning that I can always tell her, but I can't un-tell her and erase the knowledge from her mind. When we are all together, I would feel even more awkward, constantly thinking that she's thinking about it. And anyway . . . it is over. There is really nothing to talk about.

We go downstairs. Our housemates have already assembled around the kitchen table.

'It's kick-ass outside,' Darcy says, standing, stretching, and showing off her flat stomach under a cropped T-shirt. She sits back down at the table, returning to her game of Solitaire.

Claire looks up from her Palm Pilot. 'Perfect beach weather.'

'Perfect golf weather,' Hillary says, looking at Dex and Marcus. 'Any interest?'

'Um, maybe,' Dex says, glancing up from the sports page. 'Want me to call and see if we can get a tee time?'

Darcy slams her cards on to the table and looks around defiantly.

Hillary doesn't seem to notice Darcy's objection to a round of golf because she says, 'Or we could just pop over to the driving range.'

'No! No! No! No golf!' Darcy pounds the table again, this time with her fist. 'Not on our first day! We have to stay together! All of us. Right, Rachel?'

'Guess that means no golf today,' Dex says, before I am forced to become involved in the great golf debate. 'Darcy's orders.'

Hillary gets up from the table with a disgusted look on her face.

'I just want us all to be together at the beach,' Darcy says, putting a benevolent spin on her selfishness.

'And you make the prospect seem so pleasant.' Dex stands, walks over to the sink, and starts making coffee.

'What's your problem, grouchy bottom?' Darcy says to his back as if he is the one who just told her how to spend the day. 'You are being such an old stinkweed. Sheesh.'

'What's a stinkweed?' Marcus asks, scratching his ear. It is his first contribution to the morning conversation. He still looks half-asleep. 'I'm not familiar.'

'Just have a look at one right now,' Darcy says, pointing at Dex. 'He's been in a bad mood since we got here.'

'No I haven't,' Dex says. I want him to turn around so I can read his expression.

'Have too. Hasn't he?' Darcy demands an answer from the rest of us, looking at me specifically. Being friends with Darcy has taught me the art of smoothing over. But sleeping with her fiancé has dulled my instinct. I am not in the mood to chime in. And nobody else wants to become embroiled in what should be their private argument. We all shrug or look away.

In truth, though, Dex *has* been somewhat subdued. I wonder if I have anything to do with his mood. Maybe it bothered him watching me with Marcus. Not full-blown jealousy, just the territorial pangs that I experienced. Or perhaps he's only thinking about Darcy, seeing her for the controlling person she is. I've always been aware of Darcy's

101

demands – you can't miss them – but lately, I have been less tolerant of her. I am tired of her always getting her way. Maybe Dex feels the same.

'What are we doing for breakfast?' Marcus asks through a loud yawn.

Claire glances at her diamond-studded Cartier. 'You mean brunch.'

'Whatever. For food,' Marcus says.

We discuss our options and decide to skip the crowded East Hampton scene. Hillary says that she bought the essentials the day before.

'By essentials, do you mean Pop-Tarts?' Marcus asks.

'Here.' Hillary sets bowls, spoons, and a box of Rice Krispies on the table. 'Enjoy.'

Marcus opens the box and pours some into his bowl. He looks across the table at me. 'Want some?'

I nod, and he prepares my bowl. He doesn't ask anyone else if they want cereal, just pushes the box down the table.

'Banana?' he asks me.

'Yes, please.'

He peels the banana and then slices it into his bowl and mine, alternating every few slices. He takes the bruised section for himself. We are sharing a banana. This means something. Dex's eyes dart my way as Marcus flicks the last neat cylinder into my bowl, leaving the nasty end piece in its peel where it belongs.

Several hours later, we are finally ready to go to the beach. Claire and Darcy emerge from their rooms with their stylish canvas bags filled to the brim with plush new beach towels, magazines, lotions, thermoses, cell phones, and make-up. Hillary carries only a small bath towel from the house and a Frisbee. I am somewhere in between with a beach towel, my Discman, and a bottle of water. The six of us walk in a row, our flip-flops smacking the pavement with that satisfying sound of summer. Claire and Hillary walk on either end, flanking the house couple and the possible couple-to-be. We cross the beach parking lot and climb over the dune, hesitating for a second to take in our first collective glimpse of the ocean. I am glad that I no longer live in landlocked Indiana, where people call Lake Michigan 'the beach'. The view is thrilling. It almost makes me forget that I slept with Dex.

Dex leads the way down the crowded beach, finding us a spot halfway between the dunes and the ocean where the sand is still soft but even enough to spread our towels. Marcus puts his towel next to mine; Darcy is on my other side, Dex next to her. Hillary and Claire set up in front of us. The sun is bright but not too hot. Claire warns us all about the UV rays, that these are the days when you really have to be careful. 'You can get severe sun damage and not even realize it until it's too late,' she says.

Marcus offers to put suntan lotion on my back.

'No thanks,' I say. But as I struggle to reach the middle of my back, he takes the bottle from me and applies the lotion, meticulously maneuvering around the edges of my suit.

'Do mine, Dex,' Darcy says cheerfully, shedding her white shorts and squatting in front of Dex in her black bikini. 'Here. Use the coconut oil, please.'

Claire bemoans the lack of SPF in the oil, says we are too old to keep tanning and that Darcy will be sorry when the wrinkles set in. Darcy rolls her eyes and says she doesn't care about wrinkles, she lives in the moment. I know I will get an earful later, that Darcy will tell me that Claire is just jealous because her fair skin goes straight from white to bright pink. 'You'll regret it when you're forty,' Claire says, her face shaded by a huge straw hat.

'No I won't. I'll just get laser resurfacing.' Darcy adjusts her bikini top and then coats more oil on her calves, using quick, efficient strokes. I have watched her grease up for more than fifteen years now. Every summer her goal was to have a savage tan. Often we would lie out in her backyard with a big tub of Crisco, a bottle of Sun-In, and a garden hose for periodic relief. It was absolute torture. But I suffered through it believing that dark pigmentation was a virtue of sorts. My skin is pale like Claire's, so every day Darcy would surge farther ahead.

Claire remarks that cosmetic surgery won't cure skin cancer.

'Oh, for Pete's sake!' Darcy says. 'Stay under your damn hat then!'

Claire opens her mouth and then closes it quickly, looking injured. 'Sorry. I was just trying to help.'

Darcy shoots her a conciliatory smile. 'I know, hon. Didn't mean to snap at you.'

Dex looks at me and makes a face as if to say that he wishes both of them would shut up. It is the first direct communication we have had all day. I allow myself to smile back at him. His face breaks into a glorious grin. He is so handsome that it hurts. Like looking at the sun. He stands for a moment to adjust his towel, which has folded over in the wind. I look at his back and then down at his calves, feeling a surge of remembrance. *He was in my bed.* Not that I want a repeat performance. But *oh*, he has a nice body – lean but broad. I am not a body person, but I still appreciate a perfect one. He sits back down just as I look away.

Marcus asks if anybody wants to play Frisbee. I say no, that I am too tired, but what I am thinking is that the last thing I want to do is run around with my soft, white stomach poking out of my tankini. But Hillary is a taker and off they go, the portrait of two well-adjusted beachgoers leaving the rest of us to our trifling.

'Hand me my shirt,' Darcy says to Dex.

'Please?'

'The "please" is a given,' Darcy says.

'Say it,' he says, popping a cinnamon Altoid into his mouth.

Darcy hits him hard in the stomach.

'Ouch,' he says in a flat monotone, to indicate that it didn't hurt in the slightest.

She winds up to hit him again, but he grabs her wrist.

'Try to behave. You're such a child,' he says fondly. His edginess of this morning is gone.

'I am not,' she says, sidling over to his towel. She presses her fingers into his chest, poised for a kiss.

I put on my sunglasses and look away. To say that what I am feeling is not jealousy is a stretch.

*

105

That night we all go to a party in Bridgehampton. The house is huge with a beautiful L-shaped pool surrounded by gorgeous landscaping and at least twenty tiki torches. I scan the guests in the backyard, noticing all of the purple, hot pink, and orange dresses and skirts. It seems that every woman read the same 'bright colors are in, black is out' article that I read. I followed the advice and bought a lime-green sundress that is too vivid and memorable to wear again before August, which means it will cost me about one hundred and fifty dollars per wear. But I am pleased with my choice until I see the same dress, about two sizes smaller, on a slender blonde. She is much taller than I am, so the dress is shorter on her, exposing an endless stretch of bronzed thigh. I make a conscious effort to stay on the opposite side of the pool from her.

I go to the bathroom, and on my way back to find Hillary, I get stuck talking to Hollis and Dewey Malone. Hollis used to work at my firm but quit the day after she got engaged to Dewey. Dewey is unattractive and humorless, but he has a huge trust fund. Hence Hollis's interest. It was amusing to hear Hollis explain to us that Dewey has such a 'big heart', blah blah blah, trying in vain to disguise her true intentions. I am envious of Hollis's escape from firm hell, but I would rather be stuck billing than be married to Dewey.

'My life is so much better now,' she chirps tonight. 'That firm was poison! It was so stifling! I thought I might miss the intellectual stimulation . . . but I don't. Now I have time to read the classics and think. It's great. So liberating.'

'Uh-huh . . . That's nice,' I say, taking mental notes to share with Hillary later.

106

Hollis goes on to tell me about their penthouse on the park and how she's been working so hard on decorating it and has had to fire three designers for not adhering to her vision. Dewey contributes nothing to the conversation, just crunches his ice and looks bored. Once I catch him staring at Darcy's butt packed neatly into a pair of tight magenta capri pants.

Marcus is suddenly beside me. I introduce him to Dewey and Hollis. Dewey shakes his hand and then continues to mouth-breathe and look distracted. Hollis promptly asks Marcus where he lives and what he does for a living. Apparently his Murray Hill address and his marketing job don't quite measure up because they find an excuse to move on to more worthy guests.

Marcus raises his eyebrows. 'Dewey, huh?'

'Yeah.'

'*Dooo heee* have a stick up his ass or what?'

I laugh.

He looks proud of his joke, pleased to make me laugh.

'So, are you having fun?'

'I guess so. You?'

He shrugs. 'The people here kind of take themselves seriously, don't they?'

'That's the Hamptons.'

I survey the party. It is a far cry from neighborhood barbecues back in Indiana. Part of me feels satisfied that I have expanded my horizons. But a larger part of me feels uncomfortable every time I come to a party like this one. I am a poser, attempting to mingle with people who consider

107

Indiana to be mere flyover country – necessary terrain to cross on their trips to Aspen or Los Angeles. I watch Darcy making her rounds with Dex at her side. There is no trace of Indy left in her; to watch her you would guess that she grew up on Park Avenue. Her kids will grow up in Manhattan, for sure. When I have kids, if I ever have kids, I intend to move to the suburbs. I look at Marcus, trying to imagine him dragging our son's Big Wheel out of the street. He looks down at our little boy, whose face is streaked with dried Popsicle, and instructs him to stay on the sidewalk. The boy has Marcus's short eyebrows pointing up toward each other like an upside-down V.

'C'mon,' Marcus says. 'Let's get another drink.'

'All right,' I say, keeping my eye on the blonde in my dress.

As we walk toward the poolside bar, I think of Indiana again, picturing Annalise and Greg with their neighbors, all spilled out on the freshly cut Midwestern lawn. If somebody wore her same pair of khaki shorts from Gap, nobody would care.

After the party, we find another party, and then do our usual finale at the Talkhouse where I dance with Marcus again. Around three o'clock, we all pile into the car and go home. Hillary and Claire head straight for bed while the two couples remain in the den. Darcy and Dex hold hands on one love seat; Marcus and I sit next to each other, but not touching, on the adjacent couch.

'All right, kids. It's past my bedtime,' Darcy says, standing suddenly. She glances at Dexter. 'You coming?'

My eyes meet Dexter's. We look away simultaneously. 'Yeah,' he says. 'I'll be right there.'

The three of us talk for a few more minutes until we hear Darcy calling Dex from the top of the stairs. 'Come on, Dex! They want to be alone!'

Marcus smirks while I study a freckle on my arm.

Dex clears his throat, coughs. His face is all business. 'Okay then. Guess I'll head up. Good night.'

'All right, man. See you tomorrow,' Marcus says.

I just mumble good night, too uncomfortable to look up as Dex leaves the room. I feel an unexpected pang for Dex that is somehow reminiscent of Hunter leaving Joey and me alone in the lounge at Duke, but I push it away and smile at Marcus.

He moves closer to me and kisses me without asking first this time. It is a nice enough kiss, maybe even nicer than our first one. For some reason, I think of *The Brady Bunch* episode when Bobby saw skyrockets after kissing Millicent (who, unbeknownst to Bobby, had the mumps). When I first saw that episode I was about Bobby's age, so that kiss seemed like serious stuff. Someday I will see skyrockets like that, I remember thinking. To date, I have not seen skyrockets. But Marcus comes just as close as anyone before him.

Our kissing escalates to the next level and then I say, 'Well, I think we should go to bed.'

'Together?' he asks. I can tell he is joking.

'Very funny,' I answer. 'Good night, Marcus.'

I kiss him one more time before going to my room, passing Dex and Darcy's closed door on the way.

*

The next morning I check my voice mail. Les has left me three messages. He might as well be a Jehovah's Witness for as much attention he pays to the holidays. He says that he wants 'to go over a few things tomorrow, early afternoon.' I know he is vague on purpose, not leaving a specific time or instructions to meet him at the office or call in. This way he can be sure that my Memorial Day is slashed in half. Hillary tells me to ignore him, pretend that I didn't get the message. Marcus says to jam him with a message back, telling him to 'jack off – it's a national holiday'. But of course I dutifully check the train and jitney schedule and decide I will leave this afternoon to avoid the traffic. Deep down, I know work is only an excuse to go – I have had enough of this whole bizarre dynamic. I like Marcus, but it is exhausting being around a guy who, as Hillary would say, 'is potential'. And it is even more exhausting avoiding Dex. I avoid him when he is alone, avoid him when he is with Darcy. Avoid dwelling on him and the Incident.

'I really need to get back,' I sigh, as if it is the last thing I want to do.

'You can't leave!' Darcy says.

'I have to.'

As she sulks I want to point out that ninety percent of the time we are in the Hamptons she is completely distracted, in social butterfly mode. But I just say again that I have to.

'You're such a buzz kill.'

'She can't help having to work, Darcy,' Dex says. Maybe he says it because she often calls him a buzz kill too. Then

110

again, maybe he just wants me to leave for the same reasons I want to go.

After lunch I pack up my things and go into the den where everyone is lazing around, watching television.

'Can someone give me a lift to the jitney?' I ask, expecting Darcy or Marcus to volunteer.

But before they can, Dex says, 'I'll take you. I want to go to the store anyway.'

I say goodbye to everyone, and Marcus squeezes my shoulder and says he'll give me a call next week.

Then Dex and I are off. Alone for four miles.

'Did you have a nice weekend?' he asks me as we are backing out of the driveway. Gone is any trace of the banter that surfaced right after the Incident. And he, like Darcy, has stopped inquiring about Marcus, perhaps because it seems fairly evident that we have become some kind of item.

'Yeah, it was nice,' I say. 'Did you?'

'Sure,' he says. 'Very nice.'

After a brief silence, we talk about work and mutual friends from law school, stuff we talked about before the Incident. Things seem normal again, or as normal as they can be after a mistake like ours.

We arrive at the jitney stop early. Dex pulls into the parking lot, turns in his seat, and studies me with his green eyes in a way that makes me look away. He asks what I am doing on Tuesday night.

I think I know what he's asking, but am not sure, so I babble. 'Work. The usual. I have a deposition on Friday and I haven't even started preparing for it. The only thing I have on my outline is "Can you spell your last name for the court reporter?" and "Are you on any medications that might impede your ability to answer questions at this deposition?"' I laugh nervously.

His face stays serious. He clearly has no interest in my deposition. 'Look, I want to see you, Rachel. I'm coming over at eight. On Tuesday.'

And the way he says it – as a statement rather than a question – makes my stomach hurt. It isn't really the pre-blind date stomach pain I have before a blind date. It isn't the nervousness before a final exam. It isn't the 'I'm going to get busted for doing something' feeling. And it isn't the dizzy sensation that accompanies a crush on a guy when he just acknowledged your presence with a smile or casual hello. It is something else. It is a familiar ache, but I can't quite place it.

My smile fades to match his serious face. I would like to say that his request surprised me, caught me off guard, but I think part of me expected this, even hoped for it, when Dex offered to drive me. I don't ask why he wants to see me or what he wants to talk about. I don't say that I have to work or that it's not a good idea. I just nod. 'Okay.'

I tell myself that the only reason I agree to see him is that we have to finish sorting out what happened between us. And therefore, I am not committing a further wrong against Darcy; I'm simply trying to fix the damage already done. And I tell myself that if I do, in fact, actually want to see Dex for other reasons, it's only because I miss my friend. I think back to my birthday, our time in 7B before we hooked up, remembering how much I enjoyed his solo company, how

112

much I enjoyed Dex removed from Darcy's demands. I miss his friendship. I only want to talk to him. That is all.

The bus is here and people are starting to file onto it. I slide out of the car without another word between us.

As I settle down in a window seat behind a perky blonde talking way too loudly on her cell phone, I suddenly know what it is in my stomach. It is the same way I felt after sex with Nate in those final days before he dumped me for the tree-hugging guitar player. It is a mixture of genuine emotion for another person, and fear. Fear of losing something. I know at this moment that by allowing Dex to come over, I am risking something. Risking friendship, risking my heart.

The girl keeps talking, overusing the words 'fabulous' and 'amazing' to describe her 'woefully abbreviated' weekend. She reports that she has a 'vicious migraine' from 'bingeing big time' at the 'fab party'. I want to tell her that if she takes her volume down a notch, her headache might subside. I close my eyes, hoping that her phone battery is low. But I know that even if she stops her high-pitched chatter, there is no way I am going to be able to sleep with this feeling growing inside me. It is good and bad at the same time, like drinking too much coffee. It is both exciting and scary, like waiting for a wave to crash over your head.

Something is coming, and I am doing nothing to stop it.

It is Tuesday night, twenty minutes before eight. I am home. I have not heard from Dex all day so I assume we are still on. I floss and brush my teeth. I light a candle in the kitchen in case there is a lingering aroma of the Thai food I ordered the evening before for my Memorial Day dinner. I change out of my suit, put on black lacy underwear – even though I know, know, *know* that nothing is going to happen – and jeans and a T-shirt. I apply a touch of blush and some lip gloss. I look casual, comfortable, the opposite of how I feel.

At exactly eight, Eddie, who is subbing for José, rings my buzzer. 'You have company,' he bellows.

'Thanks, Eddie. Send him up.'

Seconds later Dex appears in my doorway in a dark suit with faint gray pinstripes, a blue shirt, and a red tie.

'Your doorman was smirking at me,' he says, as he steps into my apartment and tentatively looks around as if this were his first visit.

'Impossible,' I say. 'That's in your head.'

'It's not in my head. I know a smirk when I see one.'

'That's not José. Wrong doorman. Eddie's on tonight. You have a guilty conscience.'

'I told you already. I don't feel that guilty about what we did.' He looks steadily into my eyes.

I feel myself being sucked into his gaze, losing my resolve to be a good person, a good friend. I look away nervously, ask if he wants something to drink. He says a glass of water would be fine. No ice. I am out of bottled water so I run the tap until the water comes out cool. I fill a glass for each of us and join him on my couch.

He takes several big gulps and then puts his glass down on a coaster on my coffee table. I sip from my glass. I can feel him staring at me, but I don't look back. I keep my eyes straight ahead, where my bed is situated – the scene of the

Incident. I need to get a proper one-bedroom or at least a screen to separate my sleeping alcove from the rest of the apartment.

'Rachel,' he says. 'Look at me.'

I glance at him and then down at my coffee table.

He puts his hand on my chin and turns my face toward his.

I feel myself blush but don't move away. 'What?' I release a nervous laugh. He doesn't change expression.

'Rachel.'

'*What*?'

'We have a problem.'

'We do?'

'A major problem.'

He leans forward, his left arm draped along the back of the sofa. He kisses me softly and then more urgently. I taste cinnamon. I think of the tin of cinnamon Altoids that he had with him all weekend. I kiss him back.

And if I thought Marcus was a good kisser, or Nate before him, or anyone else for that matter, I thought wrong. In comparison, everyone else was merely competent. This kiss from Dex makes the room spin. And this time, it's not from booze. This kiss is like the kiss I have read about a million times, seen in the movies. The one I wasn't sure existed in real life. I have never felt this way before. Fireworks and all. Just like Bobby and Millicent.

We kiss for a long, long time. Not breaking away once. Not even shifting positions on my couch even though we are at an unnatural distance for such an intense kiss. I can't speak

115

for him, but I know why I don't move. I don't want it to end, don't want the next, awkward stage to come, where we might ask the questions about what we are doing. I don't want to talk about Darcy, to even hear her name. She has nothing to do with this moment. Nothing. This kiss stands on its own. It is removed from time or circumstance or their September wedding. That is what I try to tell myself. When Dex finally breaks away, it is only to move closer to me and put his arms around me and whisper into my ear, 'I can't stop thinking about you.'

I can't stop either.

But I *can* control what I'm doing. There is emotion, and then there is what you do about it. I pull away, but not too far away, and shake my head.

'What?' he asks gently, his arm partially around me.

'We shouldn't be doing this,' I say. It is a watered down protest, but at least it is something.

Darcy can be annoying, controlling, and exasperating, but she is my friend. I am a good friend. A good person. This isn't who I am. I must stop. I won't know myself if I don't stop.

Yet I don't move away. Instead, I wait to be convinced otherwise, hoping he will talk me into it. And sure enough: 'Yes. We should,' he says. Dexter's words are sure. No second-guessing, doubts, worry. He holds my face in his hands and stares intently into my eyes. 'We have to.'

There is nothing slick in his words, only sincerity. He is my friend, the friend I knew and cared for before Darcy ever met him. Why didn't I recognize my feelings sooner? Why did I put Darcy's interests ahead of my own? Dex leans in and kisses me again, softly but with a sense of absolute certainty.

But it's wrong, I silently protest, knowing that I am too late, that I have already surrendered. We have crossed a new line together. Because even though we have already slept together, that didn't really count. We were drunk, reckless. Nothing really happened until this kiss today. Nothing that couldn't have been stuffed into a closet, confused with a dream, maybe even forgotten altogether.

That is all changed now. For better or worse.

EIGHT

I have always done my best thinking in the shower. The night is for worrying, dwelling, analyzing. But in the morning, under the hot water, I see things clearly. So as I lather my hair, inhaling my grapefruit-scented shampoo, I pare everything down to the essential truth: what Dex and I are doing is wrong.

We kissed for a long time last night, and then he held me for even longer, few words passing between us. My heart thumped against his as I told myself that by not escalating the physical part we had scored a victory of sorts. But this morning, I know that what we shared was in some ways more intimate than sex. And it was wrong. Just plain wrong. I must stop. I will stop. Starting now.

When I was little, I used to count to three in my head when I wanted to give myself a fresh start. I'd catch myself biting my nails, jerk my fingers out of my mouth, and count. *One. Two. Three. Go.* Then I had a clean slate. From that point forward I was no longer a nail-biter. I used this tactic with many bad habits. So on a count of three, I will shake the Dex habit. I will be a good friend again. I will erase everything, fix it all.

I count to three slowly and then use the visualization

technique that Brandon told me he used during baseball season. He said he would picture his bat striking the ball, hear it crack, see the dust fly as he slid safely into home base. He focused only on his good plays and not the times he screwed up.

So I do this. I focus on my friendship with Darcy, rather than my feelings for Dex. I make a video in my head, filling it with scenes of Darcy and me. I see us hunkered down in her bed during an elementary-school sleepover. We are discussing our plans for the future, how many kids we will have, what we will name them. I see Darcy, ten years old, propped up on her elbows, pinkies in her mouth, explaining that if you have three kids the middle one should be a different sex from the others so everyone has something special. As if you can control such things.

I picture us in the halls at Naperville High, passing notes between classes. Her notes, folded in intricate shapes, like origami, were so much more entertaining than Annalise's notes which simply reported how bored she was in class. Darcy's were chock-full of interesting observations about classmates and snide remarks about teachers. And little games for me to play. She'd put quotes down the left-hand side of the page and people's names on the right for me to match. I'd crack up as I drew a line from, say, 'Nice brights, buddy' to Annalise's father, who made that comment every time drivers forgot to turn off their high beams. She was funny. Sometimes cutting, even downright mean. But that only made her funnier.

I rinse my hair and remember something else, a memory

119

that has not surfaced before. It is like finding a photograph of yourself that you never knew was taken. Darcy and I were freshmen, standing beside our locker after school. Becky Zurich, one of the most popular girls in the senior class (but not the nice kind of popular, more the mean, feared variety) walked by us with her boyfriend, Paul Kinser. With her virtually nonexistent chin and way too thin lips, she really wasn't pretty at all, although at the time she somehow convinced a lot of people, including me, that she was. So when Paul and Becky passed us, I looked at them, because they were popular seniors, and I was impressed, or at the very least curious. I'm sure I wanted to hear what they were talking about so that I could glean some insight into being eighteen and cool. I think it was only a casual glance in their direction, but maybe it was a stare.

In any case, Becky gave me an exaggerated stare back, making her eyes pop out like a cartoon. She followed this with a hyenalike, lip-curling sneer and said, 'What're you lookin' at?'

Then Paul chimed in with, 'Catching flies?' (I'm sure dating Becky made Paul meaner, or maybe he just figured out that being mean earned him action later.)

Sure enough, my mouth was wide open. I snapped it shut, mortified. Becky laughed, proud to have shamed a freshman. She then reapplied her pink frosted lipstick, inserted a fresh piece of Big Red into her mean little mouth and made one final face at me for good measure.

Darcy had been shuffling through books in our locker but clearly caught the gist of the exchange. She spun and eyed

120

the pair with revulsion, a look she had practiced and mastered. She then imitated Becky's shrill laughter, craning her neck unnaturally backward and rolling in her lips to make them invisible. She was hideous – and looked exactly like Becky in mid-chortle.

I stifled a smile while Becky looked momentarily stunned. She then gathered herself, took a step toward Darcy and spat out the word 'bitch'. Darcy was unflinching as she stared right back at the senior duo and said, 'It's better than being an *ugly* bitch. Wouldn't you agree, Paul?'

It was Becky's turn to stare, mouth agape, at her newly discovered adversary. And before she could formulate a comeback, Darcy threw in another insult for good measure. 'And by the way, Becky, that lipstick you're wearing? It's so last year.'

Everything about that moment is suddenly in sharp focus. I can see our locker decorated with pictures of Patrick Swayze in *Dirty Dancing*. I can smell that distinct starchy, meat-based odor of the nearby cafeteria. And I can hear Darcy's voice, forceful and confident. Of course, Paul had no response to Darcy's question, as it was clear to all four of us that Darcy was right – she was the prettier of the two. And in high school that sometimes gives you the last word, even if you are a freshman. Becky and Paul walked away and Darcy just kept talking to me about whatever it was we had been talking about, as if Becky and Paul were totally insignificant. Which they were. It just took a lot to realize that at fourteen.

I turn off the water, wrap a towel around my body and another over my head. I will call Dexter as soon as I get to work. I will tell him that it has to stop. This time I really mean it. He is marrying Darcy, and I am the maid of honor. We both love her. Yes, she has flaws. She can be spoiled, self-centered and bossy, but she can also be loyal and kind and wildly fun. And she is the closest thing to a sister I will ever have.

During my commute I practice what I will say to Dex, even talking out loud at one point on the subway. When I finally arrive at work, I have my speech so memorized that it no longer sounds scripted. I've inserted the proper pauses into my Declaration of Mindset and Future Intent. I am ready.

Just as I am about to make the phone call, I notice that I have an email from Dexter. I open it, expecting him to have reached the same conclusion. The subject line reads 'you'.

You are an amazing person, and I don't know where the feelings that you give me came from. What I do know is that I am completely and utterly into you and I want time to freeze so I can be with you all the time and not have to think of anything else at all. I like literally everything about you, including the way your face shows everything you're thinking and especially the way it looks when we are together and your hair is back and your eyes are closed and your lips are open just a little bit. Okay. That's all I wanted to say. Delete this.

I am breathless, dizzy. Nobody has ever written words like this to me. I read it again, absorbing every word. *I like literally everything about you too,* I think.

122

And just like that, my resolve is gone again. How can I end something that I have never experienced before? Something I have been waiting for my whole life? Nobody before Dex could make me feel this way, and what if I never find it again? What if this is *it*? The paradox hits me in the gut: I have never felt so content and safe with anyone and at the same time this is the riskiest thing I have ever undertaken. By a million miles.

My phone rings. I answer it thinking that it could be Dex, hoping it's not Darcy. I can't talk to her right now. I can't think about her right now. I am buzzing from my email, my electronic love letter.

'Cheers, baby.'

It is Ethan, calling from England where he has lived for the past two years. I am so happy to hear his voice. He has a smiling voice, always sounding like he's on the verge of laughter. Most things about Ethan are just as they were in the fifth grade. He is still compassionate, still has cherub cheeks that turn pink in the cold. But the voice is new. It came in high school – with puberty – long after friendship had replaced my schoolgirl crush.

'Hi, Ethan!'

'What's the statute of limitations on wishing someone a happy birthday?' he asks. Ever since I went to law school, he loves throwing out legal terms, often with a twist. 'Strawberry tort' is his favorite.

I laugh. 'Don't worry about it. It was only my thirtieth.'

'Do you hate me? You should have called and reminded me. I feel like an absolute ass, after eighteen years of never forgetting. Shit. My mind is going and I'm still in my twenties – not to rub it in.'

'You forgot my twenty-seventh too,' I interrupt him.

'I did?'

'Yeah.'

'I don't think I did.'

'Yeah – you were with Bran—'

'Stop. Don't say that name. You're right. I forgot your twenty-seventh. That makes this infraction somehow less egregious, right? I didn't break a streak . . . So how is it?' He whistles. 'Can't believe you're thirty. You should still be fourteen. Do you feel older? Wiser? More worldly? What did you do on the big night?' He fires off his questions in his frenetic, attention deficit disorder way.

'It's the same. I'm the same,' I lie. 'Nothing's changed.'

'Really?' he says. It is like him to ask the follow-up. It's as if he knows that I am holding back.

I pause, my mind racing. *Do I tell? Not tell? What will he think of me? What will he say?* Ethan and I have remained close since high school, although our contact is sporadic. But whenever we do talk, we pick up where we left off. He would make a good confidant in this emerging saga. Ethan knows all of the major players. And more important, he knows what it's like to screw up.

Things started out right for him. He did well on the SATs, graduated as our salutatorian and was voted most likely to succeed, picked over Amy Choi, our valedictorian, who was too quiet and mousy to win votes for anything. He went to Stanford, and after graduation took a job at an investment bank even though he majored in art history and had no interest in finance. He instantly despised everything about the banking culture. He said pulling all-nighters was unnatural, and realized that he preferred sleep to money. So he traded his suits in for fleece and spent the next several years drifting up and down the West Coast snapping pictures of lakes and trees, gathering friends along the way. He took writing classes, art classes, photography classes, funded by the odd bartending job and summers in Alaska's fisheries.

That's where he met Brandi – 'Brandi with an i' as I called her before I realized that he genuinely liked her, and that she wasn't just a fling. A few months into their romance, Brandi got pregnant (insisting she was part of that woefully unlucky .05 percent on birth control pills, although I had my doubts). She said that abortion was out of the question, so Ethan did what he thought to be the right thing and married her at City Hall in downtown Seattle. They sent out homemade marriage announcements featuring a black-and-white photo of the two hiking. Darcy made fun of Brandi's way too short and tight jean shorts. 'Who the hell hikes in Daisy Dukes?' she said. But Ethan seemed happy enough.

And that summer, Brandi gave birth to a baby boy . . . an adorable, bouncing *Eskimo* baby boy with eyes that turned coal black almost immediately. Brandi, with blue eyes that matched Ethan's, begged for forgiveness. Ethan promptly had the marriage annulled, and Brandi moved back to Alaska, probably to track down her native lover.

I think Brandi soured Ethan on the whole fresh-air, live-off-the-land kind of life. Or maybe he just wanted something new. Because he moved to London, where he writes for a magazine and is working on a book about London architecture, an interest he didn't acquire until he landed on British soil. But that's how Ethan is. He figures things out along the way, always ready to back up and start over, never bowing to pressure or expectations. I wish I could be more like him.

'So what did you do for your birthday?' Ethan asks.

I shut my office door and blurt it out. 'Darcy had a surprise party for me, I got wasted, and hooked up with Dex.'

I suppose this is what happens when you're not accustomed to having secrets. You don't learn the art of holding back. In fact, I am surprised I lasted this long. I hear static on the line as the news travels across the Atlantic. I panic, wishing I could suck the admission back in.

'Get the fuck outta here. You're kidding me, right?'

My silence tells him that I'm serious.

'Ohhh, *shhhit*.' His voice is still smiling.

'What? What are you thinking?' I need to know if he's judging. I need to know what he thinks of me, if he is siding with Chanel Suit.

'Wait. Whadaya mean, hooked up? You didn't sleep with him, did you?'

'Um. Yeah. Actually I did.'

I am relieved to hear him laugh, even though I tell him that it's not funny, that this is serious business.

'Oh, *trust* me. This is funny.'

I picture the dimple in his left cheek. 'And what exactly is so amusing?'

'Miss Goody Two-shoes screws her friend's fiancé. This is

126

raw comedy at its best.'

'Ethan!'

He stops laughing long enough to ask if I could be knocked up.

'No. We had that covered.'

'So to speak?'

'Yeah,' I say. Any pun I ever make is an accident.

'So no harm done, right? It was a mistake. Shit happens. People make mistakes, especially when they're wasted. Look at me and Brandi with an i.'

'I guess so. But still . . .'

Ethan whistles and then says the obvious – that Darcy would flip if she ever found out.

My other line rings. 'You need to get that?' Ethan asks.

'No. I'll let it roll to voice mail.'

'You sure? It could be your new boyfriend.'

'Ask yourself if you're being helpful,' I say, although I'm relieved that he is not preachy and serious. That's not Ethan's style, but you never know when someone is going to take the moral high ground. And there is definitely moral high ground all around here, particularly considering that Darcy is a friend of his too. Not as close as he and I are, but they still talk occasionally.

'Sorry. Sorry.' He snickers. 'Okay. Just one more substantive question.'

'What?'

'Was it good?'

'Ethan! I don't know. We were drunk!'

'So it was all sloppy?'

'C'mon, Ethan!' I say, as if I'm not thinking about the particulars. Meanwhile, a snapshot of the Incident flashes through my brain – my fingers pressed into Dexter's back. It is a perfect, airbrushed image. There is nothing sloppy about it.

'So you've spoken to him since?'

I tell him about the Hamptons weekend and the date with Marcus.

'Nice touch. Going for his friend. That way, if you marry Marcus, you guys can be swingers.'

I ignore him and continue with the rest – the ride to the jitney, last night, a summary of the email.

'Wow. Shit. So . . . do you have feelings for him too?'

'I don't know,' I say, even though I know that the answer is yes. Strong feelings that I don't want to have, but can't talk myself out of.

'But the wedding's still on?'

'Yeah,' I say. 'As far as I know.'

'As far as you know?'

'Yes. It is.'

Silence. He is not laughing anymore, so my guilt returns in full force.

'What are you thinking now?'

'I was just wondering where you want this to go,' he says. 'What do you want from it? Is it a fling, or do you want him to call off the wedding?'

I flinch at the word 'fling'. That's not what it is at all, but at the same time, I don't think I want Dex to call off the wedding. I can't imagine doing that to Darcy. I tell Ethan that

128

I don't know, I'm not sure.

'Hmm . . . Well, has he mentioned the engagement at all?'

'No. Not really.'

'Hmm.'

'What? What does "hmm" mean?'

'It means I think he should call the shit off.'

'Because of me?' My stomach drops at the thought of being responsible for Darcy's canceled wedding. 'Maybe he just has cold feet?'

I hear my voice rising hopefully at the suggestion of mere cold feet. Why does part of me want it to be that simple? And how can I be so thrilled to be near Dex, so deeply moved by his email, and still want, on some level, for him to marry Darcy?

'Rach—'

'Ethan, I know what you're going to say.'

I *don't* know exactly what he is going to say, but I have a hunch from his tone that it has something to do with where things are going to end up if I don't cease and desist. That it's going to blow up somehow. That someone – likely me – is going to get hurt. But I don't want to hear him say any of it.

'Okay. Just be careful. Don't get busted. Shit.'

I hear him laughing again.

'What?'

'Just thinking of Darcy . . . It's sort of satisfying.'

'Satisfying how?'

'Oh, come on. Don't tell me part of you doesn't like zinging her a little bit. There's some poetic justice here. Darcy's been riding roughshod over you for years.'

129

'What are you talking about?' I ask, genuinely surprised to hear him describe our friendship like that. I know I've been feeling more irritated by her recently and I know that she has not always been the most selfless of friends, but I've never thought of her as riding roughshod over me. 'No she hasn't.'

'Yeah, she has.'

'No. She *hasn't*,' I say, more firmly. I'm not sure who I am defending – me or Darcy. *Yes, there was the matter of you, Ethan. But you don't know about that.*

'Oh, please. Remember Notre Dame? The SATs?'

I think back to the day we all received our SAT scores, sealed in white envelopes from Guidance. We were all tight-lipped, but dying to know what everyone else got. Finally Darcy just said at lunch, 'Okay, who cares? Let's just tell our scores. Rachel?'

'Why do I have to go first?' I asked. I was satisfied enough with my score, but still didn't want to go first.

'Don't be a baby,' Darcy said. 'Just tell us.'

'Fine. thirteen hundred,' I said.

'What was your verbal?' she asked.

I told her 680.

'Nice,' she said. 'Congratulations.'

Ethan went next. 1410. No surprise there. I forget what Annalise got – something in the low 1100s.

'Well?' I looked at Darcy.

'Oh. Right. I got a thirteen hundred five.'

I knew instantly that she didn't have a 1305. The SAT is not scored in increments of five. Ethan knew too, because he kicked me under the table and hid a smile with his ham sandwich.

I didn't care that she lied per se. She was a known embellisher. But the fact that she lied about her score to beat me by five – that part really figured. We didn't call her on it. There was no point.

But then she said, 'Well, maybe we'll both get into Notre Dame.'

It was her Ethan power move in the fifth grade all over again.

Like a lot of kids in the Midwest, my dream growing up was to attend Notre Dame. We're not Irish or even Catholic, but ever since my parents took me to a Notre Dame football game when I was eight, I wanted to go there. To me it was what a college should be – stately stone buildings, manicured lawns, plenty of tradition. I wanted to be a part of it. Darcy never showed the slightest interest in Notre Dame and it irritated me that she was infringing on my terrain. But I wasn't too worried about her taking my spot. My grades were higher, my SATs were probably higher, and besides, more than one student from our high school got into Notre Dame every year.

That spring, the acceptance and rejection letters trickled in slowly. I checked the mailbox every day, in agony. Mike O'Sullivan, who had three generations of alumni in his family and was the president of our class, got into Notre Dame first. I assumed I would be next, but Darcy got her letter before I did. I was with her when she got the mail, although she wouldn't open the envelope in front of me. I went home, hoping guiltily that she had received bad news.

131

She called an hour later, ecstatic. 'I can't believe it! I got in! Can you believe it?'

In short, no. I couldn't. I mustered up a congratulations, but I was crushed. Her news meant one of two things: she had taken my spot, or we would both go to Notre Dame and she would upstage me for four more years. As much as I knew I would miss Darcy when I went away, I felt strongly that I needed to establish myself apart from her. Once she got in, there would be no perfect result.

Still, I wanted that acceptance more than I had ever wanted anything. And I had my pride on the line. I waited, prayed, even thought about calling the admissions office to beg. One sickening week later, my letter arrived. It looked just like Darcy's. I ran inside, my heart pounding in my ears as I sliced open the envelope, unfolded the paper that held my fate. *Close . . . you are very highly qualified . . . but no cigar.*

I was devastated and could barely speak to my friends in school the next day, especially Darcy. At lunch, as I fought back tears, she informed me that she was going to Indiana anyway. That she wanted nothing to do with a school that would turn me down. Her chasity upset me all the more. For once, Annalise spoke up. 'You took Rachel's spot, and you didn't even want to go there?'

'Well, it *was* my first choice. I changed my mind. And how was I supposed to know it would happen like this?' she said. 'I assumed she would get in; I only beat her by a few points on the SAT.'

Ethan had had enough. 'You didn't get a damn thirteen hundred five, Darcy. The SAT is scored in increments of ten.'

'Who said I got a thirteen hundred five?'

'You did,' Ethan and I said in unison.

'No I didn't. I said a thirteen hundred ten.'

'Omigod!' I said, looking at Annalise for support, but her gumption had run out. She claimed she had forgotten what Darcy said.

We argued for the rest of the lunch hour about what Darcy had said and why she had applied to Notre Dame if she didn't want to go there. We both ended up crying, and Darcy left school early, telling the school nurse she had cramps. The whole thing blew over when I got into Duke and talked myself into being happy with that result. Duke had a similar look and feel – stone buildings, pristine campus, prestige. It was just as good as Notre Dame and maybe it was better to broaden my horizons and leave Indiana.

But to this day I wonder why Notre Dame picked Darcy over me. Maybe a junior male member of the admissions staff fancied her photo. Maybe it was just Darcy's typical good luck.

In any case, I'm glad that Ethan refreshed my memory about Notre Dame. It replaces the Becky Zurich showdown in the forefront of my mind. Yes, Darcy could be a good friend – she usually was – but she also screwed me at a few pivotal moments in life: first love, college dream. Those were no small matters.

'All right,' I say to Ethan. 'But I think you're overstating the point a little. I wouldn't use the term "roughshod".'

'Okay, but you know what I mean. There's an under-current of competition.'

'I guess so. Maybe,' I say, thinking that it isn't much of a competition when one person consistently loses.

'So, anyway, please keep me posted. This is good stuff.'

I tell him I will.

'Oh, one more thing,' he says. 'When are you going to visit me?'

'Soon.'

'That's what you always say.'

'I know. But you know how it goes. Work is always crazy . . . I'll come soon, though. This year for sure.'

'Good enough,' Ethan says. 'I really do miss you.'

'I miss you too.'

'Besides,' he says, 'you might need a vacation by the time you're through with all of this.'

After we hang up, I note with satisfaction that Ethan never told me to stop. He only said to be careful. And I will do that. I will be careful the next time I see Dexter.

NINE

I avoid Darcy for three days, a very difficult thing to do. We never go so long without talking. When she finally reaches me, I blame my absence on work, say I have been unbelievably swamped – which is true – although I have found plenty of time to daydream about Dex, call Dex, email Dex. She asks if I am free for Sunday brunch. I tell her yes, figuring that I might as well just get the face-to-face meeting over with. We arrange to meet at EJ's Luncheonette near my apartment.

On Sunday morning, I arrive at EJ's first and note with relief that the place is full of children. Their happy clamor provides a distraction and makes me slightly less nervous. But I am still filled with anxiety at the thought of spending time with Darcy. I have been able to cope with my guilt by avoiding all thoughts of her, almost pretending that Dex is single, and we are back in law school before I ever got the big idea to introduce Darcy to him. But that tactic will not be possible this afternoon. And I'm afraid that spending time with her will force me to end things with Dex, something I desperately don't want to do.

A moment later, Darcy barges in carrying her big black Kate Spade bag, the one she uses for heavy errand-running, specifically the wedding variety. Sure enough, I see her familiar orange folder poking out of the top of the bag, stuffed with tear-outs from bridal magazines. My stomach drops. I had just about prepared myself for Darcy, but not for the wedding.

She gives me the two-cheek Euro kiss hello, as I smile, try to act natural. She launches into a tale about Claire's blind date from the night before with a surgeon named Skip. She says it did not go well, that Skip wasn't tall enough for Claire and failed to ask if she wanted dessert, thus setting off her cheapskate radar. I am thinking that perhaps the only radar that had gone off was Skip's 'tiresome snob' radar. Maybe he just wanted to go home and get away from her. I don't offer this suggestion, however, as Darcy doesn't like it when I criticize Claire – unless she does so first.

'She is just *way* too picky,' Darcy says as we are led to our booth. 'It's like she looks for things not to like, you know?'

'It's okay to be picky,' I say. 'But she has a pretty screwed up set of criteria.'

'How do you figure?'

'She can be a little shallow.'

Darcy gives me a blank stare.

'I'm just saying she cares too much about money, appearances, and how connected the guy is. She's just narrowing her pool a bit – and her chances of finding someone.'

'I don't think she's *that* picky,' Darcy says. 'She'd have gone out with Marcus and he's not well connected. He's from some dumpy town in Wyoming. And his hair is sort of thinning.'

136

'Montana,' I say, marveling at how superficial Darcy sounds. I guess she's been like this since her arrival in Manhattan, maybe even our whole lives, but sometimes when you know someone well, you don't see them as they really are. So I honestly think I've managed to ignore this fundamental part of her personality, perhaps not wanting to see my closest friend in this light. But ever since my conversation with Ethan, her pushy, shallow tendencies seem magnified, impossible to overlook.

'Montana, Wyoming. Whatever,' she says, waving her hand in the air as if she herself doesn't hail from the Midwest. It bothers me the way Darcy downplays our roots, even occasionally bagging on Indiana, calling it backward and ugly.

'And I like his hair,' I say.

She smirks. 'I see you're defending him. Interesting.'

I ignore her.

'Have you heard from him lately?'

'A few times. Emails mostly.'

'Any calls?'

'A few.'

'Have you seen him?'

'Not yet.'

'Damn, Rachel. Don't lose momentum.' She removes her gum and wraps it in a napkin. 'I mean, don't blow this one. You're not going to do better.'

I study my menu and feel anger and indignation swell inside me. What a rude thing to say! Not that I think there is anything wrong with Marcus, but why can't I do better? What is that supposed to mean, anyway? For our entire friendship it has been silently understood that Darcy is the pretty one, the lucky one, the charmed one. But an implicit understanding is one thing. To say it just like that – *you can't do better* – is quite another. Her nerve is truly breathtaking. I formulate possible retorts, but then swallow them. She doesn't know how bitchy her remark is; it only springs from her innate thoughtlessness. And, besides, I really have no right to be mad at her, considering.

I look up from my menu and glance at Darcy, worried that she will be able to see everything on my face. But she is oblivious. My mom always says that I wear my emotions on my sleeve, but unless Darcy wants to borrow the outfit, she doesn't see a thing.

Our waiter comes by and takes our orders without a notepad, something that always impresses me. Darcy asks for dry toast and a cappuccino, and I order a Greek omelet, substituting cheddar cheese for feta, and fries. Let her be the thin one.

Darcy whips out her orange folder and starts to tick through various lists. 'Okay. We have so much more to do than I thought. My mom called last night and was all, "Have you done this? Have you done that?" and I started freaking out.'

I tell her that we have plenty of time. I am wishing we had more.

'It's, like, three months away, Rach. It's going to be here before we know it.'

My stomach drops as I wonder how many more times I

138

will see Dexter in the three months. At what point will we stop? It should be sooner rather than later. It should be now.

I watch Darcy as she continues to go through her folder, making little notes in the margins until the waiter brings our food. I check the inside of my omelet – cheddar cheese. He got it right. I begin to eat as Darcy yaps about her tiara.

I nod, only half listening, still feeling stung by her rude words. *You can't do better.*

'Are you listening to me?' she finally asks.

'Yes.'

'Well then, what did I just say?'

'You said you had no idea where to find a tiara.'

She takes a bite of toast, still looking doubtful. 'Okay. So you did hear me.'

'Told ya,' I say, shaking salt onto my fries.

'Do you know where to get one?'

'Well, we saw some at Vera Wang, in that glass case on the first floor, didn't we? And I'm pretty sure Bergdorf has them.'

I think back to the early days of Darcy's engagement, when my heart had been at least somewhat in it. Although I was envious that her life was coming together so neatly, I was genuinely happy for her and was a diligent maid of honor. I recall our long search for her gown. We must have seen every dress in New York. We made the trek to Kleinfeld in Brooklyn. We did the department stores and the little boutiques in the Village. We hit the big designers on Madison Avenue – Vera Wang, Carolina Herrera, Yumi Katsura, Amsale.

But Darcy never got that feeling that you're supposed to

get, that feeling where you are overcome with emotion and start weeping all over the dressing room. I finally targeted the problem. It was the same problem that Darcy has trying on bathing suits. She looked stunning in everything. The body-hugging sheaths showed off her slender hips and height. The big princess ball gowns emphasized her minuscule waist. The more dresses she tried on, the more confused we became. So finally, at the end of one long, weary Saturday, when we arrived at our last appointment at Wearkstatt in SoHo, I decided that this would be our final stop. The fresh-faced girl, who was not yet jaded by life and love, asked Darcy what she envisioned for her special day. Darcy shrugged helplessly and looked at me to answer.

'She's having a city wedding,' I started.

'I just *love* Manhattan weddings.'

'Right. And it's in early September. So we're counting on warm weather . . . And I think Darcy prefers simple gowns without too many frills.'

'But not too boring,' Darcy chimed in.

'Right. Nothing too plain-Jane,' I said. *God forbid.*

The girl pressed a finger to her temple, scurried off, and returned with four virtually indistinguishable A-lines. And that's when I made a decision that I was going to pick one of the dresses to be *the one*. When Darcy tried on the second dress, a silk satin A-line in soft white with a dropped waist and beading on the bodice, I gasped. 'Oh, Darcy. It's gorgeous on you,' I said. (It was, of course.) 'This is it!'

'Do you think?' Her voice quivered. 'Are you sure?'

'I'm positive,' I said. 'You need to buy *this* one.'

Moments later, we were placing an order for the dress, talking about fittings. Darcy and I had been friends forever, but I think it was the first time that I realized the influence that I have over her. I picked her wedding dress, the most important garment that she will ever wear.

'So you won't mind running some errands with me today?' she asks me now. 'The only thing I really want to accomplish is shoes. I need my shoes for the next fitting. I figure we'll look at Stuart Weitzman and then zip up to Barney's. You can come with me, can't you?'

I plow a forkful of my omelet through ketchup. 'Sure . . . But I do have to go in to work today,' I lie.

'You always have to work! I don't know who has it worse – you or Dex,' she says. 'He's been working on this big project lately. He's never home.'

I keep my eyes down, searching my plate for the best remaining fry. 'Really?' I say, thinking of the recent nights Dex and I have stayed at work late, talking on the phone. 'That sucks.'

'Tell me about it. He's never available to help with this wedding. It's really starting to piss me off.'

After lunch and a lot more wedding conversation, we walk over to Madison, turning left toward Stuart Weitzman. As we enter the store, Darcy admires a dozen sandals, telling me that the cut of the shoes is perfect for her narrow, small-heeled feet. We finally make our way to the satin wedding shoes in the back. She scrutinizes each one, choosing four pairs to try on. I watch as she prances around the store, runway style, before settling on the pair with the highest heels. I almost ask her if she is sure they are comfortable, but stop myself. The sooner she makes a decision, the sooner I will be dismissed for the day.

But Darcy isn't finished with me. 'While we're over here, can we go to Elizabeth Arden to look at lipsticks?' she asks as she pays for her shoes.

I reluctantly agree. We walk over to Fifth, while I tolerate her yammering about waterproof mascara and how I have to remind her to buy some for the wedding day because there is no way that she is going to make it through the ceremony without crying.

'Sure,' I say. 'I'll remind you.'

I tell myself to view these tasks with an objective eye, as detached as a wedding coordinator who barely knows the bride, rather than the bride's oldest but most disloyal friend. After all, if I am especially helpful to Darcy, it might diminish my guilt. I imagine Darcy discovering my misdeeds and me saying, 'Yes, all of that is true. You got me. But may I remind you that I NEVER ONCE ABANDONED MY MAID OF HONOR DUTIES!'

'May I help you, ladies?' the woman behind the counter at Elizabeth Arden asks us.

'Yes. We are looking for a pink lipstick. A vivid yet soft and innocent bridal pink,' Darcy says.

'And you are the bride?'

'I am. Yes.' Darcy flashes one of her fake PR smiles.

The woman beams back and makes her decisive recommendations, swiftly pulling out five tubes and setting them on the counter in front of us. 'Here you are. Perfect.'

Darcy tells her that I will need a complementary shade, as the maid of honor.

'How nice. Sisters?' The woman smiles. Her big, square teeth remind me of Chiclets.

'No,' I say.

'But she's like my sister,' Darcy says, simply and sincerely.

I feel low. I picture myself on *Ricki Lake*, the title of the show 'My Best Friend Tried to Steal My Groom'. The audience boos and hisses as I babble my apologies and excuses. I explain that I didn't mean to cause any harm, I just couldn't help myself. I used to wonder how they found people who had committed such acts of despicable disloyalty (never mind how they got these people to fess up on national television). Now I was joining the lowlife ranks. Giving Brandi with an i a run for her money.

This has to stop. Right now. Right this second. I haven't yet slept with Dex consciously, soberly. So we kissed again? It was only a kiss. The turning point will be the selection of the bridal lipstick. Right now. *One. Two. Three. Go!*

Then I think of Dexter's soft hair and cinnamon lips and his words – *I like literally everything about you.* I still can't believe that Dex has those feelings for me. And the fact that I feel the same way about him is too much to ignore. Maybe it is meant to be. Words like 'fate' and 'soul mates' swirl around my head, words that made me scoff in my twenties. I note the irony – aren't you supposed to get more cynical with age?

'You like this one?' Darcy turns to me with her full lips in a pout.

'It's nice,' I say.

'Is it too bright?'

'I don't think so. No. It's pretty.'

'I think it may be too bright. Remember I'm going to be in white. It'll make a difference. Remember, Kim Frisby's wedding make-up, how she looked like a total tart? I want to look hot, but sweet, too. You know, like a virgin. But still hot.'

I am suddenly and unexpectedly on the verge of tears – I just can't stand the wedding talk another second. 'Darce, I really have to get to work. I'm truly sorry.'

Her lower lip protrudes. 'C'mon, just a little longer. I can't do this without you!' And then she says to the salesgirl, 'No offense to you.'

The girl smiles as if she totally understands, no offense taken. She recognizes the truth of what Darcy is saying and is probably wondering what kind of a maid of honor leaves the bride during such a pivotal moment.

I take a deep breath and tell her that I can stay a few more minutes. She samples more tubes, wiping her lips with a make-up removing lotion between hues of pink.

'How about this one?'

'Nice.' I smile earnestly.

'Well, nice doesn't cut it!' she snaps. 'It has to be perfect. I have to look perfect!'

As I study her pouty, berry-stained, bee-stung lips, any trace of remorse is gone. All I feel is solid, full-blown resentment.

Why does everything have to be perfect for you? Why does it all have to be handed to you in a perfect package all wrapped up with a Martha Stewart bow? What did you do to deserve Dex? I met him first. I introduced him to you. I should have gone for him. Why didn't I? Oh, right, because I thought I wasn't good enough for him. Well, I was mistaken. I obviously misjudged the situation. It can happen . . . especially when one has a friend like you, a friend who assumes she has a right to the best of everything, a friend who is so relentless in her quest to outshine you that you even begin to underestimate yourself, set your sights low. This is your fault, Darcy, for taking what should have been mine in the first place.

I am keyed up and absolutely desperate to get away from her. I look at my watch and sigh, almost believing that I really do have to go to work and that Darcy is being inconsiderate, as usual, taking advantage of my time. *I think my job is a little more important than your lipstick for an event that is still months away!*

'I'm sorry. Darce – it's not my fault that I have to work.'

'Fine.'

'It's not my fault,' I say again.

Not my fault.

My feelings for Dex are not my fault.

And his feelings for me – and I know they are real – are not his fault.

Before I can escape, Darcy calls Claire on her cell. Has she tried Bobbi Brown, I can hear Claire inquire and then state with the authority of *Bride's* magazine that they have a beautiful bridal line and their lipstick has plenty of moisture but not too much shine.

145

'Will you come meet me now?' Darcy pleads into the phone. Her sense of entitlement knows no bounds.

She hangs up the phone and tells me that I am free to go, Claire will be straight over. She waves at me; I am being dismissed.

'Goodbye,' I say. 'I'll speak to you later?'

'Sure. Whatever. Bye.'

As I turn to leave, she issues a final warning. 'If you're not careful, I'm going to have to demote you to lowly bridesmaid and give Claire your honored position.'

So much for just like sisters.

I call Dexter's cell phone the second I am out of sight. It is a low move, making the call while Darcy does wedding errands, but I am running off the steam of indignation. That's what she gets for being so demanding, domineering, and self-centered.

'Where are you?' I ask Dex after we exchange hellos.

'Home.'

'Oh.'

'Where are you? I thought you were shopping.'

'I was. But I said I had to work.'

I notice that we are both dancing around any direct mention of Darcy.

'Well, *do* you have to work?' he asks tentatively.

'Not really.'

'Good. Me either. Can I see you?'

'I'll be home in twenty minutes.'

*

Dex beats me to my apartment and is waiting in my lobby making small talk with José about the Mets. I am so happy to see him, relieved to be away from Darcy. I smile and say hello, wondering if José recognizes Dex from past visits with Darcy. I hope he doesn't. It's not just my parents from whom I want approval – I even want it from my doorman.

Dex and I ride the elevator and walk down the hall to my apartment. I am jittery with anticipation, eager for his touch. We sit on my couch. He takes my hands and we start kissing with an urgency that feels like an affair. It is a serious word – a scary word. It conjures images of Sunday school and the Ten Commandments. But it is not adultery. Nobody is married. Yet. I push it all out of my mind as I kiss Dex. There will be no more guilt, not for this next parcel of time.

Suddenly, perching on the couch seems ridiculous. My bed would be so much more comfortable. Nothing more has to happen just because we're on a bed. That is a teenager's perception. I am a grown woman with life experience (albeit limited), and I can control myself on my own bed. I stand up and lead him over to the other side of my studio. He follows me, still holding my hand. We sit on the foot of the bed. Dex slips his feet out of his loafers. He is not wearing socks. He moves his big toes up and down and then rubs his feet together. He has high, graceful arches and slender ankles.

'Come here,' he says, pulling me against him and both of us up toward my pillows. He is strong, his skin warm. We are now on our sides, our bodies against each other. He kisses me more, and we topple over in his direction. He stops kissing me suddenly, clears his throat, and says, 'It's so strange. Being

147

with you like this. And yet it also feels so natural. Maybe because we've been friends for so long.'

I tell him I know exactly what he means. I think back to law school. We weren't best friends in those days, but we were close enough to learn a lot about each other, stuff that comes out even when your focus is on contributory negligence and ways to rescind a contract. I mentally catalog all that I learned about Dex in the pre-Darcy days. That he grew up in Westchester. That he is Catholic. That he played basketball in high school and considered walking on at Georgetown. That he has an older sister named Tessa who went to Cornell and now teaches high school English in Buffalo. That his parents divorced when he was very young. That his father remarried. That his mother beat breast cancer.

And then there was all that I learned via Darcy, details of his personal life that I've found myself conjuring and pondering in recent days. Like that Dex is grouchy in the morning. That he does at least fifty push-ups before bed every night and that he never leaves dirty dishes on the counter. That he broke down when his grandfather died, the only time she has ever seen him cry. That he had two serious girlfriends before Darcy and that the one named Suzanne Cohen, who worked as a research analyst at Goldman Sachs, dumped him and broke his heart.

When I add it all up, I know a lot. But I want more. 'So tell me everything about yourself,' I say, sounding eighteen.

Dex touches my face and then draws an imaginary line along my nose and around my mouth, resting his finger on my chin. 'You first. You're the mysterious one.'

148

I laugh. 'Hardly,' I say, thinking that he is confusing being shy with being mysterious.

'You are. You were a closed book in law school. All quiet, not wanting to date anyone – despite plenty of guys trying . . . I could never get much out of you.'

I laugh again. 'What's that supposed to mean? I told you plenty in law school.'

'Like what?'

I rattle off some autobiographical details.

'I'm not talking about stuff like that,' he says. 'I'm talking about the important things. How you *feel* about things.'

'I hated Zigman,' I offer weakly.

'I know. Your fear was all-consuming. And then you did a great job when he finally called on you.'

'I did not,' I say, remembering how I stumbled my way through a long, painful line of questioning.

'Yes you did. You just didn't think you did. You don't see yourself the way you are.'

I avert my eyes, focus on a spot of ink on my comforter.

He continues, 'You see yourself as very average, ordinary. And there is nothing ordinary about you, Rachel.'

I can't look back at him. My face burns.

'And I know that you blush when you're embarrassed.' He smiles.

'No I don't!' I cover my face with one hand and roll my eyes.

'Yes you do. You're adorable. And yet you have no idea, which is the most adorable part.'

Nobody, not even my mother, has ever called me adorable.

'And you are beautiful. Absolutely, stunningly beautiful in the freshest most natural way. You look like one of those Ivory girls. Remember those commercials? . . . You're probably too young. You're like a J.Crew model. All natural.'

I tell him to please stop. Even though I love what he has just told me.

'It's true.'

I want to believe him.

He kisses my neck, his left hand resting on my hip.

'Dex.'

'Hmmm?'

'Who ever said I didn't want to date in law school?'

'Well, you didn't, did you? You were there to learn, not date. That was clear.'

'I went out with Nate.'

'Not until the very end.'

'He didn't ask me out until the very end.'

'Brave guy.'

I roll my eyes.

'I almost asked you out, you know that?'

I laugh at this.

'It's true,' he says, sounding a little bit hurt.

I give him a dubious look.

'Do you remember that time when we were studying for our torts final?'

I picture his thumb on my face, wiping away my tear. So it *had* meant something.

'You know exactly what I'm talking about, don't you?'

My face feels hot as I nod. 'I think so. Yeah.'

'And when I asked to walk you home, you said no. Shot me down.'

'I didn't shoot you down!'

'You were all business.'

'I wasn't. I just didn't think at the time . . .' My voice trails off.

'Yeah, and then you introduced me to Darcy. I knew then that you had zero interest.'

'I just didn't think . . . I didn't know you saw me that way.'

'I loved spending time with you,' Dex says. 'Still do.' He stares at me, unblinking.

I tell him he blinks less than anyone I have ever met. He smiles, says that he has never lost a staring contest. I challenge him, making my eyes as wide as his. I notice he has a dark speck in his left iris, like an eye freckle.

Seconds later, I blink. He flashes a quick, jubilant smile and then kisses me more. He changes the intensity and pressure and amount of tongue, the kissing ideals that are all too often abandoned once in a long-term relationship. Kissing Dex would never become stale. He would never stop kissing me like this.

'Tell me about Suzanne,' I say when we finally separate. 'And your high school girlfriend.'

'Alice?' He laughs, sweeps a piece of my hair behind my ear. 'What about her? Ancient history.'

Everyone knows you don't discuss exes when you're in a fledgling relationship. Even though you are dying to know those details from the very beginning, that is something you bring up much later in the game. You don't have to be a Rules

Girl like Claire to have that concept down. Dating someone new is a fresh start for both of you. No good can come from rehashing past – and by definition failed – relationships. But compared to the fact that Dex is engaged, ex-girlfriends are an innocuous topic. There is no need to strategize here in my safe studio. The rules don't apply. It might be the only advantage to our situation.

'Were you in love with them?' For some reason I need to know.

He rolls onto his back and stares at the ceiling, concentrating. I like that he thinks about my questions, just as he did during law school exams. I remember him staring into space for the first forty-five minutes of an exam. Not writing a word on his blue book until he thought through his entire answer.

He clears his throat. 'Not with Alice. But yes with Suzanne.'

No wonder Suzanne has always bothered Darcy so much. She wants to be the only one he has ever loved. I remember how she used to beat down Blaine in high school: 'You didn't love Cassandra, did you? Did you?' Until he finally just said no. 'Only you, Darcy.'

'Why not with Alice?' I ask. I'd rather hear about the one he didn't love first.

'I don't know. She was a sweet girl. As sweet as they come. I don't know why I didn't love her. It's something you can't really control.'

Dex is right. It has nothing to do with the other person's inherent worth, the sum of their fine attributes. It is something you can't will yourself to feel. Or not feel. Although I have done a pretty good job of it over the years. Just look at Joey. I dated him for two years and never felt even a fraction of what I'm feeling now.

'Of course, it was just high school,' he continues. 'How serious can you really be at that age?'

I nod, thinking of sweet little Brandon. Then I ask Dex about Suzanne. 'So you loved her?'

'Yeah. But that wasn't going to work in the long run. She's Jewish and was very upfront about her expectations of me. She wanted me to convert, raise our kids Jewish, the whole nine yards. And maybe I would have been okay with that . . . I'm not very religious . . . but I wasn't okay with the fact that she made it a bright line rule. I saw a life of her browbeating me into shit. Just like her mother does to her father. Besides, we were too young to commit . . . It still killed me when she walked, though.'

'Is she married now?'

'Funny you ask that. I actually just heard from a mutual friend that she got engaged. About a month after—' He stops, looks uncomfortable.

'After you did?'

'Yeah,' he whispers. He pulls me against him and kisses me hard, erasing any thoughts of Darcy. We undress and slide under the covers.

'You're cold,' he says.

'I'm always cold when I'm nervous.'

'Why are you nervous? Don't be nervous.'

'Dex,' I say into his neck.

153

'Yeah, Rach?'

'Nothing.'

His body covers mine. I am not cold anymore.

We kiss for a long time, touching everywhere.

I don't know the time, but it is just getting dark.

I almost stop him, for all the obvious reasons. But also because I'm thinking we should wait until we can spend a night together. Then again, that might never happen. And likely I will never shower with him, watch him shave in the morning. Or read the Sunday *Times* over coffee, whiling away the hours. We'll never hold hands in Central Park or cuddle on a blanket in Sheep's Meadow. But I can have him now. Nothing is stopping us from this moment.

I can see just a fraction of Dexter as we move together – his sideburn with a trace of gray, his strong shoulder, his seashell of an ear. My fingertips graze his collarbone, then hold on more tightly.

TEN

I can't stop thinking about Dex. I know that we won't end up together, that he will marry Darcy in September. But I am content to live in the moment, and allow myself the daily pleasure of obsessing. Nothing lasts forever, I tell myself. Especially the good stuff. Although typically you aren't faced with a hard deadline. I think of a few other examples of concrete, predetermined endings. Take college, for example. I knew that I would go away for four years, accumulate friends and memories and knowledge, and that it would all come to an abrupt end on a set date. I knew that on this day I would collect my diploma and pile my belongings into a U-Haul bound for Indiana, and the Duke experience would be done. A chapter closed forever. But that awareness didn't stop me from enjoying myself, sucking all of the joy out of the deal.

So that is what I am doing with Dex. I am not going to dwell on the end at the expense of the here and now.

Tonight I am home when Dex phones from work to say a quick hello and tell me that he misses me. It is the sort of call a boyfriend makes to his girlfriend. Nothing covert or complicated about it. I pretend that we are together for real. The phone rings again a second after we hang up.

155

'Hey,' I say, in the same hushed tone, thinking it is only a follow-up phone call from Dex.

'What's that voice?' Darcy asks, yanking me back to reality.

'What voice?' I ask. 'I'm just tired. What's going on?'

She launches into the details of her latest work crisis, which typically amounts to no more than a paper jam at the copier. This one is no exception. A typo on a flyer for a club opening. I resist the urge to tell her that the target audience won't notice a misspelling, and instead ask her who is going to the Hamptons this weekend. I feel my senses heighten, anticipating Dexter's name. He already told me he was going, convincing me that I had to go too. It will be awkward, but worth it, he said. He has to see me.

'Not sure. Claire might be having friends in town. Dex is in.'

'Oh, really? He doesn't have to work?' I ask, sounding a bit too surprised. I feel a stab of worry, but Darcy doesn't notice my false tone.

'No, he just finished with some big deal,' she says.

'Which deal?'

'I don't know. Some deal.'

Dexter's job bores Darcy. I have observed the way she can shut him down, interrupting him in the middle of a story, transitioning back to her own petty concerns. *Am I fat? Does this look good on me? Will you come there with me? Do that for me. Reassure me. Me. Me. Me.*

As if on cue, she tells me that she is considering sending in a tape to *Big Brother*, that it would be fun to be on the

156

show. Fun for an exhibitionist. I can think of few things more horrifying than being on national television, out there for the world to judge, assess, tear apart.

'Do you think I'd get picked?' she asks.

'You'd have a good chance.'

She is pretty enough to get picked, and she has a vivid personality – exactly what they look for on reality television. I study my own face in the mirror, think of Dex telling me that I look like a J.Crew model. Maybe I am attractive. But I am nowhere near as pretty as Darcy, with her precise features, incredible cheekbones, bow-shaped lips.

Now she is laughing loudly into the phone, telling me another story about her day. She hurts my ears. The word 'strident' comes to mind, and as I study my reflection again, I decide that although I'm far from beautiful, perhaps I have a softness that she lacks.

It is Thursday, the day before we leave for the Hamptons. Dex is over. We had planned on waiting until next week to see each other alone, but we both finished work early. And well, here we are together again. We have already made love once. Now I am resting my head on his chest. As he breathes, his chest lifts my face slightly. Neither of us speaks for a long time, then he asks suddenly, 'What are we *doing*?'

There it is. The Question.

I have thought of it a hundred times, worded the inquiry exactly like that, with the same intonation. But every time I answer it differently:

We are following our hearts.

We are taking a chance.

We are crazy.

We are self-destructive.

We are lustful.

We are confused.

We are rebelling.

He is afraid of marriage.

I am afraid of being alone.

We are falling in love.

We are already in love.

And the most common: we have no idea.

This is the one I offer up. 'I don't know.'

'Neither do I,' he says softly. 'Should we talk about it?'

'Do you want to?'

'Not really,' he says.

I am relieved that he doesn't. Because I don't. I am too afraid of what we might decide. Either choice is scary. 'Let's not, then. Not now.'

'Then when?' he asks.

For some reason, I say, 'After July Fourth.'

It sounds arbitrary, but it has always been a benchmark of sorts, the summer midpoint. Even though more than half the summer is left after the Fourth of July, the part that follows is the faster half, the part that always flies by. June, although a day shorter, feels so much longer than August.

'Okay,' he says.

'No examining anything until July Fourth.' I state the rule clearly, as I would at the outset of a law school exam. My voice is firm, even though I'm not sure what we've just

decided. That we are finished as of July Fourth? Or maybe . . .
no, he couldn't think that I meant that is when he will tell
Darcy he can't go through with marrying her. No, that is not
what we just decided. We simply decided to decide nothing.
That is all.

Still, picking the date scares me. I picture a giant countdown of days, hours, minutes, seconds. Like the clocks set up
in 1999 for the countdown to the new millennium. I remember
watching the seconds roll off such a clock in the post office
near Grand Central Station sometime in December. That clock
made me nervous, frantic. I wanted to attack my to-do list,
clear my desk of backed-up calls, finish it all immediately. At
the same time, watching those numbers tick by paralyzed me.
I had too much to do, so why do anything at all?

I try to calculate the number of hours left before July
Fourth. How many nights we will have together. How many
times we will make love.

My stomach growls. Or maybe it's his. I can't tell because
I am flat against him. 'Are you hungry? We can order food,' I
say, and kiss his chest. 'Or I can make us something.'

I imagine myself whipping up a tasty snack. I can't cook,
but I would learn. I would make an excellent, nurturing wife.

He tells me that he doesn't want to waste time eating. He
can get something on his way home. Or just go to bed
hungry. He says he wants to feel me against him until it's time
to leave.

The next day I ask Dex if there were any problems when he
returned home. It is a vague question, but he knows what I

159

am asking. He says that Darcy was not home when he got in, so he had time to shower, reluctantly wash me off him. Darcy had left him a message: 'It's eleven and you're not answering your cell or your phone at work. You're probably having an affair. I'm going out with Claire.'

It is her usual tongue-in-cheek accusation when Dex works late. She asks him if he's having an affair, never believing that he would do such a thing. She changes the person every time, selecting a random female name from his office. The less attractive the woman, the more amused she is. 'I know you're in love with Nina,' she'll say, knowing that Nina is a chubby word processor from Staten Island with fake nails adorned with glitter art.

I think of Dex returning home last night. A whole scene unfurls in my mind – Dex stealing into his apartment, hurrying to shower and get in bed, waiting for the key to turn in the lock, pretending to be asleep when Darcy enters their room. She hovers over him, studying him in the dark.

'How was your date with Nina?' she asks in a wry, loud voice.

He wipes his eyes with his fists as people do on television when they're awakened from a sound sleep. 'Hi,' he says wearily and then pretends to fall back asleep.

She cuddles up to him in bed, tossing out an 'I love you.'

His jaw clenches, but he says it back. What choice does he have? He falls asleep thinking about me. Thinking that her chin is too sharp against his chest.

*

I am watching them on the beach, down by the water.

Darcy and Dex standing together in the not too hot June sun. This weekend is the first that I have seen them together since Dex and I soberly, willfully made love. I am wearing dark sunglasses so I can study them from my towel without being obvious, while Claire babbles to me about – what else? – the wedding. What if the night is chilly? Should we buy matching wraps, a light, gauzy cardigan? I nod and murmur that it is a good idea.

Dex has just finished a quick swim, even though the water is freezing. Now they are talking, huddled close together. Perhaps he is giving her the report on the water temperature. She hesitantly steps closer to the ocean's reach, just enough to let the water coat her feet. They are both smiling. Dex kicks water on to her shins and she shrieks, turns and scampers a few feet from him. I can see the muscles strain in her long, tanned legs. She is wearing the nude-colored bikini. Her hair is down, blowing around her face. He laughs, and she raises her index finger as if to scold him and then walks toward him again. They are engaged in a full-fledged frolic. It pains me to watch them, but I can't stop. I can't look away.

I feel as if they are putting on a show. Well, Darcy is always putting on a show. But Dex is a willing participant. Surely he knows we are all watching. That I am watching. It is always that way when you are in a group and someone decides to go for a swim or walk to the water. The ocean is like a giant stage. It is natural that the others watch, if only for a moment. Dex must be aware of this, yet he is still in

161

full-throttle playful-couple mode. He should be brooding on his towel, napping or reading a novel – something dark, to give me the impression that he is confused, upset, torn. But instead he is splashing Darcy and grinning.

Marcus cups his mouth with his hands, yells down at them. 'How cold is it?'

'Freaking freezing!' Darcy announces, her hand stroking Dex's back, while he reports a manly, 'Nah, it feels good. Come on down!'

Rage commingles with hurt. For the first time, I completely regret having sex with Dex. I feel foolish, suddenly sure that it meant next to nothing to him. Tears sting my eyes as I force myself to turn away from them, slip on my headphones. I order myself not to cry.

Before I can hit play, Marcus asks me what I'm listening to. I have only seen him once since our date and that was just for a quick weekday lunch at a deli near my office, but we have talked several times, and one conversation lasted over an hour. The only apparent reason why date number two has not happened, at least as far as he knows, is mere circumstance. He's busy, I'm busy. Work has been crazy. That whole routine. So the door is still wide open, which I am very glad about. I need to focus more on him. There is no spark, but you never know. Sparks might emerge once I put Dex behind me. I smile and say, 'Tracy Chapman. It's a good CD. Wanna listen?'

I hand him my headphones as Dex and Darcy walk toward us. Marcus listens for a few seconds. 'That's nice.' He gives my headphones back to me and fishes a Coke out of our cooler.

162

'Want a sip?' he asks just as Darcy and Dex are standing over us.

I tell him sure, take the can and wipe the lid with the edge of my towel after I swallow.

He says with a knowing, goofy look, 'I don't mind your germs. If you catch my drift.'

I laugh and shake my head as if to say, 'Marcus, you crazy nut, you.'

Marcus winks. I laugh again.

Perfect timing. Dex catches the whole exchange. I do not look at him. I will not. 'Is anybody else getting in?' he asks.

Claire gives him the standard response. 'Not yet. I'm not hot enough.'

Marcus says he hates to swim, particularly in freezing water. 'Please make me see how that is fun.'

Darcy giggles. 'It's *not* fun. It's torture!'

I say nothing, hit the play button on my Discman.

'What about you, Rachel?' Dex asks, still hovering over me.

I ignore him, pretending the volume is too high to hear him.

He and Darcy return to their towels on the other side of Claire. Darcy brushes sand from her feet and ankles, while Dex sits cross-legged, looking at the ocean. I can see his shoulder and back out of the corner of my eye. I try not to think about his smooth skin and how he feels against me. I won't be feeling it again. I tell myself it's not the end of the world. It is for the best.

*

163

Before dinner that night, as I am dressing, Darcy comes to my room and asks me if I brought an eyelash curler. I tell her no, that I don't own an eyelash curler. Maybe Hillary does, but she is showering. She sits on my bed and sighs, her features rearranging into a dreamy expression.

'I just had the best sex,' she says.

I struggle to keep my composure. 'Oh, really?' I know I am opening the door for more sharing, but I don't know what else to say. My face is on fire. I hope Darcy won't notice.

'Yeah, it was phenomenal. Did you hear us?' It is like Darcy to share such details. She has always been explicit in her sexual reports. She will tell you what words were exchanged at the moment of orgasm. I have always listened, usually laughed, occasionally even enjoyed her stories. But those days are long over.

'No. I must have been in the shower,' I say.

'Yeah, we were in the shower too.' She finger-combs her wet hair, then shakes her head from side to side. 'Wow. Haven't had sex like that in months.'

I think of their wet bodies pressed together and can't decide who I hate more.

It is late, after two a.m. I have avoided Dex all night, at the house and then at dinner. Now we are at the Talkhouse. I have just ordered two beers, one for me and one for Hillary, when Dex finds me at the bar.

'Hi, Rach,' he says.

I am buzzed and brazen. The alcohol has dried up my hurt, leaving only resentment and anger. They are easier

164

emotions to manage, more straightforward. I have eliminated all the shades of gray: Dex is just a bad person. He used me. For what, I am not sure. I want to show that I hate him. I have my chance.

'Yes?'

'What's going on?' he asks casually.

'Nothing,' I snap, turning to leave.

'Wait a sec. Where are you going?'

'To take Hillary her beer.'

'I want to talk to you.'

'What about?' I make my voice icy.

'What's wrong?'

'Nothing's wrong,' I say, wishing I could think of something pointed and vengeful. I have not had much practice being mean, but my tone of voice must do the trick because Dex looks hurt. Not as hurt as I was today on the beach or during Darcy's sex report. Not hurt enough. I raise my eyebrows, looking at him with a slight look of disgust as if to say, 'Yes? Is there something I can do for you?'

'Are you – are you mad at me?' he asks.

I laugh – no, it is more of a snort.

'*Are* you?' he asks again.

'No, Dex, I'm not mad at you,' I say. 'I really am not concerned with you at all. Or what you do with Darcy.'

Now he knows that I know. 'Rachel . . .' he starts, flustered. Then he tries to tell me that it was her doing, that she initiated it.

'She said it was the best sex of her life,' I say as I walk away, leaving him standing alone at the bar. 'Good job. Congrats.'

Even in the fog of my buzz, I know that I have no right to confront Dex like this. All he did was have sex with his fiancée. He has promised me nothing – we were not supposed to even discuss anything until the Fourth of July. No material misrepresentation has been made. In fact, no misrepresentation has been made at all, material or otherwise. I am in this situation of my own accord, have not been duped. But I still hate him.

I scan the crowd, trying to find Hillary. Dex follows me and grabs my arm right below my elbow. I drop one of the beers. The bottle breaks.

'Nice. Look what you did,' I say, looking down at the mess.

'I'll get you another one.'

'Don't bother.'

'Rachel, please . . . I couldn't help that. It was Darcy, I swear.'

Hillary suddenly appears beside us. 'What's up?' I am not sure if she heard any of our conversation.

'Nothing,' Dex answers quickly. 'Rachel's just mad at me for dropping her beer.'

'You can have mine,' Hillary says.

'No, take this one,' I say, handing her the other beer.

She reluctantly takes it and asks where Darcy is.

'We were just looking for her,' I say.

I glance at Dex. He is trying to cover up in front of Hillary, but he is not doing the best job of it. His eyes are wide with worry, his mouth stretched into an uneasy smile. I bet he didn't have that look on his face in the shower.

It is over, I say in my head, with the dramatic flourish of a woman wronged. Then I turn around to find Marcus. Sweet Marcus, who offered me his Coke on the beach and is not engaged to anyone.

ELEVEN

'Ahh. The bunny-in-the-pot routine,' Ethan says, when I give him the update on Monday morning.

'It was *not* a bunny in the pot routine!' I protest, remembering that I saw *Fatal Attraction* with Darcy and Ethan. Darcy had major issues with the whole premise. She kept saying how unrealistic it was – no man would cheat on his wife with a much less attractive woman. I guess I am disproving her theory.

'Oh no?' Ethan deadpans. 'Well, perhaps a variation on that theme. More subtle though. You just exerted slight pressure . . . and let him know that it is unacceptable to continue relations with his fiancée.'

'Well, anyway . . . it's over,' I say, realizing that those two words lump me right in with a hoard of naïve women who say it's over while praying it's not, looking for any shred of hope, insisting that they only want closure when what they really want is that one last conversation disguised as seeking closure while they work to keep the door open for more. And the pathetic truth is I *do* want more. I wish I could undo the confrontation at the Talkhouse. I should not have said a word to Dex. I feel an ache of worry that he is going to stop seeing me altogether. He will want nothing to do with me after I

168

freaked out on him for doing something perfectly within his rights. He will probably decide that it's not worth it, the situation is just way too complicated.

'It's over, huh?' Ethan asks dubiously.

'Yes.'

'Bravo,' Ethan says in his finest English accent. 'Way to take a stand.'

'So, anyway,' I say, as if it is easy for me to transition away from Dex.

'Yeah. So anyway. Are you coming to London the week of the Fourth?' he asks.

I had mentioned it as a possibility in a recent email; before Dex and I had established our date. Now I don't want to leave. Just in case things aren't completely over. 'Um. I doubt it. I already committed to the Hamptons,' I say.

'Won't Dex be there?'

'Yes, but I still want to get my money's worth out of the share.'

'Right. Uh-huh.'

'Don't say it like that.'

'Okay,' he says, changing his tone. 'But are you ever going to visit me? You blew me off after your bar exam too. Because of that Nate guy.'

'I *will* visit. I promise. Maybe in September.'

'Okay . . . But the Fourth would have been fun.'

'It's not even a holiday there,' I say.

'Yeah. It's funny the way the Brits don't celebrate our independence from them . . . But it's a holiday in my heart, Rachel.'

I laugh and tell him that I'll look into flights for the fall.

'All right. I'll email you my free weekends – all my deets.'

He knows I hate the word 'deets'. Just as I hate people who make a 'rez' for dinner. Or ask you to get back to them 'ASAP'. And Ethan's favorite, designed especially to annoy me – 'YOYO', i.e. 'you're on your own'.

I smile. 'Sounds fab.'

'Super then.'

My phone rings as soon as I hang up with Ethan. Les's name shows up on my screen. I consider not picking up but have learned that avoidance techniques don't work well at a law firm. It only makes partners more irritable when you finally do talk.

'How did you serve the IXP papers?' he barks into the phone as soon as I say hello. Les always skips the pleasantries.

'What do you mean?'

'Your mode of service. By mail? By hand?'

I nailed it to his cottage door, jackass, I think, remembering the antiquated mode of service tested by the New York bar.

'By mail,' I say, glancing down at my well-worn copy of the New York Rules of Civil Procedure.

'Great. Fucking great,' he says in his normal snide tone.

'What?'

'What? *What*?' he shouts into the phone. I pull the receiver away from my ear but now I hear his voice in stereo, filling the hall. 'You fucked up! That's what! The papers needed to go by hand! Didn't you bother to read the Court's order?'

170

I scan the letter from the judge. Damn, he is right.

'You're right,' I say solemnly. He hates excuses and I have none anyway. 'I screwed up.'

'What are you, a goddamn first-year associate?'

I stare at my desk. He knows full well that I'm a fifth-year.

'I mean, Christ, Rachel, this is malpractice,' he growls. 'You're gonna get this firm sued and yourself fired if you don't get your head out of your ass.'

'I'm sorry,' I say, just as I remember that he hates you that much more when you're sorry.

'Don't be sorry! Fix the shit!' He hangs up on me. I don't believe Les has ever finished a conversation with a proper goodbye, even when he's in a decent mood.

No, I'm not a first-year, asshole. Thus your tirade has no effect. Go ahead, fire me. Who cares? I think back to when I first started working at the firm. A partner would raise his eyebrows, and it would send me back to my office with tears welling, panic mounting over my job security or at the very least my yearly evaluation. Over the years my skin has thickened somewhat, and at this moment, I don't care at all. I have bigger issues than this firm and my career as a lawyer. No, scratch the word 'career'. Careers are for people who wish to advance. I only want to survive, draw a paycheck. This is merely a job. I can take or leave this place. I start to imagine quitting and following my yet to be determined passion. I could tell myself that although I lacked a meaningful, intense relationship, I had my work.

I call opposing counsel, a reasonable mid-fortyish associate with a minor speech impediment who must have been passed over for partner at his firm. I tell him that our papers were served incorrectly, that I would reserve them by hand but they would arrive a day late. He interrupts me with a pleasant chuckle and says with a lisp that it is not a problem, that of course he wouldn't challenge service. I bet he hates his job as much as I do. If he liked it, he'd be all over this lapse like white on rice. Les would have a field day if the other side served a day late.

I send Les an email message, one brief sentence: 'Opposing counsel says they're fine with receiving papers by hand today.' That will show him. I can be as curt and surly as the next guy.

Around one-thirty, after I have printed a new set of papers and turned them over to our courier for delivery, Hillary comes to my office and asks if I have lunch plans.

'No plans. You want to go?'

'Yeah. Can we go somewhere nice? Get a good meal? Steak or Italian?'

I smile and nod, retrieving my purse from under my desk. Hillary could eat a big lunch every day, but I get too sleepy in the afternoon. Once, after ordering a hot open-face turkey sandwich with mashed potatoes and green beans, I actually took the subway home for an afternoon nap. I returned to six voice mail messages, including a ranting one from Les. That was my last nap, unless you count the times I turn my chair to the window and balance a paper in my lap. The technique is foolproof; if someone barges in, it just looks as if you're reading. I sling my purse over my shoulder as Kenny, our internal messenger from the mailroom, peeks around my half-open door.

'Hey, Kenny, come on in.'

'Ra-chelle.' He says my name in a French accent. 'These are for you.' He smirks as he produces a glass vase filled with red roses. A lot of roses. More than a dozen. More like two dozen, although I don't count. Yet.

'Holy shit!' Hillary's eyes are wide. I can tell that it takes tremendous effort for her not to grab the card.

'Where should I put 'em?' Kenny asks.

I clear a spot on my desk and point. 'Here's fine.'

Kenny shakes his wrists, exaggerating the weight of the vase, whistles and says, 'Woo hoo, Rachel. Some-one's diggin' you.'

I wave my hand at him, but there is no way to deny that these are from anyone other than a guy with romantic interest. If they weren't red roses, I could pawn them off on some familial occasion, tell them it was some special day for me, or that my parents are aware of my service error and are trying to comfort me. But these are not only roses, they are red roses. And bountiful. Most certainly not from a relative.

Kenny leaves after making one final remark about the roses costing someone some serious jack. I try to head out the door after him, but there is no chance that we are going anywhere until Hillary gets full information.

'Who are they from?'

I shrug. 'I have no clue.'

'Aren't you going to read the card?'

I am afraid to read it. They have to be from Dex – and what if he signed his name? It is too risky.

'I know who they're from,' I say.

173

'Who?'

'Marcus.' He is the only other possibility.

'Marcus? You guys barely hung out at all this weekend. What's the deal? Are you holding back on me? You better not be holding back on me!'

I shush her, tell her that I don't want everybody at the firm knowing my business.

'Okay, well then, tell me. What does the card say?' She is in interrogation mode. For as much as she hates the firm, she is one tough litigator.

I know I can't get out of reading the card. Besides, I too am dying to know what it says. I pluck out the white envelope, open it very slowly as my mind races to make up a story about Marcus. I slide the card out and read the two sentences silently: I AM SO SORRY. PLEASE SEE ME TONIGHT. It is written in Dexter's all-capitals handwriting, which means he had to go to the flower store in person. Even better. He did not sign his name, probably imagining a scenario like this one. My heart is racing, but I try to avoid a full-on grin in front of Hillary. The roses thrill me. The note thrills me even more. I know I will not refuse his invitation. I will be seeing him tonight, even though I am more afraid than ever of getting hurt. I lick my lips and try to appear composed. 'Yeah, from Marcus,' I say.

Hillary stares at me. 'Let me see,' she says, grabbing for the card.

I pull it out of her reach and slip it into my purse. 'It just says he's thinking of me.'

She pushes her hair behind her ears and asks suspiciously,

'Have you been on more than that one date? What's the full story?'

I sigh and head into the hallway, fully prepared to sell out poor Marcus. 'Okay, we had a date last week that I didn't tell you about,' I start, as we walk toward the elevator. 'And, um, he told me his feelings were growing . . .'

'He said that?'

'Something like that. Yeah.'

She digests this. 'And what did you say?'

'I told him I wasn't sure how I felt and, um, I thought we should keep things low-key over the weekend.'

Frieda from accounting darts into the elevator after us. I hope that Hillary will save further interrogation for after our elevator ride, but no, she continues as the doors close. 'Did you guys hook up?'

I nod so that Frieda, standing with her back to us, won't know my business. I would have said no altogether, but red roses would make less sense had there been no hook-up.

'But you didn't sleep together, did you?' At least she whispers this.

'No,' I say, and then give her a look to be quiet.

The elevator doors open, and Frieda scurries on her way.

'So? Tell me more,' Hillary says.

'It was pretty minor stuff. C'mon, Hill. You're relentless!'

'Well, if you'd told me the entire story upfront, I wouldn't need to be relentless.' Her face looks trusting again. I am out of the woods.

We talk about other things on our short walk to Second Avenue. But then, over steak at Palm Too, she says,

175

'Remember when you dropped that beer on Saturday night, while you and Dex were talking?'

'When?' I ask, feeling panicked.

'You know, when you were talking, and I came up – right at the end of the evening?'

'Oh, yeah. I guess. What about it?' I make my face as blank as possible.

'What was going on? Why was Dex so upset?'

'He was upset? I don't remember.' I look at the ceiling, wrinkle my forehead. 'I don't think he was upset. Why do you ask?'

When trapped, answering a question with a question is always a sound tactic.

'No reason. It just seemed odd, is all.'

'Odd?'

'I don't know. It's crazy . . .'

'What?'

'It's crazy, but . . . you guys looked like a couple.'

I laugh nervously. 'That *is* crazy!'

'I know. But as I was watching you two talk, I thought to myself that you would be way better with Dex. You know, better than he is with Darcy.'

'Oh, come on,' I say. More nervous laughter. 'They look great together.'

'Sure. Yes. They have all of that surface stuff. But something about them doesn't fit.' She brings her water glass to her lips and inspects me over it.

Keep your day job, Hillary.

I tell her she is nuts, even though I love what she has just

176

told me. I want to ask her why she thinks this. Because we both went to law school? Because we have some shared trait – more depth or dignity than Darcy? But I say nothing more because it's always wise to say as little as possible when you're guilty.

Les barges into my office after lunch to ask me about another matter for the same client. I have figured out over the years that this is his awkward way of apologizing. He only comes by my office after an explosion, like the one this morning.

I swivel in my chair and give him the update. 'I've checked all the cases in New York. And federal cases too.'

'Okay. But keep in mind that our fact pattern is unique,' Les says. 'I'm not sure the Court will care much about precedent.'

'I know that. But as far as I can tell the general holding we rely upon in Section One of our brief is still good law. So that's a good first step.'

So there.

'Well, make sure you check case law in other jurisdictions too,' he says. 'We need to anticipate all of their arguments.'

'Yup,' I say.

No, duh.

As he turns to leave, he says over his shoulder, 'Nice roses.'

I am stunned. Les and I do not make small talk, and he has never commented on anything other than my work, not even a 'how was your weekend?' on a Monday morning, or a 'cold enough out there for you?' when we ride the elevator together on a snowy day.

Maybe two dozen red roses make me seem more interesting. I *am* more interesting, I think. This affair has given me a new dimension.

I am shutting down my computer, about to leave work, with plans to see Dexter. We have not yet spoken, only traded a series of conciliatory messages, including one from me thanking him for the beautiful flowers.

Hillary appears in my doorway, on her way out. 'You're leaving now too?'

'Yeah,' I say, wishing I had slipped out ahead of her. She often asks me if I want to get a drink after work, even on Mondays, which virtually everybody else considers the only stay-in night of the week. She isn't so much a party girl, like Darcy, she just isn't one to sit home and do nothing.

Sure enough, she asks if I want to grab a margarita at Tequilaville, our favorite place near work despite – or maybe because of – the stale chips and touristy crowd. It is always a welcome escape from the predictable New York scene.

I say no, I can't.

Of course she wants a reason. Every reason I think of she can and will refute: I'm tired (c'mon, one drink?), I have to go the gym (blow it off!), I'm cutting back on alcohol (a blank, incredulous stare). So I tell her that I have a date. Her face lights up. 'So ol' Marky Mark's flowers worked their magic, huh?'

'You got me,' I say, glancing at my watch for good measure.

'Where are you going? Or are you staying in?'

I tell her we're going out.

'Where?'

'Nobu,' I say, because I ate there recently.

'Nobu on a Monday night, huh? He *does* dig you.'

I regret my choice; I should have gone for the no-name neighborhood Italian restaurant.

'If the date ends before two, call me and give me the scoop,' she says.

'Sure thing,' I say.

I go home forgetting all about Marcus and Hillary.

'Thank you so much for seeing me,' Dex says as I open the door. He is wearing a dark suit and white shirt. His tie is removed, likely stuffed into his briefcase, which he puts on the floor right inside my door. His eyes are tired. 'I didn't think you would.'

I had never considered not seeing him. I tell him this, realizing that it might erode my power. I don't care. It is the truth.

Both of us begin to apologize, moving toward each other awkwardly, self-consciously. He takes one of my hands in his, squeezes it. His touch is both soothing and electrifying. 'I'm so sorry for everything,' he says slowly.

I wonder if he knows to be sorry about the beach too, if that is included in 'everything'. I have replayed that scene over and over, mostly in sepia, like Don Henley's 'Boys of Summer' video. I blink, squeezing the images out of my mind. I want to make up. I want to move on.

'I'm sorry too,' I say. I take his other hand, but there is still much space between us. Enough to fit another person or two.

'You have no reason to be sorry.'

'Yes I do. I had no right to be angry at you. I was so out of line . . . We weren't going to discuss anything until after July Fourth. That was the deal . . .'

'It's not fair to you,' he says. 'It's a fucked-up deal.'

'I am fine with the way things are,' I say. It's not exactly true, but I am afraid of losing him if I ask for more. Of course, I am terrified of truly being with him, too. He's right – it is a fucked-up deal.

'I need to tell you about that afternoon with Darcy,' he says.

I know he is talking about the shower episode, and I can't bear to hear it. The sepia beach frolic is one thing, the up-close-and-color porn scene is another. I don't want a single detail from his perspective. 'Please don't,' I say. 'You really don't have to explain.'

'It's just that . . . I want you to know that she initiated it . . . Truly . . . I've been avoiding it for so long, and I just couldn't get out of it.' His face twitches, a mask of guilty discomfort.

'You do not have to explain,' I say again, more firmly. 'She's your fiancée.'

He nods, looking relieved.

'You know when the two of you were on the beach?' I ask quietly, surprising myself by bringing it up.

'Yeah,' he says knowingly, and then looks down. 'When I came back up to the towels, I knew. I knew you were upset.'

180

'How did you know?'

'You heard me say your name and ignored me. You were so cool. Chilly. I hated that.'

'I'm sorry. It's just that you looked so happy with her. And I felt so . . . so—' I struggle to find the right word.

'Angry? Jealous?'

I remember how he always finished my sentences in law school when I was trying to articulate my opinion about a particular case. It wasn't in a pushy way, just enthusiastic. He'd throw out a litany of choices until he found the right one. I'd sit back and say, 'No, no, no . . . Yes!'

'Yeah. Angry and jealous,' I confess. I hadn't planned on saying so much, but his eyes are drawing it out of me. 'And I also felt . . . well, obsolete.'

'You are not obsolete, Rachel. You are all I think about. I couldn't sleep last night. Couldn't work today. You are anything but obsolete, used.' His voice has lowered to a whisper, and we have assumed the position of slow-dancers, my arms around his neck.

'And you must know that I'm not using you,' he says into my ear. I feel the goose bumps rising.

'I know,' I say into his shoulder. 'But it's just so weird. Watching you with her. I don't think I should go to the Hamptons with you both again.'

'I'm so sorry,' he says again. 'I know. I just wanted to spend time with you.'

We kiss once. It is a soft, closed-mouth kiss, our lips barely touching. There is no connotation of lust or sex or passion. It is the other side of a love affair, the part I like the best.

181

We move over to my bed. He sits on the edge, and I am cross-legged beside him.

'I just want you to know,' he says, staring intently into my eyes, 'that I would never do this if I didn't care deeply for you.'

'I know,' I say.

'And I'm . . . you know . . '. taking this whole thing very seriously.'

'Let's not talk about it until the Fourth,' I say quickly. 'That was the deal.'

'Are you sure? Because we can talk about it now if you want.'

'I'm sure. Positive.'

And I am positive. I am afraid of any leads he might give me. I can't bear the thought of losing him, but have yet to consider what it would be like to lose Darcy. To have done something so huge and all-encompassing and wrong and final to my best friend.

He tells me that it scares him how much I mean to him, do I know how much I mean to him?

I nod. I know.

He kisses me again, more intensely this time. Then I experience my first truly unbelievable make-up sex.

The next morning Hillary visits me on the way to her office. She asks me how my date went. I tell her it was great. She plops down in one of my guest chairs, placing her bottle of Poland Spring water and her sesame bagel on my desk. She leans back and slams my door with her elbow. Her face is all business.

It turns out that Marcus did indeed opt for the no-name

Italian restaurant in his neighborhood. The same no-name Italian restaurant that for whatever reason also struck Hillary's fancy last night. A city of millions, and Marcus and Hillary were seated two tables apart, over identical plates of ravioli on a random Monday night. Welcome to Manhattan, a smaller island than you'd ever think.

'The only thing you didn't lie to me about,' Hillary says, shaking her finger at me, 'is that Marcus was, in fact, on a date. Just not with your lying ass – although the girl resembled you in the mouth and chin region.'

'Are you mad?'

'Not mad, no.'

'What then?'

'Well, for one, I'm shocked. I didn't think you were capable of such deceit.' She looks impressed by this revelation. 'But I'm also hurt that you feel you can't confide in me. I like to think of myself as your best friend – not some figurehead, a throwback from your high school days – your present-day best friend. Which brings me to my next point . . .' she says knowingly. She waits for me to fill the silence.

I look at my stapler, then my keyboard, and then my stapler again.

Although I have pictured getting busted many times, it is always Darcy doing the busting. Because after all, if you're going to let your mind wander, go for the worst scenario, not some intermediate level of doom. It's like worrying about your boyfriend getting into a drunk-driving accident – you don't think about him hitting a mailbox and splitting his lip. You picture lilies beside an open casket.

So I've had images of Darcy catching us. Not caught-in-bed-naked-in-the-act kind of busted – that is too far-fetched, particularly in a doorman building – but something more subtle: Darcy stops by unexpectedly, and José sends her up without buzzing me first (mental note to self: tell him never to do that). I answer the door assuming it is only the Chinese delivery guy bringing cartons of wonton soup and egg rolls to Dex and me, as we are understandably famished by our escapades (mental note to self number two: always look through the peephole first). And there she stands, her big eyes taking it all in. Speechless in her horror. She flees the scene. Dex dashes into the hall in his gingham boxers, bellowing her name like Marlon Brando in A *Streetcar Named Desire*.

Next scene: Darcy amid cardboard boxes packing her CDs with the ever-supportive Claire offering her Kleenexes at every turn. At least Dex would get all the Springsteen albums, even *Greetings from Asbury Park*, which someone had given Darcy as a gift. Most of the books would stay, too, as Darcy brought few books into the union. Just a few glossy coffee table numbers.

I read once, ironically in one of Darcy's magazines, that you should engage in this visualization exercise when you're having an affair, that you should imagine getting caught and the grim aftermath. These images should snap you back to reality, get you thinking straight, make you realize what it is you'd be losing. Of course, the article presupposed a lust-driven affair, and the article was not directed at the unattached person in the triangle, but rather

184

the participant in the committed relationship. Then again, the article also assumed that the third party was not the maid of honor in the upcoming wedding of the other two persons. Clearly our circumstances do not fit your typical adulterous mold.

In any event, I don't know exactly how I'd feel if Darcy busted us and my friendship with her ended. I can't really get there mentally. The fact is Darcy is one hundred percent clueless, and she and Dex are still very much engaged. And likely it will stay that way; they will get married and she will never discover the truth about our affair.

Hillary is a different story.

'Well?' she asks.

'Well, what?'

'Who were you *really* seeing last night? Who really sent you those?' She points at my roses.

'Someone else.'

'No *shit!*'

I swallow.

'Okay, look, I wasn't born yesterday. You get in a fight with Dex at the Talkhouse, you both clam up when I arrive on the scene, then you leave the Hamptons early the next day, all down in the dumps with false claims of imminent deadlines – I know your work schedule, Rach, and you had nothing due yesterday. And then these flowers arrive.' She points at my roses, still in full bloom. 'You point to Marcus, whom you basically ignored over the weekend. Which is odd, even if you did decide to play it low-key. Then you tell me you have a date with Marcus, and I see him out *sans* you –

with another woman!' She finishes her catalog of evidence with a jubilant smile.

'Was she cute?' I ask.

'The woman?'

'Yeah. Marcus's date.'

'Actually, yes, she was quite attractive. As if you care.'

She is right – I don't.

'Now quit stalling and address my point,' she says.

'What point is that?'

'Rachel!'

'It certainly does look bad,' I say, still reluctant to confess.

'Rachel. Who do you think I'm going to tell? I'm your friend. Not Darcy's. Hell, I don't even like her that much . . . and she's a terrible friend to you half the time.'

I pick up my tape dispenser, pull out two inches of tape and hold it between my index finger and thumb. For some reason, this is a harder confession than the one to Ethan. Maybe because it is face-to-face. Maybe because her past has not been as dicey as Ethan's.

'Okay.' Hillary tries again. 'Let me say the words for you, and you can just nod your head.' Her voice is like that of a mother to a child.

I nervously play with the tape, wrapping it around my thumb. She is about to spell it all out, and I have two choices – admit or deny. An admission might be a huge relief. A denial will have to be accompanied by a suitably indignant expression and a barrage of 'How could you think that? Are you crazy?' et cetera. I am in no mood for that charade.

'Dex is cheating on Darcy,' she says. 'With you.'

Drum roll.

I raise my chin and return her gaze. Then I nod the smallest of nods, my head barely moving.

'I knew it!'

I consider telling her that I don't want to talk about it, but in truth, I *do* want to talk about it. I want her to tell me that I'm not a terrible person. I want her to expound on her earlier statement that I would be better suited to him than Darcy. And most of all, I just want to talk about Dex.

'When did this all start?'

'The night of my party.'

She stares at the ceiling for a second and nods as if everything makes sense now. 'Okay, start from the beginning. Leave nothing out.' She settles into her chair and tears off a piece of her bagel.

'The first time I slept with him was an accident.'

'The *first* time? You've *slept* with him? Multiple times?' Hillary asks.

I give her a look.

'Sorry, go on. I just can't believe this!'

'Okay. So yes, the night of my party, we were the last two out . . . we went for drinks, one thing led to another, and we slept together back at my apartment. It was an accident. I mean, we were both drunk. I was, anyway.'

'Oh, I remember. You were a little bit out of it that night.'

'Yeah. I was. But, interestingly, Dex says he wasn't that drunk.' This detail not only shifts the responsibility his way, but simultaneously makes the genesis of the affair more meaningful.

187

'So he, what, took advantage of you?'

'No! I didn't mean to imply that . . . I knew what I was doing.'

'Okay.' She motions for me to go on.

I tell her about waking up the following morning, Darcy's frantic messages, our panic and Dexter using Marcus as his alibi. 'So that's it,' I say.

'What do you mean, "that's it"? Clearly not.' She gives my roses a purposeful glance.

'I mean, that was it for a while. We both felt regretful and—'

'How regretful?'

'Regretful, Hillary! Obviously!' To myself, I recall that first day, and my complete lack of penitence. 'So that was it. In my mind, it was over.'

'But not in his, right?'

I choose my words carefully and tell her about his Monday call to me and the things he said. And then everything that happened in the Hamptons. And about our first sober kiss. The turning-point kiss. Sleeping with him for the real first time.

She takes another big bite of her bagel. 'So is this – what? A purely physical thing? Or do you really like him?'

'I really like him,' I say.

She digests this. 'So he's going to break off the engagement. Right?'

'We haven't talked about it.'

'How can you not talk about it? Wait – was that what you were fighting about in the Talkhouse?'

I tell her that we weren't exactly fighting, but that I was

upset about him having sex with Darcy. Hence the roses.

'Okay. So if he's sorry for sleeping with his fiancée, that sounds like he's headed in the direction of breaking up with her, right?'

'I don't know. We really haven't discussed it yet.'

She looks confused. 'When are you going to?'

'We said we'd talk about it around July Fourth.'

'Why then?'

'Arbitrary. I don't know.'

She takes a swig of water. 'Well, you *do* think he's going to dump her, right?'

'I don't know. I don't even know if I want that.'

She gives me a nonplussed look.

'You are forgetting an important piece of this whole thing, Hillary. Darcy is my longtime, lifelong friend. And I am her maid of honor.'

She rolls her eyes. 'Details.'

'You just don't like her.'

'She's not my favorite person in the world, but Darcy is not the point.'

'She's a major point, in my opinion. She's my friend. And besides, even if she weren't, even if she were a random woman, don't you think I would have to confront the bad karma aspects of this?'

I wonder why I am arguing against myself.

She straightens in her chair and speaks slowly. 'The world is not that black and white, Rachel. There are no moral absolutes. It is complex. If you were sleeping with Dex for the sheer thrill of it all, then maybe I'd worry about your karma.

189

But you have feelings for him. It doesn't make you a bad person.'

I try to memorize her speech. *No moral absolutes.* That is good stuff.

'If the tables were turned,' she continues. 'Darcy would do the same thing in a heartbeat.'

'You think?' I ask, considering this.

'Don't you?'

'Maybe you're right,' I say. Darcy does, after all, have quite a history of taking. I give, she takes. That's the way it has always been.

Until now.

Hillary smiles and nods. 'I say go for it.'

More or less what Ethan said. That's two votes for me, zero for Darcy.

'I'm going to keep seeing him as much as I can. We'll see what happens,' I say, realizing that just 'seeing what happens' is my version of 'going for it'.

TWELVE

Darcy and I are flying home to Indianapolis for Annalise's baby shower, and I am stuck in the dreaded middle seat. Darcy was assigned the middle, but of course she wangled her way into my window seat, saying that if she can't look out the window she gets airsick. I wanted to tell her that this principle of car travel does not apply in a plane, but I didn't bother, just surrendered to her demand. In the past I would have done so mindlessly, but now I feel resentful. I think of Ethan and Hillary and their recent words about Darcy. She is selfish, plain and simple. And this is the truth, regardless of my feelings for Dex.

A forty-something man with a crew cut has the aisle seat to my left. He has glued the entire length and width of his right forearm to our shared armrest, elbow to fingertip. He drinks and turns the pages of his magazine with his left hand so as not to lose ground.

The pilot announces that the skies are clear and we will be landing ahead of schedule. Darcy announces that she is bored. She is the only person I know, over the age of twelve, who says with great regularity that she is bored.

I glance up from my book. 'Did you already read your Martha Stewart wedding issue?'

'Cover to cover. There's nothing new in there. And by the way, you're the one who should be reading it. There's an article on favors – you promised you would help me think of an original idea for favors,' she says, as she adjusts her seat the whole way back and then up again.

'How about matchbooks?'

'You said original!' Darcy crosses her arms. 'Everybody does matchbooks! That's just a given. I need a proper favor, in addition to matches.'

'What does Martha suggest?' I ask, marking my place in my novel.

'I dunno, hard stuff to make. Labor-intensive stuff.' She looks at me plaintively. 'You have to help! You know I'm no good at crafts.'

'Neither am I.'

'You're better than I am!'

I turn back to my book, pretending to be engrossed.

She sighs and chews her Juicy Fruit more vigorously. And when that doesn't work, she hits the spine of my book. 'Raa-chel!'

'Okay! Okay!'

She smiles, unabashed, like a child who doesn't care that she's made her mother miserable, only that she got what she wanted. 'So you think we should do something with *D*?'

'*D*?' I ask, playing dumb.

'You know, a D . . . for Dex and Darcy. Or is that cheesy?'

'Cheesy,' I say, which would have been my answer even before the D and R days.

'Okay – then what?' She checks the number of fat grams

in her snack mix before casting them into the seat-back pocket in front of her.

'Well, you have your sugared almonds in netting tied with pastel ribbons . . . or mints in a tin with your wedding date,' I say as I exert slight pressure with my left elbow, trying to wedge it in a tiny crevice on my left armrest. In my peripheral vision, I see Crew Cut flex his bicep in resistance. 'Then you have permanent keepsakes like Christmas tree ornaments . . .'

'Can't. We have too many Jewish guests – and honestly, I think some people who celebrate Kwanza,' she interrupts, proud of her diverse guest list.

'Okay. But you get the point. That genre. Permanent keepsakes: ornaments, homemade CDs with your favorite songs.'

She becomes perky. 'I like the CD idea! But wouldn't that be expensive?'

I give her a look that says, yeah, but you're worth it. She eats it up. 'But what's another few hundred dollars in the scheme of things, right?' she asks.

I'm sure her parents would love this statement. 'Right,' I patronize.

'So we could have, like, *The Darcy and Dex Soundtrack* and put our all-time favorite songs on it,' she says.

I wince.

'Are you sure it's not cheesy? Tell me the truth.'

'No, I like it. I like it.' I want to change the subject but worry that this will spark a discussion of my maid of honor shortcomings. So instead I strike a thoughtful pose and tell

193

her that although the CDs would be time intensive and expensive, they would make a lovely, special favor. Then I ask her if Dex would like the idea.

She looks at me as if to say, who cares what Dex wants? Grooms don't matter. 'Okay. Now help me think of some songs.'

I hear Shania Twain singing 'Whose Bed Have Your Boots Been Under?' Or maybe Diana Ross belting out 'Stop! In the Name of Love'.

No, all wrong, I think. Both songs cast Darcy in the role of noble victim.

'I can't think of one song. My mind's a blank. Help me think,' Darcy says, her pen poised over her napkin. 'Maybe something by Prince? Van Halen?'

'I can't think of any either,' I say, hoping that Bruce Springsteen doesn't make the cut.

'You sure it's not cheesy?' she asks.

'It's *not* cheesy,' I say, and then whisper, 'This guy next to me is really pissing me off. He won't give me any of the armrest.'

I turn to quickly survey Crew Cut's smug profile.

'Excuse me! Sir!' Darcy leans over my lap and pokes his arm. Once, twice, three times. 'Sir? Sir!'

He casts a disdainful eye her way.

'Sir, could you please share the armrest with my friend here?' She flashes him her most seductive smile.

He shifts his arm one centimeter. I mumble thanks.

'See?' Darcy asks me proudly.

This is the part where I'm supposed to marvel at her way with men.

'You just have to know how to ask for what you want,' she whispers. My mentor in dealing with the opposite sex.

I think of Dex and July Fourth.

'I might have to try that,' I say.

My parents call my cell right after we land – to confirm that Darcy's father picked us up and to ask if I ate on the plane. I tell them yes, Mr. Rhone showed up, and no, they stopped serving dinner on the New York to Indy flight about ten years ago.

As we pull into our cul-de-sac, I spot my father waiting for me on the front porch of our two-story, white aluminum-sided, green-shuttered house. He is wearing a short-sleeved, peach and gray plaid shirt and matching gray Dockers. By any measure, it is an 'outfit', and it has my mother written all over it. I thank Mr. Rhone for the ride and tell Darcy I'll call her later. I am relieved that she does not ask if we can all get together for dinner. I've had enough wedding talk and know that Mrs. Rhone is incapable of discussing anything else.

As I cross Darcy's yard into my own, my dad throws up his arm and gives an exaggerated, overhand wave as if signaling a far-off ship. 'Hello, counselor!' he belts out, all grins. The novelty of having an attorney daughter has yet to wear off.

'Hi, Dad!' I kiss him and then my mother, who is hovering at his side, already examining me for possible signs of anorexia, which is ridiculous. I am nowhere near too thin, but my mom does not accept New York's definition of thin.

As I field their questions about my flight, I notice that the hall wallpaper has changed. I advised my mother against wallpaper, told her paint was the way to go for a fresher look. But she stuck with wallpaper, switching from tiny floral print to slightly tinier floral print. My parents' taste has not evolved since around the time that Ronald Reagan was shot. Our home still has lots of country touches – cross-stitched expressions of good cheer like 'back door friends are best', a scattering of wooden cows and pigs and pineapples, stencil borders throughout.

'Nice wallpaper,' I say, trying to sound sincere.

My mom doesn't buy it. 'I know – you don't like wallpaper, but your father and I do,' she says, motioning me into the kitchen. 'And we're the ones who live here.'

'I never said I liked wallpaper,' my dad says, winking at me.

She shoots him a look of practiced annoyance. 'You most certainly did, John.' Then she tells me in a whisper, designed for him to hear, that, in fact, my father picked the new paper.

He gives me a 'Who, me?' expression.

They never tire of their routine. She plays the fearless leader, corralling her unruly husband, the good-natured fool. Although I spent much of my adolescence irritated by the monotony of it, particularly when I had friends over, I have come to appreciate it in recent years. There is something comforting about the sameness of their interaction. I am proud that they have stayed together, when so many of my friends' parents have divorced, remarried, morphed two families into one with varying degrees of success.

My mom points to a plate of cheddar cheese, Ritz crackers and red grapes. 'Eat,' she says.

'Are these seedless?' I ask. Grapes with seeds just aren't worth the effort.

'Yes, they are,' my mom says. 'Now. Shall I throw something together or would you rather order pizza?'

She knows that I'd prefer pizza. First, I love Sal's pizza, which I can only get when I'm home. Second, 'throwing something together' is an exact description of my mom's cooking – her idea of seasoning is salt and pepper, her idea of a recipe is tomato soup and crackers. Nothing strikes fear in my heart like the sight of my mother strapping on an apron.

'Pizza,' my dad answers for us. 'We want pizza!'

My mom pulls a Sal's coupon off the refrigerator and dials the number, ordering a large pizza with mushrooms and sausage. She covers the mouthpiece. 'Right, Rachel?'

I give her the thumbs up. She beams, proud to have memorized my favorite combination.

Before she can hang up, she is inquiring about my love life. As though all my phone updates informing them that I have nothing going on were just a ruse, and I've been saving the truth for this moment. My father covers his ears with feigned embarrassment. I give them a tight-lipped smile, thinking to myself that this inquisition is the only part of coming home that I don't like. I feel that I am a disappointment. I am letting them down. I am their only child, their only shot at grandchildren. The math is pretty basic: if I don't have children in the next five years or so, it is unlikely they will see their grandchildren graduate from college. Nothing like a little added pressure to an already stressful pursuit.

'Not one boy out there?' my mom asks, as my dad

197

searches for the ideal slice of cheese. Her eyes are wide, hopeful. The probe might seem insensitive, except she truly believes I have my choice of dozens, that the only thing keeping me from her grandchildren is my own neurosis. She doesn't understand that the simple, straightforward, reciprocated love she has for my father is not so easy to come by.

'No,' I say, lowering my eyes. 'I'm telling you it's harder to find a good guy in New York than anywhere.' It is the cliché of single life in Manhattan, but only because it's true.

'I can see that,' my dad says, nodding earnestly. 'Too many people caught up in that rat race. Maybe you should come home. At least move to Chicago. Much cleaner city. It's because Chicago has alleys, you know.' Every time my dad visits New York, he harps on the lack of alleys; why would they make a city without alleys?

My mom shakes her head. 'Everybody is married with babies in the suburbs. She can't do that.'

'She can if she wants to,' my dad says with a mouthful of cracker.

'Well, she doesn't want to,' she says. 'Do you, Rachel?'

'No,' I say apologetically. 'I like New York for now.'

My dad frowns as if to say, well, then there is no solution.

Silence fills the kitchen. My parents exchange a doleful glance.

'Well. There is *sort of* someone . . .' I blurt out, just to cheer them up a bit.

They brighten, stand up straighter.

'Really? I knew it!' My mom claps giddily.

'Yeah, he's a very nice guy. Very smart.'

'And I'm sure he's handsome too,' she says.

'What does he do?' my dad interrupts. 'The boy's looks are beside the point.'

'He's in marketing. Finance,' I say. I'm not sure if I am telling them about Marcus or Dex. 'But . . .'

'But what?' my mom asks.

'But he just got out of a relationship, so the timing may be . . . imperfect.'

'Nothing is ever perfect,' my mom says. 'It is what you make of it.'

I nod earnestly, thinking that she should cross-stitch that nugget of wisdom and hang it over my twin bed upstairs.

'On a scale of one to ten, how much do you dread this baby shower?' Darcy asks me the next day as we drive to Annalise's shower in my mom's '86 Camry, the car I learned to drive in. 'Ten is total, total doomsday kind of dread. One is, "I can't wait, this thing will be really fun".'

'Six,' I say.

Darcy makes an acknowledging sound and then flips open her compact to check her lipstick. 'Actually,' she says, 'I thought it'd be higher.'

'Why? How much do you dread it?'

She closes her compact, examines her two-point-three-carat ring, and says, 'Mmmm . . . I don't know . . . Four and a half.'

Ohhh, I get it, I think. I have more reason to dread it. I am the one going into a room full of married and pregnant women – many of whom are fellow high school classmates –

without so much as a boyfriend. Only one of us is thirty and totally alone, a tragic combination in any suburb. That is what Darcy is thinking. But I make her say it, ask her why she supposes that I dread the shower by a full point and a half more?

Shamelessly and without hesitation to consider a tactful wording, she answers me. 'Be-*cause*. You're single.'

I keep my eyes on the road, but can feel her stare.

'Are you mad? Did I say something wrong?'

I shake my head, turn on the radio. Lionel Richie is wailing away on one of my mother's preselected radio stations.

Darcy turns the volume down. 'I didn't mean that that was a bad thing. I mean, you know that I totally value being single. I never wanted to marry before thirty-three. I mean, I'm talking about *them*. They are so narrow, you know what I mean?'

She has just made it worse by telling me that she didn't even want this whole crazy engagement. She would have preferred another three-plus years of bachelorettehood. And lo and behold, it all just fell in her lap. What's a girl to do?

'They're so narrow that they don't even know they're narrow,' she continues.

Of course she is right about this. This group of girls, of which Annalise has been a member since the day she left college, lives like women in the fifties. They picked out china patterns before their twenty-second birthdays, married their first boyfriend, bought three-bedroom homes within miles, if not blocks, of their parents, and went about the business of starting a family.

'Right,' I mumble.

'So that's all I meant,' she says innocently. 'And deep down inside, they are so jealous of you. You're a big-time lawyer at a big-city firm.'

I tell her that is crazy – not one of those girls longs for a career like mine. Most don't work at all, in fact.

'Well, it's not only the career. You are free and single. I mean, they watch *Sex and the City*. They know what your life's all about. It's glamorous, full of fun, hot guys, cosmopolitans, excitement! But they won't let you see their insecure side. Because it would make their own lives that much more pathetic, you know?' She smiles, pleased with her pep talk. 'Yeah. Your life is totally *Sex and the City*.'

'Yes. I am a lot like Carrie Bradshaw,' I say flatly.

Minus the fabulous shoes, incredible figure, and empathetic best friend.

'Exactly!' she says. 'Now you're talking.'

'Look. I don't really care what they're thinking,' I say, knowing it is only half true. I only care to the extent that I agree. And part of me believes that being thirty and alone *is* sad. Even with a good job. Even in Manhattan.

'Good,' she says, slapping her thighs with encouragement. 'Good. That's the spirit.'

We arrive at Jessica Pell's – a fringe friend of ours from high school – exactly on time. Darcy consults her watch and insists on driving around for a few minutes, to be fashionably late.

I tell her it's not necessary to be fashionably late to a baby shower, but I oblige, and at her request take her the

201

McDonald's drive-through. She leans over me and yells into the speaker that she 'would love a small diet Pepsi'. Now, I know that she knows that McDonald's has Coke, not Pepsi. She has told me before that she likes to test them, see if they'll ask. That the Pepsi people always ask if you order the Coke, but the Coke people don't always ask.

But it is an opportunity to make a stir, create an exchange. Pimply Suburbanite meets Big City Supermodel.

'Is diet Coke awright?' the boy mumbles into his microphone.

'Guess it'll have to do,' she says with a good-natured chuckle.

She finishes her diet Coke as we pull up to Jessica's house. 'Well. Here goes nothing,' she says, fluffing her hair, as if this shower were all about her instead of Annalise and her unborn child.

The other guests have already assembled in Jessica's well-coordinated blue and yellow living room when we arrive. Annalise screams, waddles over to us, and gathers us in a group hug. Despite the uncommon ground, we are still her best friends. And it is clear that we are the honored invitees, a role that makes me somewhat uncomfortable and Darcy bask.

'It's so good to see you guys! Thank you so much for coming in!' Annalise says. 'You both look amazing. Amazing. You get more stylish every time you come home!'

'You look great too,' I say. 'Pregnancy agrees with you. You have that glow.'

Like my parents' house, Annalise resists change. She still

has the same hairstyle – shoulder-length with curled-under bangs – that was great in the eighties, horrible in the mid-nineties, and through sheer luck, slightly less awful now. It passes as a nice motherly cut. And her face, always round as a persimmon, no longer looks chubby, but simply part of the cute, pregnant package. She is the sort of pregnant woman that people gladly relinquish their seats to on the subway.

Darcy rubs Annalise's stomach with her jeweled left hand. The diamond catches the light and flashes in my face. 'Oh my,' Darcy coos. 'There is a little naked person in there!'

Annalise laughs and says, 'Well yes, that is one way of looking at it!' She introduces us to some of the guests, fellow teachers and guidance counselors from the school where she teaches, and other neighborhood friends. 'And of course, you know everybody else!'

We exchange hugs with Jess and our other high school classmates. There is Brit Miller (who shamelessly worshiped and copied Darcy in high school). Tricia Salerno. Jennifer McGowan. Kim Frisby. With the possible exception of Kim, who was a bubbly cheerleader and, miraculously, also in the advanced science and math classes, none of the girls were particularly smart, interesting, or popular in high school. But as wives and mothers, their mediocrity matters no longer.

Kim slides down on the sofa and offers me a spot next to her. I ask her how Jeff (who also graduated in our class and played baseball with Brandon and Blaine) and her boys are doing. She says they are all doing great, that Jeff just got promoted, which was exciting, that they are buying a new house, that the boys are just perfect.

'What does Jeff do again?' I ask.

She says sales.

'And you have twins, right?'

Yes, boys. Stanley and Brick.

Now, I know Brick is her mother's maiden name, but I wonder again how she could have done that to a child. And Stanley? Who calls a baby Stanley or even Stan? Stanley and Stan are man names. Nobody should have that name under the age of thirty-five. And even if the names were tolerable in their own right, they do not go together, my pet peeve in name selection. Not that you should choose rhyming names for twins, or even names beginning with the same letter, like Brick and Brock or Brick and Brack. Go with Stanley and Frederick – both old-man names. Or Brick and Tyler – both pretentious surnames. But Stanley and Brick? Please.

'Did you bring photos of the boys?' I ask the obligatory question.

'As a matter of fact I did,' Kim says, whipping out a small album with 'Brag Book' written on the cover in big purple bubble letters. I smile, flipping through the pages, pausing for the requisite time before I go to the next. Brick in the tub. Stanley with a whiffle ball. Brick with Grandma and Grandpa Brick.

'They're precious,' I say, closing the album and handing it back to her.

'We think so,' Kim says, nodding, smiling. 'I think we'll keep them.'

As she returns the album to her purse, I overhear Darcy telling her engagement story to Jennifer and Tricia.

Brit is egging her on. 'Tell her about the roses,' she prompts.

I had forgotten about the roses – perhaps blocked them out since the arrival of my own.

'Yes, a dozen red roses,' Darcy is saying. 'He had them waiting in the apartment for me after he proposed.'

Not two dozen.

'Where did he ask you?' Tricia wants to know.

'Well, we went out for a really nice lunch, and afterward he suggested that we take a walk in Central Park . . .'

'Did you suspect it?' two girls ask at once.

'Not *at all* . . .'

This is a lie. I remember her telling me two days before he asked that she knew it was coming. But to admit this would detract from the drama of her tale, as well as diminish her image as the one pursued.

'Then what did he say?' Brit asks.

'You already know the story!' Darcy laughs. She and Brit still keep in touch occasionally due to Brit's diligence; her fascination for her teen idol has never eroded.

'Tell it again!' Brit says. 'My engagement story is so lame – I picked out the ring myself at the mall! I have to live vicariously through you.'

Darcy puts on her pretend-modest face. 'He said, "Darcy, I can't think of anything that would make me happier than having you as my wife." Then he said, "Please share your life with me."'

A chorus of oohs and ahhs follow. I tell myself that she is embellishing the tale, that he really just uttered the standard, 'Will you marry me?'

'Take off your ring,' Brit clamors. 'I want to try it on.'

Kim says it is bad luck to remove your ring during the engagement.

Take it off!

Darcy shrugs to demonstrate that her free spirit is still very much intact. Or perhaps to point out that when you are Darcy Rhone you don't need luck. She slips off her ring and passes it around the circle of eager women. It ends up in my hands.

'Try it on, Rach,' Brit says.

It is a married girl's fun trick. Make the single girl try on the diamond ring so she can, if only for a moment, get one step closer to the unknown euphoria of betrothal. I shake my head politely as though declining a second helping of casserole. 'That's okay,' I say.

'Rachel, any prospects?' Tricia asks tentatively, as you would inquire about someone's CAT scan results.

I am ready to report a firm no, when Darcy answers for me. 'Tons,' she says. 'But no one special guy. Rachel is very picky.'

She is trying to help. But somehow it has the reverse effect, and I feel even more like an emerging old maid. Besides, I can't help but think that she is only being charitable because I so clearly look like the odd woman out, the loser in the group. If I were engaged to, say, Brad Pitt, there'd be no way Darcy would brag on my behalf. She'd be sulking in the corner, her competitive juices flowing in full force, telling Brit in the bathroom that yes, Brad is Brad, but Dex is so much cuter – just a little less pretty. Of course, with that, I

206

would actually agree.

'I wouldn't say I'm that picky,' I say matter-of-factly.

Just hopelessly alone and having an affair with Darcy's husband-to-be. *But you all do realize that I graduated from a top ten law school and make six figures? And that I don't need a man, dammit! But when I do find one and have a baby, I will sure as hell pick a better name than Brick!*

'Yeah, you are picky,' Darcy says to me, but for her audience. She takes a sip of punch. 'Take Marcus, for example.'

'Who is Marcus?' Kim asks.

'Marcus is this guy that Dex went to Georgetown with. Nice, smart, funny,' Darcy says, waving her hand in the air, 'but Rachel won't give him the time of day.'

If she keeps it up, they are going to start wondering if I'm a lesbian. Which would make me a true freak show in their eyes. Their idea of diversity is someone who attended an out-of-state school and didn't rush a sorority.

'What, no sparks?' Kim asks me sympathetically. 'You need sparks. Jeff and I had sparks in the eleventh grade and they never stopped.'

'Right,' I say. 'You need sparks.'

'Absolutely,' Brit murmurs.

Their collective advice: don't settle. Keep looking. Find Mr. Right. That is what they all did. And by God, I think they believe it. Because nobody who marries at the ripe age of twenty-three can be settling. Naturally. That is a phenomenon that only happens to women in their thirties.

'So, have you made a final decision on your baby names?'

207

I ask Annalise, desperate to change the subject. I know she is considering Hannah and Grace if she has a girl, Michael or David for a boy. Wholesome, classic, solid names. Not trying too hard.

'Yes,' Annalise says. 'But we're not telling.' She winks at me. I know that she'll tell me the final decision later, just as she has with the runner-up selections. I am safe. The friend who will never, can never, swipe your baby names.

My specialty is fiancé stealing.

After we play a few silly shower games, Annalise opens her presents. There is a lot of yellow clothing because Annalise does not know whether she's having a boy or a girl. So no pink gifts except for a pink bunny bank from Tiffany, courtesy of Darcy, who says she knows for sure that Annalise is going to have a girl, that she has a very good sense about these things. I can tell that Annalise hopes she is right.

'Besides,' Darcy says, 'even if I'm wrong – and I'm not – did you know that at the turn of the century, pink was for boys and blue was for girls?'

We all say that we did not. I wonder if she is making it up.

Annalise comes to my gift. She opens my card, murmuring to herself. Her eyes fill with tears as she reads my words – that she is going to be the most wonderful mother and that I can't wait to watch it all. She waves me over to her, as she did with the other girls, and gives me a big hug. 'Thank you, honey,' she whispers. 'That was so nice.'

Then she opens my present, an off-white cashmere blanket with a teddy bear border. I spent a fortune on it, but

Annalise and her baby are worth every penny. She gasps as she unfolds it, presses it to her cheek and tells me it is perfect, that she will use it to bring the baby home from the hospital.

'I want to fly back when she's born!' Darcy says. 'I better not be on my honeymoon!'

Whether she does it on purpose or it is simply the way she is wired, something she can't help, Darcy inserts herself into every moment. Usually I don't mind, but after spending ages finding the perfect gift for my second-oldest friend, I wish she would pipe down and stop overshadowing Annalise and me for a nanosecond.

Always the diplomat, Annalise smiles quickly at Darcy before returning her focus to me and the blanket. She passes it around as everyone agrees that it is the ideal receiving blanket, so adorable, so soft. That's what they're saying, anyway. But something tells me that they are all thinking, 'Not a bad choice from a litigator with questionable maternal instincts.'

THIRTEEN

When I return home from the shower, my mother follows me into the family room and bombards me with questions. I give her the highlights, but she is insatiable. She wants to know every detail about every guest, gift, conversation. I have a flashback to high school when I'd come home, exhausted from a day of academic and social pressure, and she would inquire about Ethan's debate-team performance or Darcy's cheerleading tryout or what we talked about in English class. If I wasn't forthcoming enough, she would fill in the gaps, rambling about her part-time job at the orthodontist's office or what rude thing Bryant Gumble said on the *Today* show or how she ran into my third grade teacher in the grocery store. My mother is an open book chatterbox and she expects everyone to be just like her, particularly her only child.

She finishes her inquisition on the shower and moves on to – what else? – the wedding.

'So has Darcy decided on a veil?' She straightens a pile of *Newsweek*s on our coffee table, waiting for an in-depth answer.

'Yes.'

She moves closer on our couch. 'Long?'

'Fingertip.'

She claps excitedly. 'Oh. That will be beautiful on her.'

My mother is, and has always been, a big Darcy fan. It didn't make sense back in high school given the fact that Darcy never put a premium on studying and promoted a certain unwholesome boy craziness. Yet my mother just plain old loved Darcy, perhaps because Darcy supplied her with the details of our life that she so craved. Even past the perfunctory parental pleasantries, Darcy would talk to my mother as a peer. She would come over to my house after school, lean against our kitchen counter, eating the Oreos my mother had set out for us, while she talked and talked. Darcy would tell my mom about the boys she liked and the pros and cons of each. She'd say things like, 'His lips are too thin; I bet he can't kiss,' and my mom would become delighted and elicit more, and Darcy would give it, and I would end up leaving the room to start my geometry homework. Now what's wrong with that picture?

I remember once in the seventh grade I refused to participate in the annual talent show, though Darcy incessantly heckled me to be one of her two back-up dancers in her outlandish rendition of 'Material Girl'. Despite her own shyness, Annalise folded quickly, but I refused to succumb, didn't care that Darcy's choreography called for a three-girl act, didn't care that she said I was ruining her chances of a blue ribbon. Often I would let Darcy talk me into things, but not that one. I told her not to waste her breath, I had no intention of ever setting foot on a stage. After Darcy finally gave up and invited Brit to take my place, my mother lectured me on becoming more involved in fun activities.

'Aren't straight As enough for you?' I asked her.

'I just want you to have fun, honey,' she said.

I lashed out, saying, 'You just want me to be her!'

She told me not to be ridiculous, but part of me believed it. I feel the same way now. 'Mom, no offense to you or the second daughter you never had, but—'

'Oh, don't start with that nonsense!' She pats her ash-blond hair, which she has been coloring with the same Clairol hue for the past twenty years.

'All right,' I say. 'But truly, I have had it up to here with Darcy's wedding.' I hold my hand four inches above my head and then raise it even higher.

'That's no attitude for a maid of honor.' My mom purses her lips and scrapes one index finger across the other.

I shrug.

My mom laughs, the good-natured parent, refusing to take her only daughter too seriously. 'Well, I should have known Darcy would be a handful as a bride. I'm sure she wants everything to be perfect . . .'

'Yeah, she deserves it,' I say sarcastically.

'Well, she *does* deserve it,' my mom says. 'And so do you . . . your time will come.'

'Uh-huh.'

'Is that why you're sick of this?' she asks, with the accomplished air of a woman who has watched far too many talk shows on confronting your feelings and nurturing your relationships.

'Not exactly,' I say.

212

'Then why, exactly? Is she being a pain in the you-know-what? What am I asking – *of course* she is! That's Darcy!' Another fond chuckle.

'Yeah.'

'Yes, what, sweetie? What's on your mind?'

'Yes, she's being a pain in the ass,' I say, reaching for the remote control to unmute the television.

'What is she doing?' my mom persists calmly.

'She's being Darcy,' I say. 'Everything is about her.'

My mom gives me a sympathetic look. 'I know, honey.'

Then I blurt out that she doesn't deserve Dexter, that he is too good for her. My mother looks at me circumspectly. Oh shit, I think. Does she know? Ethan and Hillary are one thing – my mother's quite another. I was unwilling to tell her which boys I thought were cute in high school, so this one is certainly off the table. I can't stand the thought of letting her down. I am thirty, but still very much a parent-pleaser. And my mother, a woman who finds the keys to life in cross-stitched blurbs, would never understand this breach of friendship.

'She's driving him crazy too. I'm sure of it,' I say, trying to cover.

'Did Dexter tell you this?'

'No, I haven't discussed this with Dex.' Technically this statement is true. 'You can just tell.'

'Well, be patient with her. You'll never regret being a good friend.'

I consider this gemstone from my mother. One would be hard-pressed to disagree with it. In fact, it is the way I have lived my entire life. Avoiding regret at any cost. Being good no matter what. Good student. Good daughter. Good friend. And yet I am struck by the sudden realization that regret cuts two ways. I might also regret sacrificing myself, my own desires, for Darcy's sake, in the name of friendship, in the name of being a good person. Why should I sacrifice myself for her? She would never do it for me. Why should I be the martyr here? I imagine myself alone at thirty-five, alone at forty. Or even worse, settling down with a dull, watered-down version of Dex. Dex with a weaker chin and twenty fewer IQ points. I would be forced to live with 'what if' forever.

'Yeah, Mom. I know. Do unto others. Blah, blah, blah. I'll be a good friend to precious Darcy.'

My mom looks down at her lap, smoothes her skirt. I hurt her feelings. I tell myself that I must be nice for one more evening. It is the least I can do. I don't have a sibling to pick up the slack and be the good child when I am off my game. I smile and change the subject. 'Where's Dad?'

'He went to the hardware store. Again.'

'For what this time?' I ask, indulging her in the 'Dad can't get enough of hardware stores and car dealerships' joke.

'Who knows? Who ever knows?' She shakes her head, happy again.

I am half asleep, thinking about Dex, when my cell phone rings. I have it next to my bed, the battery fully charged and the ringer on high, hoping Dex will call. His number lights up my phone screen. I press it to my ear.

'Hi, Dex.'

'Hi there,' he says, his voice low. 'Did I wake you up?'

'Um, sort of. But that's okay.'

He doesn't apologize, which I like.

'God, I miss you,' he says. 'When are you coming home?'

He knows when I'm coming home, knows that his fiancée has the identical itinerary. But I don't mind him asking. This question is for me. He wants me – not Darcy – back in his time zone.

'Tomorrow afternoon. We land at four.'

'I'm coming over to see you,' he says.

'Good,' I say.

Silence.

I ask him where he is now.

'On the couch.'

I picture him in my apartment, on my couch, although I know he is on their Pottery Barn pull-out, the one that Darcy plans to replace with 'a more high-end piece' as soon as they are married.

'Oh,' I say. I don't want to hang up, but in my sleepy state can think of nothing to say.

'How was the shower?'

'You didn't get a report?'

'Yeah. Darcy called.'

I am glad he told me she called him, wonder if he added this detail on purpose.

'But I was asking *you* how the shower was,' he says.

'Annalise was so happy . . . But it was miserable.'

'Why's that?'

'Showers are just that way.'

Then I tell him that I wish he were next to me. It is the kind of thing I don't usually say, unless he says something like it first. But the dark and the distance make me bolder.

'You do?' he asks in the tone I use when I want more. Guys aren't so different from us, I think, which no matter how many times I think it, will always seem like a remarkable revelation.

'Yeah. I wish you were right here with me.'

'In your bed at home, right there with your parents in the next room?'

I laugh. 'They're open-minded.'

'Wish I were there, then.'

'Although I have a twin bed,' I say. 'Not a lot of room.'

'A twin bed with you is not a bad thing.' His voice is low and sexy.

I know we are both thinking the same thing. I can hear him breathing. I say nothing, just touch myself and think of him. I want him to do the same. He does. My phone is hot against my face and, as usual when I'm on my cell, I wonder about the radiation I could be getting. But tonight I don't care about a little radiation.

The next day Darcy and I share a cab home from LaGuardia. I am dropped off first. I phone Dex the second I hit the pavement, finding him at the office working, waiting for my call. I am ready for you whenever, I say, happy that I already shaved my legs back in Indiana. He says he'll be right up as soon as she calls his office. You know, he says, sounding embarrassed by his newly acquired tactics. I understand. For

216

a second, I feel bad that my life consists of these sleazy, adulterous strategies. But only for a second. Then I tell myself that Dex and I aren't in that camp. That, in Hillary's words, life's not black and white. That sometimes the end justifies the means.

That evening, after Dex and I have been together for several hours, I realize that our visits are starting to run together in one delicious blur of talking, touching, dozing, and simply existing together in a warm, easy silence. Like the perfect beach vacation, where the routine is so blissfully uneventful that when you return home and friends ask how your trip was, you can't really recall what exactly you did to fill up so many hours. That is what being with Dex is like.

I have stopped counting our lovemaking but know that we are well past twenty. I wonder how many times he's been with Darcy. These are the things I think about now. So to say that she has nothing to do with us is not true. To say that it's not a contest is ludicrous. She is the measuring stick; I hold myself up against her. When we are in bed, I wonder, does she do it like this? Is she better? Do they follow a script by now or does she keep things fresh? (My vote, sadly, is fresh. And even more sadly, when your body is a ten, does it really matter if the sex is stale missionary?) I think of her afterward, too, when I often feel self-conscious about my body. I suck in my stomach, arrange my breasts when his back is turned, and never saunter around my apartment naked. I wonder how many times we'd have to be together before I would give up the pretty-lingerie routine in favor of the gray sweats or flannel Gap pajama bottoms that I wear when I am alone. We probably don't have time for that stage to develop. At least not before the wedding. Time is running out. I tell myself not to panic, to savor the present.

But I can sense a recent shift. I allow myself to think of the future now. I've stopped feeling sick when I imagine Dex canceling the wedding. I've stopped feeling that my loyalty to Darcy should always come before all else, namely what I want. I'm still not sure where things will go, where I want them to go, but my fear of breaking the rules has dulled somewhat, as has my instinct to put Darcy above myself.

Tonight Dex talks about work. He often tells me about his deals, and although I am interested in the mechanics of it all, what I really like is the color that Dex provides about the major players at his firm, the people who fill his daily life. For example, I know that he likes working for Roger Bollinger, the head of his group. Dex is Roger's golden boy and Roger is Dexter's role model. When he tells a story about Roger, he imitates Roger's Boston accent in a way that convinces me that if I ever meet Roger it will seem as though Roger is imitating Dex imitating Roger. Roger is barely five feet four (my question – guys usually don't supply details on the appearance of other guys and are far more likely to report on wit or intelligence) but it doesn't hurt him with women, according to Dex. Incidentally, Dex reported this tidbit matter-of-factly, not admiringly, which reassures me that Dex does not have womanizing tendencies. Womanizers feel either (a) impressed by or (b) competitive with fellow womanizers.

He finishes telling me a story about Roger and then asks, 'Did I tell you that Roger was engaged twice?'

'No,' I say, thinking that he knows he hasn't. It's not the kind of thing you forget sharing, particularly given our circumstances. I feel suddenly chilly, and pull the sheet up over both of us.

'Yeah. He broke it off both times. He keeps saying things to me like, "It's not ovah till it's ovah" and "The fat lady hasn't sung yet".'

I wonder if Roger knows anything about me, or if he's just doing the typical bachelor banter. 'When?' I ask Dex.

'When does the fat lady sing?' Dex curls his body around mine.

'Well, yeah. Sort of.' We are getting into sensitive territory, and I am thankful he can't see my eyes. 'When did he break off the engagements?'

'Not sure about the first time. But the second time was right before the ceremony.'

'You're kidding me.'

'Nope. The bride was getting dressed when he went to her room, knocked on her door, and gave her the news right in front of her mother, her grandmother, and her ninety-five-year-old great-grandmother.'

'Was she surprised?' I ask, realizing that it's a dumb question. Nobody expects the groom to barge in and call off the wedding.

'Apparently. But she shouldn't have been *that* surprised . . . She must've known he had done it once before.'

'Was there somebody else?' I ask tentatively.

'Don't think so. No.'

'Then why did he do it?'

'He said he couldn't see it lasting forever.'

'Oh.'

'What are you thinking?'

He must know what I'm thinking.

'Nothing.'

'Tell me.'

'Nothing.'

'Tell me.'

The dialogue of the new relationship. After a couple is established, the question becomes a relic.

'I'm thinking that I don't believe in that wedding-day, Julia Roberts *Runaway Bride* – or groom – routine.'

'You don't *believe* in it?'

I am treading carefully. 'I just think it's unnecessary . . . needlessly mean,' I say. 'If someone is going to call it off, they should do it before the wedding day.'

My message isn't exactly subtle.

'Well, I agree, but don't you think it's better to pull the cord than make a mistake? Don't you owe it to the other person and yourself and the whole institution of marriage to say something, even if you come to the realization late in the game?'

'I'm *in no way* advocating the making of that sort of mistake. I'm just saying you should figure it out before the wedding day. That's what engagements are for. And in my book, by the wedding day it's a done deal. Suck it up and make the best of it. That's a cold move, telling her when the gown is on.'

I picture Darcy in this humiliating scenario, and my empathy for her is unequivocal.

'You think? Even if it just ends up in a divorce?' he asks.

'Even if. You ask that girl if she'd rather be divorced or dissed in her dress in front of all those people.'

He makes a noncommittal 'hmmm' sound so I can't tell whether he agrees. I wonder what it all will mean for us. If he's even thinking about us at all. He has to be. I feel my muscles tense, my foot twitch nervously. I tell myself that it's not July Fourth yet. I don't want to think about it anymore at all.

I reach over Dex and turn up my stereo. Creedence Clearwater Revival is singing 'Lookin' Out My Back Door'. Talk about an upbeat song. It is exactly what I need to block out images of Dex and Darcy's wedding. Instead, I picture a road trip with Dexter. We are in a white convertible with the top down, sunglasses on, trucking along a stretch of highway with no other cars in sight.

Bother me tomorrow, today I'll buy no sorrow.
Doo, doo, doo, lookin' out my back door.

FOURTEEN

Every year over the July Fourth holiday, there is a mass exodus from Manhattan. People head for the Hamptons, the Cape, Martha's Vineyard, even New Jersey. Nobody stays. Not even Les. The summer of the bar exam when Nate and I stayed in the city to study, I was amazed at what a different, downright peaceful place it was without all the people. Of course, I plan on staying home this year too – there is no way I'm going to the Hamptons. I can't stomach the thought of seeing Dex and Darcy together. I call Dex and tell him this. He says what I have been hoping he would say.

'I'll stay too.'

'Really?' My heart races just imagining spending the night with Dex.

'Yeah. Let's do it.'

So we devise our plan: we will both 'discover' at the last moment that we have to work. We will bitch and moan up a storm but insist to Darcy that she should go on and have fun without us. By then she will have a fresh pedicure, new outfits purchased, parties lined up, and reservations made at her favorite restaurants. So there's no way she'll stay home, and Dex and I will be together, uninterrupted for days. We will fall asleep together, wake up together, and eat our meals together. And although Dex hasn't confirmed it, I assume that at some point we will have our big talk.

I share the plan with Hillary, who has high expectations. She is convinced that the long weekend will be the turning point in my relationship with Dex and he will realize that marrying Darcy would be a terrible mistake.

As she leaves work at noon on the third, she stops by my office and tells me to have a great weekend. 'Good luck.' She crosses her fingers in the air.

'What do you mean? You think we're going to get caught?'

'No. That's not what I meant. I mean good luck with your talk. You are going to talk to Dex about what's going on, aren't you?'

'Yeah. I suppose so.'

'You suppose so?'

'I'm sure we will. That is the plan.'

'Okay. Make sure that you do.' She gives me a stern look. 'It's crunch time.'

I grimace.

'Rachel, do not wimp out on this. If you want to be with him, now's the time to pipe up.'

'I know. I got it,' I say. And for a second I picture myself being Hillary-like. Strong, bold, and confident.

'I'll call you if your girl seems at all suspicious.'

I nod, feeling a stab of guilt over such plotting against Darcy.

Hillary knows what I'm thinking. 'You gotta do what you gotta do,' she says. 'Don't turn soft now.'

223

At seven sharp, just as planned, Dexter arrives at my door with a fresh haircut that further accentuates his cheekbones. He holds a bottle of red wine, a small black duffel bag, and a bunch of white Casablanca lilies, the kind you find at every Korean deli for three bucks a stem. Even though they are inexpensive and somewhat wilted, I like them as much as my expensive roses.

'These are for you,' he says. 'Sorry. They're kind of dying already.'

'I love them,' I say. 'Thank you.'

He follows me into the kitchen as I look for a vase to put them in. I point to my favorite blue one in my top cupboard, just out of my reach. 'Can you get that for me?'

He retrieves the vase and sets it on my counter as I begin trimming the stems and arranging them. I am a domestic goddess as far as he can tell.

'We did it,' Dex whispers into my ear.

Goose bumps rise on my arms. I manage to get the flowers in the vase and add a little water before turning around to kiss him. His neck is warm, and the back of his hair is still damp from his haircut. He smells of cologne, which he doesn't usually wear. Of course, I am also wearing perfume, which I don't usually wear. But this is a special occasion. When you are used to snippets of time, our stretch of days might as well be forever. The way I feel reminds me of bursting off the bus on the last day of school before summer vacation. No worries except what to do first – ride bikes, go to the pool, or play Truth or Dare with Darcy and

Annalise in my cool, unfinished basement. Today I know what I want to do first and I am pretty sure we will be doing it soon. I kiss Dex's neck as I inhale his sweet skin and the scent of lilies.

'This weekend is going to be out of control,' he says, sliding my tank top over my head, letting it fall at our feet. He unhooks my bra, cups my breasts and then my face. His fingers press the back of my neck.

'I'm so glad you're here,' I say. 'I'm so happy.'

'Me too,' he says, as he works on my button-fly.

I lead Dex over to my bed and remove his clothes, admiring his body from every angle, kissing him in new places. On the back of his knees. On his elbows. We have time.

We make love slowly, each of us stopping the other at various points until we can't stand it any longer, and then reversing in the other reckless, breathless direction. He feels more mine than he ever has, and I know why: he is not going home to her tonight. He will not have to wash off or check for signs of our togetherness. I sink my nails into his back and pull him harder against me.

After we make love, we order food from the diner and eat burgers by candlelight. Then we climb back into bed, where we talk and listen to music, fighting through waves of fatigue so that we can savor our time together, not waste it sleeping.

Our only interruption comes around midnight, when Dex says he should probably phone Darcy. I tell him it's a good idea, wondering whether I should give him privacy or stay in bed beside him. I decide to go to the bathroom, let him do his thing. I run water so I can't hear any piece of their conversation. A minute later, Dex calls my name.

I open the door a crack. 'Are you off?'

'Yeah. C'mere. You didn't have to leave.'

I get back in bed beside him, find his hand.

'Sorry about that,' he says.

'No problem. I understand.'

'Just taking precautions . . . I figure she won't call now. I told her I was on my way home to bed.'

'What is she doing?'

'They're all at the Talkhouse. Drunk and happy.'

But we are sober and happier, all tangled up in my sheets, our heads resting on one pillow. When Dex sits up to blow out the candle burning on my windowsill, I notice that trimmings from his haircut have transferred from his neck to my white pillowcase. There's something about those tiny black hairs that makes me so happy I want to cry.

I close my eyes so that I won't.

At some point, we fall asleep.

And then morning comes.

I wake up, remembering the first morning we woke up together, the panic that gripped my heart on that Sunday I turned thirty. The feeling I have now could not be more different. Calm joy.

'Hi, Rachel.'

'Hi, Dex.'

We are both grinning.

'Happy Fourth of July,' he says, his hand resting on my inner thigh.

'Happy Fourth.'

'It's not your typical Fourth. No fireworks planned, no picnics, no beach. You okay with that?' he asks.

'Yeah. I'm okay with that,' I say.

We make love and then shower together. I am self-conscious at first, but after a few minutes I relax and let him wash my back. We stay under the hot water (he likes his showers as hot as I do) long past the point of wrinkled fingers. Then we are out in the world, walking down Third Avenue to Starbucks. It is a humid, gray day, and rain feels likely. But we don't need good weather. Happiness wells inside me. Never have I felt so content before my morning coffee.

We are alone in line to order, Marvin Gaye singing over the sound system. I order a tall skim latte. Dex says, 'Give me the same thing in a large with, um . . . just regular milk.'

I like that he abandons the Starbucks terminology, skipping the word 'grande' and ordering his coffee as a guy's guy should.

The perky girl behind the register bellows our order to her colleague, who promptly marks our cups with a black marker. Starbucks employees are consistently, freakishly chipper, even during the worst of morning rush hour when they have to deal with hordes of cranky people waiting impatiently for their caffeine fix.

'Oh, wait,' the girl says, beaming. 'Are these together or separate?'

Dex answers quickly, 'We're – they're together.'

I smile at his slip. *We are together.*

227

'Will there be anything else?'

'Um. Yeah. I'll have a blueberry muffin,' Dex says, and then looks at me. 'Rachel?'

'Yeah. I'll have one too,' I say, resisting the urge to order a low-fat muffin. I don't want to be anything like Darcy.

'So two blueberry muffins.' Dex pays and drops his change into the tip mug in front of the register. The girl smiles at me as if to say, 'Your guy is not only hot but generous too.'

Dex and I both add a packet of brown sugar to our coffee, stir and find a seat at the counter facing the street. The sidewalks are deserted.

'I like New York this way,' I say, tasting my foam. We watch a lone yellow cab drift up Third Avenue. 'Listen . . . no honking.'

'Yeah. It really is dead,' he says. 'I bet we could get reservations anywhere tonight. Would you like to go out?'

I look at him. 'We can't do that.'

Getting coffee is one thing. Dinner is another.

'We can do whatever we please. Haven't you figured that out yet?' He winks and sips his coffee.

'What if somebody sees us?'

'Nobody's here.' He motions out the window. 'And so what if they do? We're allowed to eat, aren't we? Hell, I could even tell Darcy that we're going to grab a bite together. She knows we're both stuck here working, right?'

'I guess so.'

'C'mon. I want to take you out. I've never taken you out on a proper date. I feel bad about that. What do you say?'

228

I raise my eyebrows and smirk.

'What's that look for?' Dex asks. His full lips meet the rim of his cup.

'It's just that "proper" is not the word that comes to mind when I think about us.'

'Oh, that,' Dex says, waving his hand in the air, as though I have just stated an insignificant detail about our relationship. 'Well, that can't be helped . . . I mean – yes, the circumstances are . . . less than ideal.'

'That's an understatement. Let's call a spade a spade, Dex. We're having an affair.'

It is the most I have ever said about what we are doing. I know Hillary wouldn't give me any awards for forthrightness, but my heart still skips. It is a bold comment for me.

'I guess so,' he says hesitantly. 'But when I'm with you, I'm not thinking about the impropriety of our . . . relationship. Being with you doesn't feel wrong.'

'I know what you mean,' I say, thinking that there would be a few people out there who might beg to differ.

I wait for him to say more about it. About us. Our future. Or at the very least our coup this weekend. He doesn't. Instead he suggests we take our coffee home and read the paper in bed.

'Sounds perfect,' I say, wondering what section he reads first. I want to know every single thing about him.

It rains on and off all day so we stay in, moving from bed to sofa to bed, talking for hours, never checking the time. We talk about everything: high school, college, law school, our

229

families, friends, books, movies. But not Darcy or the situation. Not even when she calls his cell phone to say hello. I study my cuticles as he tells her he just stepped out of his office to get a bite to eat, and that yes, he's getting a lot done, been working on a pitch all day. He mumbles 'me too' at the end of their brief conversation so I know what he has just told her. I tell myself that many couples punctuate their calls with 'I love you's in the automatic way other people say 'goodbye'. It doesn't mean anything.

As Dex snaps his cell phone shut, looking chagrined, my cell phone rings. It's Darcy. Dex laughs. 'She just told me she had to run. Sure she did! To call you!'

I don't pick up, but I listen to her message afterward. She bitches about the weather but says that they are having fun anyway. She says she misses me. That it's not the same without Dex and me. I will not feel guilty. I will not.

That evening Dex and I separate for a few hours so that he can go home and change for dinner, as he has only packed jeans and shorts and basic toiletries. I miss him while he's gone, but I like the way the separation makes our dinner seem more like a date. Besides, I am grateful for the chance to primp alone. I can do the things that a guy you just started seeing should not see you do – pluck a stray eyebrow hair, strategically spray perfume (behind the knees, between the breasts), and apply make-up to make it look like you are wearing very little.

Dex picks me up at seven forty-five and we cab it down to one of my favorite restaurants in Manhattan, Balthazar, where it is usually impossible to get a reservation unless you call weeks in advance or are willing to take a six o'clock or eleven-thirty seating. But we get in promptly at eight o'clock and are given an ideal, cozy booth. I ask Dex if he knows that Jerry Seinfeld proposed to his wife, Jessica Sklar, at Balthazar. Perhaps this is the exact spot where Jerry popped the question with the Tiffany ring.

'I didn't know that,' Dex says, glancing up from the wine list.

'Did you know that she dumped her husband of five months for Jerry?'

He laughs. 'Yeah, I think I heard that one.'

'Soo . . . Balthazar must be the restaurant of choice for the scandalous.'

He shakes his head and gives me an exasperated smile. 'Please stop calling us that.'

'Face facts, Dexter. This is scandalous . . . We're just like Jerry and Jessica.'

'Look. We can't help the way we feel,' Dex says earnestly.

Yeah. And perhaps that is what Jessica whispered to Jerry on her cell phone, while her unsuspecting husband sat watching must-see TV in the next room.

As I scan my menu, I realize that my opinion of Jerry and Jessica might be changing. I used to subscribe to the notion that he was a heartless home wrecker and she a shameless gold digger who coldly upgraded her Nederlander husband for a wealthier, wittier model the second the opportunity presented itself, which, I read, was at the Reebok Sports Club, the Upper West Side gym that Darcy also belongs to. Now, I'm not so sure. Maybe that *was* how it all went down. Then again, maybe Jessica married Eric Nederlander, whom she thought she loved by any relative measure in her life up to that point, and then she met Jerry, days after returning from her Italian honeymoon, and quickly realized that she had never really loved before, that her feelings for Jerry far surpassed whatever she felt for Eric.

What was a girl to do? Stay in a marriage with the wrong man, all in the name of appearances? Jessica knew the shit that she would get, not only from friends and family and her own husband whom she had promised to have and to hold forever (not just a mere 120 days), but from the whole world – or at least those of us so bored with our own lives that we devour *People* magazine the second it hits the newsstands. Yet she went for it anyway, realizing that you only live once. She stuck her neck out in traffic, and like the frog in my all-time favorite video game, made it across the street, safely into the little box on top of the screen, or as it were in a six-million-dollar pad overlooking Central Park. Owning up to her mistake actually took real grit and courage. And maybe Jerry, too, deserved credit for ignoring the wrath of the world, following his heart at any price. Maybe true love just prevailed.

Regardless of what really happened with Jessica, Eric, and Jerry, my notions of rule-following in love are shifting.

'So, do you know what you'd like to have?' Dex asks me.

I smile and tell him that I am waiting to hear the specials.

232

*

After dinner Dex asks me if I want to go get another drink.

'Do you?' I ask, wanting to please him, give him the right answer.

'I asked you first.'

'I would rather just go home.'

'Good. Me too.'

The night has cleared somewhat, and as we are dropped off on my corner, we see a few fireworks exploding in the distance over the East River. Blues and pinks and golds illuminate what feels like our own private city. We hold hands and stare up at the sky, watching silently for several minutes before we go inside and say good night to José, who by now thinks that Dexter is my boyfriend.

We go upstairs, undress, and make love. It is not my imagination – it is better every time. Afterward, neither of us speaks or moves. We fall asleep, our legs and arms entwined.

In the morning, I wake up just as the light is returning to the sky. I listen to Dex breathe and study the sharp curve of his cheek. His eyes snap open suddenly. Our faces are close.

'Hi, baby.' His voice is scratchy with sleep.

'Hi,' I say softly. 'Good morning.'

'What are you doing awake? It's early.'

'I'm watching you.'

'Why?'

'Because I love your face,' I say.

He looks genuinely surprised by my comment. How could he be? He must know that he is handsome.

'I love the way you look too,' he says. His arms move around me, pulling me against his chest. 'And I love the way you feel.'

I feel myself blush.

'And the way you taste,' he says, kissing my neck and my face. We avoid mouths, as you do after sleep. 'And I guess all of that makes sense.'

'Why's that?'

'Well, because . . .'

He is breathing hard now and looks nervous, almost scared. I reach for a condom from my nightstand drawer, but he pulls my hand back, and moves inside me, and says 'because' again.

'Because why?'

I think I might know why. I hope I know why.

'Because, Rachel . . .' He looks into my eyes. 'Because I love you.'

He says those words exactly as I am thinking them, fighting a growing impulse to say it first. And now I don't have to.

I try to memorize everything about this moment. The look in his eyes, the feel of his skin. Even the way the light is slanting through my blinds. It is a moment beyond perfection, beyond anything I have ever felt before. It is almost too much to bear. I don't care that Dex is engaged to Darcy, or that we are creeping around like a couple of outlaws. I don't care that my teeth need a good brushing and that my hair is messy and limp around my face. I only feel Dex and his words and I know, without a doubt, that this is the happiest moment of my life. Snapshots flash through my mind. We are dining by candlelight, sipping fine champagne. We are curled up next to a raging fire in an old Vermont farmhouse with creaky floorboards and snowflakes the size of silver dollars falling outside. We are sharing a picnic lunch in Bordeaux in the middle of a meadow filled with yellow flowers, where he will give me a vintage diamond ring.

This might just happen. He loves me. I love him. What else is there? Surely he won't marry Darcy. They cannot do happily ever after. I find my voice and manage to say those four one-syllable words back to him. Words I haven't uttered in a very, very long time. Words that meant nothing before now.

Neither of us acknowledges what we have said, but I can feel it in the air, all around us. It is more palpable than the thick humidity. I can feel it in the way he looks at me and the way he says my name. We are a couple, and our words have made us brazen. At one point, as we are walking through Central Park, he takes my hand. It is only for a few seconds, five or six steps, but I feel a rush of adrenaline. What if we get caught? What then? A small part of me wants that result, wants to run into an acquaintance of Darcy's, a co-worker stuck in the city for work, going for a brief stroll in the park. She will play informant on Monday morning, telling Darcy that she saw Dex with a girl, holding hands. She will describe me in detail but I am generic enough that Darcy won't suspect me. And if she does, I'll just deny it, say I was at work all day, that I don't even own a pink shirt – this one is new, one that she has never seen. I will be wildly indignant, and she will apologize and then turn back to the issue of Dex cheating on her. She will decide to dump him and I will be supportive, tell her she is doing the right thing. This way Dex won't have to decide anything or do anything. It will all be handled for us.

We walk up to the reservoir, circling it as we admire all the views of the city. We pass a boy wearing head-to-toe army fatigues, walking an aged beagle, and then an overweight woman panting along in a slow jog, her elbows jutting out awkwardly. Otherwise, we have the usually populated path to ourselves. I listen to the gravel crunching beneath our sneakers as we walk in perfect rhythm. I am content. The reservoir, the views, the city, and the world belong to Dex and me.

Dark clouds are rolling in when we finally leave the park. We decide not to change for dinner, heading straight for Atlantic Grill, a restaurant near my apartment. Both of us are in the mood for fish and white wine and vanilla ice cream. After dinner, we dash back to my apartment in a downpour, laughing as we cross the streets mid-block, splashing our way through the puddles formed on the sidewalks. Back inside, we strip off our wet clothes and towel each other off, still laughing. Dex puts on a pair of boxers. I wear one of his T-shirts. Then we play a Billie Holiday CD and open another bottle of wine, red this time. We stretch out on my sofa where we talk for hours, only getting up to brush our teeth and transfer to my bed for another satisfying sleep together.

Then suddenly, as it always happens, time accelerates. And just as being with Dex on our first night felt like the start of the summer, fearing the end of our time together reminds me of late August, when those daunting back-to-school commercials for Trapper Keepers would replace the ones featuring gleeful towheaded kids sipping Capri-Sun poolside. I remember the feeling well – a mixture of sadness and panic. This is how I feel now as we sit on my sofa on Saturday while afternoon bleeds into evening. I keep telling myself not to ruin the last night by being sad. I tell myself that the best is yet to come. He loves me.

As if reading my mind, Dex looks at me and says, 'I meant what I said.'

It is the first reference to our sacred exchange.

'I did too.' I am filled with a deep longing, and am sure that our talk is coming. Our post-Independence Day Talk. It is coming. We are going to discuss ways to make this crazy thing work. How we can't bear to hurt Darcy, but that we must. I wait for his lead. It is his conversation to begin.

That's when he says, 'No matter what happens, I meant that.'

His words are like the sound of a needle dragging across a record. A sinking, sickening feeling washes over me. This is why you should never, ever get your hopes up. This is why you should see the glass as half-empty. So when the whole thing spills, you aren't as devastated. I want to cry, but I keep my face placid, give myself a psychological shot of Botox. I can't cry, for several reasons, not the least of which is that if he asks why I'm crying, I won't be able to articulate an answer.

I fight to salvage the night, bring the golden cast back. *He loves me, he loves me, he loves me*, I tell myself. But it is not helping. He looks at me worriedly. 'What's wrong?'

I shake my head, and he asks again, his voice gentle. 'Hey, hey, hey . . .' He lifts my chin, looks into my eyes. 'What is it?'

'I'm just sad.' My voice trembles tellingly. 'It's our last night.'

'It's not our last night.'

I take a deep breath. 'It's not?'

'No.'

But that doesn't really explain much. What does 'no' mean? That we will continue in this fashion for a few more weeks? Until the night before their rehearsal dinner? Or does he mean that this is only our beginning? Why can't he be more specific? I can't bring myself to ask. I am afraid of his answer.

'Rachel, I love you.'

His lips stay curled up at the end of the last word, until I lean over to kiss him. A kiss is my response. I won't say it back until we have our talk. *Way to take a stand!*

We are kissing on my couch, followed by the unzipping and unbuttoning and attempting to gracefully slide out of denim, which is impossible. We move various sections of the *Times* out of our way and onto the floor. The sure fix, I think – the panacea. We are making love, but I am not in the moment. I am thinking, thinking, thinking. I can feel the dials of my brain whirring and rotating like the inside of a Swiss watch. *What is he going to do? What is going to happen?*

The next morning, when I wake up beside Dex, I hear him saying 'no matter what happens'. But during sleep, my mind reprocessed the meaning of his words, landing on a perfectly logical explanation: Dexter just meant that whatever shit hits the fan, no matter what Darcy says or does, if we need some time apart in the aftermath of blood and guts, he will be waiting to love me and it will all be fixed in the end. That is what he must have meant. But still. I want him to tell me this. Surely he will say something more before he returns to the Upper West Side.

We get up, shower together, and go to Starbucks. Already we have a routine. It is eleven. Darcy and the others will be home soon. We are down to minutes and still no conversation, no conclusions. We finish our coffee and then stop at a toy store. Dex needs to buy a baby present for one of his work friends. Just a small token, he says. I can't decide whether I enjoy the feeling of being such an established couple that we run errands together, or whether I resent wasting our dwindling moments on this random task. It's more the latter. I just want to get back so that we have a few moments together. Time for him to share his plan.

But Dex lingers over various toys and books, asking me my opinion, laboring over a decision that doesn't matter one bit in the scheme of things. He finally decides on a big, green brontosaurus with a cartoonish expression. It's not what I would choose for a newborn, but I admire his conviction. I hope he will have similar conviction about us.

'It's cute. Don't you think?' he asks, cocking its tiny green head.

'Adorable.'

Then, as he's about to pay for the dinosaur, he spots a plastic bin full of wooden dice. He picks out two red ones with gold-painted dots and holds them up in an open palm. 'How much for a pair of dice?'

'Forty-nine cents per die,' the man at the register says.

'A bargain. I'll take 'em.'

We leave the store and walk toward my apartment. People are returning to the city in droves; traffic has resumed its normal pace. We are almost at my block. Dex is holding the bag with the dinosaur in his right hand and the dice in his left. He has been shaking them along the way. I wonder if his stomach hurts as much as mine does.

'What are you thinking?' I ask him. I want a long answer, articulating everything I am thinking. I want reassurance, some small nugget of hope.

He shrugs, licks his lips. 'Nothing much.'

ARE YOU MARRYING DARCY? The words roar in my head. But I say nothing, worrying that pressuring him is not strategically wise. As if what I say or don't say in the final minutes of our togetherness might make a difference. Maybe it is that tenuous – the fate of three people hanging in the balance like the cradle in the nursery rhyme.

'You like to gamble?' Dex asks, examining his dice while still walking.

'No,' I say. Surprise, surprise. Rachel playing it safe. 'Do you?'

'Yeah,' he says. 'I like craps. My lucky number is six – a four and two. You have a lucky roll?'

'No . . . Well, I like double sixes,' I answer, trying to mask my feelings of desperation. Desperate women are not attractive. Desperate women lose.

'Why double sixes?'

'I don't know,' I say. I don't feel like explaining that it stems from playing backgammon with my father when I was little. I'd chant for double sixes and whenever I rolled them he'd call me Boxcar Willy. I still don't know who Boxcar Willy is, but I loved it when he called me that.

'Want me to roll you some double sixes?'

'Yeah,' I say, pointing down at the filthy sidewalk, humoring him. 'Go ahead.'

We stop on the corner of Seventieth and Third. A bus lurches past us, and a woman with a baby nearly runs her stroller into Dex. He seems to ignore everyone and everything around him, shaking the dice with both hands, an expression of intense concentration on his face. If I saw him exactly like this, but in Atlantic City wearing polyester and a gold chain, I would wonder if he had his house and life savings on the line.

'What are we betting?' I ask.

'Betting? We're on the same team, baby,' he says in a Queens accent, and then blows hard on his dice, his smooth cheeks puffing out like a little boy blowing the candles out on his birthday cake.

'Roll me double sixes right now.'

'And if I do?'

I think to myself, *You roll double sixes, we end up together. No wedding with Darcy.* But instead I say, 'It will mean good luck for us.'

'All righty then. Double sixes coming right up for ya.' He licks his lips and shakes his dice more vigorously.

The sun shines in my eyes as he tosses the dice in the air, catches them easily, and then dramatically lowers his arm toward the ground as if he's about to roll a bowling ball. He opens his hand, fingers splayed, as the cubes clatter to the concrete right at the busy Manhattan intersection.

One red die lands on six immediately. My heart skips with the thought, *What if?* We are crouched over the landed die and its spinning twin, rotating on its axis for what seems like forever. If you tried to make a die go that long, you couldn't do it. But there it is, turning on its corner, a blur of gold dots and red background. And then it slows, slows, slows, and lands neatly beside the first one. Two rows of three dots on the second die.

Double sixes.

Boxcar Willy.

Holy shit, I think . . . *No wedding with Darcy!* . . . He wanted to talk about 'no matter what happens' as if someone were steering from up above, well, here you go. Here you have it. Double sixes. Our fate.

I look up from the dice at Dexter, debating whether to tell him what the roll had really been for. He looks at me with his mouth slightly open. Our eyes return to the dice as if maybe we got it wrong.

What are the chances?

Um, that would be precisely one in thirty-six. Just under three percent.

So we aren't talking one-in-a-million odds. But those

statistics are misleading when removed from our context. We have reached the end of a pivotal, meaningful weekend together. Right as we are minutes from parting ways (for the day? forever?), Dexter buys the dice on a whim, plays with them instead of putting them in the bag with his stuffed brontosaurus, and adopts his boyish gambling persona. I play along, even though I'm in no mood for games. Then I decide, albeit silently, the terms of the roll. And he rolls double sixes! As if to say, we are foolproof, baby.

I look at his ninety-eight cent (plus tax) dice with the reverence you would have for a crystal ball in a richly upholstered room with the world's greatest fortune-teller, wrinkled by the Persian sun, who has just told you how it was, how it is, and how it is going to be. Even Dex – who doesn't know what he just sealed for us – is impressed, telling me that he needs to take me to Atlantic City, Vegas, that we'd make a hell of a team.

Exactly.

He smiles at me and says, 'There's your good luck, baby.'

I say nothing, just pick up the dice and wedge them into the front pocket of my shorts.

'You stealing my dice?'

Our dice.

'I need them,' I say.

We return to my apartment, where he collects his things and says goodbye.

'Thanks for an awesome weekend,' he says, his face now mirroring mine. He is sad too.

'Yeah. It was great. Thank you.' I strike the pose of a confident girl.

He bites his lower lip. 'I better head back. As much as I don't want to.'

'Yeah. You better go.'

'I'll call you soon. Whenever I can. As soon as I can.'

'Okay.' I nod.

'Okay. Bye.'

After one final kiss, he is gone.

I sit on my sofa, clutching my dice. They are a comfort – the roll is almost as good as a talk. Maybe better. We didn't have a talk because it is all so obvious. We are in love and meant to be together, and the dice confirmed everything. I place them reverently in his empty cinnamon Altoids container, nestled in the white paper liner with the sixes still facing up. I touch the rows of dots, like reverse Braille. They tell me that we will be together. It is our destiny. All of me believes it. I close the lid of the tin and push it against the base of my vase filled with lilies that are still clinging on. The dice, the tin, the lilies – I have created a shrine to our love.

I glance around my prim, orderly studio, perfectly neat except for my unmade bed. The sheets have molded against the mattress, revealing a vague outline of our bodies. I want to be there again, to feel closer to him. I slip off my sandals and walk over to the bed, sliding under the covers, which are chilled from the air conditioner. I get up, close my blinds, and hit the remote control on my stereo. Billie Holiday croons. I get back in bed, wriggle down toward the bottom of it, hooking my feet over the end of the mattress. I let my senses fill with Dex. See his face, feel him next to me.

I wonder if he is home yet or still stuck in cross-town

traffic. Will he kiss Darcy hello? Will her lips feel strange and unfamiliar after kissing mine all weekend? Will she sense that something is wrong, unable to put her finger on exactly what has changed, never considering for a second that her maid of honor and a pair of dice might have something to do with the faraway look in her fiancé's eyes?

FIFTEEN

Hillary arrives at work the next day, shortly before eleven, wearing wrinkled pants and scuffed black sandals. Her toenail polish is badly chipped, making her big toe resemble a squat candy cane. I laugh and shake my head as she hunkers down in her usual chair in my office.

'What's so funny?'

'Your wardrobe. They're going to fire you.'

Our firm recently changed its dress code, from suits to business casual, so long as there is no client interaction. But I'm pretty sure that Hillary's ensemble is not what the managing partner had in mind when his memo referenced 'appropriate business casual'.

She shrugs. 'I wish they would fire me . . . Okay. So tell me about the weekend. Spare no details.'

I smile.

'That good?'

I tell her we had an awesome time. I tell her about going to Balthazar and Atlantic Grill and our walk in the park and how nice it was to have so much time with Dex. I am hoping that if I talk enough, I will be able to avoid the obvious question.

'So is he going to call it off?'

That's the one.

'Well, I'm not sure.'

'You're not sure? So he said he's thinking about it?'

'Well, no.'

'He's *not* thinking about it?'

'Well . . . It didn't come up per se.' I try not to sound too defensive.

She wrinkles her nose. Then she stares at me blankly. I wonder if her disapproval has more to do with my passivity or her growing suspicion that Dex is playing me for a fool. The former might be true, but the latter is not. 'I thought you guys were going to discuss specifics,' she says, frowning.

'I did too, but . . .'

'But what?'

'But he told me he loves me,' I say. I hadn't planned on sharing this private detail, but I feel as if I must.

Hillary's expression changes somewhat. 'He did?'

'Yes.'

'Was he drunk?'

'No! He wasn't drunk,' I say, glancing at my computer screen, hoping to get an email from Dex. We have not yet spoken since his departure yesterday.

She isn't sold. 'So did you say it back?'

'Yeah. I said it back. Because I do.'

She gives me a respectful few seconds of silence. 'All right. So you both love each other. What now? When does the little break-up happen?'

I take issue with the flippant characterization of his hurdle ahead. 'Calling off a wedding and ending a five-year relationship is hardly a little break-up.'

'Well, whatever. When is he going to do it?'

My stomach hurts as I say again that I don't know. I am tempted to tell Hillary about the dice, but I keep them to myself. That is between Dex and me. Besides, the story wouldn't translate well, and likely she would only be disgusted at me for relying on a dice roll instead of being direct.

I clear my throat. 'So did Darcy mention him at all?'

'Not really . . . But I must admit, I kind of fell down on my lookout job. I have a good excuse.' She grins.

'What's your excuse?'

'I met someone!'

'No way! Who? Do I know him?'

'No. He lives in Montauk. His name is Julian. Rachel – I didn't believe in the whole soul mate thing until I met him.'

'Start from the beginning,' I tell her. There is no better audience for someone in love than someone in love.

She tells me that he's thirty-seven, a writer, never been married. She met him on the beach. She was going for a walk, he was going for a walk. Both of them were alone, moving in the same direction. He kept stopping to examine shells, and she finally caught up to him and introduced herself. They ended up going back to his house, where he made her tomato, mozzarella, and basil salad. Tomatoes and basil from his garden, fresh mozzarella. She says they couldn't stop talking – that he is brilliant, handsome, sensitive.

'So did you see him after that day?'

'Oh, yeah. We hung out the whole weekend . . . Rach, it's

like we skipped all the bullshit. It's hard to explain . . . We are just together already. He is the best.'

'When can I meet him?'

'He's coming this weekend. You can meet him then.'

'I can't wait.'

I am happy for her, but a little envious. I assume Julian isn't engaged. Les calls, interrupting our moment. I don't answer, feeling incapable of dealing with him. Hillary also seems unable to move out of her chair and go to her office to check her own messages. Our firm and all the drones in it can wait. We are talking about love.

After Hillary leaves my office, I go back to obsessing over Dex. Despite my façade of calm in front of Hillary, I am filled with a sense of impending doom, a dull ache of worry that Dex will not come through in the end. I wait for him to call or email, feeling frustrated and almost angry as the minutes pass without a word from him.

The phone finally rings. I jump. But it's only Darcy, asking if I'm free for lunch.

I tell her yes. I hate the idea of seeing her, but I need to know what is going on. Maybe Dex has told her something.

We meet at Naples, a restaurant in the lobby of the MetLife Building. There is a line, so I suggest that we go across the street to a deli. She says no, that she has been dying for pizza. I say fine, we'll wait for a table. I study her face for possible break-up signs. Nothing new, although her hair looks more sun-streaked. She is wearing it in a low, neat ponytail. Aquamarine earrings dangle just below her lobes.

'Do I have something on my face?' Darcy asks, swiping at her cheeks.

'I was just looking at your earrings. They're pretty. Are they new?'

'No. Dex gave them to me a long time ago.'

'When? For your birthday?'

'No. . . I can't remember exactly. Just a random gift.'

I feel a surge of jealousy, but tell myself that much has changed since then.

Darcy asks me how my weekend was.

'Fine,' I say. My heart flutters just thinking about it. 'You know. Lots of work . . . How was yours?'

'Awesome. You should have been there. Great parties. Great bands at the Talkhouse. Omigod, it was *so* much fun. You and Dex picked the wrong weekend to work.'

You and Dex. You and Dex. You and Dex.

'Did Dex have to work the whole time?' I ask, for good measure.

She rolls her eyes. 'Yeah, what else is new? I'm marrying a workaholic.'

'He can't help his hours.'

'Yeah, yeah, yeah,' she says. 'But I bet you anything he volunteers for half the stuff he gets stuck working on. I swear he enjoys it. It makes him feel important.' Her voice is slightly snide. Perhaps this is the prelude to her story about their huge fight.

'You think?'

'I *know*,' she says, as we are led to a table outside. 'And I guess you know Hillary met a guy, right?'

'Yeah, she told me. Did you meet him?'

'Briefly.'

'What did you think?'

'He's not bad looking. Not my type – too artsy-fartsy. But still pretty cute. Wonders never cease.'

'What's that supposed to mean?' I ask, knowing full well that she means Hillary meeting a cute guy is an unlikely event.

'Look at her. She doesn't care about her appearance at all. Half the time she doesn't even act like a girl.'

'I think she's pretty.'

Darcy gives me a 'get real' look.

I think of Hillary's wrinkled pants and chipped toenail. 'Just because she's not a girly-girl doesn't mean she's not attractive.'

'She's over thirty. She needs to start wearing make-up. The au naturel crap went out in the seventies.'

'Well, apparently Julian doesn't agree.'

'Yeah, well, we'll see how long that lasts,' she says, dipping her bread into a plate of oil.

Yeah, we'll see how much longer you and Dex last. I think of the red dice, tucked safely into the Altoids tin, and am instantly overcome with remorse. I don't want her to be hurt. I wish there was a way for Dex and me to be together and for Darcy not to be hurt. Why are happy endings so hard to come by? I refocus on Hillary and Julian. 'I think she's really into him,' I say.

'Uh-huh,' she says, rolling her eyes. 'You *do* know her ex is with a new girl, right?'

'Yeah. Of course I know that. She couldn't care less about Corey anymore. And she dumped him, remember?'

'Well. Yeah. But then he started dating a twenty-three-year-old hottie and prancing around the Talkhouse right in front of her . . . and that's when she is suddenly so convinced that Julian is her guy. Coincidence? I don't think so.'

I tell her that I think she's being mean. 'Stop raining on her parade.'

'Okay. Fine. Whatever. Next topic,' Darcy says, dabbing her napkin at the corners of her mouth. 'When did you last talk to Marcus?'

'Last week sometime.'

She leans forward and tells me that he brought me up several times over the weekend.

'That's nice,' I say, my eyes still on the menu. Marcus feels like ancient history.

She makes a face. 'Why are you so lukewarm about him? Don't you think he's cute?'

'Yeah. He's cute,' I say.

Our waiter arrives at the table to take our orders. Darcy asks for an individual pizza. I tell him that I'd like a Caesar salad.

Darcy objects. 'Don't you want more than a salad?'

I can tell she's irritated that I'm getting a salad and she's ordering a pizza. She likes to be the dainty eater. So I appease her and say, 'Caesar salads are substantial, and actually very fattening.'

'Well, you'll have to eat some of my pizza. I can't eat the

252

whole thing by myself.' She is talking to me, but it is for the waiter's benefit. He smiles at her. She makes her expression friendly and open. I catch her moving her left hand under the table so he can't see her ring.

As he turns to leave, she says, 'Oh, and can you make sure they don't burn the bottom of my pizza? Sometimes they burn the bottom. And I like my pizzas – how shall I say it – rare?' She moves her ponytail in front of one shoulder.

He laughs and winks. 'No problem.'

'He's too young for you,' I say, not caring that he's still within earshot.

'What?' she says innocently. 'Oh, puh-*lease*. I wasn't flirting.'

Before she can launch into another topic, I must determine if there is any domestic trouble yet brewing. I use a wedding angle. 'So what did you decide on the CDs?'

'The CDs?' She looks confused. 'Oh, right, those things. I haven't given them another thought. I took the weekend off from wedding planning. . . Besides, I think those CDs might be too much trouble. Maybe I'll just do nuts or mints after all. They make these cute heart shaped Altoids tins. Maybe we'll get those. You know how much Dexter loves his Altoids.'

'Mmm . . . I didn't know that.'

'Yeah,' she says. 'The cinnamon kind.'

Dexter doesn't phone until late that night, and I miss the call because I am reviewing documents in a conference room. His message is brief: 'Sorry I haven't called today . . . The whole day's been a fire drill getting ready for this pitch on Thursday. I really should have done some of this work over the weekend . . . Not that I'd do it differently. It was worth it to be with you . . . I miss you. I'll talk to you soon.'

His message leaves me feeling hollow. *That's it*? A review of his work schedule? And using an annoying banker expression like 'fire drill', no less. I hate those expressions. The next thing I know he's going to be telling me he's 'in the weeds' – another one of those 'I'm so busy' banker phrases. And more important, he doesn't say anything about Darcy, about when I will see him next, about anything. Just that he misses me. It feels as though he is slipping away, my shot at happiness dissipating. I start to get panicky, but then tell myself to be patient. A lot can happen in a very short time. He will do the right thing. He will be with me in the end.

I finally see Dex on Thursday night. He arrives at my place late, exhausted from work. We talk for a few minutes before he falls asleep with his head on my lap as I watch a *Sopranos* rerun. Tony is cheating on Carmella again. My empathy for her is huge and all-encompassing; ironic, because she is the wife and not the other woman. I think of Darcy, compare our feelings for Dex. She doesn't love him as I do. She can't possibly. This will be my final rationalization in the home-stretch. I run my hand through Dexter's hair, aching with love for him and with worry about the end. I can't bear the thought of losing him.

I nudge him a little after midnight, tell him he should

probably get home. He reluctantly agrees and tells me again how sorry he is about his crazy work schedule. I tell him I understand, I know what it's like. He kisses me and gives me a long hug. And then he is off to be with Darcy again. As he's walking out the door, I ask him what he's doing over the weekend. I try to appear nonchalant, but in my heart I am grasping at straws, hoping that he will dole out a few hours for me.

'My dad and his wife are visiting. I didn't tell you that?'

'No. No. You didn't. That's nice though. What are you going to do?'

'You know – the usual. Dinners. Maybe a show.'

I picture the four of them out on the town. It hurts that I can't meet his father, driving home the point all the more: I am not with Dex. I am the other woman. I think of all the other women who get the random Thursday nights, but never the holidays or the special family occasions or the important work dinners. Excluded when it really matters. Then I think to myself that Dex hasn't even given me any of the assurances, false or otherwise, that the other woman always gets in the movies. Nothing but a couple of 'I love yous' and some red dice.

On Saturday night Hillary convinces me to join her and Julian. I feel guilty for crashing their dinner, but agree, not wanting to be alone with my thoughts about Dex. I have been obsessing about the cozy family weekend, Dex smiling amid all the inevitable wedding chatter, pretending that he is right on schedule with his nuptials. Maybe he *is* right on schedule.

I have no idea what is going on, and the waiting and wondering is so much harder to take after our weekend together.

So I trek down to Gramercy and meet Hillary and Julian at I Trulli, an Italian restaurant. We sit at a small round table in the beautiful back garden, surrounded by brownstone walls, a patch of navy blue sky above us. The patio is lit by candles, and tiny white lights are intertwined in the tree branches. The setting could not be more romantic. Except for the fact that I am the third wheel.

After fifteen minutes, I know I like Julian. He is not at all affected, but speaks slowly, choosing his words carefully – he uses 'favor' instead of 'like better', 'pleasant' instead of 'nice', and 'outset' instead of 'start'. They are simple alternatives, not flamboyant thesaurus entries, so I know he is not showing off. (I once went on a date with a guy who used the words 'salubrious', 'sartorial', and 'loquacious' in one evening. I declined his invitation for date number two for fear that he would show up wearing an ascot.) And although Julian is not traditionally handsome, I like the way he looks. His curly, longish hair, tanned skin, and dark-brown eyes make me think of a Portuguese fisherman.

I watch Julian laughing at something Hillary just said, leaning toward her. Nobody would ever guess that they only met a week ago. Their interaction is fluid and natural, and she is doing none of the things that women do in the new stages of a relationship. She asks him twice if she has spinach in her teeth and she eats every last bit of her pasta, then insists that we order dessert.

Over our slices of cheesecake, Hillary and I tell Julian how much we hate our jobs. He asks why we don't just quit. We say it's not that easy, golden handcuffs, paying off our loans, blah blah blah. And besides, what else would we do? He looks at me and says, yes, what else would you do? I glance at Hillary, wanting her to answer first.

'Hill would open an antiques shop,' he says, touching her wrist. 'Right?'

Hillary smiles at him. They have covered her dreams already. My bet is that she opens her shop in downtown Montauk.

'So what about you, Rachel?' Julian asks again, his dark eyes probing.

It is a common question during law firm interviews, right up there with 'Why did you decide to go to law school?', at which point you give the pat answer about the pursuit of justice when what you are really thinking is 'Because I'm a type A high achiever with no idea of what else to do; I would have gone to med school, but blood makes me squeamish.'

I tell him that I don't know, embarrassed by the truth of it.

'Maybe if you quit your job, you'd figure it out more quickly,' Julian says in his calm voice. 'Poverty, hunger – these things help you think more clearly.'

My cell phone rings. It is a jarring note. I apologize, say I thought I had it turned off before dinner. Maybe it is Dex. Maybe he sneaked off to the bathroom to call me.

'Who is it?' Hillary asks. I can tell that she, too, is wondering if it's Dex.

'I'm not sure.'

'Well, check it out,' she says. 'We don't mind, do we?'

Julian shrugs. 'Not at all.'

I can't resist. I remove my phone from my purse and listen to the message. It's only Marcus. He says he knows it's late but wondered what I was up to.

'Marcus,' I say, unable to hide my disappointment.

Hillary reminds Julian of who Marcus is – the guy from our house. He nods, says of course he remembers him.

'Why don't you call him. Ask him to come over,' she says. 'We'll order another bottle of wine.'

She is sweet to offer, but I can tell that she is ready for the shared part of the evening to be over. And I don't want more charity. I say no, I'm tired, it has been a wonderful dinner but I should really get home. Julian makes eye contact with our waitress and asks for our check with a scribbling flourish in the air.

When we leave the restaurant, Hillary asks me if I'm going to take a cab. I tell her no, I think I'll walk.

'Forty-some blocks?'

'It's a nice evening.'

We say goodbye on Twenty-seventh and Lexington. Julian kisses my cheek. He is about my height, a full two inches shorter than Hillary. I'm surprised Darcy failed to mention this. I tell Julian it was a pleasure to meet him. He says likewise, and looks forward to seeing me in Montauk. I hug Hillary and give her an excited smile to let her know I wholeheartedly approve of her new beau. As I turn for home, I realize that although I am truly happy for Hillary, her fledgling relationship makes me feel even emptier, more alone.

The cozy foursome is likely leaving the theater now, headed to a nice dinner out, strolling the avenues, laughing and singing the catchiest tunes from the show. Resentment fills me up. How can he leave me out in the cold like this? He must know I am spending every minute thinking about him, wondering what is going on. If I had the dice with me now, I would throw them in a gutter.

I continue on toward Third, checking my watch. It is just after ten and suddenly I don't want to go home. I consider calling Marcus back, but worry that it would be unfair, and I'd only be using him to get over Dex. But I am so miserable and angry that I dial Marcus's number anyway.

He answers on the first ring.

'What are you doing?' I ask.

'Hey! You got my message?'

'Yeah, I did. I was at dinner. I'm in your neighborhood. You want to meet me for a drink?'

'I'd love to. Where are you?'

I tell him Twenty-seventh and Third.

'Right there at Rodeo Bar?'

I look up. He has the correct coordinates. 'Yeah, it's right across the street.'

'Well, go in and get me a Pete's Summer Brew, would ya? I'll be right over.'

His voice is animated and cheerful and it makes me smile. I tell him I'll be at the bar waiting for him with his Pete's.

Rodeo Bar is as hillbilly as it gets in Manhattan. Old

license plates frame the bar and a huge stuffed bison hangs from the ceiling. Peanut shells litter the floor.

'Hey, good-lookin',' I hear Marcus ask behind me. 'This seat taken?'

I laugh and tell him no, he is welcome to it. 'Here's your beer.'

'And it's still cold,' he says, taking a long drink. 'Thanks.'

'You're very welcome.'

'So where were you?'

'I Trulli.'

He nods to say he knows the place. 'Nice. Were you on a date?' he asks, with feigned jealousy. He lifts his fist as if he's about to become violent toward the guy who infringed on his territory.

I laugh. 'No. I was with Hillary and Julian, her new boyfriend. You met him last weekend, right?'

'Oh, yeah. That dude Hillary picked up on the beach.'

I laugh again. 'Something like that.'

'She did. For real. It was a strong move.'

'Hillary is more like a guy than a girl in a lot of ways,' I say, thinking that I could never approach a stranger on the beach like that.

'Yeah,' he says. 'It's great, really. I'm still waiting for you to be aggressive with me.'

I smile. 'Oh, really?'

'Yes, really.' He smiles, looking right at me.

'So,' I say.

'So.' He moves his arm against mine.

'I'm pasty,' I say, comparing our skin tones.

'I like pale,' he says. 'It's feminine.'

'So let me get this straight,' I say, 'you like aggressive women who look feminine?'

He snaps his fingers in the air and points at me. 'You got it. Can you deliver?'

I laugh and sip my beer, wonder if Marcus will kiss me tonight. If he does, I might kiss him back. I might even enjoy it. *If you can't be with the one you love . . .*

We finish our beers. I say I am tired of country music and ask Marcus if he is ready to go. He says sure, do I want to go to another bar? There are plenty of good ones in the neighborhood. Have I been to Aubette? It's only a few blocks away.

'Yeah. It's on the same block as I Trulli, right?'

'Yeah. I've only been there on week nights so I don't know if it will be any good. But they have these killer apple martinis that would be right up your alley. You want to go?'

I laugh. How does he know what is up my alley? Dex is up my alley. 'Sure. Let's go.'

We walk quickly to Aubette, past the musclebound doorman clad in black at the entrance. We move inside. The crowd is hard to pinpoint – there is a bridge-and-tunnel element with a dash of Euro wannabes. I follow Marcus toward the cigar bar in the back and sit next to him on a buttoned leather couch with high arms. It is cozy, but would be cozier with Dex. I force him from my mind.

'What do you want?'

'An apple martini.' I can feel the red wine and beers moving toward my head. A martini probably isn't a good idea, but I don't care.

261

'You won't be sorry. Be right back.'

He returns with my apple martini and a glass of Scotch for himself.

'How is it?' he asks, after I take a sip.

'It's good.'

'Yeah. Tastes just like a jolly rancher, doesn't it?'

I take another sip. 'Yeah. It does. Want a taste?'

He sips from my glass and then licks his lips and looks at me. It is an invitation. For a second, in my semidrunk state, I am confused, unsure what to do next. I think of Dex. He hasn't broken off the engagement yet. He might never. I can kiss Marcus in the meantime. I must protect my heart. And something tells me that Marcus wouldn't mind being used in this manner. I lean toward him, initiate a kiss.

'Wow.' He grins. 'Didn't see that coming.'

I kiss him again.

'Or that,' he says.

I wonder if he will tell Dex. Part of me hopes he will. I kiss him a third time and add a little tongue for good measure. We talk some more. I am buzzed and vaguely attracted to him. He has nice forearms, with just the right amount of hair. We kiss several more times and it feels good, but nothing stirs inside me. And every time our lips touch, I miss Dexter a little bit more.

We finally leave Aubette and stand awkwardly in the street. A cab sails down Twenty-seventh toward Lex. Marcus doesn't stop me from hailing it, doesn't ask me to go back to his place. I am relieved, because I think I might have said yes. And that would be a mistake. It would only be the apple martini talking – that and a growing resentment in my chest that here I am, six days postroll, playing third wheel at a romantic dinner and kissing the wrong guy in a windowless lounge filled with cigar smoke.

SIXTEEN

Kissing Marcus is what I need to give Dex more time. The logic is convoluted, but I feel that the small act of betrayal puts Dex and me on equal footing, at least in the short run. He is engaged; I kissed his friend.

Hillary doesn't buy the rationale. She is beside herself, telling me to cut it off. No more. Enough.

'Just a little more time,' I say. 'It's still only July. We're only in July.'

She looks at me skeptically.

'Come on, Hill,' I say. 'Patience is a virtue . . . Good things come to those who wait . . . Time cures all things.'

'Uh-huh,' she says. 'How about "No time like the present"? Ever heard that one?'

'I'll say something soon. I will.'

'Okay. Because you really can't put this off any longer. You need to nail him down,' she says. 'Move on with your life one way or the other. This waiting around stuff just isn't good for you, Rach. I'm seriously worried about you . . .'

'I know. I'll say something,' I tell her. 'You have to remember that I've only seen him one time since our weekend together. And that was late one night after work. He fell asleep on my couch.'

'Well,' she says knowingly.

'Well *what*?'

'Well, isn't that somewhat telling?'

I know what she is implying. That if Dex loved me enough, he'd make more time for me. That I have lost momentum since July Fourth.

'No, actually it's *not* telling,' I say defensively. 'Work has been crazy for both of us. Les is on a rampage. You know that. We've literally had no time to see each other.'

'All right,' she says. 'But I'm giving him one more week. Then no more excuses.'

'Two more weeks,' I negotiate, and then explain that only a very shallow person would find it so incredibly easy to cancel an engagement. That the situation is vastly more complicated than she is acknowledging. That Dex would not string me along for the hell of it. That he values our friendship, at the very least. That he also values my friendship with Darcy. That he has integrity. That he told me he loved me. And meant it. I pull out all the stops, trying to convince myself along the way.

'All right then,' she says. 'Two weeks. Absolute max.'

I smile and nod, thinking that two weeks should just about do it. One way or the other.

In the meantime, I must face another hurdle: Darcy's shower-bachelorette party. It has been on the calendar forever – the third Saturday in July – but for obvious reasons I have yet to plan the evening. Claire calls that afternoon to press me on details. 'Should we go to the Hamptons or stay in the city?'

'I don't know. What do you think?' I am distracted, noticing that my secretary put two c's in 'recommend' on a fax cover sheet that I failed to proofread. If Les sees it, he will go postal.

'It depends on what Darcy wants,' Claire says.

'Right,' I say.

'*So*? What does she want to do?' Claire asks, in a tone that says, 'You should know this. You are the maid of honor.'

I admit that I'm not sure.

'Let's conference her in and find out,' Claire suggests in her sorority social chair voice. She puts me on hold and returns with Darcy on the line.

We present Darcy with her option: Manhattan or Hamptons. Claire outlines the pros and cons of each and assures her that either way it is going to be the best bachelorette party ever.

Darcy says she doesn't care. Both options sound great. She is subdued. Something is wrong. Maybe there is trouble brewing at home, a visible crack emerging in their relationship. Maybe Dex said something to her. I feel a surge of hope which is followed by a larger dose of guilt. How can I so easily root for my friend's unhappiness?

'You don't care?' Claire asks. 'That's a first.'

'You guys decide. I'm fine either way.'

'What's Dex doing?' Claire asks. Of course, I am wondering the same thing.

'I'm not sure,' Darcy says. 'He mentioned going to the Hamptons to golf.'

'Well, if he does that, we should stay in the city. You

don't want him around for your big night, do you?' Claire asks.

'No,' Darcy says. 'I guess not.'

Something is definitely wrong. She does not sound the slightest bit excited about a night in her honor. My instinct to soothe her kicks in. 'Claire and I will put it together and let you know where to show up,' I say. 'Does that sound good to you?'

'Yeah. That's fine.' Her voice is flat.

'Is everything all right?' Claire asks.

'Yeah. I'm just a little tired.'

'Okay. We'll work on this, Darce. It's going to be a great party,' I say.

We all say goodbye and hang up. Claire calls me right back. 'What is wrong with her? She sounds upset.'

'I don't know.'

'You think she's mad at us because we don't have this planned yet? It is pretty slack of us,' Claire says, sounding worried. It is a scary thing to have Darcy mad at you.

'No. That can't be it. She knows we told everyone about the date weeks ago . . . Everyone will be there. It's just a matter of nailing down final plans. I'll talk to her,' I say.

I hang up with Claire and call Darcy back. She answers, her voice lifeless.

'You sure you're okay?' I ask, utterly conflicted as I wait for her answer.

'I'm fine. Just tired . . . Maybe a little down.'

'Why? How was your weekend?' I ask tentatively.

'It was okay.'

'Did you have fun with Dex's father?'

'Yeah. He's nice,' she says.

'Do you like his stepmother?'

'She's okay. She can be a pain in the ass though.'

'What did she do?'

'Well, for example, she kept complaining about how cold she was at the theater. You should have heard her carrying on and on during the whole intermission, even after Mr. Thaler gave her his jacket. Dex and I were like, well, that's what you get for wearing a skimpy dress.'

Dex and I were like . . . My stomach drops. I hope I'm not in for a lifetime of those words.

'But overall the weekend was okay?' I probe, pressing the phone against my ear.

'Yeah. It was okay.'

'Then why are you down?'

'Oh, I don't know. I think it's just PMS. I'll be fine.'

Ordinarily I would try and wheedle Darcy out of her mood, find a way to perk her up, but instead I just say, 'Well, I better go. Got some party planning to do.'

She giggles. 'Yeah. You sure do. Make it a good one.'

'Okay,' I say, knowing that I will let Claire do the bulk of organizing. She will be happy to undertake the project. I know she likes pretending that she is more important to Darcy than I am, that she would have been named maid of honor but for the fact that I've known Darcy longer. She is probably right. The major thing Darcy and I have in common is the past. The past and Dex.

*

The rest of the week passes quickly. I don't see Dex, but only because he is in Dallas on a business trip. I try to convince Hillary that his deadline should be extended by three days because he can't really do anything about his situation while in Texas (although Dex and I do manage to log over four hours of phone time). She tells me that, if anything, the time away should give him the chance to really sort through his feelings and come up with a plan of action. I tell her I'm sure that's what he's doing.

On Friday morning, only hours after Dex arrives back in New York, he calls and suggests we meet for lunch before he heads out to the Hamptons. We arrange to meet at the Pick A Bagel near my apartment, to avoid the Midtown lunch crowds. I feel nervous as I take the uptown subway. I have not seen him in over a week – not since I kissed Marcus. I know that kissing Marcus was not a significant event (apparently it wasn't significant to him either as we have barely talked since), yet I feel somewhat strange when I kiss Dex hello. Not quite guilty, just reticent.

'I've missed you *so* much,' Dex says, shaking his head. 'I kept hoping you'd fly down to Dallas and surprise me.'

I laugh because the thought had actually occurred to me. 'I missed you too,' I say, feeling myself relax.

We stand there on the corner, grinning like crazy at each other, before moving inside the bagel shop. The place is jammed full of people, which gives us an excuse to touch. His fingers brush mine, the sides of our legs graze, his hand rests on my back as he guides me forward in line. I am basking in being near Dex, too distracted to order. We let three people

269

go in front of us before we both decide on egg salad sandwiches to go. We pay for the bagels and two Snapple lemon iced teas and then walk briskly toward my apartment. I tell myself not to get too swept up in emotion when we are finally alone. I really need to bring up Darcy before her bachelorette festivities get under way. I must do this over our egg salad. Unless of course he does it first.

Just as we are approaching my building, I spot Claire descending upon us a half block away. I hear Dex curse under his breath, just as I see a look of confusion on Claire's face. There is no time to consult Dex and formulate a story. Five steps later, she is upon us. We are cold busted.

'Hi, Claire!' Dex says robustly.

'What are you two doing here?' She switches her mustard-colored Prada bag from one shoulder to the other and smiles a bewildered smile.

I laugh nervously. 'What are *you* doing here?' I ask. It is a feeble attempt to buy a few seconds. I am terrible under pressure, an absolute disaster. I should not be a litigator, at least not the kind who might ever see the light of a courtroom. I am better suited to my big boxes of documents in overair-conditioned conference rooms.

'I left work early today to get ready for the party tomorrow. I was just at Kate's Paperie buying wrapping paper and a card for Darcy.' She glances at our brown paper bags. I am carrying our Snapples; Dex has the sandwiches. 'Are you having lunch?'

'No,' Dex says. He is perfectly composed. 'Well, yes, we just bought lunch. But I'm headed to my car – about to leave for the Hamptons.'

270

'Oh,' she says, but is still not satisfied. Luckily she keeps her eyes on Dex. I have more faith in him than in myself.

'I had to give Rachel something to give to Darcy,' Dex says.

She cocks her head to the side. 'What's that?'

I don't think she's suspicious; she simply does not consider that what we are doing may not be her business. In her eyes, she is in the inner Darcy circle, privy to any information that concerns her friend. And Dex and I most certainly concern Darcy.

'A note,' Dex says. 'A little something I want Darcy to have before her wild and crazy night on the town.'

'Oh.' Claire smiles, clearly not wondering why Dex couldn't just leave the note in their apartment, why he would need to designate me as his messenger. 'Well, it is going to be wild and crazy. Count on that.'

'I can only imagine . . .' Dex says.

'So, Rachel, are you taking the afternoon off then?'

I stammer and stutter and say no, yes, I'm not sure, maybe.

'Oh, screw work. Just come with me and run my last-minute errands for the party. I'm on my way to Lingerie on Lex to get a few extra things,' she says. We have designated tomorrow evening a hybrid lingerie shower-bachelorette party. 'Please come?'

'All right. Sure. I just need to run up and change my clothes and make one phone call. I'll meet you in fifteen?'

'Great!' Claire says.

I wait for her to leave first, hoping that I can have a

271

moment alone with Dex, but she is firmly rooted to the sidewalk. After a few seconds, Dex gives up and tells us goodbye. I am careful not to look at him as he leaves.

'All right then,' I say to Claire. 'See you in a few.'

I walk home in a panic, telling myself we are fine, that surely Claire doesn't suspect such a monumental betrayal. Dex calls just as I close my apartment door. I answer the phone, my hands shaking.

'Hey,' Dex says. 'Can you believe that?'

'Omigod,' I say. 'I feel like I'm going to faint. Where are you?'

'Around the corner. In the car . . . Think we're okay?'

'I hope so,' I say, feeling my pulse slowly return to normal. 'You were good . . . How'd you come up with that excuse so quickly?'

'I don't know. She bought it, didn't she?'

'Seemed to . . . but what are we going to do about the note?'

'I'm writing one now . . . Shit, I have no idea what to write. This is ridiculous . . . I'm going to come up, okay?'

I tell him it's not a good idea, that I have to go meet Claire.

He sighs. 'I wanted to spend some time with you. Can't you get out of it?'

I feel myself weakening. 'Don't you think it might look suspicious if I blow her off?'

'C'mon. Just for a few minutes?'

'Okay,' I say. 'Come up. But only to give me the note. Then I really have to go meet her.'

272

He arrives at my door minutes later, handing me my sandwich and the folded note. I put them both on my coffee table next to our Snapples. We sit on my couch.

'How does stuff like that always happen in this city?' I ask.

'I know,' he says, taking my hands. He tries to kiss me, but I am still too shaken to really reciprocate. I cannot relax. It is as if Claire is still with us.

'I really should go,' I say, angry that she ruined our chance to have the big conversation, but also somehow relieved.

He keeps kissing me, as he removes my suit jacket and rubs my shoulder.

'Dex!'

'What?'

'I *have* to go.'

'In a minute.'

'No. *Now*.'

But as he runs his fingers over my collarbone, I stop thinking about Claire. Moments later we are making love.

My cell phone rings immediately afterward. I jump. 'Oh shit. That's gotta be Claire. I *really* have to go,' I say, sitting up.

'But I wanted to talk about this weekend,' he says.

'What about it?' I ask, avoiding his gaze as I button my shirt.

'Well, it's just that . . . I'm really sorry about this bachelorette party and everything . . .'

I interrupt him. 'I know, Dex.'

273

'Something has to be done soon. I just haven't had a free moment. I haven't had a chance . . . But I want you to know that I think about it – and you – all the time. I mean, *all* the time . . .' His expression is sincere, tortured. He waits for me to speak.

This is my opening. Words form in my head, they are right on my tongue, but I say none of them, reasoning that this is not the moment to delve. We don't have enough time for a real conversation. I reassure myself that I'm not a coward, I'm just being patient. I want to wait for the right moment to discuss the destruction of my best friend. So I give him and myself an out. 'I know, Dex,' I say again. 'Let's talk next week, okay?'

He nods somberly and hugs me hard.

After he leaves, I call Claire and tell her that I got stuck on a work call but will be right over. I finish dressing, down my Snapple, and put my egg sandwich in the refrigerator. I walk to the door as I eye the folded note. I can't help myself. I go back, unfold it, read it:

DARCY,
JUST WANTED YOU TO HAVE A LITTLE SOMETHING FROM
ME BEFORE YOUR BIG NIGHT OUT. I HOPE YOU HAVE A
GREAT TIME WITH YOUR FRIENDS.
LOVE, DEXTER

Why did he have to insert the word 'love'? I comfort myself by thinking that he didn't just make love to her, and we will talk next week, still within Hillary's deadline. Then I scurry off to meet Claire, to help her prepare for Darcy's big weekend.

The whole situation is completely out of control, the stuff that happens to other people. Not to people like me.

The shower bachelorette party is agony from start to finish, for the obvious reasons, and also because I have nothing in common with Darcy's PR friends, all of whom are materialistic, shallow, bitchy egomaniacs. Claire is the best of the lot, which is scary. I tell myself to smile and suck it up. It is only one evening.

We meet at Claire's first to give Darcy her lingerie, an arsenal of black lace and red silk that I simply cannot compete against. If Darcy decides to wear any of this stuff before the wedding – particularly a La Perla garter with fishnet stockings – I am dead. Unless she only debuts my gift, a long ivory nightgown with a high neckline, something that Caroline Ingalls might have worn on *Little House on the Prairie*. It screams sweet and wholesome, in contrast to the other sultry, skimpy gifts that scream, 'Bend me over a chair and bust out the whipped cream.' Darcy pretends to like my gift, as I catch a knowing glance between Claire and Jocelyn, an Uma Thurman lookalike. For one paranoid second, I believe that Claire suspects the truth after our chance meeting yesterday and has shared her suspicions with Jocelyn. But then I just chalk it up to this sentiment: *Darcy's dowdy friend Rachel strikes again. How can she be the maid of honor when she doesn't even know how to give a proper piece of lingerie?*

After the shower segment of the evening, we cab it to Churrascaria Plataforma, an all-you-can-eat Brazilian rotisserie in the Theater District, where waiters bring you an endless servings of skewered meat. It is an amusing choice for a bunch of paper-thin women, half of whom are vegetarians and subsist on celery and cigarettes. Our group parades proudly into the restaurant, fetching plenty of stares from a predominantly male patronage. After a painful round of overpriced cocktails (put on my credit card) we are seated at a long table in the center of the restaurant where the PR girls continue to work the room, pretending to be oblivious to the attention they are garnering from all angles.

I watch a nearby table of women in conservative, Ann Taylor attire eye our group with a strange mix of envy and condescension. I make a bet with myself that before the evening is over the Ann Taylor women will complain to their waiter that our table is being too loud. Our waiter will give us a saccharine suggestion that we bring the volume down just a tad. Then our table will get all huffy and declare the Ann Taylor women a bunch of fat losers. *I am seated at the wrong table*, I think, as Claire and I flank Darcy upon her command. She is still wearing a little veil constructed out of the ribbons and bows from her gifts, happy to be conspicuous, the hottest girl at a table full of gorgeous women. Except for me, that is. I pretend to care about the flimsy conversation swirling about me as I sip my sangria and smile, smile.

After dinner, we make our way to Float, a Midtown dance club complete with velvet ropes and self-important bouncers. Of course we are on a VIP list – compliments of Claire – and are able to power our way past the long line of nobodies (Darcy's description). The evening follows the stale, silly script for the typical twenty-something bachelorette party. Which would be okay, I guess, except for the fact that most of us are no longer twenty-somethings. We are too old for the shrieking and the shots and the wild dancing with any guy self-confident (or self-destructive) enough to penetrate our group of nine women. And Darcy is too old for the scavenger list that Claire has prepared: find red-haired boy to buy her a sex-on-the-beach, dance with a man over fifty (imagine this species who still frequents dance clubs), kiss a guy with a tattoo or body piercing.

The whole event is overplayed and unsophisticated, but Darcy shines. She is on the dance floor, glistening, her hair curling slightly from perspiration. Her tanned, flat stomach shows between her low-slung pants and halter top. Her cheeks are rosy, dewy. Everyone wants to talk to the bride-to-be. Single girls ask wistfully what her dress looks like, and more than one guy tells her she should reconsider the marriage, or at the very least have one final fling. I dance on the outskirts of the group, biding my time.

When the night is finally over, I am exhausted, sober, and five hundred bucks poorer. We file out of the club as Darcy turns to me and says that she wants to sleep over at my place, just the two of us, like old times. She is so thrilled with the idea that I cannot refuse. I smile. She whispers in my ear that she wants to shake Claire, that it won't be the same if she comes along. It reminds me of high school and how Darcy would decide who she wanted to include and exclude.

277

Annalise and I seldom had a say and often could not figure out why someone failed to make the cut.

We hail a cab as Darcy thanks Claire, tells her the evening was a blast, and says to me loudly, with a nudge, 'Why don't we share a cab back uptown? I'll drop you off first.'

I say sure, and we head up to my apartment.

José is on duty. He is happy to see Darcy, who always flirts with him. 'Where you been, girl?' he asks. 'You don't visit me no more.'

'Planning my wedding,' she says in her beguiling way. She points to her now crumpled veil that she is clutching like a precious souvenir.

'Aww. Say it ain't so! You gettin' maah-ried?'

I clench my teeth and hit the up button on the elevator.

'Yeah,' she says, cocking her head to the side. 'Why, do you think I shouldn't?'

José laughs, showing all his teeth. 'Hell, no. Don't do it!' Even my doorman wants her. 'Blow that guy off,' he says.

Clearly he hasn't put the pieces of this puzzle together.

Darcy takes his hand in hers and twirls herself around. She finishes the move with a hip-to-hip bump.

'C'mon, Darce,' I say, already in the elevator, holding the door-open button with my thumb. 'I'm tired.'

She twirls one last time and then joins me in the elevator.

On the ride up, she waves and blows kisses into the security camera, just in case José is watching.

When we get into my apartment, I immediately turn down the volume on my answering machine, and switch off my cell phone in case Dex calls. Then I change into shorts and a T-shirt and give Darcy clothes to wear.

'Can I have your Naperville High shirt instead? So it will feel like old times.'

I tell her that it is in the wash, and she will have to make do with my '1989 Indy 500' T-shirt. She says it is good enough, as it reminds her of home too.

I brush my teeth, floss, and wash my face as she sits on the edge of my tub and talks to me about the party, how much fun it was. We trade places. Darcy washes her face and then asks if she can use my toothbrush. I say yes even though I think it's disgusting to share with anyone. Even Dex. Okay, maybe not Dex, but anyone else. Through a mouthful of toothpaste, she remarks that she is not drunk, or even very buzzed, which is surprising considering the amount of alcohol we consumed. I tell her it must be all the meat we ate.

She spits into the sink. 'Ugh. Don't remind me. I probably gained five pounds tonight.'

'No way. Think of how much you burned off dancing and sweating.'

'Good point!' She rinses her mouth, splashing water everywhere, before she leaves the bathroom.

'Are you all ready for bed?' I ask, wiping up her mess with a towel.

She turns and watches me, unapologetic. 'No. I want to stay up and talk.'

'Can we at least get in bed and talk?'

'If we keep the light on. Otherwise you'll fall asleep.'

'All right,' I say.

We get in bed. Darcy is closer to the window, on Dexter's side of the bed. Thank goodness I changed my sheets this morning.

We are facing each other, our bent knees touching.

'What should we discuss first?' she asks.

'You choose.'

I brace myself for wedding talk, but instead she starts a long gossip session about the girls at the party, what everyone wore, Tracy's new, short haircut, Jocelyn's struggle with bulimia, Claire's incessant name-dropping.

We talk about Hillary not showing up for her party. Of course, Darcy is red-hot mad about that. 'Even if she is in love, she should have blown off Julian for one night.'

Of course, I can't tell her that the real reason for Hillary's boycott has nothing to do with a new boyfriend.

Then we are on to Ethan. She wants to know if he's gay. She is always speculating about this, proffering flimsy bits of evidence: he played four square with the girls in grade school, he took home ec in high school instead of industrial arts, he has a lot of women friends, he dresses well, and he hasn't dated anyone since Brandi. I tell her no, that I am almost completely certain that he's not gay.

'How do you know?'

'I just don't think he is.'

'There's nothing wrong with it if he is,' Darcy says.

'I know that, Darce. I just don't think he is gay.'

'Bisexual?'

'No.'

'So you really don't think he's ever made out with

another guy?'

'No!' I say.

'I have trouble picturing Ethan touching some guy's penis, too.'

'Enough,' I say.

'Okay. Fine. What is your latest analysis on Marcus?'

'He's growing on me,' I say, for added insurance – just in case she has the slightest intuition about my feelings for Dex.

'He is? Since when?'

'I kissed him on Saturday night,' I say, and instantly regret it. She will tell Dex.

'You did? I thought you went out with Hillary and Julian on Saturday night.'

'I did. But I met up with Marcus afterward . . . for a few drinks. It was no big deal, really.'

'Did you go back to his place?'

'No. Nothing like that.'

'So where did you kiss him?'

'At Aubette.'

'And that was it? You only kissed?'

'Yeah. What do you think, we had sex at Aubette? Jeez.'

'Well, this is noteworthy . . . I thought things had sort of tapered off with you two. So can you see yourself marrying him?'

I laugh. This is classic Darcy – taking a little bit of information and running like crazy with it.

'Why are you laughing? Is he not marriage material?'

'I don't know. Maybe . . . Now can we please turn out the light? My eyes hurt.'

281

She says okay, but gives me a look of warning to say it's not yet time for sleep.

I turn off my bedside lamp, and as soon as we are in the dark, she brings up Dex and his note. She had been fairly dismissive of it when I gave it to her at the start of her party, but now she calls him thoughtful.

'Hmm-mmm,' I say.

A long silence follows. Then she says, 'Things have been sort of weird with us lately.'

My pulse quickens. 'Really?'

'We haven't had sex in a long time.'

'How long?' I ask, crossing my fingers under the sheets.

She tells me the answer I want. Since before the Fourth.

'Really?' My palms are sweaty.

'Yeah. Is that a bad sign?'

'I don't know . . . How often did you have sex before?' I ask, grateful for the dark.

'Before what?'

Before he told me that he loves me. 'Before the Fourth.'

'It comes and goes. But when things are going well we have sex every day. Sometimes twice a day.'

I force the sickening images out of my head, struggling to find something to say. 'Maybe it's the pressure of the wedding?'

'Yeah . . .' she says.

And maybe it's because he's having an affair with me. I have a pang of guilt, which increases tenfold when she switches topics again and asks out of the blue, 'Can you believe how long we've been friends?'

'I know it's been a long time . . . Think of all the

sleepovers we've had. How many sleepovers would you say we've had?'

'I'm not good at estimating things . . . A thousand?'

'That's probably close,' I say.

'It's been a while since we've had one,' she says.

My eyes have adjusted to the dark so I can vaguely see her now. With her face freshly scrubbed and her hair pulled back into a ponytail, she looks like a teenager. We could be in her bed back in high school, giggling and whispering, with Annalise snoring softly beside my bed in her Garfield sleeping bag. Darcy always let Annalise fall asleep. I think she almost hoped she would. I know I sometimes did.

'You wanna play twenty questions?' I ask. It was one of our favorite games growing up.

'Yeah. Yeah. You go first.'

'Okay. I got one.'

'Same rules?'

'Same rules.'

Our rules were simple: you must choose a person (instated after Annalise tried to do neighborhood pets), someone we knew personally (no celebrities, dead or living), and you must ask yes-no questions.

'From high school?' she asks.

'Yes.'

'Male?'

'No.'

'Our graduating class?'

'No.'

'Class above us or below us?'

'That's two questions.'

'No, it's a compound,' she says. 'If the answer's yes, I still have to break it down and use another question. Remember?'

'Okay, you're right,' I say, remembering that nuance. 'The answer is no.'

'Student?'

'No. That's five questions. Fifteen to go.'

Darcy says she knows she's on five, she's counting. 'Teacher we both had?'

'No,' I say, six fingers hiding under the covers. Darcy has been known to 'miscount' during this game.

'Teacher you had?'

'No.'

'Teacher I had?'

'No.'

'Guidance counselor?'

'No.'

'A dean?'

'That's ten. No.'

'Other staff?'

'Yes.'

'Janitor?'

'No.'

'The nark?'

'No.' I smile, thinking about the time the nark busted Darcy leaving school to go to Subway with Blaine at lunch. Darcy told him to get a real job as he escorted them to the dean's office. 'What are you, thirty? Isn't it time you left high school?' The comment earned her an extra pair of demerits.

'Ohh! I think I got it!' She starts giggling uncontrollably. 'Is she a lunch lady?'

I laugh. 'Uh-huh.'

'It's June!'

'Yep! You got it.'

June was a high school icon. She was about eighty years old, four feet tall, and massively wrinkled from years of heavy smoking. And her main claim to fame was that she once lost a fake nail in Tommy Baxter's lasagna. Tommy ceremoniously marched back to the lunch line and returned the nail to June. 'I believe this belongs to you, June?' June grinned, wiped the sauce and cheese off the nail, and stuck it back on her finger. Everybody cheered and clapped and chanted, 'Go, June! Go, June!' Other than reapplying her nail, I'm not sure what she did to earn the respect of our student body. I think it was more that somebody in the popular crowd just decided along the way that it was cool to like June. Maybe it had even been Darcy. She had that sort of power.

Darcy laughs. 'Good ol' June! I wonder if she's dead yet.'

'Nah. I'm sure she's still there, asking kids in her raspy voice if they want marinara or meat sauce on their rigatoni.'

When she finally stops laughing, she says, 'Aww. This feels just like a sleepover from way back.'

'Yeah. It does,' I say, as a wave of fondness for Darcy washes over me.

'We had fun as kids, didn't we?'

'Yeah. We did.'

Darcy starts laughing again.

'What?' I ask.

285

'Do you remember the time we spent the night at Annalise's house and hanged her sister's Barbie dolls?'

I crack up, picturing the Barbies, tied with yarn around their necks, dangling from the doorways. Annalise's little sister cried hysterically to her parents, who promptly met with the two other sets of parents to come up with a suitable punishment. We could not play together for a week, which is a long time in the summer. 'That was sort of sick now that I think about it,' I say.

'I know! And remember how Annalise kept saying it wasn't her idea?'

'Yeah. Nothing ever was her idea,' I say.

'We always thought of the cool stuff. She was a big-time coat-tailer.'

'Yeah,' I say.

I am quiet, thinking about our childhood. I remember the day we were dropped off at the mall with our paltry sixth-grade savings, racing to the Piercing Pagoda to purchase our 'best friend' necklaces, a heart inscribed with the two words, split down the middle, each side of the charm hanging from a gold-plated chain. Darcy took the 'Be Fri' half, I got the 'st end' half. Of course, we were so worried about Annalise's feelings that we only wore the necklaces in secret, under our turtlenecks, or nightgowns. But I remember the thrill of tucking my half of the heart inside my shirt, against my skin. I had a best friend. There was such security in that, such a sense of identity and belonging.

I still have my necklace buried in my jewelry box, the gold plate turned green with grit and time, but now also tarnished

with something impossible to remove. I am suddenly overcome with profound sadness for those two little girls. For
what is now gone between them. For what might never be
regained, no matter what happens with Dex.

'Talk more,' Darcy says sweetly. There is no trace of the
brash, self-centered bride-to-be whom I have come to resent,
even dislike. 'Please don't sleep yet. We never get to hang out
like this anymore. I miss it.'

'Me too,' I say, meaning it.

I ask her if she remembers the day we bought our best
friend necklaces.

'Yes. But remind me about the details,' she says in her
charming way.

Darcy loves to hear my accounts of our childhood,
always praising my more complete memory. I tell her the
story of the necklaces, give her the longest version possible.
After I am finished, I whisper, 'Are you asleep?'

No answer.

As I listen to Darcy breathing in the dark beside me, I
wonder how we got to this. How we could be in love with the
same person. How I could be sabotaging my best friend's
engagement. In the final seconds before sleep, I wish I could
go back and undo everything, give those little girls another
chance.

SEVENTEEN

The next morning, I am awakened by the sound of Darcy rummaging through my medicine cabinet. I listen to her bang around as I try to piece together my dreams from the night before, a series of incoherent vignettes featuring a wide cast of the usual characters – my parents, Darcy, Dex, Marcus, even Les. The plot is unclear, but I recall a fair amount of running and hiding. I almost kissed Dex a dozen times, but never did. I can't even be satisfied in my dreams. Darcy emerges from the bathroom with a happy face.

'I'm not hungover at all,' she announces. 'Although I took some Advil just in case. You're out. Hope you didn't need any?'

'I'm fine,' I say.

'Not bad for the day after a bachelorette party! What do you want to do today? Can we spend the day together? Just doing nothing. Like old times.'

'Okay,' I say, somewhat reluctantly.

'Awesome!' She walks toward my kitchen, starts rooting around. 'Do you have any cereal?'

'No, I'm out. You want to go to EJ's?'

She says no, that she wants to eat sugar cereal right here in my apartment, that she wants it to feel just like old times, no New York brunch scene. She opens my refrigerator and surveys the contents. 'Man, you're out of everything. I'll just run out and get some coffee and some essentials.'

'Should we really drink coffee?' I ask her.

'Why wouldn't we?'

'Because I thought we were going to be authentic. We didn't drink coffee when we were in high school.'

She thinks for a second, missing my sarcasm. 'We'll make an exception for coffee.'

'Do you want me to come with you?' I offer.

'No. That's okay. I'll be right back.'

As soon as she leaves, I check my voice mail. Dex has left me two messages – one from last night, one from this morning. In the first, he says how much he misses me. In the second, he asks if he can come over tonight. I call him back, surprised at how grateful I feel when I get voice mail. I leave him a message, telling him that Darcy is over and plans to stay for a while, so tonight won't really work out. Then I sit on my couch thinking about last night, my friendship with Darcy. Can I really do this to her? Can I continue to violate the most sacred code of female friendship? Will I be able to live with myself if I get what I want at my friend's expense? What would life be like without her? I am still thinking about it all when Darcy returns. Bulging plastic bags hang from her forearms. I take the coffees from her hands as she dramatically drops the bags to the floor and shows me the red indentations the bags made on her arms. I make a sympathetic noise until she smiles again.

'I got great stuff! Froot Loops! Root beer! Cranapple

juice! And Ben and Jerry's Chocolate Chip Cookie Dough ice cream!'

'Ice cream for breakfast?'

'No. For later!'

'Aren't you worried about your wedding weight?'

She waves her hand at me. 'Whatever. No.'

'Why not?' I ask, knowing that she will eat now and ask me later why I let her do it.

''Cause I'm just not! Don't rain on my parade! . . . Now. Let's eat Froot Loops!'

She busies herself in the kitchen finding bowls, spoons, napkins. She brings them out to the coffee table. She is in her giddy, high-energy mode.

'Wouldn't you rather eat over there?' I say, pointing to my little round table.

'No. I want it to be just like my house after a sleepover. We always ate in front of the TV. Remember?' She aims the remote control at the television and flips through the channels until she finds MTV. Then she pours our cereal into bowls, carefully making sure we have the same amount. I am not in the mood for Froot Loops, but it is clear that I do not have a choice in the matter. Although I find it somewhat touching that she wants to re-create our childhood, I am also annoyed by her bossiness. *Running roughshod*, Ethan said. Maybe it is a precise description after all. And here I am, a willing participant, letting her steamroll me.

'Tell me when,' she says, pouring whole milk on my cereal. I hate whole milk.

'When,' I say, almost instantly.

She stops pouring and looks at me. 'Really? They're barely moist.'

'I know,' I say, appeasing her, 'but this is how I liked it in high school too.'

'Good point,' she says, pouring milk in her own bowl. She fills it to the brim.

I take a few bites as she stirs her cereal with her spoon, waiting for the milk to turn pink.

Dido's 'Thank You' video is on. *I want to thank you for giving me the best day of my life, oh just to be with you is having the best day of my life.*

Of course, it makes me think of Dex.

'This song,' Darcy says, still stirring. 'You know the part when she says, "I'm home at last and I'm soaking through and through, then you handed me a towel"?'

'Yeah.'

'That line totally reminds me of you.'

'Of me?' I look at her. 'I think it's supposed to be a romantic song.'

She rolls her eyes. 'Duh! I know that. Don't worry.' She takes a bite and continues to talk with her mouth full. 'I'm not dyking out or anything. I'm just saying you really are always here for me. You know, when the chips are down.'

'That's sweet.' I smile, push away the guilt, sip my coffee.

We listen to the rest of the song as Darcy noisily eats her cereal. As she finishes her last few bites, she raises the bowl to her lips, gulping the pastel milk.

'Am I being too loud?' she asks, glancing up at me.

I shake my head. 'You're fine.'

'Dex calls me the Slurper whenever I eat cereal.'

I get a pang as I always do when I glimpse a private part of their relationship – which I like to pretend does not exist. Then I realize with an even sharper pang that Dex doesn't have a nickname for me. Perhaps I am too bland to deserve one. Darcy doesn't have a bland bone in her body. No wonder it is hard to leave her. She is the type of woman who draws you in, holds your attention. Even when she is annoying, she is compelling, captivating.

Jennifer Lopez appears on the screen in all her volupt-uousness. We watch wistfully as she gyrates over a rural landscape. 'Is her butt that great?' Darcy asks.

'I'm afraid so,' I say, although I actually enjoy telling Darcy this. She even views celebrities as competition, whereas no part of me begrudges Jennifer Lopez her fantastic ass.

Darcy makes a clicking sound. 'Don't you think it's kind of fat?' she asks.

'No. It's great,' I say, knowing that both of Darcy's cheeks equals one of Jennifer's.

'Well, I think it's kind of fat . . .'

I shrug.

'Dex loves her. He thinks she's totally hot.'

New Dexter information. *Ding! Ding! Ding!* What might this mean in the equation? I am fuller-figured than Darcy, but she is darker. I decide to discard the tidbit as not particularly helpful. I mean, most guys appreciate J-Lo no matter what their type. It's like Brad Pitt for us. You might not like blond men with pretty features, but c'mon, it's Brad. You wouldn't kick him out of bed for eating crackers.

292

'Don't worry, though, I'm sure she's not that pretty in real life,' Darcy says, assuming all women are like her and need to be consoled whenever they run across a prettier woman.

'Uh-huh,' I say.

'I mean, make-up artists can work absolute wonders,' she says knowingly, as if she has been in the industry for years. She pulls the blanket down from the back of my sofa and wraps herself in it. 'I like it here.'

So does Dex.

'You cold?' I ask.

'No. I just want to be all comfy-cozy.'

We watch videos until I almost forget about Dex. As much as you can forget someone you're in love with. Then, out of the blue, during a Janet Jackson video, Darcy asks me a question I never anticipated.

'Should I marry Dexter?'

I freeze. 'Why are you asking that?'

'I don't know.'

'There must be some reason,' I say, trying to appear calm.

'Do you think I should be with someone more laid back? Like I am?'

'Dex is laid back.'

'No he's not! He's totally type A.'

'You think?' I ask. Maybe he is. I guess I just don't see him that way.

'Totally.'

I mute the television and look at her as if to say, go on, I am ready to be a really good listener. I think of putting on your 'listening cap' in elementary school, fastening the

293

imaginary strap under your chin as the boys always did. I swallow, pause, and then say, 'It concerns me that you're asking this question. What's on your mind?'

I can feel my heart thumping as I await her answer.

'I don't know . . . Sometimes the relationship just seems a bit tired. Boring. Is that a bad sign?' She looks at me plaintively.

This is my chance. I have an opening. I consider what I could say, how easily I could manipulate her. But somehow I can't do it. I am already doing the unspeakable, but at least I will be fair about it. I am conflicted out, as they say at my firm. I can't take her case.

'I really don't know, Darce. Only you and Dexter can know whether you are right for each other. But you should really examine your concerns carefully – marriage is a very serious step. Maybe you should postpone,' I say.

'Postpone the wedding?'

'Maybe.'

Darcy's bottom lip protrudes and her brow furrows. I am sure that tears are imminent, when her eyes dart over to the television. She brightens. 'Oh! I love this video! Turn it up! Turn it up!'

I unmute the television and turn up the volume. Darcy bobs up and down, doing a head and torso dance, singing a song I have never heard by some boy band. She knows every word. I watch her, marveling at her sudden transformation. I wait for her to bring up Dex again, but she does not.

I blew my chance to tell her to call the whole thing off, that Dex is all wrong for her. Why didn't I steer her in that direction, water the seed of discontent? I never play my hand right. Then again, I don't think Darcy really wants my advice. Other than to tell her everything will be all right, that she should marry Dexter. And if I won't say what she wants to hear, she will find a video to cheer her up instead.

'That song's the bomb,' Darcy says, tossing aside the blanket. She gets up and shuffles across my apartment. She surveys my bookshelf where I recently put the Altoids tin and dice.

'What are you doing?'

'Looking for your high school yearbook. Where is it?'

'Bottom shelf.'

She squats and runs her fingers over the spines, stopping at the Husky Howler. 'Oh yeah. Here it is.' She stands back up and notices the tin placed foolishly at eye level. 'Can I have one?'

'It's empty,' I say, but she has already deposited the yearbook on the foot of my bed. Her long, sculpted arm darts toward the tin. She opens the lid. 'Why do you have dice in here?'

'Um, I don't know,' I stumble, remembering how Darcy used to tell me that I should never go on a timed quiz show. She used to lord it over me, saying that if she ever got picked to be on *The Family Feud* (never mind that we aren't in the same family) she'd have to think twice before selecting me to be on her team. And no way would I get to do the bonus round at the end.

'You don't know?' she asks.

'No reason, I guess.'

She stares at me as one might look at a babbling schizo-phrenic on the subway. 'You don't know why you put dice in an Altoids tin? Okay. Whatever, weirdo.'

She removes the dice from the tin, shaking them as if she is about to roll them.

'Don't,' I say loudly. 'Put them back.'

It is not a good idea to tell her what to do. She is a child. She will want to know why she can't roll them. She will want to roll them just because I told her not to.

Sure enough: 'What are they for? I don't get it.'

'Nothing. They are just my lucky dice.'

'Lucky dice? Since when do you have lucky dice?'

'Since always.'

'Well, why do you have them in an Altoids container? You don't like cinnamon Altoids.'

'Yes I do.'

She shrugs. 'Oh.'

I study her face. She is not suspicious, but she is still holding my dice. I will run across the apartment, tackle her, and wrestle them from her before I let her re-roll them. But she just looks at them one more time and replaces them in the tin. I am not sure if they still have sixes facing up. I will check later. As long as they are not rolled again, I am okay.

She picks up my yearbook and carries it back over to the couch, flipping to the sports and intramural pages in the back. This will keep her busy for hours. She will find a thousand things to comment upon: remember this, remember that? She never tires of our high school yearbook, discussing the past and speculating about what has become of so and so who didn't show up at the reunion because either (a) he has now become a total loser or (b) the opposite phenomenon has occurred and he is so spectacularly successful that he doesn't have time to return to Indiana for a weekend (the category Darcy says I am in because, of course, I had to work that weekend and missed it). Or she plays one of her favorite games where she opens the book to a page, closes her eyes, scribbles her index finger over the page until I say stop, and whichever guy is closest to her finger will be the one I must have sex with. Those are classic Darcy games, and when our senior yearbook first came out twelve years ago they were grand fun.

'Oh, my goodness. Look at her hair! Have you ever seen such big bangs?' Darcy gasps as she scrutinizes Laura Lindell's photo. 'She looks so ridiculous. They must be a foot high!'

I nod in agreement and wait for her next prey: Richard Meek. Only she decides to give him more credit than she gave him in the twelfth grade. 'Not bad. He's sort of cute, isn't he?'

'Sort of. He has a nice smile. But remember how he spit all over you when he talked?'

'Yeah. Good point.'

Darcy flips the pages until she finally grows tired of it, casts it aside, and resumes control of the remote. She finds *When Harry Met Sally* and squeals. 'It's just starting! Yes!'

We both recline on my couch, feet to head, and watch the movie we have seen together countless times. Darcy talks out loud constantly, quoting the parts she knows. I don't shush her once. Because even though she says talking during movies irritates Dex, I don't mind. Not even when she gets the line slightly wrong, so that I can't tell what Meg Ryan is really saying. It's just Darcy. This is what she does.

And like a favorite old movie, sometimes the sameness in a friend is what you like most about her.

EIGHTEEN

The next evening Darcy calls me just as I am returning home
from work. She is hysterical. A cold, calm feeling overcomes
me. Could this be it? Has Dex told her that the wedding is
off?

'What's wrong, Darcy?' I ask. My voice sounds tight and
unnatural, my heart filled with conflict – love for Dex versus
friendship with Darcy. I brace myself for the worst, although
I'm not sure what the worst would be – losing my best friend
or the love of my life. I can't fathom either.

Darcy says something that I can't understand, something
about her ring.

'What is it, Darce? Slow down . . . What about your ring?'

'It's gone!' she sobs.

It doesn't seem possible that your heart can sink just as
you feel tremendous relief, yet that is what happens as I
register that this conversation is only about a missing piece of
jewelry. 'Where did you lose it? It's insured, right?'

I am asking the responsible-friend questions. I am being
helpful. But I sound rote. If she were any less hysterical, she
might be able to tell that I don't care a lick that her ring has
been misplaced. I tell her that she is a slob, that she probably
just put it somewhere and forgot. 'Remember the time you

thought it was gone and then found it in one of your slippers? You're always misplacing things, Darce.'

'No, it's different this time! This time it's gone! It's gone! Dex is going to kill me!' Her voice is trembling.

Maybe not, I think. Maybe this will be the opening he has been waiting for. And then I hate myself for thinking such a thing. 'Have you told him?'

'No. Not yet. He's still at work . . . What am I going to do?'

'Well, where did you lose it?'

She doesn't answer me, just keeps crying.

I repeat the question.

'I don't know.'

'Where did you see it last?' I ask. 'Did you have it at work today? Did you take it off to wash your hands?'

'No, I never take it off to wash my hands! What kind of dumbass would do that?'

I want to tell her not to snap at me, that she is the dumbass who lost her engagement ring. But I stay sympathetic, tell her that I'm sure it will turn up.

'No, it won't turn up.' More loud sobs.

'How do you know?'

''Cause I just know.'

I have run out of suggestions.

'Can I come over? I really have to talk to you,' she says.

'Yes, come right over,' I say, wondering if there is more to this than a missing ring. 'Have you eaten?'

'No,' she says. 'Can you order some wonton soup for me?'

'Sure.'

'And an egg roll?'

300

'Yes. Come over now.'

I call Tang Tang and order two wonton soups, two egg rolls, two Sprites, and one beef and broccoli. Darcy arrives at my door fifteen minutes later. She is disheveled, wearing a pair of Levi's that I recognize from high school – they still fit her perfectly – and a white tank top. She is wearing no make-up, her eyes are bloodshot, and her hair is thrown up in a sloppy ponytail, but she still manages to look pretty. I tell her to sit down and tell me everything.

'It's gone.' She shakes her head, holding up her bare left hand.

'Where do you think you lost it?' I ask calmly, recalling that I have gone through this exercise a hundred times with Darcy. I am always helping her, cleaning up her messes, trailing loyally after her in her wake of turmoil and angst.

'I didn't lose it. Somebody stole it.'

I've no idea what she means. 'Who stole it?'

'Someone.'

'How do you know?'

'Because it's gone!'

We are getting nowhere. I sigh and tell Darcy again to give me all of the facts.

She looks at me, her eyes filling with tears and her lips quivering slightly. 'Rachel . . .'

'Yes?'

'You're my best friend.' She starts to cry again, tears streaming gracefully down her glistening cheeks and falling on her lap. She has always been a pretty crier.

I nod. 'Yes.'

301

'My best friend in the world. And I have to tell you something.'

'You can tell me anything,' I say, feeling overcome with worry, suddenly sure that Dex has laid the preliminary breaking-up groundwork.

She looks at me and makes a whimpering sound. As confident as Darcy is, she can seem so pitiful and defenseless when she is down. And my instinct has always been – still is – to help her. 'Tell me, Darce,' I say gently.

'Rachel— I— I took off my ring in somebody's apartment.'

'Okay.'

'A guy's apartment.'

I feel as though I'm looking through a camera, trying to focus. Is she saying what I think she's saying?

'Rachel,' Darcy says again, this time in a whisper. 'I cheated on Dexter.'

I stare at her, unable to mask my shock.

Yes, Darcy is a flirt. Yes, she lives life on the edge. Yes, she is selfish. And yes, she loves male attention. The attributes add up and it makes sense. I should not be surprised that she would cheat. I mean, Dex is none of the above, and he is doing it. Still, I am floored. She is getting married in less than two months. She is a glowing bride-to-be with a stunning gown, the kind that you dream about when you're a little girl. And she is with Dexter. How in the world could anyone cheat on Dexter?

The five w's and one h of journalism pop into my head. I am in high school reporter mode, interviewing for the *North Star*. 'Who with?'

302

She sniffs. Her head is down. 'This guy at work.'

'When?'

'A couple of times. Today.' She rubs her eyes with her fists and looks at me sideways.

I don't know what my face is giving away. And I'm not even sure exactly how I feel. Relieved? Outraged? Disgusted? Hopeful? I haven't had time to consider the implications for Dex and me.

'And that's how you lost your ring?'

She nods. 'I went over there today after I left my apartment, on the way to work.' She swallows and then lets out a small sob. 'We hung out, you know, fooled around—'

'Did you sleep with him?'

Her ponytail jerks up and down.

'I took my ring off because . . . well, I felt too guilty wearing it while I had sex with someone else.' She blows her nose into an already soggy tissue.

'You want a fresh one?'

She nods again. I jog the few steps to the bathroom to retrieve my Kleenex box.

'Here,' I say, handing her the box.

She takes a tissue and blows her nose again loudly. 'So anyway, I took off the ring and put it on his windowsill, next to his bed.' She points to my bed in its alcove. 'He has a studio sort of like yours.'

A studio. So he's probably not an executive, which surprises me. I would have guessed that Darcy would go for the power type. An older man. I had been picturing Richard

Gere in *Pretty Woman*. I change my mental image to Matt Damon in *Good Will Hunting*.

'So we hang out, you know.' She waves her hand in the air. 'Then we get dressed and walk to the subway. Go to work.'

'Uh-huh . . .'

'So when I get to work, I realize that I forgot to put on my ring. So I call him and tell him I need to go back and get the ring. He says no problem, but that he has a meeting at three that is going to last a couple of hours. Can we meet there at seven? I tell him sure . . . So we meet back at his place at seven. And when we go in, the place is, like, totally clean. And when we left it was a total dump. And he goes, 'Shit. The cleaning lady was here.' And we go over to the windowsill and the ring is gone!' She is crying harder now. 'The bitch took it.'

'Are you sure? I can't believe someone would do that . . .'

She gives me a 'Don't be such a Pollyanna' look. 'The ring is gone, Rachel. Gone. Gone. Gone!'

'Well, can't he just call his cleaning lady and tell her he knows she took it?'

'We tried that. She doesn't speak English very well. She just kept saying that she "didn't see no ring".' Darcy imitates the maid's accent. 'I even took the phone. I told her I would give her a big, big reward if she finds it. The bitch isn't stupid. She knows that two carats are worth about twenty million dirty toilets.'

'Okay,' I say. 'But it's insured, right?'

'Yeah, it's insured. But what the hell am I going to tell Dexter?'

'I don't know. Tell him that it fell down the drain at work . . . Tell him that you took it off at the gym and somebody broke into your locker.'

She gives me a half-smile. 'I like the gym one. That's believable, right?'

'Totally.'

'I just can't believe this happened.'

That makes two of us. I can't believe that Darcy cheated on Dex with some random guy. I can't believe that I am helping Darcy cover up her affair. Does everyone cheat when they're engaged?

'Is this a full-fledged affair?' I ask.

'Not really. Just a couple of times.'

'So it's not serious?'

'I don't know. Not really. I don't know.' She shakes her head and then rests her forehead in her hands.

I wonder if Darcy's recent moodiness has anything to do with this guy. 'Are you in love with him?'

'God, no,' she says. 'It's just fun. It's nothing.'

'Are you sure you should be getting married?' I ask.

'I knew you would say something like that!' Darcy starts to cry again. 'Can't you just help me without being all pious?'

Trust me, I'm not being pious.

'I'm sorry, Darce. I'm not trying to be pious . . . I was just offering you an out if you wanted one.'

'I don't want an out. I want to get married. I just – I don't

305

know – I just panic sometimes that this is *it*. That I will never be with anyone else ever again. And so I just had this little fling. It was nothing.'

'Okay,' I say. 'All I meant was that if you are unsure of this whole marriage thing . . . I just want you to know that I fully support whatever decision—'

She interrupts me. 'There's no decision to make! I'm getting married. I love Dex.'

'Sorry,' I say. And I *am* sorry. I'm sorry that I love Dex too.

'No. *I'm* sorry, Rachel,' she says, touching my leg. 'It's been a horrible day.'

'I understand.'

'I mean, *do* you understand? Can you imagine what it is like to be weeks away from a promise that is supposed to last forever?'

Oh, poor you. Does she have any idea how many girls would kill to make a promise like that to someone like Dexter? She is looking at one of them.

' "Forever is a mighty long time",' I say, with a hint of sarcasm.

'Are you quoting a Prince song? You better not be quoting a Prince song in my time of need!'

I tell her no, although that was precisely what I had been doing.

'It *is* a long time,' she says. 'And sometimes I don't know if I can do it. I mean, I know I want to get married, but sometimes I don't know if I can go forty more years or however long it is and never feel that thrill of kissing someone new. I mean, look at Hillary. She is on cloud nine, isn't she?'

'Yeah.'

'And it's not like that with Dexter anymore. Ever. It's all just the daily grind – him going to work all the time, leaving me with all the wedding plans. We're not even married and the fun part is already so far gone.'

'Darce,' I say. 'Your relationship has evolved. It's not about the initial frenzy, the lust, the newness.'

She looks at me as if she's really paying attention, taking mental notes. I can't believe what I'm saying. I'm convincing her that her relationship is this great, special thing. I don't know why I'm doing it. Probably just nerves. I keep going. 'The thrill of the chase is always exciting. But that's not what a real, lasting, loving relationship is all about. And the initial infatuation, the "I can't keep my hands off you" routine, it fades for everyone.'

Except for Dex and me, I think. It would always be special with Dex and me.

'I know you're right,' she says. 'And I do love him.'

I know she believes what she's saying, but I'm not sure she does love him. I'm not sure she's capable of truly loving anyone but herself.

José buzzes my intercom to tell me that my food has arrived.

'Thanks. You can send him up,' I say into the speaker.

As I step into the hall to pay the delivery guy, my home phone rings. I panic. What if it is Dex? I thrust my bills at the guy and dash back inside, throw the bag on my coffee table and lift up the phone right as the answering machine is about to click on. Sure enough, it's Dex.

'Hi,' he says. 'I'm so sorry I haven't called you today. It's been a nightmare of a day . . . Roger had me—'

'It's okay,' I say, interrupting him.

'Can I come over? I wanna see you.'

'Um, no,' I say.

'I can't?'

'No . . .'

'Okay . . . Why? . . . Do you have company?' He lowers his voice.

'Yeah,' I say, trying to monitor my tone of voice for both listening parties. 'Actually I do.'

I look at Darcy. She mouths, 'Who is it?'

I ignore her.

'Okay . . . All right then . . . It's not Marcus, is it?' Dex asks.

'No . . . Darcy's here,' I say.

'Ohhh. Shit. Good thing I called first,' he whispers.

'So we'll talk tomorrow?'

'Yeah,' he says. 'Definitely.'

'Sounds good.'

'Who was that?' Darcy asks, as I hang up the phone.

'It was Ethan.'

'C'mon, was it Marcus?' she asks. 'You can tell me.'

'No, it really *was* Ethan.'

'Maybe he's calling to tell you that he's gay.'

'Uh-huh,' I say, opening our cartons of food.

As we eat our Chinese food, I ask about Dex. 'How is he doing?'

'What do you mean?'

'I mean, does he suspect that anything is going on?'

She rolls her eyes. 'No. He works too much.'

I note that she does not change my word choice of 'is going on' to 'was going on.'

'No?'

'No. He's just the same, normal old Dex.'

'Really?'

'Yes, really. Why?' She opens her Sprite, sips from the can.

'I just wondered,' I say. 'I've read that when someone is cheating, the other person usually knows it on some deep, inner level.'

She slurps wonton soup from her plastic spoon and looks at me blankly. 'I don't believe that,' she says.

'Yeah,' I say. 'I guess I don't either.'

After we finish our dinner, I hold up two fortune cookies. 'Which one do you want?'

She points to my left hand. 'That one,' she says. 'And it better be good. I can't take more bad luck.'

I feel like telling her that choosing to sleep with a co-worker and carelessly leaving your ring behind in his apartment has nothing to do with luck. I pull the plastic wrapper off the stale cookie, crack it open, and silently read my sliver of paper. 'You have much to be thankful for'.

'What's it say?' Darcy wants to know.

I tell her.

'That's a good one.'

'Yeah, but it's not a fortune. It's a statement. I hate when they pass statements off as fortunes.'

'Then pretend it says, "You *will* have much to be thankful

for,"' she says, opening her wrapper. 'Mine better say, "You will get your ring back from the Puerto Rican bitch".'

She silently reads her fortune and then laughs.

'What?'

'It says, "You have much to be thankful for" . . . That's bullshit. Mass-produced fortunes!'

Yeah, and only one of us will have much to be thankful for.

Darcy tells me that she better get going, that she has to go face the music. She tears up again as she reaches for her purse. 'Will you tell Dex for me?'

'Absolutely not. I'm not getting involved,' I say, amusing myself with the absurdity of the statement.

'What do I say again?'

'That you lost it at the gym.'

'Is there time to get a new one before the wedding?'

I tell her yes, realizing that she has not once expressed any sentimentality over *the* ring that Dexter picked for her.

'Rachel?'

'Hmm?'

'Do you think I'm a terrible person? Please don't think I'm a terrible person. I have never cheated on him before. I'm not going to do it again. I really do love Dex.'

'Okay,' I say, wondering if she will do it again.

'Do you think I'm awful?'

'No, Darcy,' I say. 'People make mistakes.'

'I know, that's what it was. A *total* mistake. I really, really regret it.'

'You did use a condom?' I ask her.

I picture the chart in health class explaining that for

310

every sexual partner you have, there are essentially dozens of others you don't even know about: everyone he slept with and so on and so on . . .

'Of course!'

'Good.' I nod. 'Call me later if you need me.'

'Thanks,' she says. 'Thank you so much for being here for me.'

'No problem.'

'Oh, and this goes without saying . . . don't tell anyone. I mean, anyone. Ethan, Hillary . . .'

But what about Dex? Can I tell Dex?

'Of course. I won't tell anyone.'

She hugs me, patting my back. 'Thanks, Rachel. I don't know what I'd do without you.'

When Darcy leaves, I formulate my answer to the obvious dilemma – to tell or not to tell. I approach it as I would an exam question, keeping emotion to the side:

At first blush, the answer seems clear: tell Dexter. I have three major reasons for this decision. First, I want him to know. It is in my best interest for him to know. If he has not already decided to call off his wedding, having this piece of knowledge likely will sway him against marrying Darcy. Second, I love Dexter, which means that I should make decisions with his best interest at heart. Thus, I want him to have a full set of facts when making a pivotal life decision. Third, morality dictates that Dex be told; I have a moral obligation to tell Dexter the truth about Darcy's actions. (This should be distinguished from a retributive point of view, although certainly Darcy deserves a sound snitching.) As a corollary, I value and respect the institution of marriage, and Darcy's infidelity certainly doesn't bode well for a long and lasting union. This third point has nothing to do with my self-interest, as the same reasoning would apply even if I weren't in love with Dex.

The logic of point three, however, seems to indicate that Darcy should also know that Dex has been unfaithful, and that I should not be hiding my actions from Darcy (because she is my friend and trusts me, and because it is wrong to be deceitful). Thus, one might argue that thinking that Dex should know the truth about Darcy is fundamentally at odds with intentionally leaving Darcy in the dark about my own misdeeds. However, this reasoning ignores an essential distinction and one that my final analysis is dependent upon: there is a difference between thinking a person should know/be told and being that messenger. Yes, I think Dex should know what Darcy has done, and (perhaps? likely?) will continue to do. But is it my place to tell? I would argue that it is not.

Furthermore, although Dex should not marry Darcy, it is not because he cheated or because she cheated. And it is not because he loves me and I love him. These things are all true but are mere symptoms of the larger problem, i.e. their flawed relationship. Darcy and Dex *are wrong for each other. The fact that both of them have cheated, although driven to do so by separate motivations (love versus a self-serving mixture of fear of commitment and lust) is just one indicator. But even if neither had cheated, the relationship would still be wrong. And if Darcy and Dex can't determine this essential truth based on their interactions, their feelings, and their years together, then it is their mistake to make and not my place to play informant.*

And I might also drop a footnote, maybe under the morality discussion, where I would address the betrayal of Darcy:

Yes, telling Darcy's secret would be wrong, but in light of my far greater betrayal, telling a secret seems hardly worth discussing. On the other hand, however, one could argue that telling the secret is worse. Sleeping with Dex has nothing to do with Darcy, per se, but telling Darcy's secret has everything to do with Darcy. Yet considering that the ultimate decision is not to tell, this point becomes moot.

So there's my answer. I think my reasoning might be a little shaky, particularly at the end, where I sort of fall apart and essentially say 'so there'. I can just see the red marks in the margin of the blue book. 'Unclear!' and 'Why is it their mistake to make? Are you punishing them for their stupidity or for their infidelity? Explain!'

313

But regardless of my flawed rationale and the knowledge that Ethan and Hillary would accuse me of being my usual passive self, I'm not saying a word about this to Dex.

NINETEEN

The next day I return home from work, pick up my dry cleaning from José, and check my mailbox to find my Time Warner cable bill, the new issue of *InStyle* magazine, and a large ivory envelope addressed in ornate calligraphy affixed with two heart stamps. I know what it is even before I flip it over and find a return address from Indianapolis.

I tell myself that a wedding can still be called off after invitations go out. This is just one more obstacle. Yes, it makes things stickier, but it is only a formality, a technicality. Still, I am dizzy and nauseated as I open the envelope and find another inner envelope. This one has my name and the two humiliating words 'and Guest'. I cast aside the RSVP card and its matching envelope as a sheet of silver tissue paper floats to the floor, sliding under my couch. I don't have the energy to retrieve it. Instead, I sit down and take a deep breath, mustering the courage to read the engraved script, as if the wording can somehow make things better or worse:

Our joy will be more complete
if you share in the marriage of our daughter
Darcy Jane
to
Mr. Dexter Thaler

I blink back tears and exhale slowly, skipping to the bottom of the invitation:

We invite you to worship with us,
witness their vows, and join us
for a reception at the Carlyle following the ceremony.
If you are unable to attend, we ask your
presence in thought and prayer.
Dr. and Mrs. Hugo Rhone
R.S.V.P.

Yes, the wording can indeed make things worse. I put the invitation on my coffee table and stare at it. I picture Mrs. Rhone dropping the envelopes off at the post office on Jefferson Street, her long, red nails patting the stack with motherly smugness. I hear her nasal voice saying 'Our joy will be more complete' and 'We ask for your presence in thought and prayer.'

I'll give her a prayer – a prayer that the marriage never happens. A prayer for a follow-up mailing to arrive at my apartment:

Dr. and Mrs. Hugo Rhone
announce that the marriage of
their daughter Darcy to
Mr. Dexter Thaler
will not take place.

Now that is some wording that I can appreciate. Short, sweet, to the point. 'Will not take place'. The Rhones will be forced to abandon their usual flamboyant style. I mean, they can't very well say, 'We regret to inform you that the groom is in love with another' or 'We are saddened to announce that Dexter has broken our dear daughter's heart.' No, this mailing will be all business – cheap paper, boxy font, and typed computer labels. Mrs. Rhone will not want to spend the money on Crane's stationery and calligraphy after already wasting so much. I see her at the post office, triumphant no more, telling the mailman that no, she will not be needing the heart stamps this time. Three hundred flag stamps will do just fine.

I am in bed when Dex calls and asks if he can come over.

On the day I receive his wedding invitation, I still say yes, come right on over. I am ashamed for being so weak, but then think of all the people in the world who have done more pathetic things in the name of love. And the bottom line is: I love Dex. Even though he is the last person on earth I should feel this way about, I truly do love him. And I have not given up on him quite yet.

As I wait for his arrival, I debate whether to put the invitation away or leave it on my coffee table in plain view. I decide to tuck it between the pages of my *InStyle* magazine. A few minutes later, I answer the door in my white cotton nightgown.

'Were you in bed?' he asks.

'Uh-huh.'

'Well, let me take you back there.'

We get in bed. He pulls the covers over us.

'You feel so good,' he says, caressing my side and moving his hand under my nightgown. I start to block him, but then acquiesce. Our eyes meet before he kisses me slowly. No matter how disappointed I am in him, I can't imagine stopping this tide. I am motionless as he makes love to me. He talks the whole time, which he doesn't usually do. I can't make out exactly what he is saying, but I hear the word 'forever'. He wants to be with me forever, I think. He won't marry Darcy. He can't. She cheated on him. They aren't in love. He loves me.

Dex spoons me as tears seep onto my pillow. I am careful not to make a noise.

'You're so quiet tonight,' Dex says.

'Yeah,' I say, keeping my voice steady. I don't want him to know that I'm crying. The last thing I want is Dexter's pity. I am passive and weak, but I have some – albeit limited – pride.

'Talk to me,' he says. 'What's on your mind?'

I come close to asking him about the invitation, his plans, us, but instead I make my voice nonchalant. 'Nothing really . . . I was just wondering if you're going to the Hamptons this weekend.'

'I sort of promised Marcus I would. He wants to golf again.'

'Oh.'

'I guess you wouldn't consider coming?'

'I don't think it's a good idea.'

'Please?'

'I don't think so.'

He kisses the back of my head. 'Please. Please come.'

Three little 'pleases' is all it takes.

'Okay,' I whisper. 'I'll go.'

I fall asleep hating myself.

The next day Hillary bursts into my office. 'Guess what I got in the mail.' Her tone is accusatory, not at all sympathetic.

I completely overlooked the fact that Hillary would be receiving an invitation too. I have no response prepared for her. 'I know,' I say.

'So you have your answer.'

'He could still cancel,' I say.

'Rachel!'

'There's still time. You gave him two weeks, remember? He still has a few more days.'

Hillary raises her eyebrows and coughs disdainfully. 'Have you seen him recently?'

I start to lie, but don't have the energy. 'Last night.'

She gives me a wide-eyed look of disbelief. 'Did you tell him you got the invitation?'

'No.'

'Rachel!'

'I know,' I say, feeling ashamed.

'Please tell me you aren't one of *those* women.'

I know the type she is talking about. The woman who carries on a relationship with a married man for years, hoping, even believing, that he will one day come to his senses and leave his wife. The moment is just around the corner – if she only hangs in there, she won't be sorry in the end. But time passes, and the years only create fresh excuses. The kids are still in school, the wife is sick, a wedding is being planned, a grandchild is on the way. There is always something, a reason to keep the status quo. But then the excuses run out, and ultimately she accepts that there will be no leaving, that she will always be the second-place finisher. She decides that second place is better than nothing. She surrenders to her fate. I have new empathy for these women, although I do not believe that I have yet joined their ranks.

'That's not a fair characterization,' I say.

She gives me an 'oh really?' look.

'Dexter's not married.'

'You're right. He's not married. But he *is* engaged. Which might be worse. He can change his situation like *that*.' She snaps her fingers. 'But he's not doing a damn thing.'

'Look, Hillary, we are talking about a finite timetable . . . I can only be one of *those* women for a month more.'

'A month? You're going to let this thing go down to the wire?'

I look away, out my window.

'Rachel, why are you waiting?'

'I want it to be his decision. I don't want to be responsible . . .'

'Why not?'

I shrug. If she knew about Darcy's infidelity, she'd be over the edge.

She sighs. 'You want my advice?'

I do not, but nod anyway.

'You should dump him. Now. Do something while you

still have a choice. The longer this goes on, the worse you are going to feel when you're standing in front of that church, watching them seal their vows with a kiss that Darcy will drag on for longer than is tasteful . . . then watching them cut the cake and feed one another while she smears icing on his face. Then watching them dance the night away . . . and then—'

'I know. I know.'

Hillary isn't finished. 'And then darting into the night on their getaway to frickin' Hawaii!'

I wince and tell her that I get the picture.

'I just don't want you to get more hurt. I don't understand why you won't do something, force his hand. Something.'

I tell her again that I don't want to be responsible for their break-up, that I want it to be Dexter's decision.

'It *will* be his decision. You won't be brainwashing him. You'll simply be going for what you want. Why aren't you being more assertive about something so significant and important?'

I have no explanation for her. At least none that she would find acceptable. I'm not used to going for what I want, and I'm incapable of being assertive. My phone rings, interrupting our awkward silence.

I glance at the screen on my phone. 'It's Les. I better take it,' I say, feeling relief that the inquisition is over. It is a sad day when I am grateful to hear from Les.

Later that afternoon, I take a break from my research and roll my chair over to the window. I peer down on Park Avenue, watching people move about their daily life. How many of them feel desperate, euphoric, or simply dead inside? I wonder if any of them are on the verge of losing something huge. If they already have. I close my eyes and picture the wedding scenes that Hillary painted for me. I then add my own honeymoon reel – Darcy clad in her new lingerie, posing seductively on their bed. I can see it all so perfectly.

And suddenly, all at once, it is clear to me why I won't force Dex's hand. Why I said nothing over July Fourth, nothing in the time since, nothing last night. It all comes down to expectations. In my heart, I don't actually believe that Dex is going to call off the wedding and be with me, no matter what I do or say. I believe that those Dex and Darcy wedding and honeymoon scenes will unfold while I am left on the sidelines, alone. I can already feel my grief, can envision my final time with Dex, if it hasn't happened already. Sure, I have occasionally scripted a different ending, one in which Dex and I are together, but those images are always short-lived, never escaping the realm of 'what if'. In short, I have no real faith in my own happiness. And then there is Darcy. She is a woman who believes that things should fall into her lap, and, consequently, they do. They always have. She wins because she expects to win. I do not expect to get what I want, so I don't. And I don't even try.

It is Saturday afternoon, and we're in the Hamptons. I took the train out this morning, and now our whole group is reunited in the backyard. The togetherness is a recipe for disaster. Julian and Hillary are playing badminton. They ask if anyone wants to challenge them in a doubles match. Dex says sure, he will. Hillary glares at him. 'Who do you want to be your partner, Dexter?'

Until this point, Dexter did *not* know that I told Hillary anything about us. I had two reasons for keeping him in the dark on this: I didn't want him to feel uncomfortable around her, and I didn't want him to have free license to tell a friend.

But Hillary makes her snide remark in such a way that you simply cannot miss it if you are aware of the situation. Which apparently Julian is, because he gives her a look of warning. It has become clear that he will be the steadying force in their duo.

She does not stop there. 'Well, Dex, who is it going to be?' She rests her hand on her hip and points at him with her racquet.

Dex stares back at Hillary. His jaw clenches. He is pissed.

'What if two people both want to be your partner, then what?' Hillary's voice is dripping with innuendo.

Darcy seems oblivious to the tension. So are Marcus and Claire. Perhaps everyone is used to Hillary's occasional confrontational tone. Maybe they just chalk it up to the lawyer in her.

Dex turns around and looks at us. 'Any of you guys wanna play?'

Marcus waves his hand dismissively. 'Naw. Man. No, thanks. That's a girly game.'

Darcy giggles. 'Yeah, Dex. You're a girly man.'

Claire says no, she hates sports.

'Badminton is hardly a sport,' Marcus says, opening a can of Budweiser. 'It's like calling tic-tac-toe a sport.'

'Looks like it's between Darcy and Rachel. Doesn't it?' Hillary says. 'You want in, Rach?'

I am frozen at my post at the picnic table, flanked by Darcy and Claire. 'No thanks,' I say softly.

'You want me to be your partner, honey?' Darcy asks. She looks across the yard at him as she shades her eyes with her hand.

'Sure,' Dex says. 'C'mon then.'

Hillary snorts, as Darcy hops up from the table with a warning that she sucks at badminton.

Dex looks down at the grass, waiting for Darcy to take the fourth racquet and join him in the plot of grass outlined by various flip-flops and sneakers.

'We play to ten,' Hillary says, tossing the bird up for her first serve.

'Why do you get to serve first?' Dex asks.

'Here,' she says, tossing the bird over the net. 'By all means.'

Dex catches the bird and glares at her.

The game is cutthroat, at least every time Hillary and Dex have control. The bird is their ammunition and they smack it with full force, aiming at one another. Marcus does the color in a Howard Cosell voice. 'And the mood is tense here in East Hampton as both sides strive for the championship.' Claire is cheering for everyone. I say nothing.

The score is 9-8, Hillary and Julian lead. Julian serves underhand, Darcy squeals and swats with her eyes closed and through sheer luck happens to make contact with the bird. She sends it back across the net to Hillary. Hillary lines up her shot and hits a vicious forearm that conjures Venus Williams. The bird sails through the air, whizzing just over the net toward Darcy. Darcy cowers, preparing to swat at the bird, as Dex yells, 'It's out! It's out!' His face is red and covered with beads of sweat.

The bird lands squarely beside Claire's flip-flop.

'Out!' Dexter yells, wiping his forehead with the back of his arm.

'Bullshit. The line is good!' Hillary shouts back. 'That's match!'

Marcus offers good-naturedly that he doesn't think a badminton game should be called a match. Claire is up off the bench, trotting over to the bird to examine its alignment with her shoe. Hillary and Julian join her from their side of the net. There are five pairs of eyes peering down at the bird. Julian says that it is a tough call. Hillary glares at him before she and Dex resume their shouting of 'out' and 'in', like a couple of playground enemies.

Claire announces a 'do-over' in her best 'let's make peace' voice. But clearly she was not an outdoor girl growing up, because declaring a do-over is one of the biggest causes of dissension in the neighborhood. Hillary proves this to be the case. 'Bullshit,' she says. 'No do-over. The line has been in all day.'

'All day? We've been playing for twenty minutes,' Dex says snidely.

'I don't think it's landed on the line yet,' Darcy offers. But not as if she cares. As competitive as she is in real-life matters, sports and games do not concern her. She bought properties

325

in Monopoly strictly based on color; she thought the little houses were so much cuter than the 'big, nasty Red Roof Inns'.

'Fine. If you want to *cheat* your way through life,' Hillary says to Dex, disguising her true intent with a friendly smile, as though simply engaging in playful banter. Her eyes are wide, innocent.

I think I might faint.

'Okay, you win,' Dex says to Hillary, as if he could not care less. Let Hillary win her stupid game.

Hillary doesn't want it this way. She looks disoriented, unsure whether to reargue the point or savor her victory. I am afraid of what she will say next.

Dex tosses his racquet in the grass under a tree. 'I'm gonna take a shower,' he says, heading for the house.

'He's pissed,' Darcy says, offering us a blinding glimpse of the obvious. Of course, she thinks it's about the game. 'Dex hates to lose.'

'Yeah, well, he can be a big baby,' Hillary says with disgust.

I note (with satisfaction? hope? superiority?) that Darcy does not defend Dex. If he were mine, I'd say something. Of course, if he were mine, Hillary would not have been so merciless in the first place.

I give her a measured glance as if to say, enough.

She shrugs, plops down in the grass, and scratches a mosquito bite on her ankle until it bleeds. She swipes at the blood with a blade of grass, then looks up at me again.

'Well?' she says defiantly.

That night Dex is so quiet at dinner that he borders on surly. But I cannot tell if he is mad at Hillary, or at me for telling her. He ignores both of us. Hillary ignores him right back, except for an occasional barb, while I make feeble attempts to talk to him.

'What are you ordering?' I ask him as he scans his menu.

He refuses to look up. 'I'm not sure.'

'Go figure,' Hillary mumbles. 'Why don't you order two meals?'

Julian squeezes her shoulder and shoots me an apologetic look.

Dex turns in his chair toward Marcus and manages to avoid all conversation and eye contact with me and Hillary for the rest of our dinner. I am seized by worry. *Are you mad? Are you mad? Are you mad?* I think as I struggle to eat my swordfish. *Please don't be mad.* I am desperate, frantic to talk to Dex and clear the air for our remaining time together. I don't want to end on such a sour note.

Later at the Talkhouse, Dex and I are finally alone. I am ready to apologize for Hillary when he turns on me, his green eyes flashing. 'Why the hell did you tell her?' he hisses.

I am not well trained in conflict and feel startled by his hostility. I give him a blank look, pretending to be confused. Should I apologize? Offer an explanation? I know we had an unspoken vow of secrecy, but I had to tell someone.

'Hillary. You told her,' he says, brushing a piece of hair off his forehead. I note that he is even hotter when he's angry – his jaw somehow more square.

327

I push this observation aside as something snaps inside me. How dare he be angry with me! I have done nothing to him! Why am I the one feeling frantic, desperate to be forgiven?

'I can tell anyone I want,' I say, surprised by the hardness in my voice.

'Tell her to stay outta this,' he says.

'Stay out of what, Dex? Our fucked-up relationship?'

He looks startled. And then hurt. Good.

'It's not fucked up,' he says. 'The situation is, but our relationship is not.'

'You're *engaged*, Dexter.' My indignation boils into fury. 'You can't separate that from our relationship.'

'I know. I'm still engaged . . . but you hooked up with Marcus.'

'*What?*' I ask, incredulous.

'You kissed him at Aubette.'

I can't believe what I'm hearing – he is engaged and is finding fault with a nothing little kiss! I fleetingly wonder how long he has known and why he hasn't said anything before now. I fight back the instinct to be contrite.

'Yeah, I kissed Marcus. Big deal.'

'It's a big deal to me.' His face is so close to mine that I can smell the alcohol on his breath. 'I hate it. Don't do it again.'

'Don't tell me what to do,' I whisper fiercely back. Angry tears sting my eyes. 'I don't tell you what to do . . . You know what? Maybe I should tell you what to do . . . How about this one: marry Darcy. I don't care.'

I walk away from Dex, almost believing it. It is my first

free moment of the summer. Perhaps the freest moment of my life. I am the one in control. I am the one deciding. I find a space on the back patio, alone in a massive crowd, my heart pounding. Minutes later, Dex finds me, grips my elbow.

'You don't mean what you said . . . about not caring.' Now it is his turn to be anxious. It never ceases to amaze me how foolproof the rule is: the person who cares the least (or pretends to) holds the power. I have proven it true once more. I shake his hand off my arm and just look at him coldly. He moves closer to me, takes my arm again.

'I'm sorry, Rachel,' he whispers, bending down toward my face.

I do not soften. I will not. 'I'm tired of the warring emotions, Dex. The endless cycle of hope and guilt and resentment. I'm tired of wondering what will happen with us. I'm tired of waiting for you.'

'I know. I'm sorry,' he says. 'I love you, Rachel.'

I feel myself weakening. Despite my tough-girl façade I am buzzing from being this near him, from his words. I look into his eyes. All of my instincts and desires – everything tells me to make peace, to tell him that I love him too. But I fight against them like a drowning person in a riptide. I know what I have to say. I think of Hillary's advice, how she has been telling me to say something all along. But I am not doing this for her. This is for me. I formulate the sentences, words that have been ringing in my head all summer.

'I want to be with you, Dex,' I say steadily. 'Cancel the wedding. Be with me.'

There it is. After two months of waiting, a lifetime of

passivity, everything is on the line. I feel relieved and liberated and changed. I am a woman who expects happiness. I *deserve* happiness. Surely he will make me happy.

Dex inhales, on the verge of responding.

'Don't,' I say, shaking my head. 'Please don't talk to me again unless it's to tell me that the wedding is off. We have nothing more to discuss until then.'

Our eyes lock. Neither of us blinks for a minute or more. And then, for the first time, I beat Dex in a staring contest.

TWENTY

It is two days after I delivered my ultimatum and one month before the wedding. I am still invigorated by my stand and filled with a soaring, positive feeling, stronger than hope. It is more akin to faith. I have faith in Dex, faith in us. He will cancel. We will live happily ever after. Or something close to that.

Of course I worry about Darcy. I even worry that she might do something crazy when faced with her first dose of rejection. I have visions of her languishing in a hospital bed, hooked up to an IV, dark circles under her eyes, her hair stringy, her skin gray. In these scenes, I am there by her side, bringing her magazines and black licorice, telling her that everything is going to be okay, that everything happens for a reason.

But even if these scenes play out, I will never regret telling Dex the truth about what I want. I will never be sorry for going for it. For once, I did not put Darcy above myself.

As the days tick by, I go to work, come home, go back to work, waiting for the bomb to drop. I am sure that Dex will call at any moment with news. Good news. In the meantime, I steel myself, refusing to give in to my temptation to call him first. But after a full week passes, I start to worry, and feel the shift back to my former self. I tell Hillary that I want to call him, knowing that she will talk me out of it. I remind myself of a woman on the wagon, dragging herself to an AA meeting in a last-ditch effort to resist her urges.

'No way,' she says. 'Don't do it. Don't contact him.'

'What if he was drunk and doesn't remember our conversation?' I ask her, grasping at straws.

'His tough luck.'

'Do you think he remembers?'

'He remembers.'

'Well. I wish I hadn't said anything.'

'Why? So you could have a few more nights with him?'

'No,' I say defensively.

Even though that is exactly the reason.

After another few days of torture, of being unable to eat or work or sleep, I decide that I must get away. I have to be somewhere else, away from Dex. Leaving town is the only way that I will keep myself from calling him, retracting everything for one more night, one more minute with him. I consider going to Indiana, but that is not far enough. Besides, home will only remind me of Darcy and the wedding.

I call Ethan and ask if I can visit. He is thrilled, says come anytime. So I call United and book a flight to London. It is only five days away, so I must pay full fare – eight hundred and ninety dollars – but it's worth every penny.

After I type my vacation memo, I go to drop it off at Les's office. Mercifully, he is away from his desk.

'He's at an out-of-the-office meeting. Thank gawd,' his

secretary, Cheryl, says to me. She is my ally, often warning me when Les is in a particularly foul mood.

'Just have a few things for him,' I tell her, heading into his den of horrors.

I put a draft of our reply papers on his chair, the vacation memo under them. Then I change my mind and move the memo to the top of the pile. He will be so pissed. This makes me smile.

'What's that smirk for?' Cheryl asks as I leave his office.

'Vacation memo,' I say. 'Let me know how much he curses me.'

She lifts her eyebrows and says, 'Uh-oh,' without losing her place on the document she is typing. 'Someone's gonna be in *trou-ble*.'

Les calls me that evening when he returns to the office. 'What's the big idea?'

'Excuse me?' I ask, knowing that my calm will nettle him further.

'You didn't tell me you were going on vacation!'

'Oh. I thought I did,' I lie.

'When was that?'

'I don't know exactly . . . Weeks ago. I'm going to a wedding.' Two lies.

'Christ.' He breathes into the phone, waiting for me to offer to cancel my trip. In the old days, back when I was a first-year, the passive-aggressive trick might have worked. But now I say nothing. I outwait him.

'Is it a family wedding?' he finally asks. This is where he draws the line. Family funerals and family weddings. Likely only immediate family. So I tell him that it's my sister's wedding. Three lies.

'Sorry,' I say flippantly. 'Maid of honor, you know.'

I let him rant for a few seconds and make an idle threat about getting another associate to take over the case. As if everyone is chomping at the bit to work with him. As if I would care if he replaced me. Then he announces with pleasure that this means no life outside the office for me until Friday. I think to myself that that won't be a problem.

Darcy calls minutes later. She is just as understanding. 'How can you book a trip so close to my wedding?'

'I promised Ethan I'd visit him this summer. And the summer is almost over.'

'What's wrong with the fall? I'm sure London is even more beautiful in the fall.'

'I need a vacation. Now.'

'Why now?'

'I just need to get out of here.'

'Why? . . . Does it have anything to do with Marcus?'

'No.'

'Have you seen him?'

'No.'

'Why not?'

'Okay. Maybe it does have something to do with Marcus . . .' I say, just wanting her to shut up. 'I don't think it's going to work out with him. And maybe I'm a little bummed. Okay?'

'Oh,' she says. 'I'm really sorry it didn't work out.'

The last thing I want is Darcy's sympathy. I tell her that

it really has more to do with work. 'I need a break from Les.'

'But I need you here,' she whimpers. Apparently her ten seconds of sympathy have expired.

'Claire will be here.'

'It's not the same. You're my maid of honor!'

'Darcy. I need a vacation. Okay?'

'I guess it'll have to be.' I see her pouting face. 'Right?' She adds this with a note of hope.

'Right.'

She sighs loudly and tries another tactic. 'Can't you go the week I'm in Hawaii on my honeymoon?'

'I could,' I say, picturing Darcy in her new lingerie. 'If my world revolved around you . . . but I'm sorry. It doesn't.'

I never say things like this to Darcy. But there is a new order now.

'Okay. Fine. But meet me at the Bridal Party tomorrow at noon to pick up your bridesmaid dress . . . Unless you have plans to go to Venice or something.'

'Very funny,' I say, and hang up.

So now Dex will know that I am going to London. I wonder how he will feel when he hears this news. Maybe it will make him decide more quickly. Tell me something good before I fly far away.

I keep waiting, feeling increasingly tortured with every passing hour. No word from him. No call. No email. I constantly check my messages, looking for the blinking red light. Nothing. I start to dial his phone number countless times, compose long emails that I never send. Somehow I stay strong.

Then, on the night before my flight, José buzzes me. 'Dex is here to see you.'

A flood of emotion rushes over me. *The wedding is off!* For once, my glass is not only half-full, but it runneth over. My joy is temporarily clouded as my thoughts turn to Darcy – what will happen to our friendship? Does she know of my involvement? I push thoughts of her away, focus on my feelings for Dex. He is more important now.

But when I open the door, his face is all wrong.

'Can we talk?' he asks.

'Yes.' My voice comes out in a whisper.

I sit stiffly as if I'm about to be told that someone very close to me has died. He might as well be a police officer, coming to my door with hat in hand.

He sits beside me and the words come. *This has been a really hard decision . . . I really do love you . . . I just can't . . . I've given it a lot of thought . . . feel guilty . . . didn't mean to lead you on . . . our friendship . . . incredibly difficult . . . I care too much about Darcy . . . can't do it to her . . . owe it to her family . . . seven years . . . summer has been intense . . . meant what I said . . . I'm sorry . . . I'm sorry . . . I'm truly sorry . . . always, always will love you. . . .*

Dex covers his face with his hands, and I have a flashback to my birthday, how much I admired his hands while we were riding in the cab up First Avenue. Right before he kissed me. And now here we are. At the very end. And I will never kiss him again.

'Say something,' Dex says. His eyes are glassy, his lashes wet and jet black. 'Please say something.'

I hear myself say that I understand, that I will be fine. I do not cry. Instead I concentrate on breathing. In and out. In and out. More silence. There is nothing more to say.

'You should go now,' I tell him.

As Dex stands up and walks to the door, I consider screaming, begging. *Don't go! Please! I love you! Change your mind! She cheated on you!* But instead I watch him leave, not hesitating or turning back for one final look at me.

I stare at the door for a long time, listening to the loud silence. I want to cry so that something will fill the scary blank space, but I can't. The silence grows louder as I consider what to do next. Pack? Go to sleep? Call Ethan or Hillary? For one irrational second, I have those thoughts that most people don't admit to having – swallowing a dozen Tylenol PM, chasing it with vodka. I could really punish Dex, ruin their wedding, end my own misery.

Don't be crazy. It's just a little heartbreak. You will get over this. I think of all the hearts breaking at this moment, in Manhattan, all over the world. All of the overwhelming grief. It makes me feel less alone to think that other people are getting their insides torn to tiny bits. Husbands leaving wives after twenty years of marriage. Children crying out, 'Don't leave me, Daddy! Please stay!' Surely what I feel doesn't compare to that kind of pain. It was only a summer romance, I think. Never meant to last beyond August.

I stand up, walk over to my bookcase, and find the Altoids tin. I have one final hope. If I get double sixes, maybe he will change his mind, come back to me. As if to cast a magic spell, I blow on the dice just as Dex did. Then I shake

337

them once in my right hand and carefully, carefully roll them. Just as it happened with our first roll, one die lands before its mate. On a six! I hold my breath. For a brief second, I see a mess of dots, and think I have boxcars again. I kneel, staring at the second die.

It is only a five. I have rolled an eleven. It is as if someone is mocking me, saying, *Close, but no dice.*

TWENTY-ONE

I am somewhere over the Atlantic Ocean when I decide that I will not tell Ethan all of the gory, pathetic details. I will not dwell and wallow once the plane lands on British soil. It will be the first step in getting over Dex, moving on. But I will give myself the duration of the flight to think about him and my situation. How I put myself on the line and lost. How it's not worth it to take risks. How it's better to be a glass-half-empty person. How I would have been so much better off if I had never gone down this road, setting myself up for rejection and disappointment and giving Darcy the chance to beat me again.

I rest my forehead against the window as a little girl behind me kicks my seat once, twice, three times. I hear her mother say in a sugary voice, 'Now, Ashley, don't kick the nice lady's seat.' Ashley keeps kicking. 'Ashley! That is against the rules. No kicking on the plane,' the mother repeats with exaggerated calm, as though to demonstrate to everyone around her what a competent parent she is. I close my eyes as we fly into the night, don't open them until the flight attendant comes by to offer us headphones.

'No thanks,' I say.

No movie for me. I will be too busy cramming all of the misery I can into the next few hours.

*

I told Ethan not to come to Heathrow – that I would take a taxi to his flat. But I am hoping that he comes anyway. Even though I live in Manhattan, I am intimidated by other big cities, particularly foreign ones. Except for the time I went to Rome with my parents for their twenty-fifth wedding anniversary, I have never left the country. Other than Niagara Falls on the Canadian side which hardly counts. So I am relieved to see Ethan waiting for me just outside of customs, grinning and boyish and happy as ever. He is wearing new, horn-rimmed glasses, like Buddy Holly's, only brown. Otherwise he looks the same. He rushes toward me and hugs me hard around the neck. We both laugh.

'It's so good to see you! Here. Give me your bag,' he says.

'You too.' I grin back at him. 'I like your glasses.'

'Do they make me look smarter?' He pushes the frames on his nose and strikes a scholarly pose, stroking a nonexistent beard.

'Much.' I giggle.

'I'm so glad you're here!'

'I'm so glad to be here.'

A summer full of bad decisions, but at last I made a good one. Just seeing Ethan soothes me.

'It's about time you visited,' he says, maneuvering my roller bag through the crowd. We make our way outside, into the cab line.

'I can't believe I'm in England. This is so exciting.' I take my first breath of British air. The weather is exactly what I imagined – gray, drizzling, and slightly chilly. 'You weren't kidding about the weather here. This feels like November, not August.'

'I told you . . . We actually had a few hot days this month. But it's back to normal now. It's relentless. But you get used to it. You just have to dress for it.'

Within minutes we are in the back of a black cab, my bags at our feet. The taxi is dignified and spacious compared to New York's yellow cabs.

Ethan asks me how I feel, and for a second I think he is asking about Dex, but then I realize it's the standard post-flight questioning.

'Oh, fine,' I say. 'I'm really psyched to be here.'

'Jet-lagged?'

'A little.'

'A pint will fix that,' he says. 'No napping. We have a lot to do in a week.'

I laugh. 'Like what?'

'Sightseeing. Boozing. Reminiscing. Time-consuming, intense stuff . . . God, it's nice to see you.'

We arrive at Ethan's basement flat in Kensington, and he gives me the brief tour of his bedroom, living room, and kitchen. His furniture is sleek and modern, and his walls are covered with abstract paintings and posters of jazz musicians. It is a bachelor pad but without the I'm-trying-at-every-turn-to-get-laid feel.

'You probably want to shower?'

I tell him yes, that I feel pretty grimy. He hands me a towel in the hallway outside of his bathroom and tells me to be quick, that he wants to talk.

As soon as I am showered and changed, Ethan asks, 'So how's the Dex situation? I take it they're still engaged?'

It's not as if I have stopped thinking about him for an instant. Everything vaguely reminds me of him. A sign for Newcastle. *Drinking Newcastles with him on my birthday*. Driving on the left side of the street. *Dex is left-handed*. The rain. *Alanis Morissette singing, 'It's like rain on your wedding day.'*

But Ethan's question about Dex still causes a sharp pain in my chest. My throat tightens as I struggle not to cry.

'Oh God. I knew it,' Ethan says. He reaches up and grabs my hand, pulling me down into his black leather couch.

'Knew what?' I say, still fighting back tears.

'That your stiff upper lip, "I don't care" thing was just a lot of bluster.' He puts his arm around me. 'What happened?'

I finally cry as I tell him everything, no editing. Even the dice. So much for my vow over the Atlantic. My pain feels raw, naked.

When I am finished, Ethan says, 'I'm glad I RSVPed no. I don't think I could stomach it.'

I blow my nose, wipe my face. 'Those are the exact words Hillary used. She's not going either.'

'You shouldn't go, Rachel. Boycott. It will be too hard. Spare yourself.'

'I have to go.'

'Why?'

'What would I tell her?'

'Tell her that you have to have surgery – you have to have an extraneous organ removed . . .'

'Like what kind of organ?'

'Like your spleen. People can get by without their spleen, right?'

'What's the reason for removing your spleen?'

'I dunno. A spleen stone? A problem . . . an accident, a disease. Who cares? Make something up. I'll do the research for you – we'll come up with something plausible. Just don't go.'

'I have to be there,' I say. I am back to rule-following.

We sit in silence for a minute, and then Ethan gets up, switches off two lamps, and grabs his wallet from a small table in the hall. 'C'mon.'

'Where are we going?'

'We're going to my local pub. Getting you good and loaded. Trust me, it will help.'

'It's eleven in the morning!' I laugh at his exuberance.

'So? You got a better idea?' He crosses his arms across his narrow chest. 'You want to sightsee? Think Big Ben's going to do you any good right now?'

'No,' I say. Big Ben would only remind me of the minutes ticking down to what will be the most horrible day of my life.

'So c'mon then,' he says.

I follow Ethan over to a pub called the Brittania. It is exactly how I expect an English pub to be – musty and full of old men smoking and reading the paper. The walls and carpet are dark red, and bad oil paintings of foxes and deer and Victorian women cover the walls. It could be 1955. One man wearing a little cap and smoking a pipe even resembles Winston Churchill.

'What's your pleasure?' Ethan asks me.

Dex, I think, but tell him a beer would be great. I am beginning to think that the boozing idea is a pretty good one.

'What kind? Guinness? Kronenbourg? Carling?'

'Whatever,' I say. 'Anything but Newcastle.'

Ethan orders two beers, his several shades darker than mine. We sit down at a corner table. I trace the grain in the wood of the table and ask him how long it took for him to get over Brandi.

'Not long,' he says. 'Once I knew what she did, I realized that she wasn't what I thought. There was nothing to miss. That's what you have to think. He wasn't right for you. Let Darcy have him . . .'

'Why does she always win?' I sound like a five-year-old, but it helps to hear my misery simplified: *Darcy beat me. Again.*

Ethan laughs, flashing his dimple. 'Win what?'

'Well, Dex for one.' Self-pity envelops me as I picture him with Darcy. It is morning in New York. They are likely still in bed together.

'Okay. What else?'

'Everything.' I gulp my beer as quickly as I can. I feel it hit my empty stomach.

'Like?'

How do I explain to a guy what I mean? It sounds so shallow: she's prettier, her clothes are better, she's thinner. But that is the least of it. She is happier too. She gets what she wants, whatever that happens to be. I try to articulate this with real examples. 'Well, she has that great job making tons of money, when all she has to do is plan parties and look pretty.'

'That schmoozing job of hers? Please.'

'It's better than mine.'

'Better than being a lawyer? I don't think so.'

'More fun.'

'You'd hate it.'

'That's not the point. She loves her job.' I know I am not doing a good job of showing how Darcy is always victorious.

'Then find one you love. Although that's another issue altogether. One that we will address later . . . But, okay, what else does she win?'

'Well . . . she got in Notre Dame,' I say, knowing that I sound ridiculous.

'Oh, she did not!'

'Yes she did.'

'No. She *said* she got in Notre Dame. Who picks IU over Notre Dame?'

'Plenty of people. Why do you always dump on IU?'

'Okay. Look. I hate Notre Dame more. I'm just saying if you apply to those two schools and get into both, presumably you want to go to both. So you'd pick Notre Dame. It's a better school, right?'

I nod. 'I guess.'

'But she didn't get in there. Nor did she get a, what did she say, thirteen hundred five and a half or something on her SATs? Remember that shit?'

'Yeah. She lied about her score.'

'And she lied about Notre Dame too. *Trust* me . . . Did you ever see the acceptance letter?'

345

'No. But . . . well, maybe she didn't.'

'God, you're so naïve,' he says, mispronouncing it 'nave' on purpose. 'I assumed we were on the same page there.'

'It was a sensitive topic. Remember?'

'Oh yeah. I remember. You were so sad,' he says. 'You should have been celebrating your escape from the Midwest. Of course, then you pick the second most obnoxious school in the country, and go to Duke . . . You know my theory about Duke and Notre Dame, right?'

I smile and tell Ethan that I have trouble keeping all of his theories straight. 'What is it again?'

'Well, aside from you and a few other exceptions, those two schools are filled to the brim with obnoxious people. Perhaps only obnoxious people apply there or perhaps the schools attract obnoxious people. Probably a combination, a mutually reinforcing issue. You're not offended, are you?'

'Course not. Go on,' I say. In part, I agree with him. A lot of people at Duke – including my own boyfriend – were hard to take.

'Okay. So why do they have a higher ratio of assholes per capita? What do those two schools have in common, you ask?'

'I give up.'

'Simple. Dominance in a division one, revenue-generating sport. Football at Notre Dame and basketball at Duke. Coupled with the stellar academic reputation. And the result is an intolerably smug student body. Can you name another school that has that combination of characteristics?'

'Michigan,' I say, thinking of Luke Grimley from our high

school, who was insufferable in his chatter about Michigan football. And he still talks about Rumeal Robinson's clutch free throws in the NCAA finals.

'Aha! Michigan! Good one, nice try. But it's not an expensive, private school. The public aspect saves Michigan, makes Michigan alums slightly less obnoxious.'

'Wait a minute! What about your own school? Stanford. You had Tiger Woods. Great swimmers. Debbie Thomas, that skater, didn't she win a silver medal? Tennis players galore. Plus great academics – and it's private and expensive. So why aren't you Stanford grads as irritating?'

'Simple. We're not dominant in football or basketball. Yeah, we're good some years, but not like Duke in basketball or football at Notre Dame. You can't get as jazzed over nonrevenue sports. It saves us.'

I smile and nod. His theory is interesting, but I am more intrigued with the realization that Darcy got rejected by Notre Dame.

'Mind if I smoke?' Ethan asks as he removes a carton from his back pocket. He shakes a cigarette free, rolling it between his fingers.

'I thought you quit.'

'For a minute,' he says.

'You should quit.'

'I know.'

'Okay. So back to Darcy.'

'Right.'

'So maybe she didn't get into Notre Dame. But she did get Dex.'

He strikes a match and raises it to his lips. 'Who cares? Let her keep him. He's spineless. Sincerely, you're better off.'

'He's not spineless,' I say, hoping that Ethan will convince me otherwise. I want to latch on to a fatal flaw, believe that Dex is not the person I thought he was. Which would be a lot less painful than believing that I am not the woman he wanted.

'Okay, maybe "spineless" is too strong. But, Rach, I'm *sure* he'd rather be with you. He just doesn't know how to dump her.'

'Thanks for the vote of confidence. But I actually think he just decided that he'd rather be with Darcy. He picked her over me. Everybody picks her.' I gulp my beer more quickly.

'Everybody. Who besides spineless Dex?'

I smile. 'You picked her.'

He gives me a puzzled look. 'Did not.'

I snort. 'Ha.'

'Is that what she told you?'

After all these years, I have never aired my feelings about their two-week, elementary-school romance. 'She didn't need to tell me. Everybody knew it.'

'What are you talking about?'

'What are *you* talking about?'

'The reunion?' he asks.

'Our ten-year?' I ask, knowing of no other reunion. I remember the disappointment I felt when Les insisted that I had to work. Those were the days before I knew to lie. He had scoffed at me when I said I couldn't work, that I had to go to my ten-year reunion.

348

'Yeah. She didn't tell you what happened?' He takes a long drag, then turns his head, exhaling away from me.

'No. What happened?' I say, thinking that I am going to fall apart and die if Ethan slept with her. 'Please tell me you didn't hook up with her.'

'Hell no,' he says. 'But she tried.'

As I finish the rest of my pint and steal a few sips of Ethan's, I listen to him tell the story of our reunion. How Darcy came on to him at Horace Carlisle's backyard after-party. Said she thought they should have one night together. What would it hurt?

'You're kidding me!'

'No,' he says. 'And I was like, Darce, *hell* no. You have a boyfriend. What the fuck?'

'Was that why?'

'Why I didn't hook up with her?'

I nod.

'No, that's not why.'

'Why then?' For a second, I wonder if he's going to come out of the closet. Maybe Darcy is right after all.

'Why do you think? It's Darcy. I don't see her that way.'

'You don't think she's . . . beautiful?'

'Frankly, no. I don't.'

'Why not?'

'I need reasons?'

'Yes.'

'Okay.' He exhales, looks up at the ceiling. ''Cause she wears too much make-up. 'Cause she's too, I don't know, severe.'

'Sharp-featured?' I offer.

'Yeah. Sharp and . . . and overplucked.'

I picture Darcy's skinny, high-arched brows. 'Overplucked. That's funny.'

'Yeah. And those hipbones jutting out at you. She's way too skinny. I don't like it. But that's not the point. The point is – is that it is *Darcy*.' He shudders and then takes his beer back from me. 'Hold on. Let me get another round.' He crushes out his cigarette and strolls over to the bar, returning with two more beers. 'There you are.'

'Thanks,' I say, and then set about chugging mine.

He laughs. 'Man! I can't let you out-drink me.'

I wipe the foam from my lips with the back of my hand and ask why he didn't tell me about Darcy and the reunion before now.

'Oh. I dunno. 'Cause it was no big deal. She was wasted.' He shrugs. 'Probably didn't even know what she was doing.'

'Yeah, right. She always knows what she's doing.'

'I guess so. Maybe. But it really wasn't significant.'

That explains why she thought Ethan was gay. Turning her down – it must be the only explanation. 'Guess her fifth-grade charms wore thin on you.'

He laughs. 'Yeah. We did go out once upon a time.' He makes little quotes in the air as he says 'go out'.

'See. You picked her over me, too.'

He flashes his dimple. 'What the hell you talking about now?'

'On the note. The check-the-box note.'

'What?'

I sigh. 'The note that she sent you. The "Do you want to go out with me or Rachel?" note.'

'That's not what the note said. It didn't say anything about you. Why would it say anything about you?'

'Because I liked you!' Somehow I am embarrassed admitting it, even after all these years. 'You knew that.'

He shakes his head firmly. 'Nope. Did not.'

'You must have forgotten.'

'I don't forget shit like that. I have a bomb-ass memory. Your name was *not* in the note. See. I'd know because I liked you back then.' He peers at me from behind his glasses and then lights another cigarette.

'Bullshit.' I feel myself blush. It's only Ethan, I tell myself. We are adults now.

'Okay.' He shrugs and inverts the cover of his matchbook. Now he looks embarrassed too. 'Don't believe me.'

'You did?'

'Big time. I remember always helping you out in four square so that you'd get to be king. I'd always pound the king when you were in the queen position. Tell me you didn't notice that.'

'I didn't notice that,' I say.

'As it turns out, you're markedly less perceptive than I once thought . . . Yeah, I liked you. I liked you all through junior high and high school. And then you dated Beamer. Broke my heart.'

This is big news, but I still can't get past the fact that my name wasn't in that note. 'I swear I thought Annalise saw it.'

'Annalise is a sweet girl but such a lemming. Darcy

351

probably told her to say that your name was in the note. Or somehow tricked her into thinking it. How is Annalise anyway? Did she have her kid yet?'

'No. But any minute now.'

'Is she going to the wedding?'

'If she's not in labor,' I say. 'Everybody is but you and Hilary.'

'And you. Terrible thing about your spleen.'

'Yeah. Tragic.' I smile. 'So you're sure my name really wasn't in the note?'

I am focusing on evidence from twenty years ago. It is absurd, but I ascribe all kinds of meaning to it.

'Positive,' he says. 'Pos-i-tive.'

'Damn,' I say. 'What a bitch.'

He laughs. 'I had no clue that I was the man. Thought it was all about Doug Jackson.'

'You were not the man. It *was* all about Doug Jackson,' I say. 'That's the point – I was the only one who liked you. She copied me.' Again, I notice how juvenile I sound whenever I describe my feelings about Darcy.

'Well, you didn't miss much. Going out with me consisted of sharing a few Hostess cupcakes. Wasn't very exciting. And I still helped you out in four square.'

'So maybe Dex will help me out the next time we all play four square,' I say. 'That would be really . . .' I can't think of the right word. I can feel myself getting drunk.

'Nifty? Brilliant? Smashing?' Ethan offers.

I nod. 'All of those. Yes.'

'Feeling better?' he asks.

He is trying so hard. Between his efforts and the beer, I feel somewhat healed, at least temporarily. I consider that I am thousands of miles away from Dex. Dexter – who *did* have my name as an option when he chose, instead, to check the box next to Darcy's name. 'Yes. A little better. Yes.'

'Well, let's recap. We determined that I never picked Darcy over you. And that she didn't get in Notre Dame.'

'But she did get Dex.'

'Forget him. He's not worth it,' Ethan says, and then glances up at the menu scrawled on a blackboard behind us. 'Now. Let's get you some fish and chips.'

We eat lunch – fish, fries, and mushy peas that remind me of baby food. Comfort food. And we have a couple more pints. Then I suggest that we go for a walk, see something England-y. So he takes me into Kensington Gardens and shows me Kensington Palace, where Princess Diana lived.

'See this gate? That's where they piled all the flowers and letters when she died. Remember those photos?'

'Oh yeah. That was here?'

I was with Dex and Darcy when I found out that Diana had died. We were at the Talkhouse and some guy walked up to us at the bar and said, 'Did you hear that Diana died in a car crash?' And even though he could only have been talking about one Diana, Darcy and I both asked, 'Diana who?' The guy said, 'Princess Diana.' Then he told us that she died in a high-speed crash while the paparazzi chased her through a tunnel in Paris. Darcy started bawling right on the spot. But for once it wasn't give-me-attention tears. They were genuine. She was truly devastated. We both were. Several days later we watched her funeral together, waking at four a.m. to see all of the coverage, just as we had done with her wedding to Prince Charles sixteen years earlier.

Ethan and I meander through Kensington Gardens in a drizzle, without an umbrella. I don't mind getting wet. Don't care that my hair will frizz. We pass the palace and circle a small, round pond. 'What's this pond called?'

'Round Pond,' Ethan says. 'Descriptive, huh?'

We walk past a bandstand and then over to the Albert Memorial, a huge bronze statue of Prince Albert perched on a throne. 'You like?'

'It's pretty,' I say.

'A grieving Queen Victoria had this thing built when Albert died from typhoid fever.'

'When?'

'Eighteen sixty- or seventy-something . . . Nice, huh?'

'Yeah,' I say.

'Apparently she and Al were pretty tight.'

Queen Victoria must have been sadder than I am now, I suppose. I then have a fleeting thought that I'd prefer losing Dex to illness than to Darcy. So maybe it's not true love if I'd rather see him die . . . Okay, I wouldn't rather see him die.

The rain starts to come down harder. Other than a few Japanese tourists who are snapping pictures on the steps of the memorial, we are alone.

'You ready to head back?' Ethan points in the opposite direction. 'We can explore Hyde Park and the Serpentine another day.'

'Sure, we can go back now,' I say.

'Your spleen acting up in this weather?'

'Ethan! I have to go to the wedding.'

'Just blow it off.'

'I'm the maid of honor.'

'Oh, *right*! I keep forgetting that,' he says, wiping his glasses on his sleeve.

As we walk back to his flat, Ethan chuckles to himself.

'What?'

'Darcy,' he says, shaking his head.

'What about her?'

'I was just thinking about the time she wrote to Michael Jordan and asked him to our prom.'

I laugh. 'She actually thought he was going to come! Remember how she was worried about how she would break the news to Blaine?'

'And then Jordan wrote back to her. Or his people did, anyway. That's the part that I found unreal. I never thought she'd get a response.' He laughs. No matter what he says, I know he has a soft spot for her, in spite of himself. Just as I do.

'Yeah. Well, she did. She still has the letter.'

'You've seen it?'

'Yeah. Don't you remember how she taped it up in our locker?'

'And yet,' he says, 'you never saw the letter from Notre Dame.'

'Okay. *Okay*. You might be right. But where were you twelve years ago with that insight?'

'As I said, I thought we were on the same page there. The

355

whole thing was pretty transparent . . . You know, for a smart woman you can be pretty dim.'

'Why, thank you.'

He tips an imaginary hat. 'Don't mention it.'

We return to Ethan's flat, where I succumb to my jet lag. When I wake up, Ethan offers me a cup of Earl Grey tea and a crumpet. Lunch at a pub, a walk past Diana's old pad, an afternoon nap where I don't dream once about Dex, and tea and crumpets with my good friend. The trip is off to a good start. If anything can really be good with a broken heart.

TWENTY-TWO

That evening we meet up with Ethan's friends, Martin and Phoebe, whom he met during his stint writing for *Time Out*. I have heard much about both of them: I know that Martin is very proper, went to Oxford, and comes from a ton of money, and that Phoebe hails from East London, once got fired for telling her boss to 'piss off', and has slept with a lot of men.

They are exactly as I imagined. Martin is well dressed and attractive in an unsexy way. He sits with his legs crossed at the knee, nods and frowns a lot, and makes a 'hmm' sound whenever anyone else speaks, showing rapt attention. Phoebe is Amazon-tall with untamed, tomato-red hair. I can't decide whether her orange lipstick clashes with her hair or complements it. I also can't decide whether she is very pretty or just plain weird looking. Her body is definitely not ideal, but she doesn't try to hide it. One roll of her big white stomach shows between her shirt and jeans. Nobody in Manhattan would expose her stomach unless it was as hard as bedrock. Ethan told me once that British women are much less obsessed with appearances and being thin than American women. Phoebe is evidence of this, and it is refreshing. All night she talks about this bloke she wants to shag, and that bloke she has already shagged. She makes all the statements matter-of-factly, as you would tell someone that work has been very busy or that you are tired of all the rain. I like her candor, but Martin rolls his eyes a lot and makes dry comments about her being uncouth.

After Phoebe has carried on for a while about this guy Roger, who 'deserves to have kerosene poured on his balls', she turns to me and asks, 'So, Rachel, how do you find the men in New York? Are they as bloody dreadful as English men?'

'Why thank you, darling,' Martin deadpans.

I smile at Martin and then turn back to Phoebe. 'It depends . . . widely varies,' I say. I have never thought in terms of 'American men'. They are all I know.

'Are you involved with anyone now?' she asks me and then blows smoke up toward the ceiling.

'Um. Not exactly. No. I'm . . . unattached.'

Ethan and I exchange a look. Phoebe is all over it. 'What? There is a story here. I know there is.'

Martin unfolds his arms, waves smoke out of his face, and waits. Phoebe makes a hand motion to say, come on, out with it.

'It's nothing,' I say. 'Not worth discussing really.'

'Tell them,' Ethan says.

So now I have no choice in the matter, because Ethan has established that there is, indeed, something to tell.

I don't want to annoy everyone with a long session of 'it's nothing', 'tell', 'really nothing', '*c'mon* tell', and Phoebe does not seem the type to tolerate that evasive charade. She is Hillary-like in this regard – Hillary is fond of saying, 'Well then, why'd you bring it up?' Only in this instance, Ethan brought it up. In any case I am stuck, so I say, 'I've been seeing this guy all summer who is getting married in . . . less than two weeks. I thought he might call the wedding off. But he didn't. So here I am. Single once again.' I tell my story without emotion, a fact that makes me proud. I am making progress.

Phoebe says, 'Usually they wait until they're married to cheat. This bloke has a head start, eh? . . . What's his wife-to-be like? Do you know her?'

'Yeah. You could say that.'

'A real bitch, is she?' Phoebe asks solicitously.

Martin clears his throat and waves away her smoke again. 'Maybe Rachel doesn't wish to discuss it. Have we considered that?'

'No, we haven't,' she says to him, and then to me, 'Do you mind discussing it?'

'No. I don't mind,' I say. Which I think is the truth.

'So? The girl he's marrying – how do you know her?'

'Well . . .' I say. 'We've known each other a long time.'

Ethan cuts to the chase. 'In a nutshell, Rachel is the maid of honor.' He pats me on the back and then rests his hand on my shoulder in a congratulatory way. He is clearly pleased to have offered his mates this nugget of transatlantic gossip.

Phoebe isn't fazed. I'm sure she's seen worse trouble. 'Bloody mess,' she says sympathetically.

'But it's over now,' I say. 'I made my feelings known. I told him to call the wedding off. And he picked her. So that's that.' I try to mask the fact that I am a rejected mess; I think I am doing a good job of it.

359

'She's moving on marvelously,' Ethan says.

'Yes. You don't look a bit ruffled,' Phoebe says. 'Never would have guessed.'

'Should she be crying in her Carling?' Martin asks Phoebe.

'I would be. Remember Oscar?'

Ethan groans, and Martin winces. Clearly they remember Oscar.

Then Ethan tells them that he thinks that I should blow off the wedding. Phoebe wants to know more about the bride, so Ethan gives the rundown on Darcy, including some color on our friendship. He even throws in the bit about Notre Dame. I answer questions when directly asked, but otherwise I just listen to the three of them discussing my plight as if I'm not present. It is amusing to hear Martin and Phoebe using Dex's name and Darcy's name and analyzing both in their British accents. People whom they have never met and likely will never meet. Somehow it helps put everything in perspective. Almost.

'You don't want to be with him anyway,' Phoebe says.

'That's what I tell her,' Ethan says.

Martin offers that maybe he'll still call it off.

'No,' I say. 'He came over to my place the night before I left and told me in no uncertain terms. He's getting married.'

'At least he told you outright,' Martin says.

'At least,' I say, thinking that that was a good thing. Otherwise I would be filled with hope on this visit. I have to give Dex limited credit for telling me face to face.

Suddenly Phoebe gets this fabulous idea. Her friend

James is newly single, and he loves American women. Why not set that up and see what happens?

'She lives in New York,' Martin says. 'Remember?'

'So? That's just a minor logistical problem. She could move. He could move. And at the very least, they both will have a good time. Perhaps have a good shag.'

'Not everyone sees a shag as therapy,' Martin says.

Phoebe raises one eyebrow. I wish I could do that. There are times when it is such an appropriate gesture. 'Oh really? You might want to give it a go, Marty.' She turns back to me, waiting to hear my position on this topic.

'A good shag can never hurt,' I say, to win favor with Phoebe.

She runs her hands through her tousled hair and looks smug. 'My point precisely.'

'What're you doing?' Ethan asks, as Phoebe retrieves her cell phone from her purse.

'Calling James,' she says.

'Fucking *hell*, Pheebs! Put your mobile down,' Martin says. 'Have some tact.'

'No, it's okay,' I say, fighting against my prudish instincts. 'You can call him. Why not?'

Phoebe beams. 'Yeah. You boys stay out of this one.'

So the next night, thanks to Phoebe, I am eating Thai food on a blind date with James Hathaway. James is a thirty-year-old freelance journalist. He is nice looking, although Dexter's opposite. He is on the short side with blue eyes, light hair, and even paler eyebrows. Something about him reminds me of Hugh Grant. At first I think it's just the accent, but then I realize that like Hugh he has a certain flippant charm. And like Hugh I bet he's slept with a ton of women. Maybe I should let him add me to his List.

I nod and laugh at something James just said, a wry comment about the couple next to us. He's funny. It suddenly occurs to me that maybe Dex is not very funny. Of course, I've always subscribed to the notion that if I want to laugh out loud, I'll watch a *Seinfeld* rerun, that I don't need to date a stand-up comic, but I contemplate revising my position. Maybe I *do* want a funny guy. Maybe Dex is lacking some crucial element. I try to run with this, picturing him as humorless, even boring. It doesn't really work. It's hard to trick yourself like that. Dex *is* funny enough. He is perfect for me. Other than the small, bothersome part about him marrying Darcy.

I realize that I have missed what James has been going on about, something about Madonna. 'Do you like her?' he asks me.

'Not especially,' I say. 'She's okay.'

'Usually Madonna elicits a stronger response. Usually people love her or hate her . . . Ever played that game. Love it or hate it?'

'No. What is it?'

James teaches me the rules of the game. He says that you throw out a topic or a person or anything at all, and both people have to decide whether they love it or hate it. Being neutral isn't allowed. What if you are neutral? I ask. I don't love *or* hate Madonna.

362

'You have to pick one or the other. So pick,' he says. 'Love her or hate her?'

I hesitate and then say, 'Okay then. I hate her.'

'Good. Me too.'

'Do you really?' I ask.

'Well, actually yes. She's talentless. Now you do one.'

'Um . . . I can't think. You do another one.'

'Fine. Water beds.'

'So tacky. I hate them,' I say. I'm not on the fence with that one.

'I do as well. Your turn.'

'Okay . . . Bill Clinton.'

'Love him,' James says.

'Me too.'

We keep playing the game as we finish our wine.

As it turns out, we both hate (or at least hate more than we love) people who keep goldfish as pets, Speedos, and Ross on *Friends*. We both love (or love more than we hate) Chicken McNuggets, breast implants (I lie here, just to be cool, but am surprised that he does not lie in the other direction – maybe he fears that I have them), and watching golf on television. We are split on rap music (I love; it gives him headaches), Tom Cruise (he loves; I still hate for dumping Nicole), the royal family (I love; he says he's a republican, whatever that means), and Las Vegas (he loves; I associate it with craps, dice rolling, Dex).

I think to myself that I like (I mean, love) the game. Being extreme. Clear-cut. All or nothing. I do Dex in my mind, flip-flopping my decision twice – hate, love, hate, love. I remember that my mother once told me that the opposite of love isn't hate, it's indifference. She knew what she was talking about. My goal is to be indifferent to Dex.

James and I finish our dinner, decide to skip dessert and go back to his place. He has a nice flat – larger than Ethan's – full of plants and cozy, upholstered furniture. I can tell that a woman recently moved out: half of the bookshelf is bare. The whole left side. Unless they kept their books segregated all along, which is doubtful, he has pushed all of his to one side. Maybe he wanted an exact percentage of how much more empty his life is without her.

'What was her name? Your ex?' I ask gingerly. Maybe I shouldn't be bringing her up, but I'm sure he assumes that Phoebe told me his situation. I'm sure she filled him in on mine as well.

'Katherine. Kate.'

'How are you doing?'

'A bit sad. More relieved than anything. Sometimes downright euphoric. It's been over a long time.'

I nod, as if I understand, although my situation could not be more different. Maybe Dex and I saved ourselves years of effort and pain only to end like James and Kate anyway.

'And you?' he asks.

'Phoebe told you?'

I can tell that he is considering a fib, and then he says, 'More or less . . . yes . . . How are you?'

'I'm fine,' I say. 'It was a short-lived situation. Nothing like your break-up.'

But I don't believe my words. I have a flashback to July

Fourth and feel a wave of pure, intense grief that catches me off-guard with its intensity. I panic, thinking that I'm going to cry. If James asks another thing about Dex, I will. Luckily, serious conversations seem not to be James's thing. He asks if he can get me something to drink. 'Tea? Coffee? Wine? Beer?'

'A beer would be great,' I say.

As he leaves for the kitchen, I breathe deeply and force Dex from my mind. I stand and survey the room. There is only one photograph in view. It is of James with an attractive older woman who appears to be his mother. I wonder how many photographs of Kate and James were uprooted with the break-up. I wonder if he threw them away or saved them. That fact can tell you a lot about someone. I wish that I had a few photos of Dex. I have none of us together, only a few of him with Darcy. I'm sure I'll have a lot more after the wedding. Darcy will force me to order some, maybe even give me one in a frame, as a wedding keepsake. How will I ever get through it?

James returns with linen cocktail napkins, two beers poured into mugs, and a small glass bowl of mixed nuts. All nestled neatly on a square pewter tray. Well trained by Kate.

'Thanks,' I say, sipping one of the beers.

We sit close to each other on the couch and talk about my job, his writing. It's not perfectly comfortable, but not horrible. Probably because we are in a dead-end situation. There will be no second date, so there is no pressure to perform. No expectations. We will never have to deal with that awkward period after all the getting-to-know-you topics are covered, the lulls in conversation that usually come on

365

the second date, at which point both people must decide whether to fight their way through to the comfort zone or throw in the towel. Of course Dex and I didn't have to deal with that. Another great thing about Dex. We were friends first. *Don't think about Dex. Think about now, being here with James!*

James leans in and kisses me. He uses a little too much tongue – working it in frantic circular motions – and his breath smells vaguely of cigarettes, which is odd because he didn't smoke this evening. Maybe he had one in the kitchen. I kiss him back anyway, faking enthusiasm. I even moan softly at one point. I don't know why.

How many times will I have to endure kissing someone for the first time? Although Darcy says she will miss this element of single life, I have no fondness for it. Except for my first real kiss with Dex, which was absolute magic. I wonder if James is thinking about Kate as much as I am thinking about Dex. After a reasonably long time, James's hand drifts up my shirt. I do not object. His touch is not altogether unpleasant, and I think, why not? Let him sample an American breast.

After a half-hour of minor to significant groping, James asks me to spend the night, says that he doesn't want to sleep with me – well, he does, he says, but he won't try. And I almost agree, but then I learn that James has no saline solution. I can't sleep in my contact lenses, and I left my glasses at home. So that is that. It seems amusing that James's twenty-twenty vision prevents me from a potentially promiscuous move.

We kiss for a bit longer, listening to his Barenaked Ladies CD. The songs remind me of graduating from law school, dating Nate, being dumped by Nate. I hear the lyrics and remember the sadness. *You think it's only fair to do what's best for you and you alone.*

Songs and smells will bring you back to a moment more than anything else. It's amazing how much can be conjured with a few notes of a song or a solitary whiff of a room. A song you didn't even pay attention to at the time, a place that you didn't even know had a particular smell. I wonder what will someday bring back Dex and our few months together. Maybe the sound of Dido's voice. Maybe the scent of the Aveda shampoo that I've been using all summer.

Someday being with Dex will be a distant memory. This fact makes me sad too. It's like when someone dies, the initial stages of grief seem to be the worst. But in some ways, it's sadder as time goes by and you consider how much they've missed in your life. In the world.

As James walks me back to Ethan's flat, he turns to me and says, 'Do you want to go to Leeds Castle with me tomorrow? Ethan too?'

'What's Leeds Castle?' I ask, realizing that it's probably like asking what the Empire State Building is.

'It's a castle that was a Norman stronghold, a royal residence for six medieval queens. It's really quite lovely. There's an open-air theater nearby. It is a bit touristy, but you are a tourist after all, aren't you?'

I am beginning to notice that Brits put a little question tag at the end of every statement, looking for affirmation.

I give it to him. 'I *am* a tourist, yes.'

Then I tell him that Leeds Castle sounds perfect. Because it does sound nice. And because everything I do, every person I meet, puts a certain distance between Dex and me. Time heals all wounds, particularly if you pack a bunch of stuff into that time.

'Ask Ethan what he thinks about it, and call me.' He writes his phone number down on the back of a gum wrapper I find in my purse. 'I'll be around.'

I thank him for a nice night. He kisses me again, his hand on the back of my neck.

'Snogging someone new right after a big break-up. Love it or hate it?' he asks.

I laugh. 'Love it.'

James smirks. 'I concur.'

I unlock Ethan's door, wondering if James is lying too.

The next morning Ethan stumbles bleary-eyed into the kitchen, where I am pouring myself a glass of pulp-free orange juice.

'So? You in love with James?'

'Madly.'

He scratches his head. 'Seriously?'

'No. But it was fun.' I realize that I can't even recall exactly what James looks like. I keep picturing this guy from my federal income tax class in law school instead. 'He wants to meet up with us today. Go to some palace or castle together.'

'Hmmm. A palace or castle in England. That narrows it down.'

'Leeds or something?'

Ethan nods. 'Yeah, Leeds Castle is nice. Is that what you want to do?'

'I don't know. Why not?' I say.

It seems like a waste of time and a lot of effort to make more conversation with James, but I call him anyway, and we all end up going to Leeds Castle for the day. Phoebe and Martin come too. Apparently all of Ethan's friends make their own work schedules because none of them seems to think twice about taking off on a random Wednesday. I think of how different my life is back in New York with Les looming over me, even on the weekends.

It is a warm day, nearly hot by London standards. We explore the castle and grounds, have a picnic lunch in the grass. At one point, Phoebe asks me, loud enough for everyone to hear, if I've taken a shine to James. I look at James, who rolls his eyes at Phoebe. Then I smile and tell her, at the same volume, that he is quite nice, if only he lived in New York. I figure, what does it hurt to compliment him? If he genuinely likes me, he'll be happy to hear it. And if he doesn't, he will feel safe because of the distance.

'So why don't you move to London?' she asks. 'Ethan says you positively despise your job. Why not move here and find something? It would be a nice change of scenery, wouldn't it?'

I laugh and tell her I can't do that. But it occurs to me, as we sit by a peaceful lake and admire the fairy-tale castle in the

369

English countryside, that I could, in fact, do exactly that. Maybe the thing to do after you roll the dice – and lose – is simply pick them up and roll them again. I imagine handing Les my letter of resignation. It would be incredibly satisfying. And I wouldn't have to deal with seeing Dex and Darcy on a regular basis. I wonder how a good therapist would characterize the move – as running away or creating a fresh, healthy start?

On my last night in London, Ethan and I are back at his favorite pub, which is starting to feel like my local. I ask Ethan what he thinks of the idea of my moving to London. Within fifteen minutes he has me all moved into his neighborhood. He knows of a flat, a job, and several guys, if James isn't ideal, all of whom have straight, white teeth (because I have commented on the Brits' poor dental work). He says do it. Just do it. He makes it sound so simple. It *is* simple. The seed is more than just planted. It is growing and sprouting a tiny bud.

Ethan continues. 'You should get away from Darcy. That toxic friendship . . . It's unhealthy. And it's only going to be more destructive when you have to see them after the wedding.'

'I know,' I say, pushing a fry through mushy peas.

'And even if you stay in New York, I think it's *essential* that you pare back that friendship. It's not even a real friendship if she only wants to beat you.'

'It's not as malicious as you make it sound,' I say, wondering why I am defending her.

'You're right. It's not just for the sake of defeating you. I think she just respects you so much that she wants to beat you to win your respect . . . You'll note that she's not going out of her way to show up Annalise. It's just you. But sometimes I think you get sucked into it, and your whole dynamic becomes more about competing than true friendship.' He gives me a knowing, parental look.

'You think I like Dex for the same reason – to compete with Darcy. Don't you?'

He clears his throat and dabs his napkin to his lips, replaces it on his lap. 'Well? Is it possible?' he asks.

I shake my head. 'No way. You can't trick yourself into the feelings I have. Had,' I say.

'Okay. It was just a theory.'

'Absolutely not. It was the real deal.'

But as I fall asleep that night in Ethan's bed (he insisted on taking the couch all week), I wonder about this theory of his. Is it possible that the thrill I felt when I kissed Dex had more to do with the titillation of being bad, breaking rules, having something that belonged to Darcy? Maybe my affair with Dex was about rebelling against my own safe choices, against Darcy and years of feeling deficient. I am disturbed by the idea, because you never like to think that you are a slave to these sorts of subliminal pulls. But at the same time, the idea consoles me. If I liked Dex for these reasons, well then I don't love him after all. And it should be a whole lot easier for me to move on.

But the next day, as Ethan takes the tube with me to Paddington Station, I know, again, that I really do love Dex, and probably will for a very long time. I buy my ticket for the Heathrow Express. The board tells us that the next train will depart in three minutes, so we walk to the designated platform. 'You know what you're doing, right?' he asks protectively.

For a second, I think he is asking me about my life, then I realize he is only inquiring about travel logistics. 'Yes. This goes straight to Heathrow, right?'

'Yeah. Just get out at Terminal Three. It's easy.'

I hug Ethan and thank him for everything. I tell him I had a wonderful time. 'I don't want to leave.'

'Then move here . . . I really think you should do it. You have nothing to lose.'

He is right; I do have nothing to lose. I'd be leaving nothing. A depressing thought. 'I'll think about it,' I say, and promise myself I will keep thinking about it once I get home, rather than falling blindly into my old routine.

We hug one last time, and then I board my train and watch Ethan wave at me through the tinted train window. I wave back, thinking that there is nothing like old friends.

I arrive at Terminal Three and go through the motions of checking in, going through security, and waiting to board. The flight feels endless, and although I try I can't sleep at all. Despite my week of distraction, I don't feel much better than I did on the flight over. Even the aerial views of New York City, which usually charge me with anticipation and excitement, don't do a thing for me. Dex is amid those buildings. I liked it better when the Atlantic Ocean separated us.

When the plane lands, I make my way through passport control, baggage, and customs to find a long cab line. It is meltingly hot outside, and as I get in my cab I discover that the air conditioning is barely blowing through the vent into the backseat.

'Could you make it cooler back here, please?' I ask my driver, who is smoking a cigarette, an offense which could fetch him a $150 ticket.

He ignores me and lurches us sickeningly sideways. He is switching lanes every ten seconds.

I ask him again if he will please turn the air up. Nothing. Maybe he doesn't hear me over his radio. Or maybe he doesn't speak English. I glance at my Passenger Bill of Rights. I am entitled to: a courteous, English-speaking driver who knows and obeys all traffic laws . . . air-conditioning on demand . . . a radio-free (silent) trip . . . smoke, and incense-free air . . . a clean trunk.

Maybe the trunk is clean.

See? It's all about low expectations.

The backseat keeps getting hotter, so I roll down the window and endure the dirty wind whipping my hair around my face. Finally I am home again. I pay my not-so-courteous cabbie the flat rate from JFK, plus toll and tip (even though the placard also states that I may refuse a tip if my rights weren't complied with). I heave my roller bag out of the backseat.

It is five-thirty. By this time on Saturday, Darcy and Dex will be married. I will have already helped Darcy into her gown and wrapped the stems of her calla lilies with my lace handkerchief, her something borrowed. I will have already assured her a thousand times that she has never looked so beautiful, that everything is just right. I will have already walked down the aisle toward Dexter without looking at him. Well, trying not to look at him but maybe catching a fleeting look in his eyes, a mixture of guilt and pity. I will have endured that painful thirty seconds of watching Darcy, in all her glory, walk toward the altar, as I hold Dexter's platinum band in my sweaty palm. In six days, the worst will be over.

'Hello there, Ms. Rachel!' José says as I close the cab door. Then he says to someone in the lobby, 'She's back!'

I stiffen, expecting to see Darcy with her wedding folder, ready to bark demands my way.

But it is not Darcy waiting for me in my lobby, in the lone leather wing chair.

TWENTY-THREE

It is Dex. He stands as I stare at him. He is wearing jeans and a gray 'Hoyas' T-shirt. He is more tanned than when I left. I resent his healthy glow and his placid expression.

'Hi,' he says, taking a step toward me.

'Hi.' I freeze, feeling my posture become perfect. 'How did you know when I was getting home?'

'Ethan gave me your flight details. I found his number in Darcy's address book.'

'Oh . . . What do you want? What are you doing here?' I ask. I don't mean to sound bitter, but I know that I do.

'Let me come up. I have to talk to you,' he says quietly, but urgently. José is still beaming, perfectly clueless.

I shrug and push the arrow for the elevator. The ride up is endless, quiet. I look at him as he waits for me to exit first. I can tell by his expression that he is here to reapologize. He can't stand being the bad guy. Well, I will not give him the satisfaction. And I will not be patronized. If he goes down that road of telling me again how sorry he is, I will cut him off. Maybe even tell him about James. I will say that I am fine, that I will be at the wedding but after that I want minimal contact with him, and that I expect him to cooperate. *Make no mistake about it*, I will say, *our friendship is over*.

I turn the key in my lock and open the door. Entering my apartment is like opening a hot oven, even though I remembered to put my shades down. My plants have all wilted. I should have asked Hillary to water them. I turn on my air conditioner and notice that it won't operate on high. Whenever it gets above ninety-five, there is a deliberate city-wide brownout. I miss London, where it's not even necessary to own an air conditioner.

'Brownout,' Dex says.

'I can see that,' I say.

I breeze by him and sit on my couch, cross my arms, try to raise one eyebrow as Phoebe did. Both rise together.

Dex sits beside me without asking first. He tries to take my hand, but I pull it away.

'Why are you here, Dex?'

'I just called it off.'

'What?' I ask. Surely I heard him wrong.

'The wedding is off. I— I'm not getting married.'

I am stunned, remembering the first time I heard that people pinch themselves when they think they're dreaming. I was four years old and took the concept literally, pinching my arm hard, as if maybe I was still two years old and had dreamed up the second half of my life. I remember feeling relieved that my skin hurt.

Dex continues, his voice steady and quiet. He stares at his balled fists in his lap as he talks, only glancing at me between sentences. 'The whole time you were gone, I was going crazy. I missed you so much. I missed your face, your scent, even your apartment. I kept replaying everything in my head. All our time together, all our talks. Law school. Your birthday. July Fourth. Everything. And I just can't imagine never being with you again. It's that simple.'

'What about Darcy?' I ask.

'I care about her. I want her to be happy. I saw marrying Darcy as the right thing to do. We've been together, seven years and most of the time we've been pretty happy. I didn't want to hurt her.'

I don't want to hurt her either, I think.

He continues. 'But that was before you. And I just can't marry her feeling this way about you. I can't do it. I love you. And this is only the beginning . . . If you still love me.'

There is so much I want to say, but somehow I am speechless.

'Say something.'

I force a question from my lips. 'Did you tell her about us?'

'Not about us. But I told her that I wasn't in love with her and that it wasn't fair to marry her.'

'What did she say?' I ask. I need to know every detail before I can believe this is real.

'She asked if there was someone else. I told her no . . . That it just didn't feel right between us.'

'How is she?'

'She's upset. But mostly she's just upset about the damn wedding and what people are going to think. I swear that is what bothers her the most.'

'Where is she now?' I ask. 'She hasn't left me any messages.'

377

'She went to Claire's, I think.'

'I'm sure she thinks you'll change your mind.'

I am thinking this too. He will change his mind, and when he does it will be all the more cruel.

'No,' he says. 'She understands that I mean it. I called my parents and told them. And she and I are calling her parents together tonight. She says she wants me to tell them . . . and then we'll call everyone else.' There is a catch in his voice, and for a second I wonder if he might cry.

I say I'm sorry. I don't know what else to say. I can't digest this information quickly enough. I want to kiss him, to thank him, to smile. But I can't. It doesn't seem appropriate.

He nods, runs his hands through his hair and then returns them to his lap. 'It's hard, but I feel this tremendous load lifted. It's the right thing.'

He looks at me, and I hold his gaze before I kiss him. As his arms encircle me, I think, *This is real.* Then I slowly relax into him, feeling happy and whole for the first time in what feels like forever. There was always a deep calm missing before, even during our July Fourth weekend together. We now have time. All kinds of time. Maybe even forever.

I wonder what it will be like without Darcy in the picture. Will making love be different? I am about to find out because Dex is unbuttoning my shirt. My heart is pounding as we move over to my bed, where we undress.

'I missed you, Rachel,' he says. I can feel his heart beating against mine.

And then José interrupts, buzzing me, once, twice. I go to answer him, assuming that it is a package or dry-cleaning, or

378

something he forgot to tell me about. I will tell him that I will get whatever it is later. But it is not a package. It is Darcy. And she has heard my voice over the intercom.

'Tell her I'll be right down!' I say.

'Already on her way up!' José practically sings the news. Clearly he has no idea that Darcy's arrival means that my first guest and I are screwed. Then again, maybe he does know. Maybe doormen, even the ones who pretend to be your friend, secretly delight in any tenant drama.

'Oh shit!' I say, standing up and looking around. 'She's coming up! Shit!'

Dex is calm, puts his boxers back on. He walks swiftly over to my linen closet and opens the door, carrying his jeans and T-shirt. The shelves line the closet the whole way to the bottom. No good.

'Get in the other one. The other closet!' I point, frantic and wild-eyed.

He walks around the corner and opens my other closet. There is room in this one. He crouches next to my hamper, holding his clothes. I shut the closet door just as I hear her knock.

'Coming!' I shout.

I throw my underwear back on and open the door. 'Sorry. I was just changing.'

'Omigod. Thank God you're back,' she says.

I ask her what's wrong before I realize that she looks and sounds fine. No bloodshot eyes, no running mascara, no dejected gaze. Darcy moves into my apartment as I babble that I just arrived home and wanted to change into

379

something more comfortable. I put on a pair of shorts and a T-shirt.

She still says nothing.

'So. Six days to go. You must be going crazy!' I laugh nervously. 'Well, I'm here to help now. At your service. To help with any last-minute details for your wedding.'

'There isn't going to be a wedding.' She sniffs.

'What?' I gasp, widen my eyes, step toward her. Right as I am about to offer my full sympathy, I remember that I'm not supposed to know who called it off. So I ask.

'It was mutual.'

'Mutual?' I ask, my voice louder.

I lead Darcy over to my bed and sit down. The closet is next to the bed. I want Dex to hear everything. *Mutual*? Dex said he did it. If it was mutual, or if she said it first, then perhaps it doesn't mean quite as much as I thought it did. Of course, I will still be happy. But I want this choice to be Dex's. Now I want to be the reason.

'Well. Technically Dexter was the one. He told me this morning that he couldn't go through with it. That he doesn't think he loves me.' She rolls her eyes and smiles an ironic smile. I wish Dex could see the look on her face. She no more believes that he doesn't love her than she believes that I could be capable of hiding a half-naked Dex in my closet.

'You're kidding me? This is crazy. How do you feel?'

Darcy looks down at her feet. *Now* she will start to cry. And I will comfort her and tell her that it will all be okay. Then I will suggest we go for a little walk. Get some fresh air, even though it is disgustingly humid outside. Maybe I will suggest dinner. Her choice. A burger and fries now that there is no dress to fit into.

But still, Darcy does not cry. She takes a deep breath. 'Rachel . . . I have something to tell you.' Her voice is calm. She is not following the 'I've just been dumped' script. Something is going on. For a second I think that she is going to tell me that she knows everything, that she understands, that true love must prevail, and that she sees clearly that Dex and I should be together.

'Yeah?' I ask, confused.

'This is very hard for me to tell you. Even harder than when I got into Notre Dame,' she continues.

This is the first time she has brought up Notre Dame since college – which is crazy, considering my recent revelation. The conversation is definitely not making sense. Maybe she is going to confess that she, too, got rejected. That all her life she has been competing with me. And that she is finally acknowledging defeat.

'Do you remember when I told you about losing my ring?'

'Yeah?'

'How I lost it in my colleague's apartment?'

Now I am really confused. Dex must be even more confused. I am glad that I never told him how she really lost her ring. He canceled the wedding even without that information.

'How I hooked up with that guy and lost the ring?'

It's like a *Three's Company* episode where Jack and Chrissy are talking, and Janet is hiding somewhere listening to the conversation full of misunderstandings and double meanings. I remember the close-ups of Janet's face, shocked and indignant. But there is no confusion here in my studio. There is only one meaning, and Dex is getting it right: she hooked up with someone else. *Why didn't you tell me?* he will ask me, perhaps accusatorily. *It would have made everything so much easier*, he will say. I will tell him that I didn't think it was right to sway him. Maybe it will make me look noble, and Darcy all the more wrong for him.

'Well, I didn't really hook up with a guy from work.' She speaks slowly, enunciating every syllable.

'You didn't lose your ring?'

Is she about to confess to insurance fraud?

'The guy I was with wasn't a guy from work. It was someone else.'

'Who was it?'

'It was Marcus,' she says.

'Marcus?' I am floored.

'Your Marcus. Yes.'

Of course. My Marcus. The Marcus I had to fly across the Atlantic to get over.

'Do you hate me?' she asks soulfully. 'Please say something.'

'You were with Marcus the day you lost your ring? You lost it in his apartment?' I am clarifying for myself and Dexter.

She nods. Then there is a fleeting second when she looks at me sideways – a brightening in her eyes, a slight upward movement in the corners of her mouth. She is enjoying this. This is her moment to shock. Shock and shine. Win again.

I give her what she wants. Pretend to be defeated. The gracious loser again.

'So you slept with him?' I keep my voice just south of accusatory, on the hurt side.

'Yes.'

'More than once?'

'Yes,' she whispers so softly that I know Dex can't hear her answer.

So I ask loudly and clearly, 'You did?'

'Yes,' she says.

I pretend to digest it all. Actually I am digesting it all. But on a level unknown to Darcy. 'So,' I say. 'So.'

I don't ask for further explanation, but she gives it to me anyway. 'It started over the July Fourth weekend. We came back from the Talkhouse, loaded. And one thing led to the other.'

'July Fourth?' I ask.

This keeps getting better.

'Yes, but he felt terrible. And we swore that it would never happen again. Only we were totally into each other. It was intense . . . We just couldn't keep apart. We started to meet for lunch and sometimes after work. We felt awful every time because of Dex – and because of you. But then it would happen again and again . . . Do you hate me?'

I am at a crossroads. I am not sure how to play it. What would Ethan advise? Pretend to fly into a rage? *Yes, I hate you. Get out. Get out!* That would be one way to go. Or a soft, dejected, *How can I hate you? You are my best friend.* Or perhaps, *I don't know what to think. I need time.*

While I contemplate my response, she says she has something else to tell me. Something big.

'There's more?'

'Yes. There's more.' Her voice sounds fragile, but her expression gives her away. She is definitely enjoying this.

I stare at my feet. 'Go on.'

'I am a few days late for my period. And you know that I'm always on a perfect, twenty-eight-day schedule.' She is touching her stomach fondly. It is still completely flat.

My own stomach lurches. 'You're pregnant?'

'I think so. Yeah.'

I am afraid to ask who the father is. If it is Dex, all of this might be taken back from me.

'I took a test . . . it was positive.'

'Positive means you're pregnant?'

'Yes. Two pink lines. Yes, I'm pregnant.'

I hold my breath, pray, make a deal with God. Never will I ask for anything else, if only . . . 'Who is the father?' The question fills the room, circles over us, under the closet door.

'Marcus.'

I exhale, feeling light-headed with relief. 'Are you sure?'

'Yes. Positive. Dex and I haven't had sex since before my last period. Ages ago.'

'Does he know?'

'Who? Marcus?'

'Yeah. Does Marcus know?'

'Yes. But Dex doesn't. Not yet.'

He does now.

'I wanted to talk to you first.'

384

I nod, still taking it all in. 'So what are you going to do?'

'What do you mean?'

'Are you keeping it?'

'Yes. I want to have it.' She rubs her stomach in small circular motions. 'I want to marry Marcus and have his baby. I know it sounds crazy, but it just feels so right. We're in love.'

'Are you sure Marcus wants to get married?'

'Positive . . .'

'Do you think Dex suspects anything?' I ask quietly. For some reason, I don't want him to hear this question.

'No. But to be honest, I think he sensed how distant I've been. That's probably why he called it off. You know, he said he didn't love me . . . because he felt that I had turned away from him first.'

'I see.'

'I'm shocked at how calm you are. Thank you for not hating me.'

'Yeah . . . I don't hate you.'

'I hope Dex takes it as well. At least as far as Marcus goes. He's going to hate him for a while. But Dex is rational. Nobody did this on purpose to hurt him. It just happened.'

And right when I think that this story is winding up as neatly and tightly as a *Three's Company* episode, with its get-out-of-jail-free ending, I see Darcy stare at something behind me. By the look on her face, I think that Dex has emerged from his hiding place. I turn around, fully expecting to see him. But no, the door is still closed. I face Darcy again. She is still staring behind me, her expression stony and trancelike.

And then she asks, 'Why is Dexter's watch on your nightstand?'

I follow her eyes again. Sure enough, his watch is most definitely on my nightstand. Dexter's watch. My nightstand. There is no way out. At least not one that I can think of.

I shrug and stammer that I don't know. If there were any doubt before this moment as to my ability to think on my feet, that is cleared up now. I mumble, 'Oh, it's not his watch. I have one like it . . . I bought it in England.' My voice is shaking. I am a complete mess, a dying calf in a hailstorm.

Darcy leaps from my bed and grabs the watch from my nightstand, flipping it over and reading the inscription. '"All my love. Darcy",' she says. Then she looks at me with pure hatred, demonstrating how I should have reacted to her Marcus news.

'What the fuck?' she asks. It is a cold, hard question. Her eyes narrow. 'What the fuck!' she screams again, but this time it is a statement. Which means that I don't have to answer.

I stand as she pushes roughly past me into the bathroom. I follow her as she whips the shower curtain violently to the side. Only two tan Aveda bottles, a pink plastic razor, and a dwindling bar of soap.

I begin formulating a story: Dex came over to tell me about the break-up. He took his watch off, to woefully read the engraving. He was beside himself with grief. I comforted him briefly, at which point he left to wander in the park, alone.

But it is too late for explanations. The thirty-second window for explaining is over. Darcy's long, skinny fingers are gripping my closet doorknob.

'Darcy, don't,' I say, clearly indicating that her ex-fiancé is behind door number two. I stand in the way, my back against the door.

'Move!' she bellows. 'I know he's in there!'

I move, because what else am I supposed to do? She is right. We all know that he is in there. But as she opens the door, part of me actually thinks that Dex will have found a way to fold himself more neatly and tightly into a back corner of my closet. Or maybe he got out, somehow fled during the four seconds that Darcy and I stood gridlocked in my bathroom. Or maybe he miraculously found a secret opening in the back as in *The Lion, the Witch, and the Wardrobe*.

But no, he is there, crouched right where I last saw him, holding his jeans and his shirt, wearing striped navy boxers, staring up at us. He unfolds himself and stands upright.

'You liar!' she screams, thrusting her finger into his chest.

He ignores her and dresses calmly, putting one foot into his jeans and then the other. The sound of his zipper is loud in the room.

'You lied to me!'

'You have got to be kidding me,' Dex says, finding the armholes in his T-shirt. His voice is low and restrained. 'Fuck you, Darcy.'

Darcy's face grows red and she is spitting as she yells, 'You said there was nobody else in the picture! And you're *fucking* my best friend!'

I whimper her name like a broken record. 'Darcy. Darcy. Darcy.'

She ignores me, staring at Dex. I wait for him to defend us, cast a spin on the facts, tell her that there has been no fucking. Nothing at all until today when he came over to seek comfort. But Dex says calmly, 'Isn't that a bit of the pot calling the kettle black, Darce? You and Marcus, huh? Having a baby? I guess congratulations are in order.'

I expect her to make a statement about loyalty and love and friendship. I expect her to accuse us of doing it first. But she only looks at me and then Dex and then says that she knew it all along, and that she hates us both very much. And that she always will. She walks over to the door.

'Oh, Darcy?' Dex says.

'What?' She shouts the word, but the look in her eyes is needy, expectant.

'May I have my watch back, please?'

She hurls the evidence overhand at him. Clearly it is meant to strike and hurt him. But her aim is bad and it ricochets off my wall, skating across the parquet back at her feet, inscription up. She looks at it and then at me.

'And you! I never want to see you again! You are dead to me!'

She slams the door and is gone.

TWENTY-FOUR

Darcy wastes no time in getting her version of the story out. Starting with José, apparently. On our way out of the building, minutes after Darcy's departure, we pass my doorman. For once, he is not grinning. Failing in the gatekeeping function is the stuff that can get a doorman fired. He looks worried.

'Hi, José,' Dex and I say in unison.

'Aw, man, I'm really sorry I let her up,' he says. 'I, uh, didn't know . . . you know . . .'

'No. Not at all,' I say. 'Don't worry, José.'

'Did she give you an earful?' Dex asks cheerfully, as if the whole thing were just a crazy little mix-up instead of a life-defining moment for at least four people.

José has tacit permission to smile again. 'Uhh . . . you could say I got an earful. Heh, heh. But don't worry.' He laughs. 'I don't believe what she said about you . . . not most of it, anyway.'

He slaps hands with Dex as though they are old pals, which I guess they are becoming. I walk Dex to the corner. He is going home to salvage as many belongings as he can fit into his luggage – we both believe that Darcy is a slash-and-burn kind of girl, fully up to the task of taking scissors to his wardrobe.

'I'll be back as soon as I can,' he says.

I nod.

'And you're sure it's okay if I stay with you for a few days?'

He has asked me the question three times now.

'Of course. Stay as long as you want,' I say, thinking that now he not only wants me, but he *needs* me, too. It is a good feeling to be needed by Dex.

We stand facing each other in the street for a moment before Dex flags a cab and leans down to kiss me. Without thinking, I turn my head to give him a cheek. Then I remember that we no longer need to hide. I turn my face again, and our lips meet in daylight.

I return to my apartment in a state of semishock. I feel as if I should do something ceremonious. Write in my journal, which has been untouched for months (I could never bring myself to write about Dex, just in case something happened to me). Dance around my apartment. Cry. Instead, I focus on the mundane, what I am good at. I shower, unpack, water my plants, open my mail, drag two fans out of my closet and plug them in near my bed, and eat a couple of stale Fig Newtons.

Dex returns an hour later with his full array of tan Hartmann luggage and two black Nike gym bags, all stuffed haphazardly with clothes, shoes, papers, toiletries, even some framed photographs. 'Rescue mission accomplished,' he says. 'She wasn't home.'

I survey the bags. 'How did you haul all that stuff over here so fast?'

'It wasn't easy,' he says, wiping sweat from his brow. His

gray T-shirt is wet around the pits and across his chest.

'You can hang your suits in the front closet,' I say, still focusing on the practical, unable to absorb everything, although the presence of Dex's belongings is helping with that.

'Thanks.' He shakes out a few dark suits and white shirts and looks at me. 'Don't be alarmed. I'm not moving in.'

'I'm not alarmed,' I say, as I watch him hang his clothes. Although in truth, I am filled with sudden trepidation. *What next? What now?* I never planned on this – the temporary living arrangement, the end of my friendship with Darcy, the strange and sudden change in the status quo. 'I just can't believe it.'

He puts his arms around me. 'What can't you believe?'

'Everything. Any of it. Us.'

I close my eyes just as my phone rings. I jump. 'Shit. You think it's her?' I am almost afraid of Darcy, of what she will do.

'I doubt it. She's off with Marcus, I'm sure.'

I answer it.

'Is this true?' my mother asks, already in a panic. 'What I hear from Mrs. Rhone? Say it's not so, Rachel. *Please tell me!*'

'That depends on what you heard.' I choose my words carefully, and then mouth to Dex that it is my mother.

He makes a face and grabs the arm of my sofa as though bracing for a meteor to fall into my apartment. I'd prefer a meteor to this conversation.

'She tells me that Dex canceled the wedding?'

'That is correct.'

'And that you are somehow *involved* with Dex? . . . I told her there must be some mistake, but she was sure. She's very upset. Your father and I were speechless.'

'Mom, it is complicated,' I say, an admission by any measure.

'Ra-*chel*. How *could* you?' She has never sounded more disappointed in me. All of my hard work, accomplishments, years of being a good daughter – it is all down the drain. 'Darcy is your oldest friend in the world! How could you?'

I tell my mother that perhaps she would like to hear my side of the story before she casts judgment. I didn't think you needed law school to have the 'innocent before proven guilty' concept down.

She says fine, please go on. I can see her shaking her head, pacing in the kitchen, waiting for an explanation, although none could ever suffice.

I am too mad to tell her anything. How can she take Darcy's side over mine before she even hears a thing from my mouth? 'I'm not in the mood to discuss it with you,' I say. Then I add, 'Or Dad.' Because I know she will use him as the ultimate weapon, just as she did when I was a child. 'Wait until your father gets home,' an oft-heard threat to many children, wasn't employed with the same meaning in our house. It was a threat to tarnish my reputation as Daddy's perfect little girl. One stern look from my father was worse than any punishment, and my mom knew it.

'Your father is in the garage, absolutely beside himself,' she says, wavering between shrill and calm. 'I don't think he could talk even if you wanted to speak to him. Did Darcy or

Dr. and Mrs. Rhone cross your mind once?'

When I fell in love? No, they didn't! Neither did your bridge club nor my third-grade teacher!

'Mom, it's not your life. Or Dad's . . . Look, I have to go.'

I say goodbye and hang up before she can speak again. Let her be sorry when she learns that Darcy is having someone else's child. Let her do the math, subtract the months back to August. Maybe then she will phone me and apologize and toss out another one of her favorites – *people in glass houses . . .*

I hang up and contemplate phoning Annalise, getting to her before the spin doctor does. But I don't want to burden an expectant mother with this tale.

'So I gather that the news made its way west?' Dex asks me.

'Yup. Mrs. Rhone called my mom.'

'That's bullshit,' he says. 'Darcy is *pregnant* with another man's baby! Did she share that part with the old neighborhood?'

'Clearly not.'

'Think I should call Mrs. Rhone?'

'No . . . Let's just keep a low profile before everything shakes out. Screw them all.'

'You're right,' he says, and slams his fist into his palm. 'Darcy! She's *fucking* unbelievable.'

'I know,' I say.

We are both quiet. I feel uneasy. For a fleeting second, I worry that maybe Ethan's theory could be right – that I only wanted Dex to beat Darcy, and now that I have him, I'm not sure what to do. But no, there is an unmistakable feeling of love surging beneath the layers of anxiety. It will just take some time for us to be normal again. Which is ironic, because we've never really *been* normal.

'Should we order dinner?' Dex asks, breaking the silence.

'I'm not really hungry. I think I might just go to bed,' I say, even though it's only eight o'clock. 'I'm feeling pretty jet-lagged. Besides, it's too hot to eat.'

I think he knows the real reason I can't eat. 'I'm not hungry either,' he says.

I watch Dex as he listlessly tidies his belongings and finds his shaving kit. Then he showers while I brush my teeth, lock up the apartment, and climb into bed. My mind is working overtime, struggling to send a clear message to my heart. I hate feeling so much and yet being unable to categorize my dominant emotion. Am I mostly happy? Sad? Scared? I don't know. I think of Ethan. How surprised he will be. Spineless Dex isn't so spineless after all. Then I think of James. Was I kissing him when Dex was formulating a way to be with me? Should I feel guilty? Should I tell Dex?

Then I think about the four of us: Marcus was disloyal to Dex. I was disloyal to Darcy. Dex was disloyal to Darcy. Only Darcy did something to two people, to me and to Dex. She is the only one who was doubly disloyal. I think of my girl in the jury box. She is triumphant, pointing out this fact, telling Chanel Suit, 'I told you so.'

I watch Dex towel off, put on white boxer briefs, and walk toward me. He is beside the bed. I move over, taking his side. Maybe we will switch sides, our way of commemorating the change in our relationship, acknowledging its new legitimacy.

He switches off my lamp, and finds me under the sheets. His arm moves around me. Then he kisses my ear twice. But neither of us initiates anything more. Perhaps he, too, is contemplating the hugeness of what has happened.

'Good night, Dex,' I say.

'Good night, Rachel.'

For a long time, I listen to Dex breathe. When I am pretty sure he is asleep, I say his name softly.

'Yeah?' he answers, still wide awake.

'Are you okay?' I ask.

'Yes . . . Are you?'

'Yeah,' I say.

Then I hear him make a noise. It sounds like crying at first. Then I realize with relief that he is laughing.

'What?'

'You.' He imitates me. ' "I bought the watch in London." ' He laughs harder.

I allow one small smile. 'I couldn't think!'

'That was apparent.'

'You're the one who left it on the nightstand.'

'I know . . . Shit. I remembered it as soon as you let her in the apartment. Then I thought she might not see it. Then I heard the question . . . and was waiting for you to come up with something good. 'I bought it in London' wasn't what I had in mind. I was in there shaking my head in the dark, like the jig is up, baby.'

'Maybe it's for the best . . . Everything is out in the open now. She would have found out eventually.'

I don't really mean this though. Eventually would have

been better than today. And maybe she never would have known that anything was going on this summer, while she was still with Dex.

'Yeah. An engagement and two friendships finito,' he says.

I wonder which part Dex is sadder about. I hope that it is Marcus. 'You really think you won't ever be friends with Marcus again?'

He sighs and adjusts his pillow. 'I seriously doubt that we'll be grabbing a few beers anytime soon.'

'Are you sad about that?'

'What's the point of being sad?' he says. 'We're here now.'

I want to tell Dex that I love him, but I figure that it can wait until tomorrow. Or maybe even the next day.

Twelve hours later I am on my way to Hillary's office when Les ambushes me in the hall. 'Good. You're back. I need to see you.'

Yes, I had a lovely vacation. Thanks for asking.

'Now?' I ask.

'Yeah, now. Come to my office. Pronto.'

I want to tell him that normal people do not use the word 'pronto', unless they're kidding or playing Scrabble.

'I need to get a pad,' I say. So much for easing into my old routine.

Seconds later I am sitting in his office, which smells of onions, furiously scribbling instructions for three new assignments. All time-consuming, mind-numbing, bullshit first-year research projects, riddled with false deadlines. It is my punishment for taking a vacation. He talks at me in aggressive run-on sentences, his tone condescending whenever I dare to interrupt him to ask a pertinent question. As I study his bulbous nose, I am thinking that I don't need this. I remember how free I felt in London, being away from this place. I fantasize about quitting, getting another job in New York or maybe moving to London with Dex. I will resign in mid-assignment. Leave Les high and dry. Tell him what I think of him on my way out the door. Tell him that he really should do something about those hairs in his nose.

After an hour of being held prisoner (he even takes three lengthy phone calls during my sentence), I am released. I head straight for Hillary's office. It is a war zone, worse than usual. Documents clutter up every square inch of floor space. Both of her guest chairs are covered with papers, and her desk is piled high with folders, treatises, and old newspapers.

She spins around in her chair. 'Hey, you! Have a seat. Tell me about your trip!'

'Where do I sit?'

'Oh. Just dump that stuff anywhere . . . So how was England? How are you?'

'Well. Let's see,' I say, as I clear off one of her chairs. 'England was great. I made some progress in getting over Dex . . . But then I came home last night and learned that Dex called off the wedding after all.'

She gives me a quizzical look. 'He called it off? For sure?'

I tell her the whole story. She hangs on every word, and in the end she looks like one of those people who answers the door to find Ed McMahon with a big check and a television crew. She covers her eyes with her palms, laughs, shakes her head, and then comes around her desk and gives me a hug. I am not surprised by her reaction. I didn't expect her to get any of the subtleties – the fact that Darcy and I are no longer friends, the fact that my parents are upset, and that word of my treason is traveling at the speed of light all over Indiana.

'Well, that is awesome, awesome news. I owe Dex an apology. Shit. I really had him written off as another womanizing pretty boy.'

'He's not like that.'

'I can see that . . . I'm so happy for you.'

I smile. 'So what has been going on here?'

'Oh, not too much. Same old shit . . . Julian and I had our first big fight.'

'What? Why?'

She shrugs. 'We got into an argument that escalated.'

'About what?'

'It's a long story . . . but basically we have this full disclosure rule. No secrets whatsoever.'

'Secrets about your past?'

'Yeah. And just anything. So anyway, he was talking to this girl at a party, and he introduced me to her. And the three of us had a big ol' conversation about all sorts of things. And later that night, I asked him how he knew her . . . He told me he met her two summers ago . . . and that was it. Then kidding around, I said, 'Did you sleep with her?' And he just looked at me. He had!'

I don't try to hide my smirk. 'You got mad because of an ex-girlfriend?'

'No. I got mad that I had to ask him if he slept with her. He should have brought it up first! That wasn't in the spirit of our agreement. So, of course, I start to worry that he isn't as honest as he seems.'

I shake my head. 'You're a trip. So stubborn.'

'He is too . . . We haven't talked in almost twenty-four hours.'

'Hil! C'mon, you have to call him!'

'Not a chance. His finger isn't broken.'

Her words and posturing are bold and defiant, but for the first time I see her as vulnerable. Something in her eyes gives her away.

'I think you should call him,' I say. 'This is silly.'

'Maybe it is. I don't know. And then again, maybe we're not as perfect for each other as I first thought.'

'Because of one fight?'

She shrugs.

'Hillary, I think you're overreacting. Pick up the phone and call him.'

'No way,' she says, but I can tell from the way that she glances at her phone that she is weakening.

I think to myself that when you're in love, sometimes you have to swallow your pride, and sometimes you have to fight to keep your pride. It's a balance. But when the relationship is right, you find that balance. I am sure that Hillary and Julian will.

When I return to my office, I dial up my only other unconditional ally. I know that Ethan won't miss the complexity of the situation, because he knows Darcy better than

Hillary does. In some ways, he understands her better than I do.

He does not interrupt once as I tell him the story. 'So did you suspect that? When Dex called asking about my flight?' I ask him after I finish.

'I hoped . . . That's why I gave him your information. But I didn't ask any questions. I just crossed my fingers.'

'You hoped? Really? I thought you didn't like him.'

'Aw, I just didn't like him for jerking you around all summer. I like him now. I mean, I actually admire him now. He didn't take the easy way out. I really respect him for that. So many people just let the engagement tide roll over them and get washed up into the hurrah of a wedding. Dex did the stand-up thing. I give him credit. I really do.'

'I'm just glad he called it off, instead of Darcy making the decision for him after the pregnancy discovery. Then I'd always wonder, you know, if I was just the runner-up.'

'So how do you feel?' His question is gentle, and I know he is asking about Darcy.

I tell him that I am happy, of course, but devastated to lose Darcy, to realize that she will no longer be a part of my life. Although in truth, I don't think it has fully sunk in yet. 'It's just not a fairy-tale ending,' I say.

'No. It never is.'

'And it just all happened so fast. One minute I thought I was going to a wedding on Saturday. Next minute, no wedding, I get to be with Dex, Darcy is with Marcus, and she's having his baby. It is nuts.'

'I can't believe she's pregnant . . . Shit! That girl!' he says, with some amusement.

'I know.'

'Never a dull moment.'

'I know . . . I think I might miss that about her.'

'Yeah. Well. Maybe she'll come around.'

'Maybe.'

He clears his throat. 'Although I doubt it.'

'Me too.'

'So Marcus and Darcy.' He whistles. 'That's certainly a twist.'

'Yeah. You're telling me. But I can actually see it now . . . It makes sense. She's always railing on Dex for working too hard. And Marcus takes the opposite approach.'

'And you're more like Dex.'

'Yeah. So much for the "opposites attract" theory.'

'Sounds like everything may have worked out for the best. Except for James, that is. He'll be wrecked.'

'Yeah, right,' I say.

'And, of course, I'm a bit disappointed.'

'Why?'

'I thought you were going to move here.'

'Who knows? Maybe I still will.'

'And leave Dex?'

'He can come with me.'

'Think he'd do that?'

'Maybe.'

Maybe he loves me enough to follow me anywhere.

I hang up and start my assignments, signing on to Lexis, skimming and highlighting case after case. I keep checking my email and waiting for the phone to ring. At first I think it's Dex I am waiting for, but then I pick up the phone and call him, and still have an empty, aching feeling. That's when I realize that it's Darcy I am waiting to hear from. I expect her to call at any minute. Yell at me, say mean things to me, but talk to me. Communicate in some way. But my phone does not ring as I work through lunch. Around four o'clock, I finally get a call.

'Rachel?' Claire bellows into the phone.

I roll my eyes. 'Hello, Claire.'

'What in the world is going on?' she asks, pretending to be foggy on exact details. I know that Darcy has put her up to this call. Maybe she is even listening to me now. It is pure, classic Darcy. I think of all the times in high school when she cajoled Annalise and me to undertake such assignments.

I do not take the bait. I briskly tell Claire that I have to be in court in thirty minutes, and don't have time to discuss the situation with her.

'Okay . . .' Her disappointment at the lack of juice is palpable. 'Call me back when you can . . .'

Don't hold your breath.

'I just feel terrible for both of you. You've been friends for too long . . .' Her voice is dripping with false empathy. She is relishing her new position as Darcy's best friend. I picture them wearing the 'best friend' necklaces. If anyone could bring them back into fashion, it is Darcy and Claire.

'Uh-huh.' I give nothing away. Claire will be the one worthwhile casualty of my split with Darcy. I don't have to pretend to like her anymore.

402

It is Wednesday night. Three days after the confrontation. Dex and I are curled up in bed when the phone rings. This will be Darcy, I think. I both crave and fear her call, a call that might never come.

I answer nervously. 'Hello?'

'Hi, Rachel.'

It is Annalise. She sounds tired, and for a second I think it's because Darcy has dragged her into our saga. I prepare myself for a tentative, mousy Annalise-style lecture. Instead I hear a baby unleash a wail in the background.

'It's a girl,' Annalise says. 'We had a girl!'

Darcy was right, is my first thought, before I become weepy. I am overcome by the news. My friend is a mother. 'Congratulations! When?'

'Two hours ago. Eight forty-two. She's six pounds, four ounces.'

'What's her name?'

'Hannah Jane . . . Jane after you and Darcy.'

Our friendship with Annalise and the middle name Jane are two of the only things that Darcy and I still share.

'Annalise, I am so touched,' I say. 'You never told me you were considering Jane.'

'It was a surprise.'

'Hannah Jane. It's a beautiful name.'

'She *is* beautiful.'

'Does she look like you?'

'I don't know. My mom says so. But I think she has Greg's nose and feet.'

'I can't wait to see her.'

'When are you coming home?'

'Soon. I promise.'

For a moment I think that Darcy actually refrained from dragging Annalise into our scandal. But then she says, 'Rachel, you and Darce have to make up. She called me last night. I was going to call you but my water broke right afterward.'

Leave it to Darcy to induce labor.

'Whatever happened – it can be fixed, right?' she asks.

I want to ask her what she knows, what Darcy reported. But obviously I am not going to pull a Darcy. This is not the time to delve into our soap opera. 'Right,' I say. 'Don't worry about that . . . This is much more important. You have a baby!'

'I have a baby!'

'You're somebody's mother!'

'I know. It feels so nice.'

'Did you tell Darcy yet?'

'Not yet. I'm calling her now . . .'

I think to myself that if Darcy discovers that Annalise called me first, she'd be even more enraged. 'Yeah, I know you have a lot of calls to make. Tell Greg I said congratulations. And your parents . . . I'm so happy for you.'

'Thank you, Rachel.'

'I love you, Annalise.' I feel the tears welling up.

'I love you, too.'

I hang up, overcome with emotion that I don't fully understand. I knew the baby would be here sooner or later.

Yet I am still blown away by the reality of what has just happened. Annalise is a mother. She has a daughter. It is a moment that she, Darcy, and I talked about as little girls. Now Darcy is having a baby, too, and I won't even get a phone call from her when it happens. I will hear about it secondhand. It wasn't supposed to be like this. Annalise's baby makes the rift all the more tragic. Never has good news seemed so bittersweet.

'Annalise had her baby?' Dex asks, as I get back into bed.

'Yes. A girl . . . Hannah Jane,' I say, and then proceed to burst into tears. It is my first hard cry in front of Dex. The kind where your face gets all puffy and ugly and wet, and you can't breathe through your nose and you feel the pressure building in your head. I know that I am going to have a migraine in the morning if I don't stop. But I can't. I turn away from Dex and sob. Dex keeps his arms tightly wrapped around me and makes consoling sounds, but he doesn't ask me why, exactly, I am crying. Maybe because he understands. Maybe because he knows that it's not the time for questions. Whatever his reason, I have never loved him more. I let him kiss me. I kiss him back. We make love for the first time post-Darcy.

TWENTY-FIVE

The following day Darcy finally contacts Dex. He calls me straightaway with the update.

My heart jumps. I haven't let go of the fear that Darcy will somehow get Dex back, undo her pregnancy, change her mind, rewrite history. 'Tell me everything,' I say.

Dex summarizes their conversation, or rather, Darcy's demands: he is to get the remainder of his stuff out in seven days – during business hours – or it will be put out with the trash. He must leave the keys. The furniture will stay, except for the table that he 'bullied her into buying', the dresser he 'brought into the joke of a union', and the 'ugly lamps' from Dexter's mother. He must pay her parents back for her gown and the nonrefundable wedding deposits, which include just about everything, in excess of fifty thousand dollars. She will handle return of the wedding gifts. She is keeping the diamond ring he replaced only days before their break-up.

I wait for him to finish and then say, 'Pretty skewed terms, don't you think?'

'You could say that.'

'You guys should split the wedding costs,' I say. 'She's pregnant with someone else's child!'

'Tell me about it.'

'And technically, the ring is yours,' I say. 'Under New York law. You weren't married. She only gets the ring if you're married.'

'I don't care,' he says. 'It's not worth fighting about.'

'And what about the apartment? It was your apartment first.'

'I know . . . but I don't even want it now. Or the furniture,' he says.

I am glad that he feels this way. I can't imagine ever visiting him in Darcy's old apartment.

'Where do you think you'll move?'

'I'm just going to live with you.'

'Really?'

'It was a joke, Rach . . . We'll hold off on that for a little while.'

I laugh. 'Oh . . . yeah. Right.'

I am a little disappointed, but mostly relieved. I feel as if I could live with Dex immediately, but I want it to work, to be right, and I see no reason to rush things.

'I called a few places this morning . . . I found a one-bedroom on East End. I might just hit the bid.'

Hit the bid. Just as you did with me.

'How is Darcy going to pay the rent alone?' I ask, more curious than concerned, although there is a part of me that is worried about her wellbeing, how she will manage, what will happen to her and her baby. I can't turn off the caring-about-Darcy switch after a lifetime of looking out for her.

'Maybe Marcus is moving in with her,' Dex says.

'Do you think?'

'They *are* having a baby together.'

'I guess so. But do you really think they're going to get married?' I ask.

'I have no idea. I don't care,' he says.

'You haven't heard from Marcus, have you?'

'Nope . . . Have you?'

'No.'

'I don't think we will.'

'Are you going to call him?'

'Maybe someday. Not now.'

'Hmm,' I say, thinking that maybe I will someday call Darcy too. Although I can't imagine it happening for a very long time. 'So was that it? Did she mention me?'

'No. I was shocked. Tremendous restraint for her. She must be getting some big-time coaching.'

'No kidding. Restraint is not Darcy's style.'

'But enough about her,' Dex says. 'Let's forget about her for a while.'

'I will if you will,' I say.

'So what do you want to do tonight?' Dex asks. 'I think I'll be able to get out of here at a decent hour. What's your schedule?'

It is five now, and I have at least four hours of work remaining, but I tell him that I can leave whenever.

'Should we meet at eight?'

'Sure. Where?'

'Let's make dinner together at your place. We've never done that.'

'Okay, but . . . I can't cook,' I confess.

'Yeah you can.'

'No, I really can't. Truly.'

'Cooking is easy,' he says. 'You just sort of figure it out as you go along.'

I smile. 'I can do that.'

After all, that is pretty much what I have been doing lately.

An hour later, I leave my office for home, not caring if I run into Les. I take the elevator down to the lobby, then two escalators down to Grand Central Station. I pause to admire the gorgeous main terminal, so familiar and so associated with work that I somehow miss its beauty on a daily basis. I study the marble staircases at either end of the concourse, the arched windows, the dramatic white columns, and the soaring turquoise ceiling, painted with constellations. I watch the people, mostly in business attire, moving in every direction toward trains bound for the suburbs, subways reaching every corner of New York, and a multitude of exits to the busy city streets. I glance at the clock in the center of the terminal, take in its intricate face. Six o'clock exactly. Early.

I walk slowly toward Grand Central Market, a food hall comprising individual stalls selling gourmet treats, located on the east end of the concourse. I have often passed through this corridor with Hillary, buying the occasional chocolate

409

truffle to go with our Starbucks coffee. But this evening, I am on a greater mission. I move from stall to stall, filling my arms with delicacies: hard and soft cheeses, freshly baked breads, Sicilian green olives, Italian parsley, fresh oregano, a perfect Vidalia onion, garlic, oils and spices, pasta, red, green, and yellow produce, an expensive Chardonnay, and two exquisite, restaurant-perfect pastries. I exit the corridor on Lexington, passing by a makeshift cab line and throngs of harried Midtown commuters. I decide to walk home. My bags are heavy, but I don't mind. I'm not carrying a briefcase full of law books and cases; I'm carrying dinner for Dex and me.

When I get back to my apartment, I tell José to let Dex up when he arrives. 'No need to buzz for him anymore.'

He winks and hits the elevator door for me. 'Aww. So it's serious! That's good stuff.'

'Good stuff,' I echo, smiling.

A moment later, I am arranging groceries on my counter – more food than my apartment has ever seen at one time. I put the Chardonnay in the refrigerator, play some classical music, and search for the recipe book that my mother gave me at least four Christmases ago, a book I have never before used. I flip through the glossy, pristine pages, finding a salad and pasta recipe that contains my approximate ingredients. Then I find an apron – another virginal gift – and set about peeling, chopping, and sautéing. I glance at the book for guidance, but I do not follow every instruction precisely. I substitute parsley for basil, skip the drained capers. Dinner will not be perfect, but I am learning that perfection isn't what matters. In fact, it's the very thing that can destroy you if you let it.

I change my clothes, selecting a white sundress with pink embroidered flowers. Then I set the table, begin to boil water for our pasta, light candles, and open the bottle of Chardonnay, filling two glasses, sipping mine. I glance at my watch. Ten minutes to spare. Ten minutes to sit and reflect on my new life, on how it feels to be Dex's legitimate, only love. I settle into my couch, close my eyes, inhale deeply. Good smells and beautiful, clear notes fill my apartment. Peace and calm rush over me as I process the lack of any bad feelings: I'm not jealous, I'm not worried, I'm not scared, I'm not lonely.

Only then do I acknowledge that what I am feeling might actually be true happiness. Even joy. Over the past several days, when I have felt the beginning of this emotion tugging at my heart, it has crossed my mind that the key to happiness should not be found in a man. That an independent, strong woman should feel fulfilled and whole on her own. Those things might be true. And without Dex in my life, I like to think I could have somehow found contentment. But the truth is, I feel freer with Dex than I ever did single. I feel more myself with him than without. Maybe true love does that.

And I do love Dex. I have loved him from the very beginning, back in law school, when I pretended to myself that he wasn't my type. I love him for his intelligence, his sensitivity, his courage. I love him wholly and unconditionally and without reservation. I love him enough to take risks.

I love him enough to sacrifice a friendship. I love him enough to accept my own happiness and use it, in turn, to make him happy back.

There is a knock at my door. I stand to open it. I am ready.

TWENTY-SIX

It is Saturday, what would have been Darcy and Dexter's wedding night. I am with Dex at 7B, the bar where it all began, back on the eve of my thirtieth birthday. We are sitting in our same booth. It was my idea to come back here. I suggested it in a playful way, but in truth I felt a strong need to return and revisit the way I felt before it all began. I want to ask Dex if he feels at all wistful on this night, but instead I tell him a Les story – how he blasted me in the hall for not using jump cites in a draft brief.

'That guy sounds like a miserable human being . . . Can't you work with someone else?'

'No. I'm his personal slave. He monopolizes my time, and now other partners won't ask me to work on their matters because Les inevitably pulls rank and leaves them high and dry. I'm trapped.'

'Do you ever think about changing firms?'

'Sometimes. I just started revising my résumé today, in fact. Maybe I'll leave the law altogether, although I have no idea what I would do.'

'You'd be good at so many things,' Dex says, with a loyal nod. I add 'supportive' to my growing list of things I love about him.

413

I consider telling him about my idea of temporarily moving to London, wondering if he'd come with me. But tonight isn't the time for that conversation. We have enough going on right below the surface. He has to be thinking about her, thinking, *What if*. How could he not be?

'I'm going to play some songs on the jukebox,' I say.

'Want me to come with you?'

'No. I'll be right back.'

'Pick some good ones, all right?'

I give him a 'have some faith in me' look. I walk over to the jukebox, past a couple smoking in silence. I slip a nappy five into the slot. The machine spits the bill back out at me three times, but I am patient, smoothing out the edges on my thigh before it finally takes. I flip through the songs, considering each one carefully. I choose songs that Dex likes, and songs that remind me of our first summer together. And of course I play 'Thunder Road'. I glance over at Dex, who appears to be deep in thought. He suddenly looks over at me and waves, a silly smile on his face. I go sit back down, sliding in beside him. As he drapes his arm around me, a wave of emotion leaves me breathless.

'Hi there,' he says, in a way that tells me he knows exactly how I'm feeling.

'Hi,' I say back, in the same tone.

We are one of those couples I used to watch, thinking to myself that I'd never be on the inside of something so special. I remember reassuring myself that it probably looked nicer than it actually was. I am happy to be wrong about that.

I smile up at Dex, my gaze resting on a tiny patch in his

left eyebrow, a blank space where perhaps three or four hairs should be.

'What happened there?' I ask, reaching to touch his brow. My fingertips rest lightly on the spot.

'Oh, that. It's a scar. I fell playing hockey when I was a kid. Hair never grew back there.'

I wonder why I never noticed it before and realize that I never knew he played hockey. There is so much that I still don't know about Dex. But now we have time. Endless time stretches before us. I study his face for other discoveries until he laughs self-consciously. I laugh too, and then our smiles fade away in unison. We drink our Newcastles in easy silence.

'Dex?' I say, after a long while.

'Yeah?'

'Do you miss her?'

'No,' he says firmly. His breath is warm in my ear. 'I'm with you. No.'

I can tell that it is the truth.

'You aren't at all sad tonight?'

'Not one bit.' He kisses the side of my head. 'I'm a lot of things right now. But sad isn't one of them.'

'Good,' I say. 'I'm glad.'

'How do *you* feel? Do *you* miss her?' he asks.

I consider his questions. I am mostly happy, but with a soupçon of nostalgia, thinking of all that I have shared with Darcy. Until now, our lives have been so intertwined – she has been my frame of reference for so many events. Beating drums in the bicentennial parade. Tying yellow ribbons

415

around the tree in my backyard during the hostage crisis. Watching the *Challenger* fall from the sky, the wall come down in Germany, the Soviet Union dissolve. Learning of Princess Diana's death, of John F. Kennedy, Jr.'s fate. Grieving after September 11. All of it was with Darcy by my side. And then there is our personal history. Memories only we share. Things not another soul would ever understand.

Dex watches me intently, waiting for my answer.

'Yes,' I finally say, somewhat apologetically. 'I miss her. I can't help it.'

He nods as though he understands. I wonder why I miss her and Dex does not. Perhaps it is because I've known her so much longer. Or maybe it's the very nature of a friendship versus an intimate relationship. When you are in a relationship, you are aware that it might end. You might grow apart, find someone else, simply fall out of love. But a friendship isn't a zero-sum game, and as such, you assume that it will last forever, especially an old friendship. You take its permanence for granted, which might be the very thing so dear about it. Even as Dex rolled those double sixes, I never imagined the end of Darcy and me.

I picture her now, wondering what she is feeling at this very moment. Is she as melancholy as I am? Or just angry? Is she with Marcus or Claire? Or is she alone, flipping sorrowfully through our high school yearbook and old pictures of Dex? Does she miss me too? Will we ever be friends again, tentatively agreeing to meet for lunch or coffee, rebuilding one small step at a time? Maybe she and I will laugh about that crazy summer when one of us was still twenty-something. But I doubt it. This one can't be bridged, particularly if Dex and I stay together. Our friendship is likely over forever, and maybe that is for the best. Maybe Ethan was right, and the time has come to stop using Darcy as a measuring stick for my own life.

I run my hands along my glass, marveling at how much has changed in such a short time. How much I have changed. I was a parent-pleaser, a dutiful friend. I made safe, careful choices and hoped that things would fall into place for me. Then I fell in love with Dex and still viewed it as something happening *to* me. I hoped that he would make things right, or that fate would intervene. But I have learned that you make your own happiness, that part of going for what you want means losing something else. And when the stakes are high, the losses can be that much greater.

Dex and I talk for a long time, covering virtually every moment of our summer, chronicling it all – the good and the gory. Mostly we laugh, and only once do I get teary, when we get to the part where he told me he was going to marry Darcy. I tell him how I rolled our dice after he left my apartment. He says he is sorry. I say he has no reason to be sorry, that he didn't at the time and certainly doesn't now.

And then, just before midnight, comes that sweet sound of the harmonica, playing slowly at first and then building momentum before Bruce sings, 'The screen door slams, Mary's dress waves'.

A smile spreads across Dex's face, his eyes are bright and especially green. He pulls me against his chest and says into my ear, 'I'm glad we're not eating cake right now.'

417

'Me too,' I whisper.

Dex holds me as we listen to Bruce, the words rich with our meaning:

Hey what else can we do now
Except roll down the windows and let the wind   blow
back your hair
Well the night's busting open
These two lanes will take us anywhere.

It occurs to me that tonight is an ending and a beginning. But for once, I embrace both. The last line of 'Thunder Road' fills the bar:

'And I'm pulling out of here to win.'

'You want to go now?' I ask Dex.

He nods. 'I do.'

We stand and walk through the smoky bar, leaving 7B before the next song begins to play. It is a beautiful, clear night with a faint chill in the air. Fall is coming. I take Dexter's hand as we stroll up Avenue B, looking for a yellow cab headed in the right direction.

Something Blue

Emily Giffin

Thirty, successful and stunning, Darcy Rhone used to think that 'being down and out' meant not finding a size four at the Barney's Warehouse Sale. Now she is pregnant, unmarried and recovering from a series of break-ups and, for the first time in her life, completely alone.

Frantically casting around for help, she persuades an old high school friend to let her stay with him in London for a few weeks. Little does she know what she's in for when she boards the plane, but as weeks turn into months, Darcy makes a surprising discovery. Preparing for motherhood and settling into a new city, she builds herself a new life from scratch, finally finding romance – in the most unexpected place . . .

Praise for Emily Giffin

'*Sex and the City* fans will love this sassy debut novel about two best friends whose rather unlikely lifelong friendship is about to be sorely tested' *Woman's Own*

'Here's a heroine you'll root for and a book you won't want to put down. I loved it'
Lauren Weisberger, author of *The Devil Wears Prada*

'Gripping from start to finish' *Best*

arrow books

Being Committed

Anna Maxted

Hannah thinks you have to be insane to get married. She's content with her life – the job as a private investigator at Hound Dog Investigations, the boyfriend of five years, Jason, and the wonderful father (pity her mother is such a disaster). Besides which, she's tried marriage once before, but she ended up divorced before she was 21.

So, when the long-suffering Jason proposes, Hannah doesn't think twice about turning him down. Still, she's a little shaken when, a month later, the man has the nerve to get engaged to someone else. Is she not up to settling down? Hannah's family are convinced she blew her one chance of hooking a permanent man, and maybe – just maybe – there's something in Jason's theory that being committed means first coming to terms with your past.

Praise for Anna Maxted

'Always one to favour heroines who err on the quirky side, Hannah is her best to date – a wonderfully eccentric character who'll have you in stitches' *Glamour*

'Funny and inspiring, you'll be turning the pages 'til the small hours' *Company*

arrow books

The Learning Curve

Melissa Nathan

Nicky Hobbs loves teaching at the local primary school. She's idolised by her class – in particular ten-year-old Oscar Samuels – but she's starting to find she'd quite like some adult adoration for a change.

Mark Samuels is a frazzled single father working all the hours God gives to provide for his beloved son, Oscar. But he's unable to see that Oscar would prefer his presence to his presents once in a while.

Ms Hobbs knows Mr Samuels is a heartless workaholic. Mr Samuels is certain Ms Hobbs is an interfering busybody. But when they finally meet they start to discover that first impressions can be deceptive. And perhaps they've both got a bit of learning to do . . .

'Tremendous fun' Jilly Cooper

arrow books

We Are Family

Josie Lloyd and Emlyn Rees

1953, and although the coastal village of Stepmouth appears as idyllic as ever, a passionate feud threatens to shatter the small, tight community. Sixteen-year-old Rachel Vale, wilful and unconventional, has fallen in love with the man her brother hates. When the town is devastated by a vast, unstoppable flood, the Vale family is left broken and irreconcilably divided. Or so it seems.

Fifty years later, and Laurie Vale, an only child and aspiring artist, takes a phone call from an aunt she never knew existed, only to discover that everything she ever believed about her family is a lie. As the truth unfolds, the hopes and passions buried in the Vale family's past surface once more. Unknowingly, Laurie has also taken the first step towards becoming ensnared in a complex love affair of her own.

Divided between Fifties Stepmouth and the searing heat of a present day Mallorcan summer. *We Are Family* is a modern family saga which explores the conflicting relationships of two very different generations.

arrow books

Never Say Never

Melissa Hill

Sometimes hopes and dreams don't go according to plan – sometimes, real life gets in the way.

On a mild May evening, a group of friends on the verge of graduating speculate on what the future holds. Will Leah be a chef? Robin an accountant? And Olivia the one who holds it all together? The one thing they know is that they'll always be friends – no matter what – but they make a pact to meet up in years, just in case fate intervenes.

Years later it's clear that life has not gone according to plan. Why is Robin in New York determined never to go back to Dublin? Why is Olivia grieving? And why does Leah feel so left out as she heads towards the big three-o?

When Robin is forced to return, they all find themselves face to face with the past – suddenly nothing can ever be the same again. And they start to realize that sometimes it's best never to say never . . .

'An absolute joy from start to finish' *Irish Independent*

arrow books

THE POWER OF READING

Visit the Random House website and get connected with information on all our books and authors

EXTRACTS from our recently published books and selected backlist titles

COMPETITIONS AND PRIZE DRAWS Win signed books, audiobooks and more

AUTHOR EVENTS Find out which of our authors are on tour and where you can meet them

LATEST NEWS on bestsellers, awards and new publications

MINISITES with exclusive special features dedicated to our authors and their titles

READING GROUPS Reading guides, special features and all the information you need for your reading group

LISTEN to extracts from the latest audiobook publications

WATCH video clips of interviews and readings with our authors

RANDOM HOUSE INFORMATION including advice for writers, job vacancies and all your general queries answered

Come home to Random House

www.rbooks.co.uk